Newearth

A Hero's Crime

A. K. Frailey

Hardcover ISBN: 979-8-9861803-3-5

Cover design by James Hrkach and A.K. Frailey

Website
https://akfrailey.com/

Amazon Author Page
https://www.amazon.com/A.-K.-Frailey/e/B006WQTQCE

THE WRITINGS OF A. K. FRAILEY

Books for the Mind and Spirit
https://akfrailey.com/
Contact: akfrailey@yahoo.com

Historical Science Fiction Novels
OldEarth ARAM Encounter https://amzn.to/2KLhlsN
OldEarth Ishtar Encounter https://amzn.to/2OAkDQF
OldEarth Neb Encounter https://amzn.to/3iGqGlQ
OldEarth Georgios Encounter https://amzn.to/3v7w8oI
OldEarth Melchior Encounter https://amzn.to/3nyfkEJ

Science Fiction Novels
Homestead https://amzn.to/3DcTuhz
Last of Her Kind http://amzn.to/2y1HJvg
Newearth Justine Awakens http://amzn.to/2pq0vWN
Newearth A Hero's Crime https://amzn.to/3S4rROI

Short Stories
It Might Have Been—And Other Short Stories 2nd Edition https://amzn.to/2XXdDDz
One Day at a Time and Other Stories https://amzn.to/2YFtQ5r
***Encounter Science Fiction Short Stories & Novella* 2nd Edition** https://amzn.to/3dq6q5l

Inspirational Non-Fiction
***My Road Goes Ever On—Spiritual Being, Human Journey* 2nd Edition** https://amzn.to/2KvF3Ll
My Road Goes Ever On—A Timeless Journey https://amzn.to/3v5BlOM
The Road Goes Ever On—A Christian Journey Through The Lord of the Rings https://amzn.to/3rtAy6S

Children's Book
The Adventures of Tally-Ho http://amzn.to/2sLfcI5

Poetry
***Hope's Embrace & Other Poems* 2nd Edition** https://amzn.to/3cn22X8

Prologue

–Mirage-Reborn–

Truth

Cerulean awakened flat on his back, weary and struggling to remember recent events. He blinked at dust-speckled sunrays slanting before him. He wanted to move, but his body felt weighed down, practically attached to the structure under him. Swallowing back panic, he inhaled a long, calming breath.

His chest barely budged, as if gravity had increased threefold. Too weak. Forcing himself to concentrate, he faced practical reality. Since he couldn't move, he must lie still and listen. Surely, there was a good explanation. A sharp ache in his neck reassured him. *At least, I'm not dead.*

Murmuring voices traveled overhead. A woman—no—two women. Arguing.

Depressed, he closed his eyes.

Clare and Justine. At it again. They argued on Newearth. They argued aboard ship. Now they were arguing here—*Wherever that might be!* He imagined bellowing, shut up! And seeing their reaction. He tried to form words. *Nope. Not anytime soon.*

A shadow hovered nearby and blocked the warm light. A gentle hand caressed his forehead. "Cerulean?"

Using every ounce of energy at his disposal, which wasn't much, Cerulean pried his eyes open. Directly above him, a towering figure stared down, a lean figure with a clean-shaven face, bright green eyes, and a shock of thick, white-blond hair.

Concern emanated from those eyes, despite the upturned creases in the corners, which matched the smiling mouth. "So good to see you awaken naturally. I was ready to rouse you, but it's usually better to let nature take its course."

Swallowing a desert dryness, Cerulean attempted to form words. "Where—?"

Justine's flowing black hair and sculptured face rose into view, crowding out the other figure, her eyes wide and her tone authoritative. "You're on Mirage, Cerulean. We made it—though barely. I was afraid you were going to—"

Clare's round, child-like face framed by chestnut, shoulder-length hair shoved forward. Her chocolate-colored eyes flickered irritably at Justine and then returned to Cerulean. "It's Mirage-*Reborn* now. And you had us going, old friend. Abbas here"—she nodded to the white-haired man— "saved your life. Good thing he has a better disposition than that son of his. Omega would probably have played some ridiculous—"

The urge to scream closed Cerulean's eyes again. *We need to save Newearth! Cosmos is coming...*

Without another word, the gentle hand smoothed his brow. Abbas' voice, deep and confiding, pronounced final judgment. "He's still weak. You must allow him complete rest for a few more days, and then—"

"Then what?" Clare's voice rose two notches, near screech level.

Justine broke in with a husky, earthy tone that unclenched Cerulean's jaws. "Calm down, Clare. Abbas wants to save Cerulean as much as we do. He's just making sure that we don't kill him with kindness. Right, Grandfather?"

The sound of Abbas' chuckle warmed Cerulean's heart. So honest and lighthearted, something Cerulean had not felt since—when? He couldn't remember. Everything was a blur. Years of pain and turmoil. Fear evolving into interplanetary panic. The mission to find Omega and save Newearth.

He sighed. Finally, everyone finally knew. He couldn't save everyone. Maybe he would die. Maybe he wouldn't. But the truth was clear—he couldn't fight any longer.

Chapter One

–Mirage-Reborn–

Our Present Difficulties

Justine's rock-hard arms folded stiff against her body, contrasting sharply with her tapping, slippered foot. "What do you mean you're leaving?" Every millimeter of her perfectly contoured body dressed in a burgundy blouse and slim white pants strained for action.

The well-appointed ship's deck with state-of-the-art instrument panels, a large central screen, and two holograms of neighboring star systems surrounded Captain Xavier Pax as he sprang from his chair and zeroed in on the communications console. His bulky dark-green suit and tall brown boots made him appear larger than he actually was. Turning his attention to the computer, he scanned a recent log entry. "My job was to get you here before Cerulean died." His voice rose with his irritation level. "I did that. Now, if you don't mind, I'd like to complete a thorough check of the ship before I head back home."

Uncoiling herself, Justine pounded across the bridge. "You can't leave. You know why we came and why we must stay."

Pax turned and considered Justine through narrowed black eyes. "I know, 'We're chasing a riddle in hopes of finding a mirage.' I get the joke. But honestly, this place—I don't trust it. *Nothing* is what it appears to be. I did a scan of the surface, and do you know what this planet is actually made of?"

Justine pursed her lips in controlled impatience, stepped to the captain's chair, tapped the arm console, and pointed at the central screen. A rocky wasteland under clouds of vaporous mist, dotted by erupting volcanoes, materialized larger-than-life on the screen. “That right there? It’s the sister planet a few light years from here.” She clapped her hands together. “Amazing what advanced reconstruction can do.”

Blowing air through his mouth like a swimmer coming to the surface, Pax waved his arms emphatically. “Hold on! I’m not about to dive into this pool of make-believe Mirage-Reborn—or whatever they call it. It’s not just the planet, and you know it. The people living here are—”

“Varied and eccentric. Deal with it. That’s not why we’ve come, Pax!”

The bridge door slid open with a distinct high-pitched whine, and Clare marched forward, her shoulders arching as she scowled. “I thought you were going to fix that thing. I get shivers down my back every time I use it—takes me all day to straighten out my spine.” Her gaze swung from Pax to Justine, and her frown grew more pronounced. “What?”

With a dramatic arm-fling, Justine glowered. “He’s deserting us.”

Clare’s eyes widened. She zeroed in on Pax. “Oh, no you’re not!” She hurried forward and confronted him with every millimeter of her medium frame. “I have all the authority I need to lock you up, so don’t play games with me. You agreed to this little adventure—”

Pax sucked in a deep breath like a dragon preparing to toast a village. “Agreed? I didn’t know what I was *agreeing* to. Your friend Cerulean, who nearly died before explaining anything, told me to get him to this planet. I did that. And you”—he jabbed a finger at Justine—“made all sorts of clever remarks about chasing riddles, but you never actually told me anything, even though I asked about a million times.” He adopted a mocking imitation. "'We're chasing Omega to stop Cosmos.' By the Divide! What does that *mean*?"

Clare rubbed her cheek and glanced at Justine. "You know, I thought he was smarter than this. He seemed so, I don't know, *commanding* during the voyage."

Justine nodded, her arms slowly refolding over her chest like ships docking at their appointed port. "He was. He is. He just thinks that by acting imbecilic, he can get more out of us."

Pax staggered to the captain's chair and flopped down, cupping his head in his hands. "I give up. You want to play me for a fool, fine. But I'm warning you; this isn't a healthy place to hang around. We're risking our lives—maybe more than that—by staying here."

Clare stepped over and placed a firm hand on Pax's arm. "Look, Pax, you have to trust us. Like we trusted you, remember? Cerulean is alive because we arrived here in time. We owe you that. I can't think of anyone else who could've navigated so well on the little information we gave you. It was magic. Really." She titled her head and locked eyes with him. "Honestly, thank you for all you've done."

With a sniff, Justine nodded. "Okay, I'll be nice. I'll second Clare. You're a remarkable pilot and a skilled navigator, but—" Her glare seared into Pax's eyes. "If you try to leave this planet's orbit before Cerulean is ready or before we've found Omega, you're a dead man."

Squaring his shoulders, Pax leaned back. He rubbed his jaw. "Fine. I'll be your captive captain. For now. But I'm sending a public record back to Newearth authorities and stating my honest position. You two will be held responsible for the end result. I have zero interest in playing savior and dying a martyr's death."

Clare slapped her forehead. "Aye! Speaking of death,

one of the Mirage-Reborn inhabitants came down with something—a weird skin lesion—and Abbas wants us to look at it—see if we recognize it."

With a frown riding between her eyes, Justine shook her head. "Grandfather is perfectly capable of curing just about every known ailment this side of the Divide. He hardly needs our assistance."

Clare stepped toward the door. "Well, he asked for it. You can explain your laziness to him in person. He also informed me that we can visit Cerulean for a few hours today." Jutting her chin at Pax, her tone turned commanding. "You're coming."

With a playful smile, Justine stroked Pax's arm. "Of course, he's coming. He's eager to meet the townsfolk and tell Cerulean how he's been wrongfully detained."

Brushing off Justine's touch, Pax rose and lumbered after them. "Not that you deserve my help. This whole trip has been one deception after another."

The lift doors swished open, and Clare stepped into the small space.

Pax followed and found a corner. "I don't believe that a planet-eater is out there. It's just a delusional hysteria created by Cerulean's diseased mind."

Justine took her place at the center. "Believe what you want. Ignore the evidence and let conspiracy theories swirl around in your brain. As long as you keep this ship in readiness, I won't kill you."

Pax clasped his hands and stared at the ceiling. "That's the second death threat in less than an hour." He sighed. "So glad I'm here."

Justine would never admit it out loud. *Me too.*

~~~

7
~~~

Cerulean sat up and considered his environment. Light green wallpaper with scrolls of pink and blue flowers decorated the bedroom like fake ivy twined through the bars of a birdcage. His bed, wood-framed with a thick mattress worn to a slump on the left side, reminded him of the old mattress on Anne's farmstead. Running his hand over the cover, he admired the cross-stitched, homemade quilt—simple squares of what looked like old clothes.

A knock turned his attention. He stared at the white three-paneled door and cleared his throat. Lifting his chin, he clasped his hands together. *Ready for—anything.* "Come in."

A medium-sized woman with shoulder-length brown hair and severely short bangs over hazel eyes and wearing a shapeless, beige dress carried a tray into the room. Once at his bedside, she nudged a water glass aside and then placed the tray on the side table.

Upon the tray sat a rose-speckled porcelain bowl with a thick metal spoon. Steam swirled into the air. A limp piece of white bread slathered with creamy yellow butter lay next to the bowl. A peach with fuzzy pink skin brightened the stark setting.

Cerulean sniffed and leaned closer, absorbing the smells and pleased by the wholesome sight. His spirit lightened, as if someone had just taken a load off his back. He looked at the woman. "You're a sight for sore eyes. I thought I'd die of neglect in here. Does Abbas usually have so little pity on his patients?"

The woman, late thirties or early forties, flicked a towel off her shoulder and wrung it in her hands. "I don't know what you mean. Abbas is the soul of kindness. Everyone thinks so. You've just been out of your head. You don't realize—"

Surprised by her anxiety, Cerulean lifted his hand. "I've missed your name." Pointing to the food, he nodded at her. "I'd like to thank you—"

"Don't thank *me*. It's nothing. Abbas asked me to let you stay here and to feed you a home-cooked meal when you woke, so, naturally, I did what I could. Nothing special." She straightened stiffly and fixed her eyes directly ahead as if waiting for her next order.

Flummoxed, Cerulean tried to think of a comment to put her at ease.

Pounding shook the wall, and a voice rose in thunderous demand. "Grace, where've you gotten to? I'm hungry, and it's late. You promised to wheel me over to the hall this afternoon!"

Grace's pink cheeks blanched. She hurried to the door.

Cerulean snapped his fingers. "*Grace.* Yes, Abbas mentioned you. But I thought he meant—"

Grace stepped through the doorway and called out, "Be right there, Father. I'm coming." She turned and met Cerulean's inquisitive gaze. "My father was born and raised on Lux. We emigrated here when—" She shook her head. "Never mind. It's not important." She glanced at the tray. "You better eat before it gets cold. Though Luxonians don't really need food, do they? But dinner and a bed are what Abbas wanted for you."

As Grace started over the threshold, Justine stuck her head into the room and grinned.

Grace squeezed by.

Justine sauntered in, eyeing the cozy comforts. Refocusing on Cerulean, she placed her hand against her chest and practically cooed. "Be still, my anxious heart. Is my friend finally sitting up and"—she pointed to the bowl—"eating—what is that? Green gruel?"

Grace's voice called back, "It's broccoli and cheese."

Controlling an eyeroll, Cerulean considered Grace's plaintive defense before he turned his attention to Justine.

Justine sat on the edge of his bed and poked his arm.

"Be nice. You know how weak I am."

Justine ladled a scoop of the chunky soup and then let it drizzle back into the bowl. "Looks nutritious anyway." She locked eyes with Cerulean and leaned in, whispering, "What do you really want?"

"A strong cup of coffee and a dozen chocolate chip cookies."

Without flinching, Justine kept her gaze steady. "After you kill yourself with terrible food choices, you'll be the death of me; you do realize that."

Multiple heavy treads unlocked their mutual gaze.

Clare, tugging Pax along, strode through the doorway. "Sorry we took so long, but Pax thought he recognized an old friend, and I had to remind him of his primary duty." She bestowed a fake smile on Pax.

With not an ounce of pretense, Pax scowled.

Exhaustion diminished Cerulean's welcoming wave to a mere finger flutter.

Pax offered a mock salute.

Clare shoved him forward.

Cerulean gestured toward a couple of chairs. "Pull up a seat. Tell me everything."

Once Pax and Clare were seated, the room fell deathly silent.

Clare laced and unlaced her fingers.

Pax lounged in the chair and stretched out his legs.

With a quick jerk, Justine rose and paced across the room. "Abbas won't tell us anything. Omega isn't here. Apparently, he left last year and hasn't been seen or heard of since. The inhabitants of this place appear happy enough, though I gather there is some tension between the sheriff, a man named Quinn, and some citizens." Justine shrugged. "Humans hate authority figures. Anyway, Abbas won't say—or can't tell us—where Omega has gone, and he doesn't seem inclined to help us in the matter of Cosmos either."

Pax clasped his hands behind his head. "Why should he? A supposed planet-eater light years from here is no concern of his. He's probably quite happy playing god in his little kingdom." He muttered, "I know I would be."

Clare pointed at Pax as she eyed Cerulean. "He's just mad because we wouldn't let him run away. Thinks he can return to Newearth, and life will go on as usual."

Using all the strength he could muster, Cerulean studied each of his guests, considering Pax the longest. "Getting ill wasn't part of my plan, but we still have a job to do. Abbas doesn't have the faculties he used to, and to be honest, he's detached from the concerns of the universe. Pax is right; he only cares for Mirage-Reborn and his son. Little else matters. If you hadn't shown up on his doorstep with me near death, I doubt he'd even have talked to you."

Justine gripped the bed frame. "So, what now? Should we go find—?"

Cerulean shoved back his covers and attempted to throw his legs over the side, but his body wavered, shimmering and fading.

Pax sprang from his chair and forced Cerulean back. "Stop! I've already saved you once. Now don't act like an idiot. Rest until you're strong again." He glanced at Justine. "I'll go to the ship and see what our sensors tell us about Omega's whereabouts. In the meantime,"—he glared at Justine— "keep this idiot in bed." His gaze swerved to Clare. "You're a human rights investigator, right? So—go investigate. Somebody knows where Omega went or how to get a message to him. Surely, even demi-gods have a message system."

Justine smirked as she tossed a glance at Clare. "Told you he'd come in handy."

Pax pounded to the door. "Just do your job so we can get this mess straightened out. I have no plans to stay here one millisecond longer than I have to." His footsteps pounded down the stairs.

Clare shrugged an I-don't-know-what's-eating-him expression at Cerulean, then traipsed over the threshold and out the door.

Justine spread the blanket over Cerulean's legs and smoothed out the wrinkles. A frown puckered between her eyes.

Cerulean sighed as he lay back on the pillows. "What?"

"I don't get why Pax hates it here so much." Her gaze strayed up to a picture on the wall: a mother holding her baby. "But I do understand his desire to go home."

Cerulean took her hand, clasping her cold fingers in his own. With a flutter in his chest, a picture of the ebullient child filled his mind. *How Omega ever managed to combine Luxonian and Human natures…* He struggled to refocus on Justine. "Zara will be fine. Kendra and Faye will take good care of her."

Slowly pulling away, Justine squared her shoulders. "True. But I still miss her."

Cerulean exhaled a long breath. "All the more reason to find Omega and solve our problem."

Justine started for the door.

Cerulean closed his eyes and prayed for sleep. "But keep an eye on Pax—and everyone else—if you can manage it."

Chapter Two

–Newearth–

We All Have Our Weakness

Taug, a typical Cresta with a large, soft body, four tentacles, and a brain sack hidden behind a spiral shell at the back of his head, wore a slimmed-down grey-green bio-suit and matching boots. He sat at a red booth and leaned over the café table opposite his shape-shifting, Bhuaci friend. His eyes narrowed in concentrated pleasure as he slurped a large green drink from a curvy straw.

Faye, in her usual elfin style, shimmered in a sparkly cream-colored top and pink legging. While her feet swung free under the table, she swirled a significant dollop of chocolate syrup on top of a towering banana split. She scooped up a huge mouthful and moaned in ecstasy.

Late afternoon customers packed the Breakfastnook Café on a sublime mid-summer day, and the noise level rose nearly ten decibels as a group of Uanyi youth—insectine with rubbery exoskeletons, enormous eyes, and long necks—bustled to a rear booth, slapping each other on the back and calling out to another party across the room.

With his eyes following the rowdy throng, Riko, a tall, slim Uanyi wearing his standard tight white shirt and sailor-style pants, sauntered to the empty booth across from Taug and Faye and began to wipe the table with a disinfectant cloth.

Licking her lips as she savored the exquisite blend of syrup, ice cream, and fresh fruit, Faye's gaze followed Riko with interest.

Taug gurgled the last of his drink and leaned back, patting his ample stomach. He grinned in happy contentment. “That was one of the best Greens I’ve ever had. I’ll tell Riko next time—”

Faye popped the spoon from her mouth. “He’s right there.”

Taug squiggled his cumbersome body around. “Oh! Hello, Riko. That’s not your usual duty—cleaning up. What happened to your hostess—the big Ingot—the one with a passion for androids?”

Giving the table a final sanitary slap, Riko straightened and plodded over. “She’s getting married. Ups and tells me the day before the wedding. Said it was a sudden decision, and it can’t be put off.”

Faye shrugged, swirling her spoon in her empty dish. “Maybe it was a matter of necessity.” She raised her eyebrows. “A *family* matter.”

Riko shook his head, the rag dangling from his hand. “Don’t think so. The husband-to-be is itsy-bitsy—for an Ingot, I mean. Never saw such a mismatch. Can’t see them having offspring.”

Taug shoved his empty glass aside. “Size has nothing to do with Ingot reproduction. Most of it is done in a lab—” He frowned at Riko. “I’d have thought you’d know that, considering how many you have in your employment. Ignorance is never bliss, my friend.”

Faye’s gaze darted from Taug to Riko. She raised her hand in protest. “Riko is a master of his profession. I doubt there is much he doesn’t know.”

His pride puffing, Riko lifted his hands like an honest man. “Hey, I run a clean café; reproduction cycles are way off my radar. But there are other matters...” He leaned in, his gaze sweeping from Faye to Taug. “You heard anything?”

Taug pursed his lips, his gaze traveling across the

room.

A cloud passed over Faye's face, shadowing any hint of joy as she shook her head. "They left three days ago, but Cerulean hasn't been in touch." She drew Riko in with a beckoning finger. "He's *very* ill. I'm not sure he'll survive the trip."

Riko squared his shoulders. "Even if Cerulean is sick and can't find Omega, Max and Bala can still track Cosmos and destroy her before she gets within—"

Slapping a tentacle on the table, Taug harrumphed. "Max and Bala don't have the least idea what they're dealing with. By the Divide, Cosmos eats planets!"

As customers turned in their direction, Riko waved to another Uanyi at the back of the café. "Turn up the music, would you? It's too quiet in here."

An OldEarth mix of oriental meditative music and Bhuaci chimes lifted the noise level several decibels.

Taug squeezed out of the booth. "I have to go. I've got applications to fill out." *Blasted things. I might as well be a pod who never walked on land before.*

Riko snatched up the empty dishes and glared at the Cresta. "Don't tell me you're getting a job like the rest of us laboring folk?"

Faye scooted out after Taug and stood to her full height, a kitten between two Great Danes. She faced Riko. "Taug just wants to make himself useful. Though—"

Gurgling, Taug stared at her.

Faye snapped her mouth shut.

With a shrug, Riko started away. "No concern of mine. I mind my own business—just praying that my new hostess doesn't have any secret love interests."

As Riko shuffled out of range, Faye turned and poked Taug in his protruding middle. "You were quite rude."

Swinging her hand playfully in his tentacle, Taug

pulled her to the door, a grin spreading over his face. "Yes, well, I'm fond of mysteries and not saying too much. Except to you, of course."

~~~

Faye stood in the middle of a beautifully furnished apartment and arranged a miniature figurine on a two-meter board. She eyed the battle array. Two armies faced each other, one composed entirely of humans, the other of various lifeforms, including Crestas, Ingots, Uanyi, Bhuaci, and even a bright Luxonian sparkled here and there.

Taug sat scrunched at a computer station, expertly importing information into the database. He glanced at Faye and smirked. "The Luxonians should be on the human side. They're *always* on the humans' side."

Faye waved his comment away. "Not so. In the very beginning, Luxonians tried to experiment on humans. They actually—"

Taug squeezed around in the little chair. "You can be so blind sometimes—it amazes me. Luxonians need humans almost as much as humans need Luxonians. They've become interdependent to a disgusting degree."

Faye moved one human figure forward and stepped away from the game board. Sallying over to Taug, she pointed at the screen. "Any luck?"

Taug sighed and slapped at the console. "If I'm willing to be a lackey working for Human Services or the Inter-Alien Commission, I might be able to get an entry-level position, but no serious scientist in the Cresta establishment will touch me." He stared beyond the screen to the large bay window, which encompassed the
~~~

entire west wall of Faye's apartment.

With a nod, Faye scooted to the window and looked over the Vandi population as it scurried home before the late summer sun settled behind the low, eco-friendly buildings. "They're scared. Few people stop to chat, and everyone glances at the sky, fearing to see an enormous shadow ready to eat them alive." *All so familiar.*

Heaving himself to his feet, Taug plodded across the room and joined Faye. "I thought I was depressed." He laid a tentacle on her shoulder. "You have a morbid way with words."

Faye clasped his tentacle and turned, facing him in the half-light. "You could save us—if you really tried." Her own helplessness nearly strangled her will to live.

A shiver spread over Taug's body. "Little one, you think too much of your humble servant. I'm the one who failed—remember? I failed everyone—most especially myself."

Morphing into an enormous red and gold snake, Faye peered into Taug's eyes. "I can take on any shape I please. I can even become as dangerous as a Crestonian sea serpent, but nothing *I* do will stop Cosmos from coming. But you—"

Taug wrapped his tentacles around his body and waddled across the room, nearly knocking the delicate game board asunder as he went by. "Me? I'm useless. Worse than useless—no one trusts me."

Diminishing to her former shape and flittering across the room to stand before him, Faye stopped Taug in his tracks. "I trust you, Taug. We'll all die if someone doesn't save us." She glanced at the shadowed window. "I know Cerulean wants to, and Bala and the rest will do their best, but it isn't enough." She swept her arm toward the game board. "You said that only Luxonians are on humanity's side. But that's not true. What threatens them also threatens us. Bhuaci have already lost one planet to this beast; I lost my own sister—" Choking, Faye pulled a breath deep from her chest and shuddered. She collapsed to her knees.

Her assistant, a male Bhuac named Garrison who always dressed in a uniform of blue tunic and brown leggings, hustled into the room, gripped Faye's shoulders, and glared at Taug. "What've you done?"

Faye steadied herself and raised her hand. "Stop, please. I just overtaxed my strength." She offered an apologetic smile and nodded to the door. "Would you be so kind as to fix dinner? Taug has been taxing his strength, too, working industriously on his applications."

Garrison's somber eyes traveled from Faye to Taug. With a sigh, he surrendered. He backed away with a formal bow and left the room.

Faye faced Taug. Her tone hardened. "I will not surrender to that planet eater. You must stop her. There's a legend that once she gave birth and nearly died in the process. You only need to introduce something into her system that overtaxes her strength. Once she is weak, we can kill her."

Taug froze. His gaze rose to the lofty ceiling, while his voice dropped to a whisper. "Such cruel cunning from a Bhuac."

Faye slapped the game board, jostling the figures. They fell in disarray. "Is it cruel to kill a murderer?"

Rubbing a tentacle across his lips, Taug gazed at his friend. "I never thought so, and the case against Justine was dropped for that very reason. But still, Cosmos is a living organism."

Faye's voice rose hysterically. "That creature is not a sentient being! She's a virus—a cancer. No one hesitates to wipe out a disease, and we'll not hesitate to destroy her." Faye shuffled closer and burrowed her head against Taug's side, like a child nuzzling a loving parent. "Once you discover how."

Taug's tentacle curled around the petite, frail figure. His gaze wandered to the shadowed window.

~~~

Faye ignored the dark night and leaned against the café's glass door curtained by a flowered cloth. She peered into the dim interior. A figure shuffled about inside. After a timid knock, she stood back, waiting and watching.

Riko froze and frowned at the door. Sucking in a deep breath, he gripped the edge of the Dustbuster tucked into his side pocket and marched forward. He yelled at the door. "It's past closing time; try again in the morning."

Clutching every ounce of confidence she could muster, Faye lifted her voice. "Riko, it's me—Faye. Let me in. We need to talk."

After swinging the door wide and sweeping his gaze up and down the quiet street, Riko tugged Faye inside. "At this hour? What, you hear something?"

Horrors had haunted her too long, Faye sighed. *I can't just stand by and let it happen…not again.* Using every ounce of her innate courage, she shoved images of her destroyed home world from her mind. "Not from Cerulean or the others." She leaned in. "But I have a plan, and I need your help."

Scowling, Riko slapped his hands together and turned away. "By the Divide, I always attract troubled females."

Faye trotted after him. "No romantic interludes! I
~~~

want you to help save Newearth."

With long strides, Riko sauntered into his immaculate, well-organized kitchen, crossed through a narrow passageway, opened a door, and then stepped into a soft-lighted living room. Two plush chairs faced each other, while a holographic game station stood against the left wall. A computer console sat embedded in an uncluttered desk with a screen hanging from the ceiling. Two other passages led into dark interiors.

Faye stepped forward, scanned the environment, and ambled toward a colorful holographic space sector ensconced in a wall niche. An incense burner with a cold mound of ash sat at its base. She lifted a tentative finger and caressed the edge of the hologram. "Was this your home world?"

Riko tilted his head, staring at the 3-D image. "Once upon a time."

With one raised eyebrow, Faye frowned at Riko and then gazed around the room. With a slight gasp, she glided near the right passageway and stopped before a golden brazier and a minutely detailed icon hanging on the wall. It depicted a young Uanyi woman with brilliant, laughing eyes, a determined chin, and broad shoulders. *She almost looks like she has my sister's honest eyes*. "Is this—?"

Riko stepped up and clasped his hands in a meditative posture. "Mom. An extraordinary person—everyone thought so."

Faye's gaze darted between the icon and Riko. "I see the resemblance. You are definitely your mother's son."

Chuckling, Riko turned away and flopped down on one of his over-stuffed chairs. "I don't know who else would have me. Okay, flattery will get you a comfortable seat." He pointed to the plush chair. "So, what can I do for you—after I'm done saving Newearth, of course."

Faye perched on the edge of the chair frame, trying to keep from sinking into its depths. "You remember my friend Taug?"

Riko snorted. "No one could forget Taug. He's infamous."

Attempting to lean forward and make eye contact, Faye had to content herself with staying upright. "Well, he's going to save Newearth. I mean, he's going to figure out how to stop Cosmos so that she can't hurt us."

Riko leaned back and let the chair swallow him. "Then, you don't really need me? Oh, blast, I was looking forward to a little excitement."

Faye wiggled to her feet and smoothed down her blouse. "I'm not explaining myself well. Your job is to save Taug."

With a jerk, Riko shot forward, his gaze fixed on Faye. "Okay, enough joking around. I can't imagine what you've got up your little Bhuaci sleeve, but I bet it's wild—and dangerous."

Faye wrinkled her nose, a charming affectation that usually worked. "It might ruin your life. But considering that we're facing death anyway, I thought you'd be interested."

Riko rotated his hand in a so-so gesture. "Go on..."

Scooting off the chair, Faye wandered over to the portrait and stared at the figure she wished she had known. "Taug is a worthy Cresta, more so than most. I'd trust him with my life. But"—she turned and peered into a dark shadow—"not with everyone's." She sighed. "We all have our weaknesses. I'm afraid that Taug wants to regain his former position so much that he might let certain scientists know what he's doing."

Taug stroked his chin. "And that's bad?"

"Crestonian society sees Newearth as a source of

wealth—a living laboratory. They've never valued non-Cresta lifeforms; that's not in their interest. If Newearth were eaten—say—it would be unfortunate, but that's all. Those who succumbed to cruel fate would be the acceptable price one paid for scientific exploration."

Riko heaved himself from the chair and paced across the room. "They'd want to preserve Newearth resources, surely."

"Observing Cosmos devour her latest snack would be quite informative. They'd have to destroy her, certainly, but only after they'd completed their tests."

Halting in front of Faye, Riko gripped her by the arms. "Even Crestas aren't that merciless. They want to help us."

Faye pulled free and returned to the portrait. Her voice dropped to a whisper. "Who killed your mother?"

Silence fell like a knife on a chopping block.

After a long moment, Riko's breathing rose directly behind Faye, who stood facing the portrait of his mother. "It was a civil war. A long and terrible story."

Turning, Faye stared into Riko's eyes. "If Ingots can kill their own kind, a Cresta could surely watch aliens die."

"If Taug is no good, then why trust him?"

"Oh, but he is good. I just need someone to keep an eye on him." She reached out and clasped Riko's hand. "Oh, and he needs a lab—a very expensive lab—where he can work without any interference."

Riko peered down at her petite hand clasping his. "You need money?" He shrugged, disappointment as clear as a snuffed candle. "I don't have much."

Faye let his hand slip away. She lifted the brazier and placed it under the portrait. With a snap, she lit a cube of incense. Gray curls of smoke wafted before their eyes, and a heavy scent filled the air. "You have what we need.

The café's collateral will cover the expenses."

Riko squeezed his eyes shut.

However necessary, cruel demands still cut deep. Before his pain became her own, Faye hurried out the door and into the dark night.

Chapter Three

–The Merrimack–

Impossible

Bala loved ships of all kinds. Missions were another matter altogether.

The Merrimack sped through the star-speckled blackness like an asteroid careening across a night sky. On the curved sides, banks of rectangular windows lighted the interior, softening the severe outline of the gray oval structure. Various weapon ports dimpled the top and bottom, forward and aft. Being the pride and joy of Newearth's Inter-Alien Alliance Protection Program, it had taken the combined efforts of the Luxonian Diplomatic Corps, a coalition of Bhuaci for a Better World, and no less than twenty Human Services Representatives to forge an agreement, placing the ship in Roux, Max, and Bala's capable hands for exactly one hundred and eighty-four days—approximately half a year.

Sitting at a round white table in the ship's lounge, Bala choked on a well-salted French fry. He stared at his datapad and read the fine print on the final agreement.

"Under penalty of Inter-Alien Alliance law, The Merrimack *will be fully serviced before being returned to Newearth at docking bay seven, the twenty-eighth day of the second month, year fifty-five."*

He chomped on another fry and reclined on the swayback chair. "Ha! *If* we ever return."

The door hissed open, and Roux slipped inside, his gaze flicking right to left.

"What's wrong? Missing something—or someone?" Bala's eyebrows bounced up and down in sympathetic understanding.

Slapping his hands over his face, Roux stumbled to the couch and fell lengthwise. "Lord, have mercy. I swore I'd never do this to myself again—but look what I've up and done. I'm careening into uncharted territory with—"

Bala squared his shoulders, ran his fingers through his unruly hair, and stuck out his chest. "The best man in the universe to tackle an impossible mission, sir!" Gulping his last couple of fries, he rose and snapped his stocking feet together. "Reporting for duty, sir!"

Dragging his fingers down his face, Roux peered at the severely vertical Bala and groaned.

Bala remained as stiff as a statue.

Roux righted himself and leaned forward, waving Bala back to his seat. "Okay, enough." He peered into Bala's eyes. "Get serious, man. We're about to face the deadliest force this side of the Divide."

"*That* side of the Divide, too, by all accounts, sir."

Roux's jaw jutted forward. "Cerulean sent you to punish me, didn't he?"

At Cerulean's name, Bala's enthusiasm deflated like a punctured balloon. He swiveled back to the table and drummed his fingers. "Sorry. When I get nervous, I get silly. Just my way." He rose and headed to the food dispenser. Tossing a glance back at Roux, he gestured to indicate the menu. "Want something? The fries aren't half bad. The ketchup is terrible, though. Still, enough salt can fix about anything."

Roux rose and took a seat at the table. "Get me a drink—something hot and titillating."

Bala turned and tapped the console, muttering, "He doesn't mean it. Not a chance." Two steaming mugs slid through an opening, and Bala carried them over to Roux. "The word is *scintillating* not *titillating*." He handed one over and gripped the other for dear life. "Strong and hot. Should add sparkle to your life—if that's what you need—Luxonian."

Roux nodded his gratitude and took a sip. "Ah! If only we had some homemade bread to go with it." He shook his head, clearly trying to shake off a memory, and gestured. "Now sit down and tell me what you know about this Bhuac, Yelsa. I may be the one who brought her on board, but I'd like to know your impression."

Bala shrugged. "I've hardly had the chance to get to know her. But I'll admit; she isn't like other Bhuacs. Most are quiet and reclusive. But then again, Faye is cute but dangerous, probably because she was forced into leadership before she was ready. War will do that. But Yelsa—she's clearly eager for engagement. The way she dresses and her take-charge attitude—"

The door slid open, and a young woman dressed in a brown jerkin over a black shirt, gray leggings, and calf-length, laced boots stepped forward. Her mass of curly hair nearly overwhelmed her thin face. After a cursory glance around the room, she nodded respectfully to the two men and ambled toward the dispenser.

Bala's and Roux's eyes followed her every move.

I must maintain a professional demeanor... Using utmost self-control, Bala refused to smile though his eyebrows danced. He cleared his throat. "We've got room here, Yelsa. Care to join us?"

An aroma of garlic and onion filled the air, and the sound of a liquid pouring into a bowl arrested Bala's attention. He sniffed deeply as Yelsa drew near, his gaze surveying her tray.

Yelsa slid into the seat across from Bala, next to Roux, and offered a thin smile. "Thank you. I wasn't sure how strict you'd be here."

Roux peered at Yelsa as she settled her dishes into position. "Strict?"

Tearing a small loaf of bread in half, she shrugged. "You know. Separation of beings—either by race or rank. The usual."

With a laugh, Roux pushed back his chair and stood. "We'd all be eating alone if that was the case." He drummed the back of his chair and stared at the door as it slid open again.

A tall man with black hair, a sharp chin, and well-defined muscles in a crisp, dark green uniform marched into the room, his gaze locking onto Roux. "Sir? I finished calibrating Cosmos' last known location, and I—"

Yelsa leapt to her feet, her eyes wide and her brows arched. "Sir! I'm in charge of locating the creature. I've already input the data needed to ascertain her next target. You told me that I'd—"

Using a halt signal with one hand facing Yelsa, Roux stepped from the table and waved Max over. "Apparently you two haven't set things straight." He swept his gaze between the two. "*Max* is supposed to work with you to find the best—"

"I work alone!" Yelsa's hands clamped her waist as her gaze narrowed in on Max.

Enjoying the battle of wills, Bala rested his head on one hand, his gaze bouncing from one speaker to the next.

"No one works alone on board a ship, Yelsa." Roux pointed to her soup. "Sit down and finish your meal. I'm calling a meeting at thirteen hundred, and I want everyone on the bridge, ready to work—together." His gaze intercepted Max's glare. "Have you seen Dr. Jazzmarie?"

Blinking rapidly, Max squirmed. “She was on the bridge a few moments ago.”

Roux nodded. “Good. I need to check on a few things.” He pointed at Bala. “You’ll be working the communication systems primarily, so familiarize yourself with the console on the bridge. I’ll address your other duties when we’re all together.”

Rising, a new thought sped through Bala’s brain. He checked his datapad and frowned. “I’m still waiting for an important check-in. Seems messages aren’t getting through as well as I’d hoped.”

Max glanced back at Bala. “Where we’re going, messages may never get through.”

Roux and Max crossed over the threshold, and the door closed behind them.

Yelsa sipped her soup, her eyes staring vacantly across the room.

Bala tapped his datapad and then slapped it against his hand.

Yelsa glanced up. “You don’t need to worry about communication protocol. Newearth authorities aren’t going to question us, as long as we get the job done.” She stuffed a large chunk of bread into her mouth.

Wincing at the uncouth sight, Bala glanced aside. “I’m not trying to reach the governor; I’m trying to check in with my wife.”

Yelsa chewed around her words and snorted. “Wife? Ha! You have kids, too, I suppose?”

“Six.”

Shaking her head, Yelsa jabbed the air with her spoon. “No accounting for taste.”

Bala didn’t say it, but words rang in his ear. *So true.*

~~~
~~~

Jazzmarie hummed an ancient human lullaby as her eyes scanned the bridge console. Dressed in a blue and green embroidered skirt and a lacy, yellow blouse, with her thick hair tied in a smooth bun on the top of her head, she appeared regal, like a queen of Oldearth. Her black eyes and gentle smile softened her appearance, lessening the distance between herself and any mere commoner who stood before her. Her round features belied the quickness of her gaze and the speed of her mind.

When the bridge door slid open, she glanced up.

Max stood frozen on the lift.

Roux circled around him, staring in irritation at his stiff figure. "What's wrong with you, Max? Your circuits overload or something?"

Jerking forward, Max marched to a console at the far end of the room. "No, sir. Just trying to solve a problem—"

Tickled by Max's discomfort, Jazzmarie laughed. "I think he means me, Roux." She ambled over to Max. "Sorry about this morning, Maximan. I wasn't trying to be intrusive; it's just that I've never been this close to an android—of your quality—before." She grinned at his blank stare. "You are quite remarkable!"

Max leaned over the console, effectively breaking off the conversation. "Duly noted."

Scratching his head, Roux dropped down on the captain's chair. "I've called a meeting for"—he glanced at the main screen depicting date, time, current coordinates, and other significant data—"thirteen hundred. Ten minutes. Yelsa and Bala will join us. Have you been able to review everyone's medical history, Doctor?"

Jazzmarie strode to the captain's chair, placed her sculptured brown hand on the console, and nodded.

"Please, call me Jazzmarie. The title Doctor seems too cold and clinical for such an intimate setting." She glanced at the bio-console with a grin. "You certainly have a mixed crew, Roux. The Luxonian Medical Department has been kind enough to share information with us for years, so I'm quite familiar with *your* needs. I only wish I could have been of assistance to Cerulean before he was snatched off the planet."

The door swished open, and Bala ambled in, his shoulders slumped. "I'm early, but I thought I'd try to get a message through using the bridge console. Maybe, I'll have better luck."

Roux waved him along. His gaze returned to Jazzmarie. "Since you're human yourself, Bala's biology poses no mystery, but how about Yelsa?"

Jazzmarie narrowed her eyes, a spark of irritation igniting a dark mood. "Shapeshifters are all much alike. I find Bhuaci physiology rather boring, honestly. They can morph into simple forms, but they lack higher abilities."

The door opened, and Yelsa stomped forward, her searching gaze locked onto the tactical console where Max stood.

Max glanced up and stiffened. "I am in the middle of programming our first run-through."

Running over and leaning in, Yelsa scanned the screen. "You idiot! We're not taking our ship through an asteroid belt. Even an android can't be that reckless."

Roux cleared his throat noisily and rose to his feet. "Our meeting will begin now." He beckoned the crew to stand before him on the lower deck. "I realize that there has been very little preparation or consultation before we set out. That was not due to oversight but rather to ensure the safety of our mission. We can't afford to have people asking too many questions."

"And why not?" The doctor's hands were poised on her hips as her eyes locked onto Roux's uncertain gaze.

Roux lifted his chin. "Because we don't have the answers. Our mission is to track Cosmos and engage her—only if necessary. We don't know if we can even find her, or if we do find her, what her reaction will be."

Max stepped away from the console. "So, what—exactly—is our objective?"

Lifting her hand, Yelsa shook her head like a grieved teacher. Her tone vibrated with sarcasm. "Possibly to find the beast and destroy it before it can devour Newearth, you think?"

Jazzmarie clasped her hands and bowed her head in mock respect. "That objective states a great deal more about you than about this mission, Yelsa."

Bala jumped and twirled around, scrambling for his pocket, nearly tripping over Max. "Oh, ow! Stinging!"

Max gripped Bala by the shoulder, keeping him upright by sheer force.

Roux's eyes locked on Bala. "What the hell are you doing?"

Pulling his datapad from a side pocket, Bala juggled it from hand-to-hand before he finally tapped it and exhaled a deep breath. "I didn't want to miss Kendra's message, so I set it for high vibration, but it felt like getting zapped with a taser."

Roux rubbed his forehead spasmodically. "Go ahead. Read it. We won't be able to go forward until—"

Bala's eyes widened as he scrolled through the message. He squeaked and reached for the deck railing. "Oh, God!"

Max's grip on his shoulder tightened.

All eyes fixed on Bala.

Jazzmarie pulled a gauge from her skirt band and pressed it against Bala's head. "Stand still; I want to get an accurate—"

Bala waved her off. "I'm not sick! Kendra is. She's been sent to New-Mayo for tests."

Max assisted Bala to a chair, shoved him down, and tucked his legs under the console. He patted Bala on the back with one hand, keeping a firm hold with the other.

Jazzmarie watched Max in rapt fascination. *He's so sensitive!*

Roux strode to Bala and held out his hand. "Let me see that."

Bala handed over the datapad.

The room remained silent as Roux scrolled through the message.

Yelsa returned to the console, leaned in, and pressed a series of commands.

Max's gaze darted to her, and he opened his mouth, but Roux's chuckle interrupted him.

"She's being sent to the obstetrics department, Bala." He patted the drooping man on one shoulder. "You didn't tell me that she's expecting."

Bala wobbled to his feet. "She's not—she would've told me. I wouldn't have left if—" He slumped back onto the chair. "I need to go home."

Yelsa straightened and squared her shoulders. "That's not in our near future. I found Cosmos' trail. She's quite a distance, but I've locked onto it."

Max stomped over to Yelsa and peered at the console. Frowning, he tapped a series of commands. Glancing over his shoulder, he commanded the room with an authoritative tone. "Take a look, sir. Do you really want to follow this trajectory?"

A holographic scene appeared on the platform, depicting a colorful galaxy and a wavering black streak in the distance. A red line marked the trajectory through the star system but dissolved at the edge of the black miasma.

Roux turned slowly and peered at Yelsa, his hands clenching at his sides. “Yelsa? You want to take us around the Divide?”

Yelsa shook her head, her unwavering gaze fixed on the holographic image. “No, sir, that would take too long, and we’d lose her. We must go through it.”

Jazzmarie pursed her lips as she eyed the young Bhuaci. *Even the best-intentioned fools are still fools.*

Chapter Four

–Mirage-Reborn–

Happy Existence

Cerulean leaned against the window frame and watched the inhabitants of Mirage-Reborn shuffle along the street, intent on their daily duties. He could hear Grace as she bustled in the kitchen, fixing meals and carrying food to her father. The old man had a temper, but Grace appeared to take everything in a calm stride. Like the rest of the planet, Cerulean surmised her attitude reflected more illusion than truth.

The dusty street, lined with various shops, a bank, a library, and a sheriff's office, glowed in the early morning light. Apparently, no post office was needed. His gaze shifted to the brilliant blue sky. Not a star could be seen, though he knew perfectly well that they sparkled above in uncountable abundance. Was this world totally cut off from the larger universe? Anxiety pressed on him as a shimmering weakness tingled in his feet.

Movement dropped his gaze to the sidewalk, where a thin man swaggered out of the sheriff's office. His form settling again, Cerulean leaned forward, holding the curtain aside. Another man stepped off the walkway, skirted between an OldEarth DeSoto Sedan and an Oldsmobile Coupe, and tromped across the street. "Hey, Quinn! I've got something you'll want to see."

With a slow smile, Quinn faced the man and nodded. He gripped the man's arm with welcoming authority and steered him back inside the office.

Cerulean frowned. He'd seen townsfolk passing in and out of Quinn's office all day, but there never seemed to be any trouble. Why so many visitors?

Stiffening, Cerulean realized that someone stood behind him. Dropping the curtain, he made a slow turn, his gaze steady.

Abbas, broad-shouldered but with a worry-lined face, stood in the middle of the room. "Entertained?"

Cerulean let his gaze wander toward the closed door. He refocused on Abbas. "Certainly. Are you?"

Abbas' laugh shed years off his face. "I wouldn't be here otherwise. Though, I must admit, my citizens' endless demands exhaust all patience." He stepped closer and gestured toward the chair. "Please, sit. I don't want to sap your newfound strength." He glanced out the door. "Grace has taken her father to the grocery store. The original proprietor passed away last week, and I've asked her to take over the place. She's capable, and it will allow her some measure of freedom from her father's demands—don't you think?"

Rather than sit, Cerulean leaned against the back wall, his gaze still flickering to the window where the curtain ruffled in a light breeze. "I know little about Grace, this town, or any of your citizens. They appear to be content—rather like birds in a gilded cage."

Abbas strolled to the chair and sat on the edge, smoothing his wrinkled brow. "I was hoping that you'd see past the obvious and perceive our depths."

Cerulean shrugged and stepped to the window again.

Justine and Pax strolled down the sidewalk; their heads bent in earnest conversation.

His heart clenching, Cerulean glanced at Abbas. "I only know that Newearth is facing destruction, and our one hope—Omega—is not here."

Abbas interlaced his fingers and sat in the chair by the window. "Why do you say your *one* hope when surely there are many solutions to your problem?"

With a snort, Cerulean retreated to the bed and sat on the edge. "If you have any ideas…I'd love to hear them."

A car roared down the street, drowning all hope of conversation. Abbas closed his eyes. "I need to muffle those things—if not for their sake—for mine." He peered over. "Don't look to me to solve your Cosmos problem. I'm getting too old to manage this meager town." He tilted his head. "Perhaps we could do each other a service?"

Cerulean spread his hands wide, offering his services.

"You compared Mirage-Reborn to a gilded cage. But the truth is that every inhabitant living here was doomed elsewhere. Omega saved each one from a deadly fate—deserved or otherwise. I'm not always proud of my son's exuberance, but I admire his devotion. He's like his mother. While I created a world to study, he created a family to love."

"So, why did he leave? Where has he gone?"

"He didn't inform me of his plans. All I know is that these people will fall into chaos if left to their natural devices. They need a leader."

"Or a god?"

With a weary sigh, Abbas rose and approached the window. "I am Abbas—a father who cares for them in place of my son. Omega means to be responsible, but I am bearing the responsibility, like a grandfather left with abandoned children."

Cerulean joined Abbas at the window. They watched a Cresta citizen lumber along with an armload of groceries behind a Bhuaci couple. His heart warmed at the sight. "Reminds me of Newearth."

Abbas smiled. "That was Omega's vision—why we call this place Mirage-Reborn. Where I created a primitive village for one race, he modernized and blended many races into a single town. Personally, I think he's obsessed with Newearth—or at least with certain Newearth inhabitants."

Swallowing, Cerulean flicked a glimpse at Abbas. "He considers Justine his daughter, and Zara—"

Abbas waved a hand. "Stop. You're reading in your own emotions and labels. Remember, Omega has no experience. He never married and never generated life. He has only observations and experiments. He is a child."

Cerulean tapped his fingers against his thigh, his impatience rising. "It seems that we both need your son."

"Exactly!" Abbas placed his hand on Cerulean's shoulder and led him to the door. "You can't afford to wait until Omega returns, and I can't bear this weight any longer." He stopped and stared into Cerulean's eyes. "If you knew how old I am, how I long to be released from all this—you'd pity me." He opened the door and started down the dim hallway. "I must find Omega and bring him home."

Cerulean's steps quickened.

Turning at an entryway, Abbas stopped. "But I can't leave Mirage-Reborn unattended. I need you to stay and act—"

Horror filling every crevasse of his being, Cerulean froze.

"…as a counselor and friend." Abbas gripped Cerulean's arm. "You're still recovering. But I'll help you. While you're here, I'll give you a human body that won't require the Luxonian sunlight for regeneration. As soon as your mission is complete, I'll return you to Lux for deep healing."

Limp, Cerulean bowed his head to an inevitable doom. He would not find rest here.

Abbas' grip tightened. "There's no other way. You're in no condition to search for Omega, and none of your friends has the least hope of finding him or defeating Cosmos alone. Your best hope is that I can discover his whereabouts and return him to Mirage-Reborn."

Cerulean looked into Abbas' eyes and glimpsed the depth of his desperation. "Then he will help us to defeat Cosmos?"

Abbas started forward and crossed into the well-lit front room. He pulled open the front door and led Cerulean onto the porch. Gesturing toward the townsfolk passing along the sidewalk, chatting and strolling with preoccupied concerns, he grinned. "They're very much like your Newearth friends, just in a more primitive environment. He won't let either world die—if he can help it."

He glided down the steps. "They've each been snatched from a merciless fate by the generosity of my son, but they don't know how to maintain their happy existence."

Cerulean stopped on the bottom step and surveyed the bustling street.

"If left to themselves, they'd destroy everything we created here." Abbas eyed Cerulean. "If you want Omega's help—you must keep these people from killing each other."

~~~

Cerulean watched Abbas stroll away as he clenched the porch railing. The townsfolk slowed to a placid pace under the late summer sun. The steady ring of a blacksmith's hammer halted, and hungry patrons crowded into the café. On impulse, Cerulean descended the steps and started forward.
~~~

A woman's voice called out, "Cerulean!"

Cerulean turned.

Clare hurried up the street. She caught up and wrapped her arm familiarly around his. "Where're you going?"

Patting his lean stomach, Cerulean nodded to the café. "Grace tries her best, but I could use an extra meal or two."

Clare beamed. "Well, in that case, let's go. I'm dying for something sweet. The ship's version of chocolate nearly destroyed my stomach."

The two soon settled on stools at the café's counter. With a brief glance at the menu, Cerulean caught the waitress's harassed attention and ordered a cheeseburger, fries, carrot sticks, and a slice of apple pie.

Clare contented herself with a chocolate milkshake.

Cerulean studied the crowd.

Lacing her fingers with her elbows perched on the counter, Clare stared blankly ahead and sighed.

Cerulean nudged her. "What's eating you?"

"Nothing. It's just—I hate waiting. We're stuck here with no way of catching Omega and getting help—not knowing anything for certain."

A waitress squeezed near, slapped the kitchen counter, and ordered another burger and fries.

Clare leaned toward Cerulean and dropped her voice. "Perhaps it's time to take action."

Disgusted by the waitress's behavior, Cerulean snorted before responding to Clare. "What, you want to take hostages?"

Clearly scandalized, Clare poked his arm. "These people are innocent victims. But how about Abbas? He knows where Omega has gone—he's just protecting him."

"From what?" Cerulean faced Clare.

A scowling waitress with short, black hair and green eyes unloaded a tray and placed a plate piled with food in front of Cerulean and then nudged a tall shake in front of Clare. “You need anything else, just let me know.” She raced on to the next order.

Chomping into his burger, Cerulean ate in silence.

Clare twirled the straw in her shake, a dark frown building between her eyes. Finally, she flicked the straw aside. “How about we demand that Abbas—”

Infuriated by her blind insensitivity, Cerulean wiped his face with a napkin and then hissed, “How about you leave Abbas alone? You might want to try thinking before you speak.”

Clare’s jaw tightened. She crossed her arms over her chest. “I know you’ve been sick, but that’s no reason to get rude. *I am* Newearth’s Human Services representative—remember?”

“Who could forget?” Shoving the dish aside, Cerulean scowled. “How am I supposed to pay for this?”

“You’re on Abbas’ tab. You’re not about to wash the dishes, don’t worry.” She snapped her fingers at the waitress and pointed to Cerulean’s pie and her milkshake. “Could I have this to go?”

The glare she received in return made it clear that leaving was the best option.

~~~

Cerulean meandered along the sidewalk, attempting to sample his apple pie, making a mess in the process.

Clare plunged a straw deep into her cup and inhaled a long, noisy slurp. She turned toward the entrance to the shady park.
~~~

Justine and Pax sat together on a bench on the far side.

Cerulean redirected Clare onto Main Street. "Sorry I was rude, but you have no idea—"

Clare wiped ice cream off her chin and shrugged. "Tell me."

After swallowing the last of his pie, Cerulean wished he had brought along a drink to wash it down. *Too late now.* He cleared his throat. "Turns out that everyone on this planet was sentenced to certain doom before Omega saved him or her."

With a large eye roll, Clare whined, "Oh, please! Not the 'Omega is really a good guy' speech. He tried to sell me that already, but I'm not buying it."

Cerulean stared straight ahead, his tone dropping to an irritated growl. "Clare, you really need to grow up and stop thinking everything revolves around your childhood trauma."

Clare lifted her hands. "Nice, Cerulean! Sheesh. You're so sensitive today!"

As they passed the sheriff's office, the door opened.

Cerulean glanced inside, frowned at the number of guns in a glass cabinet, and quickly returned his attention to Clare. "Abbas believes that he can bring Omega home, but he needs someone to look after the inhabitants while he's gone. So, he wants my help."

Clare halted and gripped Cerulean's arm. "You're supposed to babysit this insanely primitive town?" She jabbed the air. "What's he thinking? It's not our responsibility!"

"Can you find Omega or keep me alive?"

Crushing her empty cup, Clare scowled. "He's offering to keep you alive? I thought you were better already."

Striding forward, Cerulean passed the grocery store. "I'm alive for the time being. But I'm not really healthy yet. He's not a mercenary, Clare. Abbas needs Omega as much as we do. If he goes after him, he hardly wants Mirage-Reborn to fall apart. It makes sense. And maybe—after Omega sees how well we've cared for his little world—he'll be more motivated to help us."

Clare stomped to a trashcan and dropped in her cup. She chewed her lip.

"You have any better ideas?"

Clare tilted her head back and bathed her face in the noonday sun. "What am I going to do in thc meantime—besides avail myself of Mirage-Reborn's charming cuisine?"

Cerulean slipped his empty container into the trash and took her arm. "I heard that the grocery store is under new management. My landlady, Grace, is taking over. You could be of service." He peered into her eyes. "I know this isn't what we planned. Instead of facing a planet-eating monster, we're infiltrating a town of mixed beings who don't have the slightest desire for our care—so far as I can see."

"So why?"

"Because Abbas asked. And when Omega returns, we need him in a good mood."

~~~

Justine rose from the park bench and stepped away from Xavier Pax.

Pax surveyed the empty street.

The park remained quiet with only a couple of children playing on the monkey bars. Justine peered at the lithe little girl swinging behind a boy.

Suddenly, the girl wrapped her legs about the boy's
~~~

waist and hampered his next move. He fell to the ground with a cry, but the girl laughed. "Told you to let me go first."

The wretched little power-grabber! Justine pursed her lips and started forward.

Pax gripped her shoulder. "They're kids. Let 'em be. They'll work it out."

Justine shook Pax's arm away and continued her trajectory.

The girl hung from the bars in easy competence, mocking the boy as he limped away. "Sissy. Next time you should play with babies!"

Justine came up from behind, gripped the child by the waist, and gave her a firm shake. "*That* was not kind."

The girl dropped to the ground. With a furious scowl, she turned around. Then her gaze rose, surveying Justine's powerful physique. She screamed a long, piercing wail. "Mom-my! Dad-dy!"

Pax ran forward and grabbed Justine's arm. "Uh-oh. Let's go."

Justine faced Pax. "You said that you don't trust anyone on this planet. I'm interested in seeing what these people are really like. So far, we have nothing but speculation and"—she stared down at the screaming child—"a nasty little girl."

A Cresta and two humans bustled forward.

With a pained expression, Pax closed his eyes.

Justine faced the humans and ignored the Cresta.

The man scooped up the little girl, his eyes wide with alarm. The woman pounded up to Justine, her index finger swinging. "What's going on? What've you done to my little girl?"

Justine stared at the child, who was now sniffling contentedly on her father's shoulder as he stroked her back. "Ask your daughter."

The man's eyes narrowed. "Listen, you—you—"

Justine lifted her hand. "I'm visiting from Newearth, and I watched your daughter injure a little boy without provocation. I merely pointed out that her behavior was unkind when she—"

The girl scowled, dramatically rubbing her shoulder. "That *thing* jerked my arm off." She laid her head on her father's shoulder, crying in exaggerated sobs.

The Cresta stepped forward. "I'm afraid you'll have to come with me."

A faint smile spread over Justine's face. "And you are?"

"The Official Park Officer."

Pax backed to the sidewalk, turned, and jogged toward the residential neighborhood.

Justine watched him go, one eyebrow rising. She then peered from the mother to the father, her hands placidly at her sides. *I'm never done being surprised by people.* She faced the officer. "Lead the way."

Chapter Five

–Newearth–

Worth Living For

Faye strolled along the avenue, enjoying the shivering coolness that played tag with the heat of the late summer sun on her bare arms.

A gentle breeze blew along Vandi Main Street, fluttering through the tops of the boulevard trees, swirling their leaves in all directions. The maples displayed their silver backs while the oaks rustled in warning of an oncoming storm.

A pair of cream-colored doves perched side by side on the limb of a white pine like an icon of fidelity. Their cooing barely rose against the trills of the Pine Warbler, who flew from a tree limb toward the steep slanted rooftop of the Oldearth Antique Bookshop. A Black-capped Chickadee whistled an energetic tune against the mewing of a discontented cat meandering from the bookshop toward the meat market across the street.

Faye's pixie haircut tousled by the breeze softened her serious, inward contemplation. When she turned and entered the Breakfastnook Café, her eyes locked immediately onto Riko, who stood next to a large, blinking Ingot youth wearing patched techno-armor and scuffed boots.

Riko glanced up, met her gaze, and spoke hurriedly. "Stay here, Wendell, and keep at it. I'll be right back." With an encouraging pat on Wendell's arm, Riko passed the booths to the front door.

Before Faye could speak, he nodded to a shiny, three-paneled door in the east wall and exclaimed in a jocular tone, "It's all right, my dear. Simple mistake. I'll direct you." In formal politeness, he led her to the door and leaned in. He flattened his left hand against the middle panel, his right gripped the handle, and he pressed his eye against a peephole. With a shrug, he muttered. "Triple security—Taug's idea."

The door clicked open, and the two passed through. With a stiff bow, Riko backed away, talking loudly, "No problem. Glad I could help. Remember, this new part isn't my establishment. You'll have to talk to the owner—"

A call from the kitchen forced his retreat without further ceremony.

Faye inhaled a soft breath and stepped into a miniature laboratory. Her gaze scanned the room, traveling from a boxy shelving unit on her left to a miniature Cresta pool against the north wall. She trotted forward, fascinated by the glass-paneled tank filled with Cresta sea life. Splaying her fingers across the surface, she peered in and then jumped back, startled at a pair of staring golden eyes.

Taug rose and gripped the top edge of the pool, lifting his head clear. He let the soupy liquid drip off his neck and wiped his face with the back of a tentacle. "I wasn't expecting you until this evening."

Faye stifled a laugh at his appearance. "There's a storm brewing, so I came early." She pointed at the pool. "That's hardly big enough for an eel, much less a full grown Cresta. What did you do—steal it from a Crestonian nursery?"

Swiping drips from his face, Taug pursed his lips. "If you would look around, you'd see this lab is hardly large enough for a pool of any size. I had to make sacrifices." With a sudden plunge, Taug dropped under the murky water.

Faye turned and studied her surroundings. Against the

east wall a large bank of shelves and cabinets held various laboratory equipment, a second three-paneled door stood in solemn assurance of an outside exit, and a medium-sized screen lay embedded in the wall. A holopad took up the southwest corner, while more shelves and lab equipment lined the south wall. A dissecting table stood in the center of the room and a low, steel framed dissecting tub sat ensconced near the west wall. A rolling table with various knives, pointy tools, tubes, and scopes stood off by itself.

A dripping Taug slapped across the floor with a wide towel wrapped around his middle and his breather-unit strapped into place. He bowed in mock ceremony. "It's not much, but I call it home."

Faye considered Taug in silence before she spoke. "You've become very comfortable with me, I see."

With a grin, Taug snorted, "I'd be stuck inside a cramped bureaucrat's office if it weren't for you. Instead, I'm here, doing what I do best."

Trailing her hand along the side of the dissecting table as she strolled around the room, Faye spoke to the air. "And what have you discovered? Anything new?"

Taug eyed Faye and adjusted his towel. "I planned to wait until I had completed more research to show you, but I do have a starting point."

Faye paused, her gaze still focused on the air. "What's that?"

Taug plodded to the dissecting tub and lifted a thick-rimmed top. He glanced at Faye and pointed inside. "Take a look."

Scuttling across the room like an eager child, Faye leaned forward, stared blankly, and then, in heaving, quick breaths, covered her mouth with one hand and waved frantically with the other. "Shut it! Shut it up, quick!" She backed away and landed limply on a swivel chair against the south wall.

Taug stumped over and laid a firm tentacle on Faye's shoulder. "I have to study living specimens to learn how to kill one."

With a shudder, Faye glanced at the tub and closed her eyes. "What is it? That can't be one of them. It's too small—"

"Think of it as Cosmos' younger cousin, a distant relation in its earliest stage of development. But don't worry; it'll tell me everything I need to know."

"How did you get—"

Taug removed his tentacle from her shoulder and started for the narrow passageway beside the pool. "We all have our little secrets. You must let me keep mine."

Faye stared at Taug's back. "How about if you grow fond of it—like you did with Derik?"

In mid-step, the last drops dribbled from Taug's soft form. Facing the back wall, his voice turned grave. "Derik was innocent. Cosmos is not." He continued his forward momentum and disappeared into the shadows.

Bracing herself, Faye stood and faced the tub. She squared her shoulders and marched to the vat. Using both hands, she lifted the lid a few centimeters and forced herself to peer deeply into the dark interior.

~~~

Riko glanced out the plate glass window as thunder rolled across the sky. He returned his gaze to the lean, shorthaired, and clean-faced Ingot. *Pure innocence inside a brutally confusing body. If only parents understood that...* "Listen, Wendell, it'll be a slow afternoon, and I've shown you all I can for the day. Why
~~~

don't you go on home and start early again tomorrow?"

A red blush highlighted the round scar in the middle of Wendell's forehead as he stared at his torn boots. "If you say. Mama could use help." At over two meters tall, he had to bend to be on level with Riko, but since he slouched, he rarely stood at his full height.

Riko patted Wendell's arm and smiled comfortingly. "Yeah, Zia is a marvel running that daycare. I'm sure she can use all the help she can get. But remember, when you wipe tables, you have to clear them first. Clear—then wipe."

Rubbing a round synthetic portal on the side of his head, Wendell nodded. "Like food. Chew—then swallow."

With only a millisecond's hesitation, Riko nodded. "Yeah. You got it." He approached the door and opened it.

Dark clouds scuttled across the sky, sending a cold wind into the café.

A round-figured Ingot, as unlike her youthful counterpart as night is to day, stood aside as Wendell crossed over the threshold. After a brief backward glance, she sallied inside.

Riko sighed as he watched Wendell clump down thc street in apparent indifference to the sudden rain shower. Riko turned and glanced at the last few Bhuaci customers chatting cozily in a corner booth before he turned a narrow-eyed gaze upon the sultry-eyed Ingot before him. "Okay, Lang, what'dya want?"

Like all Ingots, Lang's body from the neck down was encased in techno-armor, but her form-fitting suit outlined the fantasies of multiple beings. She sauntered to the counter, snatched up a menu, and waved it languidly at Riko. "What? Can't an innocent Ingot get service around here? Or are we only allowed to serve?"

She gazed pointedly at the door.

Oh, right, and I believe every word you say. Riko sneered. "Don't go there, Lang. I run an honest establishment, respecting the rights of all Newearth citizens. Surely, you didn't come here to start a smear campaign. There must be easier hunting on the west end."

With a snort, Lang waved the menu again. "I'm in dire need of a nutritious meal. That's all I want—really."

Riko pulled a datapad from his pocket and tapped it awake. "Okay, sure. I'll play along. What'll you have—to order—I mean?"

"You know what would be heavenly? I'd love a plate of your spicy Crestonian squid with steamed broccoli."

Riko tapped the datapad and looked up. "Anything else?"

"A small glass of apple cider vinegar."

Riko retreated toward the kitchen, tossing a wide grin at the customers departing from the booth. "Have a good evening!"

The front door and the kitchen door swung shut simultaneously.

Without hesitation, Riko turned and peered through the kitchen door window.

Lang eyed the empty café and within seconds, her gaze fixated on the three-paneled side door. She sidled over and gripped the handle. She shook it. It remained fixed in place. Frowning, she bent over and peered through the peephole.

Ah-ha! Just as I thought. Riko grabbed a utensil tray and a jug of brown liquid and hustled back into the dining room. "Ay there! Lang, I told you to hunt somewhere else." Hurrying over with the tray and container, Riko motioned the Ingot back to the counter.

Batting her eyes in schoolgirl contrition, Lang slid

onto a red stool. "I wasn't doing anything—"

Riko waved her lies away. "Keep your stories for the holoscreen and your adoring audience. You'll do anything for good ratings—even make something up and call it news."

Pinching her fingers a few centimeters apart, Lang peered through the tiny space. "There's always a bit of truth in my reports."

Riko sniffed disdainfully and retreated toward the kitchen.

A large, heavyset man with jet-black hair, a ring in his nose, and wearing a sleeveless red shirt and baggy pants strode, chest first, into the café. He swung his gaze across the counter, stopping briefly on Lang, and then swooped past the booths toward Riko. "You the owner—Riko?"

A motley crew of humans crowded into the café, some holding bags of dark liquid, others wielding thick cudgels.

A knot forming in his stomach, Riko cocked his head and strutted forward. "Yeah? What do you want? It's almost closing time—"

The spokesman stomped forward and leaned into Riko's personal space. "I've heard rumors—gonna-get-you-killed rumors. You're working with a Cresta who made some kind of treaty with that planet-eater that's heading our way."

Riko blinked, no coherent thoughts coming to mind. He froze in place.

Lang slid off her seat and sashayed over to the angry human. Purring her words, she wiggled her way between the two, turned her face toward the man, and grinned mischievously. "What's your name? Maybe *I* can help you."

Riko glared at Lang's back.

The black-eyed human refocused his gaze on Lang. "Rufinius."

Lang lifted her hands, wiggling her fingers in welcome, and addressed the assembly. "You all know me—Lang—from *Newearth News Reports*. I'm already investigating this case for the Inter-Alien Alliance, so you needn't worry. At this point—there's nothing but rumors. But trust me"—she twirled around and gripped Riko by his starched, white shirt—"if I discover a traitor, I'll personally feed him to Cosmos—before I blow her to bits!"

The crowd roared their approval, and one woman slammed her putrid bag against the counter, splattering a sulfurous muck. Several agitators backed away.

Eyeing the mess, Riko groaned.

Rufinius ran his gaze up and down Lang's form, his eyes squinting in appraisal. "You work alone, little lady? I do my own thing. Safer that way."

Lang unceremoniously dropped Riko's shirtfront, offered a surprising look of contrition, and turned on Rufinius. She drew herself up to her full height—nearly thirty centimeters taller than her opponent—and her face mutated into an ugly snarl. "You interfere with my story, human, and I'll eat you alive." Gripping him by the throat, she shoved him toward the front door.

The crowd parted to let them through.

With a final thrust, Lang shoved Rufinius to the ground, where he sprawled on the sidewalk, rain pelting his prone body.

Recovering from the shock, Riko pounded forward and held his datapad out to the crowd. "I've already called for Interventionists to handle this, so feel free to stick around—"

In a desperate exodus, the throng elbowed their way away from the café and scattered onto the quiet street.

Riko stood aside, huffing. After watching the departing crowd through the window, he dropped the curtain with disgust and turned around.

Lang leaned against the door. "Marvelous! I've never met anyone like you."

I could say much the same. Straightening his shirt, Riko sighed. "Well, for once, your lies came in useful."

Lang perched on the stool and leaned against the counter. "Who said I was lying? I am a reporter."

"Not for the IAA."

"No, but I'll pass along everything I learn—once the story breaks across every holoscreen on the planet." She rubbed her jaw, a starry-eyed glint animating her features. "Maybe it'll go universal."

Riko slapped his forehead and started toward the kitchen.

"Where are you going?"

"To get your meal."

Lang clapped her hands and grinned. "You're a consummate café businessman. I'm impressed."

Pleased beyond reason, Riko shrugged. "Don't be. It's probably jelly by now."

~~~

Riko, wrapped in a dark blue bathrobe and black slippers, strode across his living room and tapped the computer console. He squared his shoulders and faced the screen. *Please, for once, give me eloquence...or at least the strength to say no.*

The storm outside settled into a steady, drumming rainfall.

A pale green face with an unusually long neck stared
~~~

back at Riko, breaking into a wide smile. “Hey, Riko. I’m just setting a few things in order, and I’ll be heading off-planet without further ado. Nothing like a family reunion to—”

Riko’s trembling hands clenched into a tight ball behind his back. “Listen, Uncle Clem, I can’t let you come. Not with the way things are now. I don’t think you realize how dangerous Cosmos—”

A thick-fingered hand waved at the screen. “Cosmos, schmazmos! You think I’ll be scared off by some overgrown space blob? I’m coming to help you out.” He blinked, his lips wavering. “Don’t you want me?”

Jumping forward, Riko nearly ran into the screen. “No! I mean, yeah, of course. I need you more than ever—but there’s been trouble. I’ve gotten sort of involved—”

Uncle Clem smirked, one eyebrow rising. “Oh, well! It’s about time you found yourself a companion. Don’t worry; I’ll be discreet. You’ll hardly know I’m around.”

While rubbing his forehead, Riko searched for words, fighting his traitorously meek personality. “Not that. It’s—well, hard to explain. But I would hate for you to risk your life. After Mama—I’d never forgive myself if—”

“Listen, Riko; you’re family—and my kind of Uanyi. I don’t care about planet-eaters or Newearth troubles. I care about you. And I might be able to help. Remember, I was awarded First Citizen in charge of public relations for the—”

Wringing his hands, Riko huffed. “Yeah, I remember. But this involves some unscrupulous characters. You can’t trust anyone. I even had to mortgage—” Coughing, Riko recovered himself and chewed his lip. “Well, I just want to be sure that you’re ready for whatever happens. It might get ugly.”

Uncle Clem beamed across the light years. “Remember what your wise mother used to say. ‘If it’s worth dying for, it’s probably worth living for too.’”

Riko’s eyes filled with tears. “I sure hope so.”

Chapter Six

–The Merrimack–

Where Are We?

Max couldn't understand his reaction to medicine, doctors, and all matters related to healthcare. He might hate them. He just wasn't sure.

Sickbay aboard a small vessel could never hope to attain the grandeur of a larger spacecraft and certainly wouldn't dare to compare itself to a planetary hospital.

The Merrimack's sickbay, though, ranked among the best of its kind and proudly displayed, among the usual tools of its trade, several extraordinary accoutrements. An unusually large specimen case with reinforced quarantine locks stood on the far end of the room, while scopes of extreme power and magnitude lined the right wall. High-capacity bio-computers and data processors lay embedded in a sterile console on the left. Three flexible beds, each made to adjust to the needs of various species, stood in isolated sections of the room, facing a large window to the starry universe.

Max sat ramrod straight on one bed, his gaze wandering from the colorful array of a distant galaxy to the merciless black Divide. He shuddered. "Everyone knows it is death to go there."

Jazzmarie peered through the instrument in her grasp, pointed a laser-like beam at Max's face, and squeezed. She grinned. "That's a good one."

Swiveling, Max peered at Jazzmarie. "You're not worried about entering the Divide?"

Jazzmarie tapped data into the console at her side. "Why? Do you really believe the Bhuac is a suicidal maniac determined to kill us?" She stopped and leaned forward, her gaze delving into Max's worried eyes. "Are you afraid to die?"

Jumping off the bed, Max shook himself. "Yes, but that's not the point." He straightened his uniform and ran his fingers over his short, thick hair. "The Divide is the largest black hole in the known universe. And it's growing. You know as well as I that death is not the worst thing that can happen. Existing in an eternal emptiness might be. I'd rather not find out."

Jazzmarie straightened and considered Max. "A spiritually self–aware android! Have you always had trust issues?"

Max clenched his fists and wished his eyes were lasers. "There is nothing to trust in the Divide!" He swung his gaze over the medical equipment. "Are you so caught up in your experiments—measuring limbs, testing limits, questioning mental and social abilities—that you don't see the danger in front of us?"

With a sly grin and a beckoning finger, Jazzmarie swayed her way over to a small wall panel.

Tilting his head to one side, his curiosity piqued, Max followed.

After tapping in a code and pressing three fingers to a pad, the doctor unlocked a small door. She turned and faced Max. "I'm not without resources. I suppose you don't realize—I am second in command of this ship. If at any time I sense a threat, I can reroute the bridge controls from here."

Max's eyes widened. "You can take over the ship?"

"Anytime I want."

"So—you *do* see the danger of going into the Divide?"

"Of course. That would be insane. But we won't be going into the Divide."

"According to Yelsa's coordinates, we'll go very near."

"We'll just get close enough for me to report the evidence needed to dismiss her from her post." Jazzmarie shrugged. "Then I'll take over the directional controls."

Max jerked back. "But that's supposed to be my job. I'm trained—"

"If I can't trust a Bhuaci—should I trust an android?"

"But Roux—"

Jazzmarie shook her head as she closed the panel. She strolled to the exit. "Luxonians are noble creatures, and I have nothing against them in principle. But Newearth is at risk, and as a human, it's my duty to see that a human takes charge."

"Why are you telling me this? You clearly don't trust androids."

Slipping her arm into Max's, she gently led him to the threshold. "That's the beauty of these extensive tests, Maximan." At her approach, the door slid open. "You aren't just an android—not by any measurement that really matters. In my way of thinking, you're as human as I am."

~~~

Roux stood in the center of his quarters and studied the coordinates laid out on a large holopad. Striding around the holograph, he dragged his fingers down the side of his face. Then he closed his bleary eyes in exhaustion. Throwing back his head, he groaned.

A quick succession of three musical notes forced him to open his eyes as he turned to the door. "Come in."

The door opened, and Yelsa strode in. "You sent for me?"

Roux motioned for her to sit on one of two matching,
~~~

steel-frame chairs.

She frowned at the furniture as if uncomprehending their purpose.

Roux shrugged. "Stand then." He pointed to the hologram. "I've studied your—shall we say—inventive idea, but I don't believe it'll work."

Yelsa's chin hardened. "Sir, forgive me if I sound rude, but you're not a locations expert. I know a great deal more about—"

Roux rounded on her, one hand flying upward. "It's not what you know; it's what you *don't* know that worries me. You can't possibly realize how things might turn out if you catapult us off the edge of the Divide!"

Standing at attention with her hands clasped behind her back, Yelsa lifted her chin. "I *can* know, sir. I've done it before."

Roux caught his breath. "When? How? Who was with you?"

With a quick shake of her head, Yelsa blocked Roux's questions. "I can't share that information. But I know what I'm doing. I have no desire to commit suicide—especially not when we're so close to finding Cosmos."

After backing away, Roux toured his room and stopped at a shelving unit with a tiny portrait framed in black. "Would you ever consider suicide, Yelsa?"

Yelsa inhaled. "If we fail this mission, I'll consider it then." She locked eyes with Roux. "But not until then, sir."

After a long, intense gaze, Roux broke the connection and strode back to the holograph. "Okay. You have one chance to explain this to me. Go slow." He offered a lopsided grin. "As you said, I'm not an expert."

~~~
~~~

Jazzmarie slid onto a comfortably padded chair in the lounge and nudged a tall drink toward Max. She sniffed, miffed. "There's no joy here." Waving one hand at the bare walls, she shrugged and pulled a tall glass filled with dark red liquid toward her. "I couldn't even get one itsy-bitsy picture for the walls. Strict regulations. Pity." She took a sip, leaned back, and refocused on Max. "But you—you're some comfort, at least. I want to know all about you, Maximan."

Tugging at his collar, Max straightened and set a hard, deadpan expression—a man facing his interrogator. "You must already know that I was created by—"

With a huff, Jazzmarie exhaled a long dreary breath and sing-songed her next words. "Yes, beings of extraordinary imagination and skill." She leaned in. "I know *of* them. But like everyone else, all I've ever heard are mere rumors—the stuff they report on that dreadful scandal—Newearth News." Dangerous ideas danced in her head. "I'd much rather wiggle the truth out of you." She pointed to his glass. "Drink up. A little liquor won't hurt you."

With steady hands, Max took a large gulp and sat back. A puzzled expression passed over his face. He patted his chest and coughed, a pink blush warming his otherwise cold expression. He peered closely at the glass and then, with a shrug, shifted his gaze across the room. "I can't tell you much about my creator. Justine was the one who caught Omega's interest, not me. I was created first but considered inferior. He never expected me to develop." Max paused, his eyes surprisingly unfocused.

Twirling her glass, Jazzmarie stared at the light playing across the smooth surface. "So, how did you discover your *human* side?"

In an official manner, Max pulled out his datapad. "It

was an accident. My leg was blown off, and my head was damaged. The doctors planned to turn me off, but a medical assistant insisted that they check my brain functions. They discovered that my mechanical brain was overgrown with the human neurons implanted in me." He tapped his pad and turned a picture of a middle-aged woman with stylishly short hair and a wide smile toward Jazzmarie. "She was an exceptionally skilled nurse." He frowned, and his voice dropped low, meditative. "Wonder what ever happened to her."

Jazzmarie stiffened. A brittle sensation tightened her muscles.

Max slipped the datapad back into his pocket and shrugged. "Omega probably had no idea that the embryotic elements would overwhelm my android superstructure, but—"

Jazzmarie whistled low, the full-blown reality hitting her like icy water after being tossed into an ocean. "So, when they realized your true nature—they saved your life?"

Blinking, Max licked his lips. "They gave me my life. Once I knew I was human-ish, I wanted to know more about my creator. Justine and I had met years before—arranged by Omega, most certainly—though he never interfered. She had abilities I never imagined. And ambitions. I'd have been content to work as a ship's guard and occasional mercenary—you know—android for hire. But when I learned that Justine had been accused of murder and was being held for trial, I found her and discovered—"

In overwhelming excitement, Jazzmarie pounced and clasped Max's hand. "Her humanity!"

Max stared for a moment at Jazzmarie's hand then drew his gaze up to her face. With an intake of breath, he slipped his hand free and rose to his feet. Leaning over the table, he spoke low. "Omega never cared for me. I was merely a practice model. Justine is as close to family as I'll ever get, but since Omega gave her a daughter, she has no need for anyone else." Max gazed at Jazzmarie's hand. "Don't look to me for a future." He crossed over the threshold.

Jazzmarie froze.

The door slid shut behind him.

Tapping her fingers together, Jazzmarie stared at the wall and held in a scream.

~~~

Bala slumped on his bridge chair, his head resting on one hand, his vision glazed with exhaustion.

The door slid open, and Max strode through. He started for the directional console, glanced at Bala, halted, and changed trajectory. He leaned in. "Are you ill?"

Waving him off, Bala straightened. "I'm always ill when my wife is pregnant. There's a name for it, but I can't remember. Besides, I'll be dead in a few days, so it hardly matters."

Shocked by a clenching sensation in his chest, Max grimaced and turned to his console. He tapped the screen. Reports started flying before his eyes.

Bala staggered over and leaned on the railing for support. "We're still heading into the Divide?"

Max frowned. "Not exactly. Yelsa has made a few adjustments to her trajectory." He tapped, scanned, and tapped again. He faced Bala. "According to these coordinates, we'll arrive at the very edge of the Divide before we are sucked to our doom."
~~~

"Oh, well. That's better. I thought—" Eyes opening wide and face contorting, making him look like an insane clown, Bala made a diving motion with his hand. "We were going straight to h—"

The door slid open. Roux stepped in and settled on his chair. He swiveled around. "You've got the new coordinates, Max?"

Max glanced at Bala. "Yes, sir."

Leaning forward, Roux clasped his hands together, an expectant schoolteacher before a promising student. "So, Max, you understand what we're doing?"

"No, sir."

Roux scoured his forehead. "Didn't Yelsa brief you on her plan?" Meeting Max's blank stare, Roux slapped his armchair console and leaned over the intercom. "Yelsa Prater!"

Yelsa's bell-toned voice rang over the speaker. "Yes, sir?"

"Weren't you supposed to inform Max and Bala about your plan?"

A long pause and Yelsa's voice dropped. "I thought about that, sir, and it occurred to me that you might explain it to them better than I."

Roux's back straightened like a spring released from its case. "Yelsa, I gave you a clear direction. Apparently, you've chosen to disregard it."

Yelsa's voice hardened. "Not disregard, exactly. I just thought it would be wiser if you told them."

Squeezing his head, Roux closed his eyes. "Yelsa, report to the bridge, where we will complete this discussion." He slapped the arm console. "Damn!"

Max stayed stiffly in place.

Bala nudged him and pointed to the directional console with bouncing eyebrows. "Back to our doom, old man."

~~~

Jazzmarie lay across a plush chair with a datapad clenched in her hands in a stiflingly small room with only one computer station, a plain bed, and a tiny counter. Her loose floral tunic and white pantaloons splayed across the arms of the chair. She stared at an old news report about the trial of Justine Santana. Focusing in on the picture of Justine, she tapped and magnified. Justine's face grew twice as large. Squinting, Jazzmarie traced Justine's eyebrows with a finger. "It's the eyes. Challenging yet vulnerable. Men can't resist." Jazzmarie stroked her own face and then dropped her feet to the floor.

A chime rang, and Roux's voice intoned. "Doctor, come to the bridge immediately."

Rising, Jazzmarie tossed her datapad aside. "What's happened?"

Silence stole a moment and then Roux responded, "You'll need to see this for yourself."

~~~

Roux took a deep breath as the door slid open.

Jazzmarie strode over to him, her multi-colored outfit rippling with every move. With a set mouth and piercing eyes, she clapped her hands together. "What's this all about? Has Cosmos—"

"Already been here." Roux tapped the console, and the main screen shifted into high magnification. Bits of rock and debris sailed serenely through silent space.

Jazzmarie pursed her lips and stomped to the locations console, shoving Yelsa aside. "Where are we?"

Scowling, Yelsa folded her arms over her chest and stepped back. "We're close on her trail. Closer than any of us realized."

Jazzmarie glared at Yelsa. "So, your idea of going into the Divide was what? A test of bravery?"

Yelsa sneered. "*I* don't play games." Pointedly, her gaze swung from Jazzmarie to Max.

Roux sliced through the moment of tension and waved at Bala. "You tell them!"

Bala scuttled over to the screen and gestured to indicate the edge of the Divide still visible in the corner. "Yelsa planned to have us ricochet off the edge of the Divide, about here, giving us the momentum to go"—he tapped another section of the screen—"into space where she thought Cosmos was feeding." He turned and traipsed over to the stationary, holographic space image, and with a few adjustments, he brought the reddish-blue hologram into sharp focus and pointed. "But apparently, we've been off-track. Cosmos must've needed a snack, and she changed—"

A red light flashed on a panel at the communications station.

Bala's eyebrows rose. He rushed over, peered at the screen, and his eyes widened.

Irritated, Roux snapped, "If it's about your wife, it can wait. We've—"

Bala turned and stared at Roux. "It's not Kendra. It's a planetary distress call."

Roux clenched his jaw. *If I can't run a ship, how am I going to save a planet?*

Chapter Seven

–Mirage-Reborn–

Positively Insightful

Cerulean peered up, shading his eyes from the sun, his heart pounding.

A hawk flew in close, swirling just above a gnarled oak tree where, on an overhanging limb, a nest of hatchlings, unaware of their imminent danger, chirped in a desperate plea for their next meal.

Gravity oppressed him as he stood rooted to the spot. Being encased in a biological body without his Luxonian luminosity had certain advantages—his physical senses were heightened—but now there was no escape. For him or the baby birds.

A small speck catapulted from the left—a tiny sparrow torpedoed the hawk, diving in for a stinging retaliation, which soon turned the enemy away.

Stymied by the smaller bird's daring and the larger bird's cowardice, Cerulean continued watching until a hand pressed his shoulder. He turned.

Abbas grinned. "Remarkable, aren't they? Small but courageous beyond prediction. Prudence would dictate self-preservation, but they charge into battle with only their will and a determined beak." Abbas' gaze landed on Cerulean's face. "Apparently, it's enough." He chuckled as he pointed to the hawk retreating into a copse of woods with the sparrow in hot pursuit.

Cerulean nodded. "Enough for a bird's survival, perhaps. But what is enough for me?"

Abbas patted Cerulean's arm as he turned away. "That we have yet to see."

Exhaling a long sigh, Cerulean followed Abbas into

the woods. "I've accepted my fate. How about you?"

Stooping under low hanging branches, Abbas made his way, heading steadily toward a fallen tree. He soon perched on an angled trunk and folded his arms inside his long sleeves. "I have one task to complete before I let fate have its way with me. I must find my son and remind him of his duty. Then, I will gladly pass beyond the borders of the living and join the spirits of my ancestors."

Cerulean leaned against a tall pine tree and peered at the elderly figure with a raised eyebrow. "So powerful yet you'd succumb to death so easily?"

Running his fingers along the rough bark, Abbas appeared to shrink. "*You* can ask such a thing?" He peered at Cerulean, his eyes grieved. "When is a lifetime long enough?" He stood and waved at the fallen tree. "Surely, there comes a moment when death is no longer the enemy." He blinked back tears. "I want to be released from toil, Cerulean. I've shaped worlds, fashioned cultures, supported and entertained vast life systems, but now I crave an end." Tears filled the old man's eyes. "Is that wrong?"

Cerulean snapped a twig and peered at the jagged ends. "It depends." He glanced up and frowned at Abbas. "Who releases you?"

Abbas smacked the log and stood tall again, his eyes narrowing. "You're playing with words. I have the authority to decide my own coming and going."

Cerulean shook his head. "You were created without your permission. You live by your Creator's will. Does He have no say in your end?"

Like an evening sunset fading into night, Abbas' eyes dimmed from rage to solemnity. "You never cease to amaze me. I thought in human form your perceptions might darken, but you are positively insightful."

Shrugging away from the tree trunk, Cerulean started back toward town. "When will you begin searching for Omega?"

Abbas fell in step alongside Cerulean. "I've been searching for him a long while, fruitlessly, unfortunately. But tomorrow afternoon, we'll gather at the hall, and I'll introduce you. That night, when the townsfolk sleep secure under their new governor, I shall depart to the furthest ends of the universe to find my son."

Cerulean held a vine out of the way, allowing Abbas to pass ahead. "You will return?"

The old man squinted, staring into twilight. "Before death finds me. I hope."

~~~

Cerulean entered the hall and stopped inside the doorway, amazed.

For many years, the majority of citizens in Mirage-Reborn had lived in a medieval village more simply named Mirage. Omega—despite designing Mirage-Reborn as an OldEarth, 1950s, American town—had decided to give the inhabitants a free hand at the construction of the town hall. The two histories conflicted mightily.

The hall's street front, Omega had insisted, had to conform to the style of the rest of OldEarth, 1950s, small-town America, but on the inside, they could let their imaginations soar. The townsfolk had fled to the ancient past. They integrated heavy oak beams, plank tables, a straw-strewn dirt floor, open fireplaces large enough to roast a whole hog, and a central skylight,
~~~

allowing smoke to escape and sunlight to filter in.

After inspecting the hall and allowing his shock to settle into uneasy acceptance, Cerulean returned outside and crossed Main Street to Nelson's Grocery Store. He glimpsed inside the front plate glass window.

Clare, dressed in a skirt, blouse, and flowered apron, stood on a stepstool stacking fruit jars in pyramid formation on a table centered in the main aisle.

Cerulean breezed through the doorway and stopped by her side, stroking his chin thoughtfully. "Your artistic skills are improving."

Peering at her creation with her hands held aloft, Clare stepped off the stool and elbowed Cerulean in the side. "Shut up. You'll jinx me."

Chuckling, Cerulean tugged her aside. "Jinx? If you're thinking like that, you've been in Mirage-Reborn too long." He peered down the empty aisle and leaned in. "I'm to be introduced as the new governor in about an hour at the town hall, and I'd like you there. For protection if not moral support."

Her hands on her hips, Clare shrugged. "No doubt they'll be disgruntled to hear that Abbas is leaving, but there's no reason they'll take it out on you. Still, nothing's happening around here." Satisfied that her creation would hold, Clare wiped her hands on her apron and grinned at her handiwork. "It's perfectly proportional, isn't it?"

Cerulean nodded with a reassuring murmur as he swept his gaze across the empty registers. "Not much business, eh?"

Swiping a stray lock of hair out of her eye, Clare pursed her lips. "Not since Grace took over. People don't trust her." Clare rubbed her cheek thoughtfully. "There's something going on. She's nice enough on the surface but cold as ice underneath. Her father's a regular curmudgeon." She gripped Cerulean's arm and locked eyes with him. "I think he's a murderer."

Cerulean exhaled like a sprung tire. "You're not a human services detective here, Clare. You're just a—"

Unexpectedly, Grace stepped forward from the dairy aisle. A gray pallor had fallen over her normally pink cheeks as she reached for the checkout counter.

Cerulean jogged forward, concern speeding his heart rate. "Are you all right, Grace?"

With a wave, Grace stopped him. "Just a bout of indigestion. Had the meatloaf at the café today. Stupid of me." She winced, embarrassed.

Untying her apron, Clare stepped forward. "Well, Cerulean tells me there's going to be a big announcement at the hall. We don't want to miss the excitement." Clare eyed her boss. "You'll come?"

With a nod, Grace straightened. "In a bit. I'll check on my father first. He'll probably want to go. Can't be left out of anything, you know." Her flashed smile faded in an instant.

As the door shut behind Clare, Cerulean glanced back through the window.

Grace wiped her eyes and headed to the cash register.

~~~

Cerulean stood against the north wall inside the hall as Clare mingled through the crowd.

Dozens of murmured conversations rumbled through the milling throng. Every time someone entered, the room tensed, only to give rise to another burst of anxious whispering as they recognized a familiar face.

Justine entered and meandered through, her eyes
~~~

locking on Clare. She stepped beside Cerulean. "What is she doing?"

Clearing his throat, Cerulean nodded toward Grace, who pushed her father's wheelchair toward an open place against the west wall. "Clare has a theory about Grace and her father." He sighed. "She sees villains everywhere."

Justine shrugged. "I'm hardly one to defend Clare's myopic views, but I thought you trusted her instincts."

They both watched as Clare chatted with Old Man Nelson—an innocent man, never. But innocent of murder, perhaps.

Grace stood at her father's side, staring into space, her face pale as death.

Anxiety gnawing at him, Cerulean's heart beat faster. "I trust her instincts. Usually. But I suspect that her real interest in Grace and Old Man Nelson is to dig up evidence of Omega's nefarious nature."

Justine chuckled. "He's hardly nefarious. He created me, after all. I'm proof of his highest qualities."

With an assenting nod, Cerulean decided to change the subject before Clare wandered over. "Where's Pax? I told him to be here."

All conversation fell silent as Abbas stepped into the hall.

Leaning over, Justine whispered. "Pax has control issues. You sure you got him on good authority? He's not some kind of escaped convict or anything?"

Annoyed, Cerulean scowled and crossed his arms.

Abbas ambled to the dais and beckoned Cerulean to come forward.

As soon as they were positioned front and center, the crowd grew tense. Abbas raised his arm. "Thank you all for gathering here today. I have important news." He held a dramatic breath. "I have found Omega."

Loud chatter spread across the assembly.

Abbas waved his hand. "Please, I know you are excited, but let me finish. He's being held prisoner, and I must attend to his release."

A roar of questions erupted like lava spouting from a volcano.

Shock slammed Cerulean, tightening his throat.

In matching intensity, Clare and Justine stared wide-eyed from opposite ends of the room.

A father trying to placate his anxious children, Abbas lifted both hands. "I realize this is a surprise, but there are some who lack—shall we say—my generous spirit. Their interest is merely domination. In his inexperience, Omega fell prey to their deceptive ploys, but I'll arrange his release soon." Abbas searched the crowd as if peering into each and every soul. "Have no fear; I'm not abandoning you." He drew Cerulean to his side. "I'm entrusting you into the care of a man of unquestionable ability and resolve, Cerulean. He'll act as governor until Omega's return."

Wide eyes glared from every dark corner of the room.

Abbas nudged Cerulean forward.

Straightening as tall as humanly possible, Cerulean gazed at the crowd. "I'm quite certain that we'll work well together." His gaze landed on Sheriff Quinn. He swallowed a lump forming in his throat. "Feel free to advise me on how best to serve your interests."

A few nods and grunts set a more genial tone, while whispering groups huddled together.

Abbas leaned in toward Cerulean. "See, that wasn't so bad." As he strode to the door, the crowd parted like sheaves of wheat in a windstorm.

Just as Cerulean joined Justine, Clare hustled over and joined them. His irritation level jumped two notches. "Where's Pax?"

Justine shrugged and tapped his shoulder. "Haven't seen him for hours. But Quinn was watching you like a snake sizing up dinner. He has nearly everyone in town spying for him."

A headache pounded at the back of Cerulean's head. *Spies. Just what I need.*

Clare yanked his sleeve like a child trying to get his attention. "There's Pax!"

Squeezed against the left wall by the crowd, Pax stood with one hand covering his face, as if to block the dim light.

Justine frowned. "He doesn't look too good. Is he ill or something?"

Pax darted forward, bumping into a Cresta citizen, who smacked Pax's arm and grunted, "Watch where you're going, human!"

Pax stood frozen, terror in his eyes.

With a sudden look of interest, the Cresta peered into Pax's face. "Do I know you?"

Pax bolted for the door.

Conversation stopped as citizens crowded the door, watching Pax flee.

Clare started forward, but Cerulean gripped her arm and held her back. "Don't—not yet."

Thrusting one hand on her hip, Clare pouted. "Why not? I can find him. And when I do, I'll tell him a thing or two about keeping his mind on business."

Cerulean lowered his voice. "No. Instead, you'll keep your eye on Grace. Find out what's going on with her father. I don't think he's a murderer, but there's something off about them. If I have to govern here, I need to understand these people." He turned to Justine.

Lifting her hands in mock surrender, Justine grinned. "I'll investigate Quinn. I already know what's going on; I just don't know how to stop it." She scanned the crowd.

"At least, not yet. Give me a few days."

Cerulean heaved a sigh. "That'll free me to chase down Pax and find out what's wrong with our ship's captain." He waved Justine and Clare toward the door. "Just keep everyone alive until Omega gets back."

He watched the two women traipse away and rubbed his jaw. *If Omega gets back.*

~~~

Cerulean wandered up a dead-end road toward the last farmhouse as a moonless night blanketed the countryside. His head ached. He'd accidentally scraped his arm on a stone wall, his throat was parched, and exhaustion frayed his all-too-human nerves. He rubbed his neck as he muttered to himself, "God, how did I ever get myself into this?"

When a woman's voice murmured sympathetically from the dark, he jerked aside, putting his hand over his heart as if to keep it in place.

A pool of light and a tiny woman stepped from the shadows and lifted a lamp. "Sorry, I didn't mean to scare you."

Cerulean heaved in a couple of convulsive breaths and waved off any hint of offense. "I'm the one who's sorry. I don't usually go wandering around on private property in the middle of the night."

The slight figure drew closer and raised the lamp higher. "You're the new Governor—Cerulean?"

Snorting a half-chuckle, Cerulean nodded. "So, I'm told."

"You appear exhausted. Would you like to come to my home and have a glass of lemonade? It's something
~~~

of a tonic here on Mirage-Reborn."

With a sigh of relief, Cerulean stepped forward. "I'd love to."

The simple kitchen reminded Cerulean of Anne's farmstead, with a wooden table, herbs hanging from the rafters, lacy curtains, and plain white cups and saucers in neat rows on a shelf.

He took a grateful sip of the cool drink and smiled. "I don't even know your name."

The woman slid onto a ladder-back chair and lowered her gaze. "Vera. I live here with my brother, Dimi."

Cerulean's eyes swept over the diminutive figure before him, tripping only slightly over the three-fingered hands with the thickened middle finger. His gaze traveled across the neat rills running along her neck, and her shy face averted from his own. "I don't think I've met your kind before."

Vera's gaze stayed glued to her glass. "We are LuKan. My brother and I were orphaned when Cosmos destroyed our world. Omega found us before we perished and offered us a new life here." A frightened glance darted over Cerulean. "I've heard about you. You're not human, are you?"

Cerulean leaned back and let his gaze wander around the comforting sights of a well-cared-for home. "No. I'm Luxonian. Originally. Though for the time being, I'm in human mode. My friends and I are tracking Cosmos to stop her before she reaches Newearth."

"But why come here? We have no power over such a beast, surely."

"Not you, but Omega…"

Vera's gaze lifted toward the star-filled window. "Perhaps." She turned and studied Cerulean's face. "But tonight, you're looking for a friend—Pax?"

Surprised, Cerulean nodded. "Yes. Do you know

him?"

Vera stood and placed her glass in the sink. "I believe he is still in the barn. He's frightened." She wrung her hands and dropped her gaze. "I know what it is to be frightened. Be gentle—no matter what he's done."

Cerulean looked from Vera's anxious face to the window. *Just what has he done?*

~~~

Cerulean slid the barn door aside, holding the lantern in the other hand, and called out softly, "Pax? Are you here? It's me—Cerulean."

Scattered straw fell from the hayloft.

Pax's voice rose from the dim interior. "Are you alone?"

Cerulean waved Vera behind him. "Pretty much. Now come out here and tell me what's going on. You already have Clare and Justine jumping to all sorts of unpleasant conclusions."

Pax leapt down from the loft and landed in front of Cerulean. Brushing straw from his dusty clothes, he sneezed. "You've caught me." He held out his wrists as if waiting to be taken into custody.

Cerulean frowned. "Have you committed a crime, Pax?"

Throwing back his head, Pax laughed. "More than you'd believe." Suddenly, he peered into the dark doorway.

Vera stepped into the light.

Pax rushed forward. "No!" Brushing past Cerulean, he attempted to slip around Vera, but a tall, thin LuKan stopped him in his tracks.
~~~

Vera held up her hand and stepped closer, her gaze glued to Xavier Pax. "Don't be afraid. My brother Dimi and I understand what it is to be hunted."

Cerulean spun around and gripped Pax's arm, alarm spreading through him. "Good Lord, man, you're being hunted?"

Vera placed her small hand over Cerulean's and, with surprising strength, lifted it off Pax's arm. "He's *not* a man. He's an Ingot."

Chapter Eight

–Newearth–

A Cresta with the Besta

Riko stood with an eager crowd at the dirty, disheveled docking bay and swallowed his pride. He thrust his past behind him and faced his future.

Uncle Clem's face glowed with joy as he disembarked from the daub-gray landing tube. His gaze searched the small crowd.

With a stiff wave, Riko stepped forward, catching Clem's eye.

Bounding steps and, before Riko knew what hit him, Uncle Clem enveloped him in a bear hug.

"Gosh, it's good to see you!" Uncle Clem pulled back, holding Riko at arm's length, his eyes traveling over Riko's crisp white outfit and firm exoskeleton. Clem grinned. "You're eating well and dressing neat—that much is clear!"

Darting a glance at the luggage depository, Riko maneuvered Uncle Clem away from the stream of passengers. "Your stuff should be coming through at any moment. Let's—"

Uncle Clem jogged beside Riko as he maneuvered through the crowd. "Sure, but listen. I got news! A brainstorm, really. I've created the best slogan in the universe—Listen!" Clem thrust out his chest and spread his hands across the air, outlining an imaginary banner. "The Breakfastnook Café—Delicious Food Every Day!" Uncle Clem beamed.

With a tight smile, Riko nudged his uncle forward and pointed to the luggage wheel.

Uncle Clem pounced and captured a brown bag

bulging at odd angles. "Ah, a little bit of home. You remember this? Your Uncle Sem used it when he went on his first—"

Riko bustled forward, dragging his uncle through the crowd. "Sorry, but we're in a bit of a hurry. Taug wants to meet you, and I hate to keep him waiting."

Tossing his bag over his shoulder, Uncle Clem threw one arm around Riko and kept up with the quick pace. "Taug? I don't remember hearing about him. He's one of your workers?"

Riko swallowed. "Sort of. We have a shared goal."

Uncle Clem's perpetual grin widened. "Great! He can help me place our new banner right over the café in bright—what? You think sunset-orange will get some attention?"

Trying to keep tears at bay, Riko squinted ahead.

~~~

Riko scanned the crowd, inventorying his workers, and found everyone in place. Even Wendell, wearing a clean outfit, wiped an empty table with a disinfectant swab. The noontime crowd had arrived in full force, and the café bustled with hungry customers wanting quick service and a breather from life's troubles.

Exhaling a relieved sigh, Riko led his uncle down the main aisle between the crammed central tables.

Not one to miss an opportunity, Uncle Clem stopped at the first table and began shaking hands. "Hi! I'm Clem, Riko's uncle. Feel free to call me Uncle Clem, too. I'm going to be helping out from now on, so let me know if I can be of—"

Riko yanked Uncle Clem by the arm and pulled him
~~~

the length of the café, mumbling, "I should've known," under his breath.

Uncle Clem ambled along behind, finally pulling free by the back wall. "Hey there, Riko. I know I'm new here, but really, a little respect won't hurt your reputation. Never bodes well if customers see you mistreating your own family."

Blowing air between his lips, Riko turned and faced his uncle. "Sorry, but you don't understand. I don't need help with the café; I need help with another business venture."

Uncle Clem's already large eyes widened to alarming size—clearly fascinated by a world of possibilities. "Other business? You never told me—"

Thrusting one eye against the pupil-scan and wrapping his fingers around the print-scanner, Riko unlocked the side door and, with a commanding tug, ushered Uncle Clem over the threshold.

Uncle Clem stopped short, facing the stark white laboratory like a Uanyi gone snow blind. He rubbed his eyes.

Taug stood beside a deep sink with a swan neck faucet rushing at full capacity. He turned slowly with a dark scowl lowering over his features and turned off the water. He thrust his dripping tentacles on his hips, and tilted his head at Riko, skewering him with a piercing stare.

Riko charged forward, clapping his hands together like a coach readying his team for the big game. "Ah, yes, Taug. I'm so glad you're in."

Glued to the spot, Taug's eyes narrowed as his gaze zeroed in on Uncle Clem. "Where else would I be?"

Uncle Clem began to wander the perimeter, his mouth open—his innocent fingers tentatively reaching for the shiny instruments.

In imitation of a Crestonian boar, Taug growled deep in his throat.

Gripping Uncle Clem's hand, Riko pulled him front and center. "I mentioned I might have a surprise weapon." His stiff grin matched his formal wave. "Well, here he is."

Taug's gaze narrowed another notch, his growl dropping to a mere vibration.

Uncle Clem swiveled toward Riko, his mouth as wide as a black hole.

Scrambling back to the door, Riko did a quick check and peered through the eyehole. Satisfied that no one was near, he straightened and refocused on Taug. "You remember what happened the other day? If Lang hadn't been there, the whole café would've been reduced to Cresta slime and Ingot acid-rocks." Riko jogged forward jabbing his finger in the air. "Like it or not, I've made an investment in you. I don't intend to see you fail." He glanced back at his uncle. "Besides, you might figure out how to stop Cosmos and become Newearth's greatest hero. Never hurts to have a PR man working on your image ahead of time."

His hand shaking, Uncle Clem pointed at Taug. "I'm going to represent—*him*?"

Stretching his neck like an athlete preparing for action, Taug unwound his tentacles and ambled toward the dissection tub. "In that case, you ought to know exactly what you're representing." Taug lifted a heavy lid and wiggled a tentacle, beckoning him closer.

Both Uanyi ambled forward. Riko peered down while Clem leaned in. Within seconds, they both staggered backward.

Riko pinched his nose.

Uncle Clem covered his mouth. "What in the universe are you doing?"

With a smirk, Taug slid the lid back into place. "I'm applying acidic compound combinations on little Cosmos cousins." He looked up and grinned. "Try saying that five times fast."

Uncle Clem gripped Riko's sleeve, his neck and face deepening to a dark green. "I'm gonna be sick."

Riko wrapped his arm around his uncle's shoulders and braced him against the wall. He threw a wrathful glare at Taug. "You think that was funny or something?"

Taug ambled across the lab and picked up a datapad. Scrolling through, he found what he wanted and tossed it to Riko. "A message you might like to know about—they've found Cosmos. She just ate another planet. And it looks like she's pregnant. Oh, joy. At least, we shan't be lonely when we're devoured. We'll be part of a family feast."

~~~

Faye watched a throng of children as they chased each other across the dying lawn and smiled. Early autumn always pleased her with its cool temperatures, the hint of things to come, and the leaves changing from faded green to scarlet and orange. A vivid memory of Bala being chased by a gang of kids at Cerulean's last party sent a chill over her slender arms. She stared up at the bright sky. Where was he now? Had he found Omega?

A shout claimed her attention.

Kendra stood in the doorway, calling to the kids. They jostled forward like a herd of antelopes.

Faye held back, watching, when Kendra's gaze found her.

"Faye? Goodness, girl, get yourself in here and help a
~~~

desperate woman before she succumbs to madness."

Grinning in delight, Faye skipped up the last steps into Kendra's warm kitchen. She stopped short.

Zara sat hunch-shouldered at the table, staring blankly at a bowl of steaming soup.

With a quick motion, Kendra gestured Faye to the other side of the table. "Here, sit yourself down and have a bowl of my famous vegetable stew." She glanced to the doorway. "Don't worry; the kids are going back to school. You're safe."

Still eyeing Zara, Faye slid onto the bench. After a moment of awkward silence, Faye focused on Kendra. "You appear alive and well."

Kendra slid a spoon across the table.

Faye caught it and leaned over the soup, sniffing the delectable aroma. "From the hysterical messages Bala sent, I was afraid you were half-dead with—"

With a warning shake of her head, Kendra's gaze glanced off Zara. "Oh, you know Bala. He exaggerates every little thing. I'm fine. The kids are healthy, and considering they've been back in classes for almost a month, it's a miracle they haven't caught anything." She took a minuscule sip of water. Her hand shook as she set the glass back on the counter. "Now, eat up. I know you—always hungry."

Avoiding any prolonged stare, Faye focused on the soup and took several bites. She glanced up, her eyes gleaming. "You have a way with vegetables—never known the like. I'd swear I was eating—"

A low hum from the other end of the table interrupted the conversation. Zara began rocking back and forth, slowly, the hum rising like a swarm of bees.

Her nerves tightening, Faye's spoon clattered in the bowl. She pushed back her chair and started to rise.

Kendra ran aside and gripped Faye's shoulder,

holding her in place. “It’s okay. It only lasts a bit. She’ll stop in a minute.”

Faye stared into Kendra’s face, noticing dark circles under tight, anxiety-filled eyes. Resisting Kendra’s pressure, Faye stood and leaned in. “What’s wrong with her?”

Dropping her voice, Kendra stayed fixed on Zara. “I don’t know. Without warning, she’ll suddenly stiffen and turn all Dr. Jekyll and Mr. Hyde on me.”

Faye frowned and raised an eyebrow. “I don’t understand the reference.”

Kendra sighed. “It’s an OldEarth classic. Good guy—bad guy complex all mixed up in the same man.”

Stepping around the table, Faye closed in on Zara. A Luxonian-human with uncontrolled powers… She placed her hand lightly on the child’s shoulder.

The humming grew louder and higher, more urgent.

Faye glanced at Kendra. “Does she ever get violent?”

Kendra shook her head. “No. Just hums till she’s over her spell. Then right as rain.”

The humming slowed to a murmur, and the rocking ceased.

With a long sigh, Kendra turned toward the sink. “I never could understand my own children. No reason in the universe I should understand a Luxonian-andr—”

A husky boy with bright eyes trotted into the room, huffing. “Hey, Mom! I can’t find Reginald. I was going to introduce him to my bio class.”

Placing a clean bowl on the shelf, Kendra shrugged. “I haven’t seen him. But if I find him in my kitchen, you’ll hear about it all right.”

The boy turned and hustled out the door.

Faye watched the child retreat with a perplexed frown. “You don’t like Barni’s friend?”

Kendra draped a dishtowel over the sink. “Friends, I

enjoy. Mice—not so much." She motioned Faye toward the doorway. "Let's take a breather outside. I've been cooped up all day."

Faye took one step toward the door but suddenly doubled back and scooted around the table, slipping behind Zara's chair. A brief glance at Zara's hands forced a slight gasp. She hurried on and caught up with Kendra.

Kendra held the door open. "Something wrong?"

Faye nudged Kendra forward and shook her head. As she took the last step out, she darted one more glance at Zara, and her heart froze.

Dangling a dead mouse in front of her glassy eyes, once again, Zara hummed.

~~~

Faye sauntered into Taug's lab with her hands clasped behind her back and her gaze trailing along the floor.

As the door shut behind her, Taug straightened up from the dissecting table. "Ah! You're early. I wanted to have more results verified by the time you came, but—" Taug's ample middle wiggled in glee as he grinned. "I think you'll like what I've learned."

Faye strolled over. "Something interesting. Deadly, even?"

Taug pointed with a long, razor-thin blade. "When they're in their reproductive stage, they are the most vulnerable. If I had enough acidic compound, I could just spray her with this." He pointed to a clear vial of liquid. "But of course, Newearth would have to endure months of acidic rain."

Dread filling her, Faye's fixed stare didn't waver.
~~~

"But if she is shot with—" Taug bent low and stared into Faye's eyes. "Are you even listening?"

Breaking away from her innate repugnance, Faye strolled to the dissection tub and lifted the lid. *Leaders must protect their own, even at the cost of...* "Of course. Go on."

Taug's eyes followed her every move. "Well, it wouldn't take much of anything poisonous to send her off balance, and she'd miscarry. Then we'd blast her with interplanctary missiles. She'd be weak, so—" He pushed aside his medical instruments. "You don't look well."

Staring at the tub contents—wiggling worms? *Is this all Cosmos really is?* She forced a nonchalant shrug. "I'm fine." She dropped the lid in place with a clatter. "Our problem is solved. You can kill the mighty beast."

"Theoretically. Yes. The problem is just how much damage she can do while under attack." With a concerned frown, Taug ambled across the room and threw a tentacle over Faye's shoulder. "It's getting late. Let's see if Riko can fix us a couple of tall glasses of Green." Taug huffed. "Just hope that his uncle isn't in sight. That Uanyi will kill me before Cosmos even arrives."

Faye halted. "How?"

Taug passed a tentacle through the air, highlighting an invisible banner. "He has a wonderful marketing idea: 'Taug—A Cresta with the Besta!'" He dropped his tentacle to his side, his shoulders slumping. "He'll be the destruction of my sanity. See if he won't."

Faye stopped at the doorway, blocking Taug. "Before we go to the café, I'd like you to visit Kendra."

Taug chuckled. "Bala brags that her cooking is renowned throughout Newearth, but I hardly think her stew can compare to Riko's Green."

"Not that. It's Zara—Justine's daughter. Omega's *other* creation."

Taug's grin died abruptly. "What about her?"

"She might not be as big as Cosmos, but she might be dangerous just the same." Faye traced a small circle on his middle, a target of sorts. "Just imagine the combination of a being who can take any shape, move fast as light, and has the super-intelligence of an android. Then put her in a child's body—and make her very angry."

Chapter Nine

–The Merrimack–

Life Without Risk

Roux stood on deck, gripped the railing, and stared at the bridge screen, stupefied.

Enormous, jagged rocks and planetary debris hurtled through star-riddled blackness on their eternal journey to nowhere in particular. No scream accompanied them, for the terror—left far behind—lost its voice in the vast emptiness of open space.

The torn planet hung lopsided, still turning but knocked off its natural orbit around its distant sun. Clumps of planetary matter clung haphazardly like shreds of dirt from an uprooted plant. Shards bled through the rent atmosphere, draining the broken core still further.

Max rose from his chair, his mouth open but silent.

Her eyes glued to the image, Jazzmarie stepped forward like a sleepwalker and placed a trembling hand on Max's shoulder.

Bala, draped against the arm of his chair like a wrung-out rag, held his face in his hands as if to shade his eyes from blinding grief.

Only Yelsa manned the directional console, her gaze fixed on the data stream. With a triumphant snort, she straightened and faced Roux. "We can catch her, sir."

Unheeding, Roux stepped forward and ran his fingers through the air as if tracing the missing section of the planet. "My father brought me here once when I was very young. We visited the wild-animal park. It was the best month of my life. Amphibians as big as mountains, flying creatures decorated with every color of the rainbow, and these cute little—" Roux's voice broke, and his shoulder drooped. "God Almighty."

As if on cue, a fiery spout erupted, and volcanic cracks opened vast fissures, further renting the planet's surface.

Max cleared his throat, blinking rapidly. "It's hopeless. No one could survive."

Frowning, Jazzmarie dropped her hand to her side and trotted across to the communications console. She jabbed Bala in the ribs. "Get to work and send a message. See if anyone responds."

Bala straightened and focused his attention on the console, his fingers darting in every direction.

Jazzmarie bent over his shoulder. "And send messages out to every ship in the area that might be able to lend assistance—Luxonian, Cresta, Ingilium, Sectine"—she dashed a glance at Yelsa— "even Helm." She shrugged. "Someone might be able to get here in time."

After stepping behind her, Max leaned in. "You really think anyone could have survived this?"

Jazzmarie turned and tapped her fingers together. "We won't know until we try—will we?" Peering intently at Roux, she strode forward and took a position between her captain and the main screen. "Don't you agree, Roux?"

Without taking his eyes off the desolation, Roux nodded.

Yelsa's eyes widened, her mouth puckering. "If we don't hurry, Cosmos will get away again."

Jazzmarie's eyebrows rose as she stared at Yelsa. *"Again?"*

Shaking himself out of his stupor, Roux turned from the screen. "Max, I want a full analysis of the planetary destruction. There's something not right here." He waved his hand in the air. "Obviously, a lot is wrong, but

I mean—" He locked eyes with Jazzmarie. "Doctor, consider the scene dispassionately. What does it look like to you?"

The hologram panel before her, Jazzmarie pulled the screen image up on the holoplatform. The massive scene of destruction slowly turned in vivid three-dimensional form. She circled around, her gaze sweeping from the planet core to the flying debris. "It looks like someone took a bite and left."

Roux snapped his fingers. "Exactly!" Charging over to the holoplatform, he traced the planet core with his finger. "She attacked here." He tapped the area of greatest destruction. "Granted, one Cosmos bite can do a great deal of damage, but still, this planet should cease to exist. It should be—"

Max jumped forward. "I have it, sir. There's a great deal of Technetium on this planet. When I checked the debris, I discovered that it's almost completely Technetium. In fact, it seems as if the other elements were devoured, but this was"—Max took a breath—"spat out."

"Gave her a tummy ache, did it?" A gleam entered Roux's eye. "This information might come in handy. Thank you, Max."

Yelsa tapped her foot and gripped the directional console. "If she's sick, then we have no choice but to give chase now. There might never be a better time."

Bala lifted his arm. "Wait! I've got a signal."

Roux rushed to the communications console. "From a passing ship or the planet?"

Bala met Roux's gaze. "From the planet, sir. Someone is still alive down there."

~~~
~~~

Jazzmarie watched Bala and Max playing a heated game of table tennis as she sprawled across the lounge couch. She scooped ice cream into her mouth at intervals. After catching a drip, she wiped her face and pointed at Max with her spoon. "Watch his left hand, Maximan. Bala has got a wicked return that'll knock you out of the game if you're not careful."

Without taking his gaze from the bouncing ball, Max frowned. "I should have gone down."

Bala sent the ball whizzing to Max's right corner. "The Cresta Commander made it quite clear that he'll assess the situation on the surface and call us if he can utilize our *limited* assets."

Catching the ball with one hand, Max straightened. "I'm not sure that he should have the right to stop us from doing our part. It's possible there are human and android survivors."

After dropping his paddle, Bala set off for the food dispenser. "It's a Cresta colony—they'll have the Inter-Alien Alliance on their side." He tapped the wall and looked over his shoulder. "You want anything?"

Max shook his head. "I don't know how you can eat after what you saw today."

"I'm sickened by it, but the truth is, I need to keep my strength up." He tapped in a code and waited. "We'll need to keep our wits about us if we're going to stop Cosmos." A tray slid forward with a flat, bright orange pizza in the center and a round packet to the left. Bala sniffed. A pouting scowl creased his forehead. "Oh, well. It looks real. Kinda."

Jazzmarie tossed her empty container into a recycle depository. "How do you plan on stopping Cosmos, Bala? You have a secret weapon?"

Sliding onto a chair, Bala set his tray squarely down, pulled a napkin out of the dispenser, and confronted his food like a bear facing a beetle. "I've been thinking. Why don't we try to communicate with her?" With a glint in his eye, he tore open the packet and rhythmically zigzagged spice over the pizza.

Max wandered over and focused on Bala's ministrations. "It's been tried. She never responds. I doubt anything so primitive can understand advanced language."

Jazzmarie sidled up, leaned against a chair, and gazed at Max. "Primitive or not, I have a theory that may change everything."

Halting his pizza before his mouth, Bala glanced at Jazzmarie. "Do tell."

Jazzmarie slipped onto the chair next to Bala, and with an inviting glance at Max, patted the seat next to her. "She's pregnant."

Bala dropped his pizza on the tray, his eyes wide as saucers. "How in interstellar madness can you tell that?"

Jabbing her index finger in the air like a scolding professor, Jazzmarie sniffed. "Surely, you've noticed that she's erratic and grown enormously fat—"

Max blinked and sat down. "Eating whole planets could have that effect."

Jazzmarie stroked Max's arm. "You're still a child, aren't you, Maxi?"

Staring forlornly at his food, Bala huffed. "You'll have to do better than that, Doctor. Lots of women act crazy and get big without the least chance—" He cleared his throat and bounced his gaze on the ceiling.

Jazzmarie lifted a second finger for further emphasis. "She also spewed out the Technetium. It's radioactive stuff that would hardly suit a growing life. And"—Jazzmarie cocked her head at Bala—"I can feel it. Call it a sixth sense."

Max rose and paced across the room. "If that's the case, then we have no choice. Yelsa's right; we must kill her now before she gives birth to another planet eater."

Jazzmarie's gaze hardened.

Squaring his shoulders, Bala lifted his pizza and shoveled in a huge bite. While he chewed, he glanced from Max to Jazzmarie. "How about we consider my idea? Cosmos may not understand language, but she must understand survival. A little stimulus response, maybe? Splash the way to Newearth with that dreadful Technetium, and she might find other roads to travel." He took another bite and shrugged. "Though I have to admit, taste isn't everything."

~~~

Yelsa followed Roux into his quarters, her head down and her gaze sweeping the floor.

Roux retreated to the other side of his console and turned around, crossing his arms over his chest. "Look, Yelsa, I understand your feelings. But I need to make it clear once and for all that I'm the captain of this ship, and we're not leaving orbit until I know that there is nothing that we can do to help the survivors down below."

Frustration building to her breaking point, Yelsa paced forward. "The Crestas don't want us here. Two Ingoti passenger ships are turning this way, and even the Luxonian Supreme Council has offered their support." She narrowed her eyes in contempt. "We are wasting valuable time. Cosmos will get away, and it will be our fault when she attacks another planet."
~~~

Roux leaned against the wall, his back to the window, where stars ran riot over a sea of blackness. "What are you suggesting we do, Yelsa? Our missiles might annoy her, but she'd kill us long before we injure her." He heaved a sigh. "Besides, I was told to track and relay messages back to Newearth about her coordinates. I haven't been given leave to kill her—officially." He waved at the starry universe. "There are other considerations involved—protocol that must be followed."

Rage shaking her thin body, Yelsa stomped to Roux. "How many more innocent people must die before someone takes a stand?" She flapped her arms. "I know—the Inter-Alien Alliance has threaded 'Respect all lifeforms' into the fiber of our beings so that it's nearly impossible to even contemplate the destruction of another life. But this is war. Kill or be killed."

Roux's shoulders sagged. "We make moral choices. She can't."

"My point exactly!" Yelsa took the position on the right side of the window, forcing Roux to turn toward her. With her palms flat against the smooth surface, she peered into the starry blackness. "There are untold innocents who will die tragic deaths because this beast must feed. If it were a plague, you wouldn't hesitate. Just because she's of enormous size doesn't change her nature. Cosmos is a blight on the universe."

Roux paced silently behind Yelsa and faced the same view. His gaze slipped from the window to Yelsa's face and rolled along her shoulder.

She glanced at him. "What are you afraid of?"

Swallowing, Roux took one step backwards. "I'm not afraid. I'll just have to think about what you've said. It's not like we can kill her without risk."

Yelsa's gaze met Roux's at close range. "Life without

risk is death."

Roux passed his hands caressingly down her arms—just barely touching her. He sucked in a deep breath and turned away. "True."

Chapter Ten

-Mirage-Reborn-

Bet You Didn't Know

Cerulean sat at the wooden kitchen table and watched Vera sweep onion, tomato, and green pepper pieces into a frying pan of sizzling scrambled eggs. Her bowed head and diminutive body made her appear more like a child at play in the kitchen than the mistress of the farm. He turned to Pax and gestured toward the window. "The sun's rising. You better start explaining so I'll have a decent story to tell Clare and Justine."

Sitting across from Cerulean, Pax stared through red eyes, his face dirty and haggard. His shoulders slumped as he ran his hand across his smeared brow. "My birth name was Induit Seven-Zero-Five. On Ingilium, you aren't really considered a viable life form until your synthetic enhancements are in place. In my case, I was considered too weak to process, so I was sold to a Cresta Lab."

Clenching his clasped hands on the table, Cerulean steeled himself.

Vera stood frozen in mid-stir.

With a heaving breath, Pax tipped back the creaking chair and stared at the ceiling. "By some strange fate, the Cresta who got ahold of me had just lost a child. In an unaccountably kind manner, he treated me like an adopted—"

"Son?" Hope rose in Cerulean.

Pax grimaced. "Pet."

Rubbing his temple, Cerulean muttered, "Maybe, you're lucky he didn't have you for lunch."

A smile quivered on Pax's lips. "On the contrary, he

took excellent care of me. He adapted my physiology to appear human and trained me to be a very effective thief."

Vera turned around, her mouth gaping, her eyes wide.

Fury rushing through him, Cerulean stared at Pax. "He sent you into the black market?"

Dropping his chair back on all four legs, Pax nodded. "Certainly." His grin widened. "Direct service between Crestar and Ingle and all points in between. I was quite good, too." His gaze fell, and his smile disintegrated. "Until I was caught."

Rising, Cerulean traipsed across the room. "So, you're telling me that I put a fugitive in charge of an interstellar crew to save Newearth?"

The sound of a glass breaking turned both Cerulean and Pax toward Vera.

Vera stared at the broken shards of glass as a puzzled frown etched across her brow. Slowly, she looked up and locked her eyes on Cerulean. "You call him a *fugitive*?" She blinked. "You've already found him guilty?"

Pax jerked to his feet and loped across the room. He retrieved a broom from the corner and began sweeping up the pieces. "No false modesty here. I am a fugitive and a guilty one too. Ask any Cresta." He dumped the broken glass into the trashcan and peered at Cerulean. "Once the authorities threatened me with Bothmal, I turned over every bit of evidence to the Inter-Alien Alliance Committee." He smacked the broom back into the corner. "Trust me—I'm not welcome on Crestar or Ingilium. Both worlds would sooner have my head mounted on a rack than let me live another day."

Cerulean leaned against the stove. "Hence your paranoia at the sight of every Cresta and Ingot."

Pax glanced at Vera. "Can't blame me for wanting to live a little longer. Even if I'm a failed thief made from waste material."

Using her miniature body like a wedge, Vera displaced Cerulean from near the stove and scooped a mound of scrambled eggs onto a plate. She laid the plate at Pax's place and nodded decisively, wiping her hands on her apron. "Eat."

Cerulean raised an eyebrow.

Pax opened his mouth and choked on his words. "You've already been too kind. I'd better go—"

Vera's scowl rivaled the petulance of a ruffled hen. Her hands flew to her hips. "Yes, I've been kind, and you'll be kind, too, if you have any sense. Dimi could use help in the field today—there are tomatoes and peppers to get in the ground and a row of zucchini to hoe. Eat up, or he'll have the job done before you get out there."

Dimi stared blankly at his sister.

Relief washing over him, Cerulean swiped a fork from the counter and tossed it to Pax. "Better hurry."

~~~

Clare hefted the box in her arms as she walked down the aisle and stole a glance at Grace.

Mid-morning and a handful of customers roamed the aisles of Nelson's store, looking for their day's necessities. Two cashiers manned the check-out lanes, chatting with the customers as they moved them through.

Grace and Clare carted supplies to their proper shelving units in the back of the store.

Grace turned and intercepted Clare's glance. "What?"

Blushing, Clare dropped her carton of cereal boxes
~~~

and rubbed her back. “Nothing. I was just thinking about someone I knew on Newearth. You look like her.”

Grace sniffed. “Poor woman. Bet she never had any luck either.”

Shoving empty boxes aside, Clare made room for the new inventory, then she ripped open the full carton, and started filling the shelf. “No, actually, she became Newearth’s leading archeologist and married one of handsomest men this side of the Divide.” Clare leaned in. “I was jealous for years.”

Grace smirked as she stacked sugar bags on a high shelf. “Not anymore?”

“I’ve got my work and Cer—” Clare caught herself, blushed, and turned back to her boxes.

Grace shook her head. “I was wondering if there was anything between you two. He’s certainly attractive—in a Luxonian sort of way.”

Moving on to another shelf, Clare shrugged. “It’s not like that between us. We’re just friends. Now Justine—” Clare sneered and blew air between her lips.

Grace chuckled.

Clare straightened, composing herself. “I’m talking too much. Hardly the trait of a good detective, eh?”

Stiff, Grace cleared her throat. “A detective?” She righted the tipped sack of sugar and squinted in concentration. “How do you like that line of work? I’ve always wondered what it’d be like.”

Clare kicked an empty carton aside. “It’s great, so long as you don’t love the victims or hate the villains—too much.”

Loading two empty containers into her arms, Grace retreated toward the back door.

Clare traipsed along behind, tugging along three empty cartons.

In silence, they broke the cartons down and smashed

them into a large outdoor dumpster.

Grace headed back inside, grabbed another full box, nodded to indicate a smaller box to the left, and headed to the middle of the store.

Like an obedient child, Clare grabbed the box of goods and traipsed right behind. In a few moments, they both got to work unpacking the goods. Clare plunked cans onto a metal rack while Grace arranged loaves of bread decoratively on a plastic center table.

Clare stood back and admired Grace's work. "You have a talent—for arranging things, I mean." She lowered her voice. "I sure wish your father wouldn't yell at you so much. He has no idea how talented—"

Raising her hand, Grace stifled the comment. "He cares, in his own way. But I'm not really talented at anything—just determined." A somber expression spoke more than her words.

A lump rose in Clare's throat as she placed the last can on the shelf. "So, tell me about Omega. What's he like?"

Grace's lips pursed, and she appeared perplexed. "You've never met him?"

"Yeah, sort of. He's haunted me since childhood."

Grace blinked. "Haunted? That hardly seems possible. Omega saved my life. From what I understand, he has saved nearly everyone on Mirage-Reborn."

A sinking sensation made Clare dizzy. "Saved you? Perhaps he simply arranged it so that he appeared to rescue you."

Grace tapped the last loaf in line with the others. "Hardly." She stared Clare right in the eyes. "I murdered my father's wife. It was Omega who helped me escape Bhuaci justice." Turning, she scooped the last two empty cartons into her arms, then she walked away.

Cold with shock, Clare stood alone in the middle of the produce aisle.

~~~

Justine stood on the sidewalk and observed a young woman wearing a form-fitting, calf-length dress glance timidly through the front window of the Sheriff's office,

Inside, Quinn, with his blond hair slicked back and wearing a tan vest over a cream-colored sheriff's uniform, caught the woman's gaze and pointed to the door.

Glancing wide-eyed at Justine, the woman thrust the door open and charged forward.

Justine strolled in after her.

The sheriff's grin reached from ear to ear as he welcomed the woman from behind a high counter. "Hello, Madge. Nice to see you." He glanced at Justine's entrance, and a scowl shadowed his face.

Justine sauntered to a bench by the window, sat down, and flipped through a day-old newspaper.

With a trembling hand, Madge dug an envelope out of her purse and handed it to the Sheriff. "Billy said it's all he's got for now. He'll get more as soon as he can." Her twitchy smile slipped into a grim line that seemed to be held firm by sheer force of will.

Quinn's sunny side returned as he ambled around the counter. He took the envelope and smoothly slid it into a vest pocket. His eyes traveled over the young woman, a man taking the scenic route. "You sure look nice in that dress. Bet your husband gets jealous easy, don't he?"

Madge dropped her gaze and cleared her throat. "Well, that's all Billy told me to say. So, I'd better go."

As she turned away, Quinn reached out and grabbed her hand.
~~~

Unabashedly, Justine peered over the top of the newspaper.

Madge stiffened like a terrified rabbit.

Twisting Madge's wrist upward, Quinn's voice turned authoritative. "Let me take a look at that cut there, sweetheart. Why, that looks infected."

Madge jerked away. "It's not a cut, just some kind of rash or something."

Quinn gripped Madge's elbow and steered her to the far end of the counter. "No. That's an infection. But I have just what you need." He plucked a plain blue jar off a shelf and unscrewed the lid. "Here. Just the thing. My mother used to make all sorts of remedies. This cures all kinds of sores and lesions." He scooped out a fingerful, dragged Madge's arm forward, and slathered it across the inflamed skin. He looked at her as he caressed her arm. "Now—doesn't that feel better?"

With a nervous shake, Madge sniffed and tugged her arm free.

Enough is enough. Justine laid the newspaper aside and stood up.

Exhaling a long, drawn-out breath, Quinn eyed Justine.

Madge scurried to the door, a quick glance darting from Quinn to Justine. "Billy's waiting. Bye."

As the door shut behind Madge, Justine sauntered to the counter. "Could I see that magic potion, please?"

Quinn snatched the jar off the counter and tucked it back on the shelf. "Nothing you need to bother about."

Justine fixed her gaze on Quinn, watching his every move. "Really? How do you know? I could have lesions all over my body and be in desperate need of your mama's secret tonic."

Quinn turned around, faced Justine, and rubbed his lips thoughtfully. "You've always been a troublemaker, haven't you? One of those bad-girl types that likes to get attention at any cost."

With her hand against her chest in mock horror, Justine's eyebrows sky-rocketed. *"Moi—mauvaise fille?"*

Quinn stared at her through narrowed eyes. "That some kind of slang?"

Chuckling, Justine shook her head. "I could ask you much the same. You've been reviewing OldEarth Westerns?"

Quinn squared his shoulders, his chin jutting forward. "Don't be stupid. My roots go all the way back to OldEarth New York. I'm authentic."

Laughter bubbled inside Justine. "Good heavens, you cut yourself short. Why, the particles in your body reach back to the dawn of the universe."

Turning beat-red, Quinn retreated behind the counter. "Listen, I was gentle on you last time, but don't fool with me. I don't care where you come from—"

Justine's voice turned icy as she straightened. "Oh, but I think you do." Strutting around the counter, Justine gripped Quinn's hand and pinned it—and the gun he held—to the counter. "You see, I'm Omega's creation, his daughter, we'll say. Abbas' granddaughter." She grinned as she pried the gun out of his hand and shoved it across the counter. "That makes me worth knowing—don't you think?"

A tremor ran over Quinn's body.

Justine released Quinn and returned to the bench by the window. After picking up the newspaper, she flapped it open and perused its contents.

With a huff, Quinn circled the counter and stopped in front of Justine. His eyes narrowed. "You're one of *them*?"

"I'm unique. An android-Human." Dropping the

paper onto the bench, she met his gaze. “Is that good enough?”

Whistling low, Quinn paced across the room, stopped, and stared out the window. “I knew he was powerful, but I never—”

Justine yawned through a smile. *This wasn’t so hard after all. Just had to show the fool who’s in charge.*

Quinn turned and considered Justine, one eyebrow rising. “You must be an early model.” With a swagger, he paced toward Justine then propped one boot on the bench and leaned in. “You see, he’s got a little girl—a beautiful thing. He sent her to some off-planet school, but he was going to bring her back and settle her here at Mirage-Reborn. Told me so himself.”

Justine’s eyes narrowed, lasers ready to fire.

His gaze traveling across the ceiling, Quinn mused. “He’s so besotted, he’ll probably marry her.” Boyish dimples appeared as his gaze swung over Justine. “Didn’t know you had a rival—did you?”

Chapter Eleven

–Newearth–

A Good Man

Taug leaned back on his swivel chair in his lab and stared at the central screen. His body relaxed while his tentacles intertwined behind his back—a great mind contemplating his existence. He shifted his gaze higher.

Across the ceiling, a long, arched skylight peered into a black night replete with millions of twinkling stars. A comet hit the atmosphere and streaked across the sky, its bright tail streaming like a kite string.

Movement from the screen snagged Taug's attention.

Jazzmarie's beaming face filled the frame. "I appreciate your quick work, Taug. With these findings, I'll have no trouble producing the proper formula. You just make sure that they shoot her exactly as I direct. We don't want her disintegrating, now do we?"

With a tilt of his head, Taug acknowledged the point. "What is Roux's plan?"

"We're following her trail, trying to get a little closer. Yelsa has a plan to obliterate her on sight, but I'll make sure that won't happen."

His tentacles swinging to the front, Taug recomposed himself. "I won't ask how."

"Wise of you."

A sliver of apprehension stabbed Taug. He rubbed the side of his face. "You're quite sure this will immobilize her?"

"I'm the most qualified person in the entire universe to make this breakthrough. Are you frightened?" Jazzmarie held up a datapad. "With this information, I'll stop her in her tracks. We'll be able to study her for years. What a trove of information she carries inside her swollen body! The Cresta world will be very grateful to the scientist who brings this treasure home, am I right?"

Happiness wiggled through Taug's middle. "They'll be delighted."

"Maybe someone will be treated with a little more respect?"

Taug tilted his head in consideration of the woman before him; it was time to stop playing the fool. "Maybe someone will further her studies?"

Jazzmarie laughed. "Oh, Cosmos means more than professional advancement. I expect she'll do wonders for my personal life as well."

"Intriguing, but I best not get nosey." Taug frowned. "Too bad she wasn't really pregnant. That would've added a great deal to her value."

With a shrug, Jazzmarie tossed that loss aside. "Honestly, I haven't a clue how she reproduces. I just brought the idea forward to see how the others would react."

"You have charming subtleties."

"Reactions reveal reality."

Unsettled by a new fear, Taug struggled to his feet and paced in front of the screen. "You're certain that tranquilizers shot from Newearth will be enough?"

"They had better be. I'm not about to reveal my plan to Roux. He'd reject it out of hand and destroy any opportunity of adjusting the weapons' schema." Her gaze fastened on Taug. "You just pass the word along that you have the perfect weapon against her. Give them the formula at the last possible moment, so they have no time to review it, and tell them to hit her dead center. Believe me, there isn't a biological creature alive that can't be tranquilized. If by some bloody chance we do kill her, we'll still have saved the day. Either way, you'll have first dibs on the carcass."

Appeased, Taug stopped pacing and stood where he started. "Yes. It's a perfect plan."

Jazzmarie frowned. "You don't look particularly happy about it."

Fear nuzzling at the back of his mind, Taug tried to suppress it. "Perfect plans often have unpredictable results. It's Newearth that's at stake."

Jazzmarie rolled her eyes. "That's what makes this whole thing exciting. High stakes, you might say. Now, I have a meeting with a very unpredictable friend." She grinned. "Wish me good luck."

With the charming manners of an old-world ambassador, Taug bowed low. "You hardly need luck." He tapped the screen, and it blinked to black.

Turning, he murmured, "But you could use a heart."

~~~

Riko stood beside Wendell at the checkout counter and kept a firm hold of his patience. "So, the customer steps up, and what do you say?"

"Good morning." Wendell frowned. "If it's not morning?"

Riko's jaws clenched.

A bright sun shone in the east window, and the café sparkled in the early morning light.

With a stiff finger, Riko pointed to the front window. "If the sun is coming from the east, it's good morning, and if it's coming from the west, it's good afternoon. See?"

"If it is raining?"

Riko glared at the floor. "Just say good day, all right?"
~~~

He rolled his shoulders like a boxer ready for the third round. "Okay, now what do you do next?"

The door swung open, and Lang strolled in.

Riko glanced up, his heart thumping a little harder. "We're not open yet."

Lang smiled. "Fine. I'm not hungry yet." She sauntered to a front table and perched on the edge. "Go about your work. I'm just here to annoy you for a bit."

Scratching his head, Riko glanced from Lang back to Wendell, who was staring open-mouthed at the gorgeous Ingot. Applying one finger under the chin, Riko closed Wendell's mouth. "So, you check the datapad, confirm the table number, and then hand the scanner over for the transaction."

Wendell's eyes never moved off Lang, though he nodded his head vigorously.

Riko sighed.

With a twinkling-eyed smirk, Lang sauntered forward. "Let me help." She peered at Wendell's blushing face. "I'd like an Ingoti breakfast special and a cup of blackberry tea. Table three." She smiled. "Got that?"

Glancing at the datapad, Wendell tapped the surface and handed it over.

Lang finished the transaction and handed it back with a glow. "You better watch out, Riko. This boy will have your job someday."

Surprised but pleased, Riko straightened, facing Wendell. "Well, that's enough for now. You'd better go in the kitchen and get things ready." He watched Wendell stride through the swinging door. Circumventing Lang, he straightened the table service she had knocked askew. "Your breakfast will be ready in a bit."

Lang waved his words aside. "Breakfast can wait. The

IAA is getting nervous. When they get nervous, Newearth News trembles."

Moving on to the next table, Riko stayed focused. "What's the problem? Not enough infighting to keep everyone happy?"

Lang perched on a stool at the counter. "No one has heard from *The Summons,* and *The Merrimack* sent word that Cosmos took a bite out of another planet. Apparently, it wasn't to her liking—she left before dessert."

Returning to the register, Riko tapped the console. "They've got destroyers ready to launch. Their grand plan is on every holoscreen across the planet." He gestured toward the window. "You see anyone panicking?" He glanced at Lang and froze, alarm sending chills along his arms. "Don't tell me—it's all a sham?"

Lang slid off the stool. "No. They have destroyers. And they might actually *sting* her. But sadly, she'll have eaten us long before we do any real damage." Lang pointed to the door leading to Taug's lab. "What about *him*? Any solutions yet?"

"We're not exactly buddies. He doesn't share with me."

"Oh, really? Well, he's sharing with someone. He's sent coded messages to *The Merrimack.*"

Riko's face darkened as he marched around the counter and crossed his arms over his chest. "*The Merrimack*? Why?"

"That's what I and the IAA would like to know." Lang leaned in, gripping Riko's shoulder. "They'll come in and confiscate every chair and bit of cutlery if they think you've put Newearth at risk."

"I'd never do that!"

"No one knows who to trust these days." She glanced

at the door and patted Riko's arm. "You better find out what's going on. See if Taug has a solution to Cosmos and pass it to me in a hurry, or you'll find yourself accused of treason."

Riko's knees turned to water.

Lang swung toward the door with a wave. "Oh, I'll be back for breakfast in an hour. Keep it hot, would you?"

Gathering his courage and squaring his shoulders, Riko shut the door behind Lang and swung toward the kitchen, shouting, "Wendell!"

Wendell hurried through the doorway with a white apron lopsided around his waist. "Sir?"

"I have a message. You'll have to carry it to Taug for me—quick!"

Wendell stood stiff and still, a hot-pad limp in one hand.

Riko pounded forward. "Take that apron off and—" He swiped the hot-pad out of Wendell's hand and stared into his eyes. "Listen to me carefully. Taug is the Cresta who works next door. He's at Kendra Impala's house, but he needs to come back here right now. Tell him it's an emergency."

Wendell pulled the apron free and held it at arm's length. He nodded. "Taug, come. Riko say it an emergency."

Riko draped the apron over his arm and patted Wendell's shoulder with a relieved smile. "You're a good man to have around, Wendell. No one in the universe would ever suspect you—of anything."

~~~

Taug inched toward the plush couch in Kendra's
~~~

living room, behind which a low hum grew louder.

Morning light streamed through the window, highlighting the scuffed floor and polished tables and chairs.

Faye crouched close by Taug; her eyes stayed glued to a shadow stretching from the couch's backend.

Standing in the kitchen doorway, Kendra wrung a towel in her hands.

The hum's pitch rose to a siren level, and the couch jerked in awkward thrusts from side to side.

Kendra jumped forward, her arms wide, barring Taug from taking another step. "You're frightening her. She's not usually this bad, but Crestas naturally make her uneasy." She glanced beyond Taug to Faye. "I know you mean well, but I think you two better go."

Eyeing Kendra, Taug dropped his tentacles limply at his sides. "You'd be very foolish to leave this child untreated. You have children of your own to protect." His gaze moved to Kendra's middle.

Kendra caressed her protruding tummy and shook her head. "She'd never hurt me."

Faye stepped forward, moving in front of Taug. "You don't know that. In truth, you have no idea what she is capable of. I doubt she even knows." Faye took another step closer, her hands imploring. "Let us help her. Let us help you, before—"

A blond streak flew out from behind the couch and tackled Faye.

Taug spun around, his tentacles wrapping about the frantic child.

Without warning, the couch slid across the floor and knocked Taug off his feet, sending sharp pain through his body as he landed awkwardly. An end table catapulted across the room and sent Kendra spinning backwards.

Zara stood, her ragged blond hair falling over her eyes. She pinioned Faye's arms behind her back. With a grunt, she thrust Faye into Taug, knocking them both back. Growling like a feral child, Zara screeched, "Leave me!"

Faye morphed into a giant version of herself, the top of her head all but scraping the ceiling. She glowered terrible and fierce, her eyes glowing in red fury.

Taug grappled with Faye, wrapping his tentacles about her waist. "No! Not now. She's right. We must stop before someone gets hurt."

Staggering forward, Kendra enveloped Zara in a gentle hug, smoothing back her hair and caressing her cheek. "It's all right, sweetheart. I'm here. No one's going to hurt you."

Huffing, Faye returned to her usual shape, her eyes still red and fierce. She turned to Taug. "Telekinesis is dangerous for anyone—more so in an angry child."

"Certainly," Taug murmured. "But we need to think this through. We've approached her badly. Look." He pointed as Zara cuddled into Kendra's embrace, her eyes squeezed shut like a frightened child.

Kendra waved Faye and Taug toward the door. She mouthed the word, "later" and directed Zara into the hallway leading to the kids' bedrooms.

A chime rang through the house.

Kendra froze and peered at Faye imploringly.

Faye nodded, marched to the front door, and swung it open.

Standing ramrod straight on the porch, silhouetted against a glorious array of autumn leaves, Wendell looked every inch the expectant messenger. "Taug?"

Faye scowled and shook her head. She pointed to Taug, who stepped up behind her.

Wendell straightened his shoulders, his gaze swinging

to the ceiling. “Taug, Riko say to come. Emergency.” He carried his gaze back to Taug, his own face glowing with accomplishment.

Snapping a tentacle toward Wendell, Taug huffed. “Why? What’s wrong?”

In stupefaction, Wendell stiffened. “Don’t know. Sorry.” He pointed to his head. “Empty pool.” His gaze shifted to something behind Taug. He tilted his head, and a slow smile spread across his face.

Taug turned, as did Faye. They both stared as Zara, now wide-eyed, stepped away from Kendra’s embrace and stopped in the center of the living room. Her face glowed as she grinned at Wendell.

Chapter Twelve

-The Merrimack-

Waiting For You

Bala sucked in a bracing breath as Roux stepped into his quarters.

Roux glanced around and stopped dead in his tracks.

The allotted space was exactly the same as all standard quarters on the ship—except for the captain's, which was significantly larger—yet it appeared to loom in limitless space. Pictures, portraits, trailing vines, exercise equipment, and even an ornamental, dwarf pine tree created a homey niche in what should have been a Spartan living space.

Roux tapped his fingers together. "Bala? You want to explain *this*?"

With a white towel swung nonchalantly around his neck like a fighter pilot of OldEarth, Bala bowed and swept an imaginary helmet off his head. "Welcome to my abode, Captain. I told you I had the solution to all your problems. Well, here it is." He backed up, feeling for a large metal frame.

Roux stepped forward and scowled. "What the—?"

As if giving tribute to a good buddy, Bala hugged the metal post. "It's a full-body exercise machine. Just step in and every millimeter of your physique will get a workout. Your nervous system will finally leave you in peace—trust me. You'll be so exhausted; you'll sleep like the dead and wake surprisingly refreshed."

Glancing from the machine back to Bala's beaming face, Roux pursed his lips. "Does the fact that I'm Luxonian mean anything to you?"

With a boyish beckoning gesture, Bala drew Roux

closer. "I spent enough time with Cerulean to know that he responded in a much more human fashion to his physical sensations than he'd ever admit." Bala's eyebrows danced.

Roux swallowed.

"Come on—give it a try. I'm going to jog in place as you work out. You talk about whatever's bothering you, and I can run around. It's perfect."

Laboriously, Roux climbed the two steps into the apparatus.

Bala positioned Roux's hands on a front bar and his feet on fixed pads. Then he tapped an arm console. "Pretend you're strolling along in the woods."

Roux's feet began to move in a slow rhythm with his arms.

Raucous bird song broke through the air, making Roux jump.

Slapping the console, Bala turned down the volume and began jogging in miniature circles before Roux. "Part of the program, don't worry. I would've added the full hologram effect, but I didn't have enough room." His head swiveled as he tried to maintain eye contact with Roux. "I have to stay in shape, you understand. I'll be outnumbered eight to one when I get back." *I can hardly keep up with Kendra as it is...much less the kids...*

"I thought this was Kendra's seventh?"

Bala swallowed the vestiges of his pride. "Yeah, but she usually sides with our offspring." Bala sucked in a deep breath and pounded his chest in mock manliness. "So, what's our next move? You know Yelsa's—"

Roux picked up speed. "What about Yelsa?"

"Well, I—"

"She may be a perfect example of Bhuaci beauty and brilliance, but *I'm* the captain."

Bala's head dropped; his shoulders hunched as he picked up speed.

Roux's fingers clenched the bar tighter. "Cerulean should have checked in by now. I'm getting worried. He didn't look well before we left."

"He's probably just—"

"Last thing I heard, they had settled on Mirage-Reborn, Omega was gone, and someone named Abbas was in charge." The machine surged faster, and Roux upped his pace.

Trying to keep his steps even, Bala avoided a rough spot on the floor. "Clare can handle—"

The whirl of the machine grew louder as the speed increased.

"Did you know that Faye heard about Cosmos' pregnancy? She mentioned it in a report to the IAA, which they sent to me to confirm." Roux wiped sweat off his brow. "How in the universe did anyone on Newearth hear about that? I never said anything because it was just one of Jazz—I mean—the doctor's pet theories."

"Maybe Taug—"

"Yeah, and what about that Cresta? I'd like to know what he's been up to."

"He's a friend, really, not a typical Cresta—"

"The IAA is keeping an eye on him. He's got a secret lab—did you know that?"

Shaking his head, Bala dug in and expanded his circle. "I sure hope Zara isn't too much for Kendra—"

Daring one hand off the bar that was speeding up and down, Roux waved that concern away. "Zara's Android-Luxonian—as stable as the sun is bright. She's probably helping out in all sorts of unexpected ways. It's that android-human mother of hers that you should be worried about."

Panic flooded Bala. "What do you mean?"

"You know Justine's history. She's unpredictable. I'm glad I don't have to rely on her for support on a strange planet with a primitive culture."

Bala frowned. "Is that how you think of Max?"

Rolling his eyes, Roux huffed his words. "Max is—harmless—like a—child. He'll follow—orders—no matter—what. No worries!"

Chagrined, Bala's irritation level spiked. "Well, the doctor sure seems rather interested—"

A gleam entered Roux's eyes as he sucked in a lung full of air. "It's fascinating—isn't it? All these—lifeforms—working—for Newearth. So much—*passion*—you know?"

Bala slowed to a walk, his hands on his hips and his chest heaving. "I'm only the communications officer."

Roux jumped off the machine, sucked in a deep breath, and stood with a sheen of sweat brightening his face. "Wow! I do feel invigorated. Thanks, Bala." His eyes sparkled as he marched to the exit.

Bala waved a couple weak fingers as the door shut behind his captain. "Now, *I'll* never sleep."

~~~

Max leaned back in his cream-colored swivel chair on the bridge and tapped his fingers against the shiny surface. At first random, the tapping sounded like an insect smacking aimlessly against a window.

Though the bridge controls made no noise, lights of various colors flashed in accustomed patterns across panels and consoles.

Yelsa swung a frown from her directional console to
~~~

the communications center where Max sat.

He tapped out a playful rhythm on the edge of the console, repeating it four times to get the beat just right.

Her eyes flashing, Yelsa gripped the arms of her chair and swiveled around. "Stop!"

Freezing, Max stared at Yelsa, perplexed. "What's wrong?"

Yelsa stood and raised her arms as if to embrace the bridge. "Listen."

Max cocked his head. Nothing.

Yelsa nodded. "That's how it's supposed to be. Quiet. So, I can concentrate. We've lost our advantage, and if I'm not careful, we'll lose Cosmos altogether."

"She's heading toward Newearth—"

"She could stop for snacks twenty times along the way! Don't you understand yet? No one on that"—she wagged a finger at the screen—"innocent planet had to die. It was our fault. We dallied too long, arguing about the Divide, arguing about—"

Max shook his head. "We did nothing wrong. And we were right to stop and help. Cosmos is ahead of us. We'll find her."

"And then what?"

"We'll stop her."

Yelsa's eyes narrowed as she took another step nearer. "How?"

"Jazz—I mean the doctor—is working on a poison. We'll shoot her with it, and that'll be the end of the matter."

Yelsa folded her arms across her chest. "You're okay with that?"

Max clasped his hands, his jaw tightening. "I thought that's what you wanted."

Yelsa tromped over to the hologram of the destroyed planet and shook her fist. "It is!" She whirled around and glared at him. "But everyone on this flying bucket has been fighting me."

"No one's fighting you. We just weren't sure—"

Yelsa pointed at the medical console. "Jazzmarie—that so-called doctor. She wanted to spare the monster. You know she did. Bringing in a specimen like Cosmos would cultivate a great deal of professional prestige—"

"No." Max rose and strode over to Yelsa. "She's only being sensitive—to me." He leaned in. "You don't know what it's like. Being the monster."

Yelsa stepped backward, her eyes blazing. "Do you go around eating planets?"

"No, but I have killed people." Max swallowed and stepped to the railing, leaning against it. "I was a killer in my early years. Mercenary for hire." He blinked. "I didn't know any better."

Yelsa rubbed her chin and peered at him through a lowered gaze. "That explains your motivation. But Jazzmarie? She isn't sparing your feelings; she's playing with them."

"She's Newearth's best—"

"She's humanity's worst!"

The door slid open, and Jazzmarie stepped forward. Noting the tense expressions in a swift glance, she grinned. "What have we here? A lovers' quarrel?"

With a snort, Yelsa returned to her console.

Max sidled back to the communications station. "Yelsa doesn't believe that we're willing to destroy Cosmos if the opportunity arises."

Jazzmarie's hand flew to her chest. "I'll do whatever it takes to stop her vile path of destruction."

Max glanced at Yelsa's impassive face.

Jazzmarie sauntered to the medical console. "But sadly, I don't think we have the power to do the needful."

Both Max and Yelsa turned toward Jazzmarie.

"You see, I've been working with a fine Cresta scientist by the name of Taug on Newearth. And though we have worked out a formula to destroy her, we don't have the ability to get it deep enough into her system without risking our lives. We'll just have to wait until she gets closer to Newearth, and they can send up—"

In a deadpan tone suited to her blank stare, Yelsa tapped the directional console. "We're not going to wait. We can destroy her any time we want."

Max tilted his head. "How?"

"Blow her to smithereens."

Jazzmarie folded her arms. "Our missiles won't penetrate—"

"They don't have to. We can destroy her from the inside."

Bounding across the bridge, Jazzmarie focused a laser-like gaze on Yelsa. "And *how* will we get inside?"

"We'll let her eat us."

Max gripped the railing as a wave of an unseen force rolled over him. *If this is fear, I can't imagine courage.*

~~~

Roux leaned back in the captain's chair on deck and rubbed his face. He propped his head on one hand and glanced over at Bala. "Any news?"

"All quiet on the western front, sir."

Roux slid his gaze over to Max. "How long before she's in visual range, Max?"

"Possibly within the next hour, sir. She speeds up suddenly and then slows down, very erratic. Hard to calculate exactly."
~~~

With a sigh, Roux stared at the screen filled with stars amid the vast universe. "I wish Yelsa were on deck."

Bala and Max exchanged glances.

Jazzmarie rose and padded over to the captain's chair. "I gave her a heavy sedative. She's in a very fragile state." Though still quite audible, the doctor's voice dropped to a husky whisper. "You know about her sister?"

Closing his eyes, Roux nodded. "It's part of the reason I wanted her on board. They were very close. This pursuit is personal."

Jazzmarie pursed her lips as she toyed with a silver bracelet. "It's called survivor's guilt. Yelsa needs to die to save her sister. Or so she thinks." With a sniff, Jazzmarie pulled her sleeves even. "Unfortunately, she'd kill us all in the process." Glancing up, she met Max's gaze. "You don't want to die, do you, Maximan?"

Scowling, Max turned back to his console.

A violent lurch jerked the ship, nearly pulling them from their seats. Roux sat up and glanced around. "What just happened?"

Max's fingers appeared to blur as he speed-checked the system monitors. "We've hit some kind of mine. It's knocked out our port thrusters. We're coming to a halt, sir."

Jumping to his feet, Roux rushed to Max's side. "By the Divide, who—?"

Max pointed to the screen. "It's a trader of some kind."

A small gray ship with a yellow and red stripe over the top sailed into view on the main screen.

Bala raised his hand. "We're being hailed."

Jazzmarie retreated to the lift door, her eyes fixed on the screen.

Roux straightened and faced the screen. "Open

communications."

Larger than life appeared the faces and upper bodies of two men, one something of a giant—over two and a half meters tall and heavyset, wearing a blood-red vest—the other shorter but lean with brilliant yellow eyes.

With an intake of breath, Max rose slowly, staring at the screen. "Not traders—raiders, sir."

Roux masked his "bloody hell" reaction with a swipe of his hand. He stared at the two men and braced his legs. "What can I do for you two gentlemen?"

The yellow-eyed man, lithe with a well-toned physique, wearing a form-fitting dark green outfit, took one step forward. "We've been waiting for you, Roux."

Chapter Thirteen

-Mirage-Reborn-

Purpose Of Existence

Cerulean strolled across Main Street and stopped as Quinn stepped outside, locking the sheriff's office door behind him.

Long shadows highlighted the layers of dust on Main Street. The drowsy hum of bees mingled with the last warbles of sleepy birds as families settled in for the last meal of the day and a well-earned rest. A cool breeze swept the day's heat away, and a rosy tinge behind a line of spring-green trees drew the eye to the horizon.

"Good evening, Sheriff. You certainly put in long days."

Quinn turned with a grimace. "It's my duty." He squinted as he straightened. "Doubt you'd understand."

Suppressing a grin, Cerulean gestured down the street. "Mind if I walk with you?"

After shoving the key into a deep pocket, Quinn marched ahead. "I'd say it's a free country—but as you know, that's hardly the case."

Cerulean kept pace. "Neither Omega nor Abbas seem particularly despotic."

"Despot or god, it's all the same to me." The sheriff stopped and thrust his hands on his hips. "What'dya want?"

Cerulean motioned toward the café. "How about a cup of coffee or something?"

"Look, I'm not your friend, Luxonian, so get to the point."

Cerulean shook his head. "Your spy network isn't keeping you abreast of the local gossip. I'm not

Luxonian at present. I'm as human as you are. Price I paid to stay alive and help Abbas."

Quinn's eyes rolled over Cerulean. "Yeah, and Justine's just a friendly little concoction of Omega's imagination, right?" Quinn smirked. "I know why you're here."

Cerulean waited, trying to appear unconcerned.

"You and your little gang want to take over. Well, I'm afraid you're too late. Mirage-Reborn is growing up, and we don't need caretakers anymore."

Pursing his lips, Cerulean nodded, his heart rate quickening. *Feels strange, like I might get short of breath.* He forced himself to focus on Quinn. "You'll be their illustrious leader, I suppose?"

"Someone has to free these people from the tyranny of—"

A Cresta waddled by, his gaze sifting over them like a soldier checking a minefield.

Cerulean pointed to the empty park. "Let's be discreet, shall we?" He plodded over and sat on a garden bench beside the band stage.

Rolling his eyes, Quinn followed and propped his foot on the first step of the stage. He swiped his hat from his head and poked at Cerulean. "I'm warning you now; take your friends and go on your way. Don't wait for Omega or Abbas. The best thing you can do for this world is leave us alone."

Perched on the edge of the seat, Cerulean clasped his hands. He didn't have to fake weariness. "I gave Abbas my word that I'd stay and be of service." He peered at Quinn. "I'm not trying to change anything."

Quinn smacked his hat back on his head. "Well, I am. I care about this world—you don't. There's the difference between us."

Tapping his fingers steeple-style, Cerulean stared at

the pink horizon. “Is that why you spy on the community, pay informers, and stoop to creating skin lesions so you can offer your mother’s homemade cure?”

“Devil’s minion!” Quinn edged closer. “That android had better stay away from me, or I’ll teach her some manners.” He straightened and glanced over his shoulder across the street. “You think you understand? You don’t know the first thing about these people. They’re all criminals, vagrants, and social deviants that Omega took in thinking he could offer them a new lease on life. He chose me as sheriff because he knew I could keep order.”

“You’re good at keeping order, then?”

“I kept order in Bothmal—the largest prison system this side of the Divide.”

Tired of the posturing, Cerulean stood. “So, why did he choose *me?*”

Quinn spat on the ground. “Omega didn’t! It was Abbas. He’s always distrusted his son’s judgment. He’s afraid that we’ll fall into chaos, and then he’ll have to clean up the mess.”

A cloud passed over Cerulean’s composure. “Why would he fear that?”

“You’re not very smart, are you?” Quinn swept his arms high, embracing the park and beyond. “They nearly killed each other—in that world they used to have—the medieval village Omega first created. They got into some kind of land dispute and attacked each other. Over thirty-five percent of the population *died*.”

With a sinking sensation, Cerulean’s gaze dropped to the ground.

“There’s a lot you don’t know.”

Cerulean lifted his chin and met Quinn’s superior gaze. “True, but I do know that the spying will end, the payments will stop, and the lesions will disappear."

"Or what?"

A fresh surge of energy filled Cerulean. "You don't want to find out."

Quinn laughed. He gripped Cerulean's shoulder and squeezed. "I'm a patient man, but I've warned you. Leave while you still can—*human*."

Reflexively, Cerulean shook Quinn's hand off his shoulder. His heart raced, and his hands clenched.

Suddenly, a familiar petite figure in the distance scuttled forward. Vera stopped at the edge of the park. A concerned frown etched across her forehead.

Huffing his disgust, Cerulean shoved past Quinn and stepped toward Vera.

Quinn snorted. Laughter bubbled in an undercurrent.

Like a frightened rabbit, Vera darted across the street toward a long winding road leading out of town.

Cerulean caught up and paced alongside.

Once they were well away from Main Street, Vera glanced aside her. "Pax has been a big help, but he's depressed. He doesn't understand his place here—or anywhere."

Cerulean considered her dark hair softly gleaming in the evening light. "Few do."

"But there is someone who does understand."

Trailing his fingers along a fence line, Cerulean sighed. "Perhaps. But Abbas is a bit preoccupied at the moment."

Vera stopped and stared at Cerulean. "Not Abbas. I mean Lucius Pollex—the blacksmith. He was injured in a rescue attempt, then wrongfully imprisoned. Omega rescued him from his Bothmal prison guard."

Swallowing a hard lump in his throat, Cerulean stiffened. "Prison guard?"

"Jeremy Quinn."

After rubbing his hands over his face, Cerulean looked over his shoulder.

Quinn's office windows reflected the blood-red twilight.

~~~

Justine faced Clare across a checkerboard. She leaned forward from a ladder-backed chair in a comfortable living room, with her head propped on one hand and her eyes glued to the game. "I still don't understand why Omega didn't tell me that he plans to bring Zara back here."

A lacy window curtain fluttered in a gentle breeze as the dark of night filled the rectangular frame.

Clare sat enthroned on a curvy, Victorian-style couch and peered at the checker pieces. Slowly, she picked one and slid it across a black square. "Why do you expect honesty from Omega? He's as devious as the day is long."

Justine jumped her piece over three of Clare's and gathered them in her hand. "He's always been honest with me. Are you sure you aren't reading your human qualities into him?"

Her shoulders hunching, Clare shook her head and slid another piece across the board. "You've got me there. I've been tricked by more humans than I care to count. I certainly never would have pegged Grace as a murderer."

"There's more to that story. Humans will do surprising things to protect their own." She jumped the last of Clare's pieces and placed them on a neat pile.

Clare stretched. "Enough. You've beat me three
~~~

times, and that's as much humiliation as I care to take in one night."

"You react emotionally and don't think through your options."

Like a leaking airbag, Clare slumped against the back of the couch. "There's something to be said for human emotions."

"Perhaps the very reason why Grace killed her stepmother."

Rubbing her eyes, Clare yawned. "You're not helping."

Justine stood. "I suspect Quinn thinks the same. And Pax." She sauntered to the kitchen cabinet and pulled down a box of gingersnaps.

Clare's gaze followed her. "I'd like to help Grace. I bet you're right, and there were extenuating circumstances. Still, murder is murder. If we were on Newearth, I'd have to arrest her."

"Lucky for Grace, we're not on Newearth. To be honest, I wouldn't mind murdering her father. Such a cantankerous old man." Justine crunched a cookie.

Clare pressed her hands over her ears as she pounded across the room. "Stop! The way things are going, I'll have to arrest everyone before Omega returns."

Justine swallowed and wiped her lips. "You could arrest Quinn. There's a man begging for justice."

Snatching the box of gingersnaps, Clare sniffed. "I'd need evidence."

"I'll be your witness. I saw him take payment from Madge."

Clare waved a cookie. "Payment for what? You have any evidence it was a crime? She might have been paying back a loan."

"The lesion on her arm, then. He had the cure right there in his office."

"You can't arrest a man for offering a cure."

Her eyes narrowing, Justine peered at Clare. "I know crimes are being committed, but you just follow the law blindly?"

Nibbling the cookie, Clare shrugged. "You have another option?"

Justine peered at the bag of gingersnaps. "Possibly. But"—she grimaced—"it won't be as easy as checkers."

~~~

Vera moved like a shadow, leading another shadow down a long, winding lane. Even slight shuffling and murmuring could give away their presence. Anxious and impatient, Vera quickened her pace. "Come along. There's nothing to be afraid of."

Pax padded along behind, his voice sharp against the quiet night. "Then why are we stumping down the road in the pitch black?"

"I told you, my friend works during the day and, besides, it's best if we kept our business to ourselves."

Illuminated by lighted windows, a neat two-story house huddled on the street corner next to a large free-standing building with enormous barn doors.

Stopping before the house, Vera waved Pax along. "Here we are." She climbed the three steps, marched across the porch, and knocked on the wooden front door.

Pax retreated into the shadows.

The door opened, and a tall, muscular man with blond hair and bright blue eyes stood in a pool of yellow light. His eyes widened. "Vera?"

Suddenly shy, Vera pointed behind her. "Hi, Lucius. I brought a friend—who needs your help."
~~~

Smiling, Lucius stepped back and swept his hand toward the glowing room. "Any friend of yours is a friend of mine, Vera. You know that. Come on in."

As Pax stepped inside the living room, he rubbed his eyes and blinked in the sudden light. Then he looked around, and his mouth dropped open. He might have stepped into an art museum.

Glorious figures gleamed in aged copper, polished silver, and golden hues. A medieval knight bedecked in shiny armor stood at attention with a pike stiff in his hand. A meter-high copper hound dog leaped in the corner—forever frozen in an expression of doggy joy. A bird with outstretched winds dangled from a chain, seeming to fly across the room. Tapestries depicting hunting scenes and bucolic meadows covered two walls, while tall sconces with lighted beeswax candles illuminated the shadowed corners.

His hand against his chest, Pax stepped forward and turned slowly, his gaze wandering the room, his eyes alight with rapture. "It's better than anything I've ever seen."

Vera stood beside Lucius, pleased with Pax's enthusiasm. She glanced at Lucius, and a warm blush worked up her face. "I took a chance bringing him here, but Pax needs *you*."

In a comforting move, Lucius gently squeezed Vera's hand, and then he stepped toward Pax. "How can I help?"

Hunching his shoulders, Pax dropped his gaze and shook his head. "I don't think you can." He jutted his chin toward Vera. "She's been letting me stay with her and Dimi, but I'm only putting them at risk. Someone'll recognize me, and the game'll be up." Sucking in a long breath, he squared his shoulders. "I didn't do anything wrong…by choice anyway." He shrugged again. "Too many people want me out of the way. I was safe in space, living as a trader. But no one can protect me here."

Stroking his temple with a thick finger, Lucius tilted his head, a man studying his next project. "It's because of Quinn, isn't it?"

Pax glanced at Vera, his brows drawing together. "Quinn? No. I'm—" He scowled. "You didn't tell him?"

Vera gripped her courage and held on. She met Pax's troubled look. "That wasn't my place. It's your story to tell." She patted Pax's arm. "Lucius is a good man. He'll understand your predicament. And he can help." Her gaze swiveled to the tall blond figure, and warmth filled her. "He always does."

Before anyone could object, she hurried to the door and slipped back out into the embracing night.

Chapter Fourteen

–Newearth–

Life's Terrible Truth

Riko stood with folded arms next to Faye, who sat in a café booth, squeezed next to Taug and across from Wendell. He chewed his lip, anxiety returning like a familiar friend. *A fine set of interrogators we make. Poor kid couldn't tell a lie if his life depended on it.*

Apparently unconcerned, Wendell stared blankly ahead.

Faye sighed.

Taug snorted.

Low rumbles of thunder reverberated across the late autumn sky, rolling closer with each pass. A gust of wind scattered leaves from colorful trees, setting a cascade into action that few could enjoy in the evening darkness. The café's locked door with closed sign checked any passerby's inquiry. Light from the kitchen slanted across the propped steel door, allowing a pool of illumination to brighten the booth where they sat.

Faye shoved the napkins dispenser aside, reached across the table, and clasped Wendell's hand. "It's not that we think you did anything wrong, Wendell. It's just that we'd like to know how you managed it."

Wendell's wide eyes stared fixedly on the shiny table. He shrugged. "I smile. She smile."

Confused, irritated, and more than a little weary, Riko cleared his throat. "Yes, they noticed that. But apparently, Zara smiled back like she knows you." Riko gripped the edge of the table and leaned in, focusing his gaze on Wendell's bowed head. "Does she?"

Pulling his hand free from Faye's grasp, Wendell

glanced up. “In street. She walk. I walk. She smile. I smile.”

Taug tapped his tentacles together contemplatively. “You take the same path each day?”

With a nod, Wendell’s gaze returned to the tabletop.

Faye sucked in an appreciative breath. “So, she’s like an acquaintance—a friend?” Faye looked up and met Riko’s gaze.

Wendell shrugged. “Smile mean friend.” He peeked a glimpse at Taug. “Like water mean life.” He turned his gaze to Faye. “Like butterfly mean free.”

Chuckling, Taug waved a tentacle in the air. “You have a philosopher here, Riko.”

Faye slid out of the booth, scampered around to Wendell’s side, and offered him a brief hug. “You’re the most remarkable Ingot in creation.”

With his back kinked from stress, Riko huffed and stepped away. “Okay, that’s enough for tonight. Head home now, Wendell. Your mama’s probably worried.”

In customary obedience, Wendell slid out of the booth and started toward the kitchen door.

Riko called after him. “Oh, and take that last apple pie. It’ll be stale before morning.”

With a quick over-the-shoulder nod and the hint of a grin, Wendell strode from dimness to light, disappearing into the cavernous depths of the kitchen.

Taug struggled from the booth and ambled toward his lab, his tentacles waving. “Come and enjoy a cup of something with me, Riko. It’s about time someone fed *you* for a change.”

Stopping short, Faye tilted her head as she stared at Taug’s retreating back. “Am I included in the offer?”

Unlocking the door, Taug turned and bowed. “You are included in everything, Faye. I could hardly exist without you.”

Slapping her hands to her blushing cheeks, Faye scooted forward. "And you're the most *gallant* Cresta in the universe."

His mood ready to drop into the abyss, Riko shook his head as he sauntered into Taug's lab. "Don't bother telling me what I am. I'll have nightmares for weeks."

Faye and Riko captured two rolling lab chairs and plunked down.

Taug poured a thick amber liquid into three glasses, then passed them around. "To health and long life!"

All three sipped, savoring the intense flavor. Finally, Riko leaned back, propping an elbow on a rolling metal table with shelves. *Not a dissecting table, I hope.* He sighed and glanced from Taug to Faye. "Look. I know you two are concerned about Zara, but we have more important things to worry about right now. Lang visited earlier, and she has news."

Faye and Taug listened attentively as Riko relayed Lang's message. He quickly summed up the situation. "No one has heard from *The Summons*, and *The Merrimack* sent word that Cosmos took a bite out of another planet!" He pounded his fist into his hand. "We can annoy her, but we can't kill her. Not yet." He forced himself to his weary feet, carried his empty glass to the counter, and placed it inside the granite sink. He avoided looking around and faced Taug. "You'd better come up with something quick, or the IAA will send *us* as a peace offering to that bloody beast."

Unperturbed, Taug shuffled over and placed his glass next to Riko's. "Never fear. I've nearly completed my work. We'll just need the power to penetrate her thick hide." He ambled to the tray, pulled open a shelf, and sorted dissecting knives.

His stomach doing flip-flops, Riko turned toward the door. "I'll set Uncle Clem on that. Maybe he can find out what the IAA plans to do. After all, we can't win this battle with slogans." Reaching the door, he stopped and turned back. "Oh, and one more thing."

Taug looked up, one tentacle clasping a razor blade.

With a sidelong glance, Riko met Faye's gaze. "Lang said something about coded messages to *The Merrimack.* You wouldn't know anything about that?"

Returning to the tray, Taug laid the blade aside. "I told you; I'm working with the doctor—Jazzmarie—to find a solution to Cosmos." He shrugged. "No mystery."

Faye slid off her chair and wandered toward the pool. "So, why are the messages coded?"

With a chuckle, Taug gleamed a wicked smile in her direction. "I don't know how to send any other kind."

Riko sighed. *I should've seen that coming.* With his stomach clenching and in serious need of sleep, he headed for home.

~~~

Kendra lay in her bed, groaned in lonely misery, and flopped her arm to the empty side where Bala should have been.

A howling wind scattered leaves across the yard, but the house remained as dark and still as an abandoned barn.

With a jerk, Kendra grabbed the blankets and pulled them tighter, snuggling closer to the pillows.

A soft chime rang through the silent darkness.

Kendra sat bolt upright, her heart beating wildly. Listening, she waited, stiff and tense. The chime repeated. Her heart leapt with joy. She kicked the blankets aside and hustled to her dresser. Lunging forward, she scooped her datapad to her breast like a
~~~

crying baby.

Once back in bed, she flicked the bedside table lamp on low and huddled over the datapad, her eyes scanning. Scraping her disheveled hair aside, she crooned, "Talk to me, man o' mine."

From a room down the hall, a child whimpered, and Kendra froze. As silence followed, she returned her gaze to the datapad with a sigh. She read Bala's message and smiled. "You did what?" Giggling, she covered her lips with a shaky hand. "Oh, Bala. Really! You didn't!" She tapped the message to play.

Bala's weak and weary voice warbled across the light years. "Oh, Love-O-Mine, I'm missing you-oo-oo. I'm dreaming of you, holding you, loving you-oo-oo…"

Her heart squeezing unbearably, she clutched the datapad to her chest, covered her mouth, and sobbed in silence.

~~~

Faye sat on her circular bed with her legs folded under her and tapped on her datapad.

I wish you were here, Cerulean.

I'm okay.

Taug's the same as ever—only more so. You can practically see through Riko; he's so transparent. I think he's scared. Really scared. His Uncle Clem leaves me speechless. Never knew anyone with so much blind goodwill. Must have a powerful spirit protecting him. Can't think what else has kept him alive so long.

More ships than ever are leaving each day, taking family and all non-essential personnel to their home-worlds or other settlements. The IAA promises that
~~~

they'll protect us, so panic is avoided, but few believe Newearth News reports. No one wants to take chances with a "Gargantuan Sky Serpent." That's Lang's term—creative as always—you've got to give her that.

In other news, Zara has developed disturbing talents, but we'll have to discuss that when you return. Don't tell Justine. She'll only worry.

The sun will rise soon, so I best prepare for another day—to our demise or our delight? You probably know better than I.

Oh, and before I skedaddle, I learned an odd thing last night—it'll make you laugh—or cry. There's a Newearth businessman, Simms, a slimy sort but reconstructed to look good, if you know what I mean. He's building an enormous, new docking bay—"the best equipped this side of the Divide." In yesterday's interview, Lang asked him if he was going to put construction on hold until after the crisis passed. He said, "No, I'm not a coward—not like some OldEarth Luxonians I could name." I believe he was referring to you. Odd—isn't it?

I need a friend I can entrust with life's terrible truth, Cerulean. Come home—soon.

~Faye

~~~

Riko clattered about the kitchen, arranging foodstuffs and utensils for the breakfast crowd.

The Breakfastnook remained locked, but morning's rosy fingers peeked through the front window, highlighting its lacy white curtains.

Wendell hummed as he trotted through the back door.
~~~

With a nod and a glance, Riko set him to work.

Without warning, Zara appeared in their midst. She wore a mini-skirt and tight pink blouse over her tall, shapely body, no longer that of a child. Her gaze fixed intently on Wendell.

Blinking back his surprise, Riko scowled as he picked up a frying pan and advanced. "Zara? You look different. What're you doing here?" He pointed to the front door. "You should use the door like everyone else."

Zara's eyes narrowed. "I'm not everyone else."

His gaze moving down her budding female physique, Riko scowled. "You look older—a lot older!"

With a flickering smile, Zara's eyes shifted from Riko to Wendell. "I'm Wendell's age now."

Riko took another slow, careful step, his elbow flexed and the frying pan at the ready. "That's not what I heard. Justine said you were—"

With a low hum building like a growl deep in her throat, Zara expanded, taking the shape of a mammoth grizzly bear. Her mouth opened, and a cavernous voice echoed. "I am what I make up my mind to be!" She swiped a sharp claw at Riko.

Despite a nimble backward leap, a scratch tore across Riko's mid-section, leaving a small, ragged gash across his shirt. Riko stared at the rent and huffed, bracing his legs for a retaliatory charge.

Wendell flew forward, his arms outstretched between the two.

Zara halted.

His hands shaking, Wendell lifted them toward Zara in surrender. "Please, friend. No."

Shrinking to her former self, Zara appeared as she had when she entered, though shaking and clearly exhausted by her exertion. She grabbed Wendell's hand and pulled him to her side. "I'd never hurt *you.*"

Like a limp doll in the hands of its mistress, Wendell yielded to her every direction. Standing close to her now, he peered at her through searching black eyes.

Surprised by the depth of emotion in the young Ingot's face, Riko held up a hand in truce and settled the frying pan on the stovetop. "Look, I've never done *you* any harm." Leaning against the sink, he folded his arms, ready for a serious chat. "I'm not interested in a confrontation, but would you be so kind as to explain what you're doing here?"

Zara dropped Wendell's hand and limped over to a stool. She pressed her fingers to her side, her body fuzzing for a moment and then solidifying. Her breathing seemed ragged as if she had trouble catching her breath. "Your friends—the Cresta and the Bhuaci—they're trying to kill me!"

Riko's eyes slid over to Wendell. He bit his lip and nodded to the half-done chores. "Uh…would you finish up the morning prep?"

Dutiful as ever, Wendell strode to the counter, flicked a white apron over his head, and began arranging the days' breakfast assortment.

Riko waved toward the door. "Walk with me?"

Her gaze rolled over him, inspecting him for hidden weapons? Zara finally glanced at Wendell as he briskly went about his work. Satisfied, she marched forward.

Riko unlocked the front door, moved aside, and allowed Zara to step into the early morning light. The storm had passed, leaving a world of glimmering autumn leaves strewn across the shiny street and reflecting pools along the sidewalk. Riko clasped his hands over the ragged tear in his clothing and strolled forward.

Avoiding the mud, Zara hopped over every puddle. "You can't protect him, you know."

Riko glanced at a passerby as he hustled to keep pace.

"From Cosmos?"

With a huff, Zara stopped, straightened her shoulders, and looked Riko in the eye. "That bag of sulfurous gasses? Ha! Omega will take care of her. I'm talking about Crestas, Bhuaci, Humans, and all the rest of Newearth. They're killers. All of them." She stared forward again, racing faster this time.

Not in the mood to play chase, Riko leaped and gripped Zara by the arm. "No one wants to kill you or Wendell. By the Divide, that boy is the most innocent person on the planet."

Slapping off Riko's grip, Zara hurried down the road. "Everyone thinks I'm dangerous, and he's too innocent for his own good. We're both expendable."

With a head ache threatening, Riko trotted after Zara. "Who told you that? *Has* someone tried to hurt you?"

Zara stopped in place and hissed, "Justine was locked away for seventy years only to be awoken and tried for another fake crime. Hundreds of beings are killed every day on this planet!" Her eyes narrowed as she peered at Riko. "Don't you ever watch Newearth News?"

A ray of illumination clarified Riko's thinking. A smile tugged at his lips. "I see. You've heard about Justine's past, and you've been catching up on the news." His eyes roaming over Zara's form, he frowned. *Not my kid. But if she were...* "So, how old are you—really?"

After stomping across the street, Zara arrived at the park entrance. She started for the swings, calling over her shoulder, "By Newearth standards, I'll be eight years soon."

Riko followed and dropped down on a bench.

Zara plunked down on a swing and scuffed the ground with her feet. "That Cresta friend of yours wants to dissect me."

With the firm seat supporting him, Riko leaned back and dropped his hands onto his lap. "He's more of an acquaintance, really. But I'll not deny the fact that Taug has probably considered the idea. Still, you must understand—he won't actually do it. He's a reformed Cresta. At least, that's what Faye says."

"Bhuacs lie. Omega says it's their nature."

Aiming a grimaced smile at a wide-eyed Bhuaci mother as she led her toddler to a miniature play castle, Riko offered a friendly wave and spoke out of the corner of his mouth. "Lower your voice, okay?"

Zara watched the child clamber awkwardly to the castle and take a tumble. "Justine would've protected me. But *you* sent her away."

Riko watched the Bhuaci mother lift the elfin-looking child onto the tower walkway and raise his arm in victory. The little one laughed.

Riko faced Zara. "Leaving was Justine's choice. She wants to save Newearth for you." He pressed his fingers together steeple style and stared straight ahead. "Omega left. Justine is gone. Kendra isn't feeling too good, is she?"

Zara pushed off and started to swing, her gaze fixed on the sky.

As clouds rolled away, Riko's shoulders relaxed. "Since no one is around to save the innocent, you've taken the job, is that it?"

Zara kept her gaze fixed on the sky. "Someone should."

Exhaling a breathy cloud, Riko looked back to the café. "Yes, you're quite right; someone should."

Chapter Fifteen

–The Merrimack–

Histrionic Tendencies

Bala had surely had worse days, but at the moment, he couldn't think of one. *We're chasing a monster across the universe, my pregnant wife is taking care of the kids all by her lonesome, the captain is getting a tad too chummy with a Bhuac with visions of death and glory, and now we've got unwelcome visitors. I hope You've got a plan, since I can't think of a thing.*

Yelsa moaned as she returned to consciousness. She tugged at her restraints, then her eyes flew open, and she glanced around the room. "Where—?"

"Oh, good. You're awake. I was getting lonely."

Tied to a chair, Yelsa swiveled her body to the right and peered at Bala, who sat slumped in a chair. "Where am I?"

Rotating his head on his neck, Bala indicated the entire room. "Normally, I would welcome you to my humble abode, but—"

Squinting, Yelsa surveyed the trailing vines, exercise equipment, and the family portraits done in childish scrawl. She pursed her lips. "I'll never understand you."

With a chuckle, Bala nodded. "It's mutual, I'm sure."

After appraising her restraints, Yelsa tested their strength. She began to morph, her body glowing in hazy colors.

Bala cleared his throat. "Excuse me. Just a bit of advice before you let *everyone* know about your talents."

Solidifying, Yelsa clenched her jaw and glared at Bala.

"You see, Jazzmarie shot you from behind because

she knew she didn't stand a chance against a Bhuac and because she's rather keen on living to see another day."

"You sided with her?"

"On the contrary, I nearly had a heart attack." Bala shook his head. "I'd have chosen a different way of presenting my argument. But Jazzmarie has her own methods—drastic though they may be. Honestly, with your histrionic tendencies and her trigger finger, you two should be the best of friends or kill each other outright."

With a huff, Yelsa grunted. "*Why* are we here?"

"I was getting to that. You see, after Max carried you off, we met unexpected trouble."

Yelsa jerked at her restraints. "I'm tired of these!"

Bala lifted his hands, revealing two thick manacles wrapped around his arms and legs. "Simmer down. You're not the only prisoner here."

"Jazzmarie restrained you?"

"Not her. Our visitors."

"Visit—"

The door slid open, and a lean, yellow-eyed man stepped into the room. Glancing away from Bala, he bestowed a polite smile upon Yelsa. "I understand you have technical skills, so I hardly think these will be necessary." With a tap on his wrist datapad, he unlocked the restraints, and they fell to the floor.

Bala leaned back, crossed his legs, and began humming a tune akin to "I'm a little teapot."

Yelsa rubbed her wrists, stood, and glared at the stranger. "Who the hell—"

"My name is Erik, and I've been sent here to locate a certain Luxonian by the name of Cerulean. I was hoping you could be of service."

"I already have a job, thank you." Yelsa marched away from the stranger.

Erik gripped her arm. "Cosmos is no longer your

concern." He nodded to Bala. "As your friend will tell you, I have full control of this ship, and your new mission in life is to assist me."

Yelsa glanced at Bala, who kept his expression modest and unchallenging. She swept her gaze over Erik. "You realize you're on the wrong ship?"

"Not at all. I am on the one ship this side of the Divide that knows where Cerulean has gone. I'd like you to lead me to him."

"For what purpose?"

"I'm afraid I haven't made myself clear. Your job is to serve me." Erik lifted a Dustbuster and aimed it at Bala. "He's rather useless, isn't he?"

Yelsa jutted her chin and folded her arms. "He's of no particular value to me, except for communication purposes." She shifted her stance. "And Newearth? You're just going to let her destroy it?"

"Cosmos will never make it to Newearth. Does that satisfy you?"

"Perfectly." Yelsa shoved Erik aside and stomped away.

Erik eyed Bala. "Communications?"

Bala leveled his gaze. "My specialty."

~~~

Max sat ramrod straight, strapped to his chair in front of the directional console.

Chained to the holographic console unit, Roux glared at the floor.

Jazzmarie sat tied to the communications console and stared at the giant across the bridge. Accenting her most sultry voice, Jazzmarie turned on the charm. "So, what's
~~~

your name?"

The giant peered over, his Dustbuster ready. "Chas."

Momentarily distracted, Max perked up. "Is that with a c-h or a k?"

Roux rolled his eyes.

Bouncing a glare off Max, Jazzmarie tried again. "So, Chas, how did you meet Mr. Erik?"

"He saved my life."

Jazzmarie's eyes grew round, wild with wonder. "Really? How heroic! I'd love to hear the details."

Max harrumphed under his breath.

Pacing over to Jazzmarie, Chas leaned in, his large face mere millimeters from hers. "It's personal. Don't you have any boundaries?"

Roux barked a sharp laugh. "Where are your boundaries, Chas?"

Chas straightened and aimed his Dustbuster at Roux.

With hunched shoulders, Roux surrendered. "Rude, sorry. But you must admit. You've boarded our ship, taken us prisoner—"

"For the good of Newearth! For the good of all beings this side of the Divide."

Surprised and rather intrigued, Max's eyebrows rose. "How does hunting Cerulean factor into your equation?"

"We're not hunting him. We just want to protect Newearth from the invasion he's planning."

Jaws dropped open across the bridge. Even his own, Max noticed with pleasurable surprise.

The lift door slid open, and Yelsa stepped forward.

Oh good, our savior. Max stiffened. *Me, dripping with sarcasm?* He began an internal system's check.

Erik sauntered in beside Yelsa.

Appraising the captive crew, Yelsa frowned. "You don't expect me to fly this ship alone, do you?" Placing her hands on her hips, she eyed Erik with a raised eyebrow. "I'm only human after all!"

Human? Max canceled his internal review.

Jazzmarie's gaze lowered and a corner of her lip lifted.

A smirk. Definitely a smirk.

"You can manage." Staring at Chas, Erik pointed at Max. "Keep an eye on that one. He almost overpowered me."

At least he has a modicum of humility. Better than some... Max shrugged. "I would have if you hadn't aimed—"

Roux coughed. "You don't have to do this, Erik. I'm willing to help—if it means saving Newearth." He glared at Chas. "If you'd just told us your reason from the start, all this trouble could've been avoided. How were we supposed to know about an invasion?"

Yelsa stepped to the console and focused her attention.

Peering through hooded eyes, Erik jutted his jaw in Roux's direction. "It's not your concern. My employer is taking care of the matter. You only need to—"

Yelsa swung around, her eyes widened in alarm. She glanced from Chas to Erik. "Did you travel through the Sinsinawa District?"

Exasperated, Erik pounded to her side. "What of it?"

"That's one of Cosmos' favorite feeding grounds."

Erik leaned over the console as data streamed by reflecting off his pale face. "So?"

Yelsa morphed into a seven-foot muscular beast and slammed Erik across the bridge. His body fell in a heap. At the same moment, Roux disappeared and reappeared at Chas's side, knocking the Dustbuster from his grasp and smashing his face with an upper right cross.

Once Roux had restrained Chas, using the chains that had moments before bound him, Roux faced Erik's limp body.

Jazzmarie, released from her bonds by Yelsa, leaned over the prone figure.

Roux exhaled an uncertain breath. "Still alive?"

Jazzmarie shook her head. "Not in this world." She climbed to her feet and hurried over to Max. "Sorry, Maximan, you've been so brave. I'll get these off you—"

Max snapped the restraints.

Chuckling, Jazzmarie appraised the broken strands. "Why didn't you do that earlier?"

"You could have been killed, and I was waiting for the captain to give the command."

Roux clasped Max on the shoulder. "Thank you, Max. You did the right thing. This whole situation could've turned out very differently." He leaned into the captain's console and slapped the intercom button. "Hang in there, Bala. I'll be right there."

"Ever so kind of you, sir."

Strolling over to Yelsa, Roux clasped his hands behind his back. A grin slid across his face. "The Sinsinawa question was a terrific diversion. How'd you ever think of it?"

Yelsa tapped a red blip on the screen moving in their direction. "Because it's true. Cosmos loves that place—and anything carrying traces of it."

Max frowned. "Are we still towing their ship?"

Flopping onto her chair, Yelsa nodded. "Yep. Now, Cosmos is hunting us."

Max eyed the red blip. Apparently, sarcasm wasn't the only thing he could feel.

Chapter Sixteen

–Mirage-Reborn–

Let the Nightmare End

Vera tossed in her sleep, her dreams disturbed by flickering flashes of light and an acrid smell that wrinkled her nose. Sweat prickled her arms and legs till she panted and threw off her covers. Suddenly, she sat bolt upright, her eyes wide and staring.

Heavy smoke stung them instantly. Flames danced and darted like flickering fingers from under the door.

Skittering to the chair by her desk, she pulled on her skirt and blouse and began yelling, "Dimi! Dimi, where are you? Help me!"

In the echoing emptiness, she heard only the fire crackling on the other side of the door. She reached for the door handle, but the hot metal seared her hand at first touch.

After grabbing another shirt from her dresser, she wrapped her throbbing hand and darted forward. She gripped the handle again, her whole body trembled. With a snapping click, the knob turned, and the door flew open. A rush of heat and flame knocked her backward.

In horrified amazement and with sharp pain on her face and arms, Vera stared at the flames. With a natural fear of fire, knowing how the LuKan skin burned so easily that even sunburn could cause serious health issues, she crawled to the opposite side of the room and scrambled to her feet.

The flames flickered toward her.

"Dimi?" She clutched at her throat, inched over to the window, and stared down. It was a six-meter drop at least. In the dark, it looked like an endless abyss.

The sound of clattering boots running up the steps made her glance at the doorway. The door had swung shut again, but now flames engulfed the wood.

A man called through the smoke and fire. "Vera? Where are you?"

Vera's shoulders slumped in relief. Lucius Pollex. "I'm here, Mr. Pollex! I can't get out, and Dimi's not answering!" Vera clapped her hands together and winced as the blisters made contact.

A grunt and pounding shattered the air. Lucius shouted, "Dimi? Dimi, can you hear me?" A splintering thwack thudded against the door to the next room.

Vera closed her eyes and wiped sweat from her face.

More splintering crashes and the sound of boots running across the floor. Shouts, grunts, and then silence, except for the roaring fire.

Wrapping her long, three-fingered hands around her middle, Vera hugged herself. She swallowed against the bile that rose in her throat and ran to the window, sucking in fresh air.

Boots on the move again and then heaving grunts stopped outside her door. "Vera? Vera, stand back!"

Vera pressed her back against the window frame, her shoulders shaking.

A thwack smashed through the wooden door, and a sharp, red-tipped blade shone through the flames. Uncounted thrusts tore at the wood until it fell aside like a torn curtain.

Wearing a heavy coat, Lucius Pollex stepped through the flames. His red-rimmed eyes scoured the room and then landed on Vera, huddled against the back wall. He ran to her, gripped her arm, and lifted her to her feet. "Hurry, this timber frame won't hold much longer."

She froze at the flaming doorway.

Without a word, Lucius stepped around Vera and scooped her into his arms, enfolding her little body within his. He sprang through the red and orange darts of fire. Once through the doorway, he dropped her in a clear space on the landing and bent over a prone figure.

Vera gasped. "Dimi!"

Before she could step closer, Lucius lifted Dimi's limp body over his shoulder and reached for Vera. She shook herself, fighting nausea that bubbled up from her middle. As they descended the steps, she tripped and toppled forward.

Instantly, Lucius grabbed her around the waist. Squeezing her body against his, he jogged down the last steps and through the front doorway into the smoky, night air.

Falling to her knees, Vera choked and sobbed, her hands over her face. She rocked back and forth, oblivious to everything except overwhelming pain and fear.

Shouting to her left forced her to look up. A small crowd huddled over a prone form laid out on the grass. A primal scream rose inside her, and Vera scrambled like an injured animal toward the body. "Dimi! Dimi, get up. Talk to me! Dimi!"

The crowd backed away.

Blinded by tears, Vera felt along Dimi's body, and finally, she stared into his face. If only she could make a connection.

Dimi lay with arms flung awkwardly at his sides, legs limp and sprawled, face turned up, and eyes open wide—eyes that saw nothing, not the stars that twinkled overhead nor his sister's tears as they landed on his cheek.

A firm but gentle hand gripped Vera's shoulder.

She slid to the ground, her head landing on her

brother's chest, sobbing, clinging with blistered and bleeding fingers.

The hand stayed with her, gentle, undemanding, warm and real in a nightmare of searing pain.

The murmuring crowd shuffled away. Someone bent low. A woman's voice whispered, "You want me to take her home with me? I've got room—"

Vera shivered.

Lucius tightened his grip, gently lifting her off her brother's body and wrapped his arm around her. "Give her time. I'll watch over her tonight."

The woman nodded and slipped off her coat. She laid it over Dimi's body, stifling a sob.

A man stepped forward. "You want me to lay him somewhere proper—in the town hall, maybe?"

Lucius murmured, "No, not there. Lay him in my front room. I'll tend to him in the morning."

Footsteps padded away, voices murmuring. "Poor thing. Wonder how it started…"

Two men laid Dimi's body on a stretcher and carried him into the dark night.

Vera shivered and blinked, tears slipping down her blistered cheek.

Lucius limped backward and braced himself against a shed wall. He wrapped his muscled, fire-seared, blackened arms around her and pressed her head to his chest. "I'll take you somewhere to rest."

Trembling, Vera closed her eyes and burrowed into Lucius' strong embrace. His chest rose and fell, his heart beating in a steady rhythm. Warmth settled over her. She closed her eyes. "Just make the nightmare end."

~~~
~~~

Vera felt a fresh breeze blow gently over her face. She opened her eyes and stared over Lucius' charcoal-blackened coat into a hazy yard of drifting smoke, trampled grass, treetops, and a red sunrise.

An early bird chirped in the treetops.

Rising on her elbow, Vera studied the stubble-bearded face of Lucius Pollex. His rhythmic breathing remained stable and unhurried. She shifted her arm and looked around.

Her hands stung. Blisters oozed on one, and angry red blotches had swollen over the other. Wiggling her toes, she was amazed that they didn't hurt—nothing like her hands. Her gaze drifted over Lucius. She sucked in a horrified gasp.

Lucius' legs ended in blackened boot remnants and burned stumps. "Oh, God, no!" Fresh tears welled in her eyes.

Lucius stirred and groaned. His eyes snapped open, and his arm squeezed protectively around Vera. When their gazes connected, he sucked in a deep breath and darted a glance around the field and smoldering ruins. "You're still alive then?"

Vera nodded. She wiped her face with the back of her hand and sat up, her eyes searching for assistance. She attempted to stand but fell.

"Wait. I'll help." Lucius tottered to his feet, gripped her hand, and helped her up.

Gaping at his burned stumps, Vera choked in horror.

Lucius pulled up a charred pant leg and revealed a metal band connecting an artificial limb to the stump of his leg. "They were burned in an accident some time ago." He raised his gaze to the blue sky and exhaled. "I was never happy about it—till now. If I didn't have such feet, I could never have walked across a burning floor to save you."

Tears trickled down Vera's cheeks.

Peering at her face, Lucius pursed his lips. "You need care, too, or I'll be digging more than one grave this day." With a careful touch, he wiped her tears away, his gaze somber. "And I won't have that." His gaze traveled to the spot where Dimi's body had lain. He sighed. "I wish I'd had wings. Maybe, I could've got there in time."

Vera stepped over the trampled ground to her devastated home and surveyed the ruins. Only a few timbers still stood as grey-blue smoke spiraled lazily into the sky.

Looking over her shoulder, a shaky smile trembled on her lips. "The LuKan believe in the Immortal Life." She watched a hawk soar above the smoky drifts. "Today—Dimi has wings for us both."

~~~

Grace Nelson winced at the memory of Pav as he lay dead on the grass and tried to keep her heart from pounding out of her chest. She pounded across the street and nearly tackled Clare as she entered the grocery store. "There you are! I've been waiting since dawn for you to show up."

Gripping the handle, Clare stiffened. "I always come in at six. Why are you worried?"

Grace dragged Clare away from the door and jogged her halfway down the alley between Nelson's Grocery and the bakery. "Because of what happened last night!" She dragged a breath from the depths of her despairing soul. "Surely, you've heard?"
~~~

Clare folded her arms across her chest and leaned back against the grimy, brick wall.

Wiping a moist brow, Grace lowered her gaze. "Someone torched Vera's house and killed her brother Dimi." Tears welled in Grace's eyes. "No gentler a creature ever existed—"

Jerking forward, Clare gripped Grace's arm. "Torched—are you sure? Where's Vera?"

With a shudder, Grace pulled free and wrapped her arms about her waist. "I tried to help. Flames engulfed the place. I offered to take her home, but Lucius Pollex—the blacksmith—had taken over. Literally. He was holding her in his arms."

Clare paced across the alley. "It could've been an accident. Some of these timber frames—"

"Quinn smirked on the sideline and never lifted a finger to help." *If only someone would*— Their gazes locking, Grace rubbed her hands together. "He hates Vera for siding with Cerulean and your friend, Justine." Striding forward, she nudged Clare toward the store's back entrance. "You'd better watch yourself. Quinn has a mean streak longer than an Ingoti rat snake. And he's not the forgiving type. As long as you stay here, you're hate-bait."

Clare swiveled on her heel and clamped her hand against the back door. "Before we go in, I have to understand your part in all this. How do I know that—?"

"*I* didn't torch her house?" Drawing in a long breath, Grace leaned back and stared at the brightening sky. "I could've once—maybe—if I was angry enough." Her gaze dropped to the ground. "But not now. I'm not that person anymore." Wiping the back of a hand against her dripping nose, she sniffed back welling tears. "My stepmother was a conniving manipulator who played my father to gain a miserable little fortune. But she couldn't wait for him to die. A dainty thing with high-maintenance needs, she was too smart to kill him outright. No—her specialty was haranguing a person till he wished he were dead." Swallowing back a shuddering sob, she ran her fingers across her trembling lips. "My father went from a strong, fun-loving man with a lusty appetite and fire in his eyes to a stifled, raging, tormented old hothead."

With her hand still fixed firmly against the door, Clare shook her head. "So, you murdered the wench." Clare's eyes bored into Grace. "How?"

"Poison."

"But you've reformed?"

Grace turned away. "I hate myself more than anyone else ever could. Why do you think I live like I do? I deserve every sarcastic, biting remark my father throws my way." Her jaws clenching, Grace wrenched the door free from Clare's hand. "The most decent being I've ever known was just murdered. Judge me if you like, but make Quinn pay for what he's done. He'll never repent on his own."

~~~

Pax stood beside the window on the second floor of Lucius' home and watched the gentle blacksmith tuck Vera into a high, soft bed. Standing aside, he slipped his cold hands into his armpits and chewed his lip. "Anything I can do?"

Ignoring Pax for the moment, Lucius swept a stray lock of hair from Vera's face and smiled down at her petite figure swallowed up by the enormous quilt. "Comfortable?"
~~~

With a nod, Vera turned, closed her eyes, and burrowed deep under the thick blanket. "I'm so tired."

"Sleep then." Lucius turned and, with a simple gesture, swept Pax out of the room before him.

Marveling at the man's gentleness, Pax scratched his jaw. "What're you going to do with her?"

Placing a finger over his lips, Lucius motioned Pax from the hall to the living room. Once stationed before the front door, Lucius grabbed a satchel and swung it over his shoulder. "You'll have to stay here while I go to town. I have questions that need answering." His gaze swung to the bedroom. "She's exhausted, so let her sleep. There's food in the pantry. Fix whatever you like." Lucius gripped the door handle.

Suddenly frightened, Pax ran forward. "Wait! You can't just leave me here. What if she needs something? Or someone comes looking for you?" *Or me?*

Lucius met Pax's gaze. "Listen, Quinn took me through hell. Maybe I deserved it; maybe I didn't. But the fact is, Vera and Dimi did nothing but offer kindness since the first day they came." Gripping Pax's shoulder, he leaned in. "You know what evil does; it spreads."

Pax shuffled his feet. "I'd like to help. Cerulean could come and—"

Lucius shook his head. "Not him. That other friend of yours. The android. I want a chat with her. She could put Quinn in his place without breaking a sweat."

Amused by the idea, Pax smirked. "Rumor has it, Justine was once a hired killer."

A dark scowl distorted Lucius' face. His mouth curled into a snarl. "I'm not stooping to that." He jabbed Pax's chest. "And neither are you!" After swinging the door wide, he stepped across the threshold. "Remember, everything you do leads one of two places: to hell—or away from it."

Lucius hurried across the porch and pounded down the porch steps.

After shutting the door with a soft click, Pax's stomach growled. He turned toward the pantry and tried to ignore the hunger in his heart.

~~~

Grace couldn't push her anxiety away any longer. She had to do something, to act now, or live with the consequences—all of Newearth would have to live with the consequences. Readying herself for action, she peered out the store window and surveyed the scene.

Mid-morning light poured down from a bright blue sky, while Quinn hurried across the street and into his office. Lucius followed along behind, entering after him, a grim expression hiding nothing.

Anxiety burrowed into Grace's brow, giving her a throbbing headache. Fighting the fear that rose in her middle, she wrung her hands as she stepped into the sunshine and crossed Main Street. Once across, she glanced into the sheriff's window.

Two men paced in front of the high counter. Lucius Pollex stood in the cell behind them.

Panting, Grace hurried inside the office. "Why is Lucius locked up?"

The taller man, thick around the middle, grinned. "Fool thought he could threaten the Sheriff and get away with it. Quinn isn't easily intimidated. Especially since might makes right around here." He chuckled as he patted the gun in his holster.

The second guard laughed. It seemed that brute force amused them to no end.
~~~

Despite a complete lack of planning, Grace launched into the best histrionics she could muster. "But there's a Cresta gone crazy! Said that he's going to take over the town!"

The larger guard grabbed her arm. "What? Where?"

With violent shaking that wasn't completely fake, Grace pointed to across the street. "He was just in the store, ripping things off the shelves—he's gone mad—planning to kill Quinn next."

Thc first guard started for the door.

Grace shrieked. "Hurry! Quinn can't protect himself against an enraged Cresta." She followed their gazes to the cell where Lucius sat quietly on a low bench. "I'll stay and watch him. You two get going!"

As soon as both guards bustled out the door, Grace scurried around the counter, snatched the keys off a hook, and unlocked the door. Hardly able to believe her audacity, Grace led Lucius through the back door and then raced to the woods bordering the café.

Once they made it into the grove, she gasped for breath and gripped Lucius' shoulder. "You know—where—their ship—is?"

Eyeing her with uncertainty, Lucius snorted. "Cerulean's ship? Who doesn't?"

Abashed, Grace pressed her hands against her heaving chest. "Me."

Flushed and clearly perplexed, Lucius crossed his arms. "What do you want with his ship?"

Grace shook her head. "Not me. *You!* You've got to send a message."

Lucius glared at Grace. "I have business with Quinn! Why would I want to send a message—and to whom?"

"To Newearth and to that other ship Clare told me about. There's got to be a way. Tell them that Cerulean's in trouble. That Mirage-Reborn is in trouble. Tell them to send help—or we're lost." She shuddered at the memory of Pav's blistered face and her own desire for revenge. *If Quinn takes over, we might as well be dead.*

~~~

Pax stood at an L-shaped counter in Lucius' kitchen and, with practiced care, built a glorious triple-decker salami and cheese sandwich. A sharp knock rapped at the back door. After tiptoeing around scattered boxes, he retreated to the back entry, lifted a heavy curtain from the door window, and peeked out.

Justine's iron glare smacked him in the face.

Barely controlling a frightened squeak, he unbolted the lock.

The door thrust open from the outside. Justine trooped over the threshold with Clare sailing in behind. Cerulean took up the rear.

With his momentary peace shattered, Pax closed his eyes. *Cerulean I can handle. Clare is acceptable. But Justine...*

Sauntering over to the counter, Clare eyed the sandwich. "I never get to eat this good. I'm lucky I can get a decent BLT at that stupid diner."

Cerulean lifted his hand. "Not now, Clare. We're here to get organized. Remember?"

"I'll be better organized on a full stomach."

Justine shook her head, her eyelids drooping in pity. "You sound more like Bala every day."

Clearly unruffled by the thought, Clare picked up the sandwich, leaned against the counter, and took an enormous bite. She groaned in base pleasure.

"Enough!" Pax grabbed a knife.
~~~

Clare stiffened.

Wiggling the implement, Pax pointed to the sandwich. "We can share. I'll cut this one in half and make more. Lucius' pantry is well supplied."

Cerulean tugged at his collar and plopped down on a stool. "Have you all gone mad?"

Pax sliced the sandwich into two even pieces and then plucked another loaf off the shelf. "You should eat, Cerulean. You're human now. Humans need to eat."

Justine toured the well-stocked larder. "I always said you'd come in useful. Though I must admit, Lucius Pollex appears to be the man of the hour." She turned and eyed Pax. "Tell me about him."

An indifferent shrug, and Pax busied himself passing around ingredients for further sandwich building. "Vera told me that he served as a governor's bodyguard, but when a fire broke out, he saved the governor's baby instead of the governor. Some maniacal judge found him in dereliction of duty and sentenced him to Bothmal, where he was lucky enough to meet Quinn."

Justine crossed her arms. "Who soon made the poor man's life hell—if I'm any judge of character."

Pax dragged a stool toward Cerulean and shoved a sandwich in his direction. "Quinn has control issues. Vera said that he thinks he's going to save Mirage-Reborn from the oppressors." He offered a sandwich to Justine.

A glint lighted in Justine's eyes. "You've become a gentleman, Pax."

Cerulean wiped his lips free of spicy sandwich dressing. "In the outlandish hope that Abbas returns with Omega someday soon, it'd be nice if we were good enough to avoid civil war while he was gone. So, what's the plan?"

After getting himself comfortable on a wooden chair

at the kitchen table, Pax took a large bite and pointed to Justine. Unconcerned by his breach of manners, he spoke between chews. "Lucius wants you to put Quinn in his place."

Clare snorted. "How? Lock him in a box?"

A chuckle turned them toward the front entrance.

"Personally, I wouldn't recommend that." Quinn sauntered in with Vera's limp body over his shoulder and a revolver in one hand, aimed at Cerulean. "I have Lucius locked away good and tight. And when I dispose of you, my troubles will be over."

Pax dropped his sandwich and jumped to his feet, his chair tipping over and crashing to the floor.

Cerulean rose and faced Quinn. "Omega won't believe your story—whatever it might be."

Justine and Clare stood frozen, their eyes following Quinn's every move.

Mad delight shone through Quinn's eyes as he fixed his gaze on Cerulean. "Omega won't have anything to say about it." Sauntering forward, he let Vera's body fall, slumping across the table. He ran one finger alongside her face. "Pretty little creature. Don't worry. She's out cold." Looking up, he grinned. "Omega wasn't kidnapped by chance. Abbas is on a fool's errand." Quinn snapped his fingers. "Judgment upon them."

Doom settled over Pax. *There is no justice in this world...*

Justine spat out her words. "No one is more powerful than—"

"Tut, tut, machine-o-matic. You forget your history. But the Crestonians haven't. They've remembered their loss, and they've bided their time." Quinn leveled his gun at Pax and motioned for him to move away from the counter.

His insides twisting, Pax lifted his hands and did as

directed. He took a few steps backward, but Quinn kept nudging him to move until he ended up in a corner.

"Revenge is at hand," Quinn said with a twisted curl to his lip. "A long time in coming but all the sweeter for that."

Cerulean shook his head. "Crestonians can't seriously believe that Omega or Abbas decimated the Crestonian population. That was an act of violence neither of them is even capable of."

Swinging around, Quinn directed Cerulean next to Pax. "Ah, but blame they will. And once Omega strayed too far, he grew weak—as did Abbas. They're guilty of their crimes, and they'll pay with their lives."

What crime? Giving people a second chance?

"It wasn't them!" With cold fury in her eyes, Justine shoved off the counter and lunged for Quinn's neck.

No! Pax jumped in between the two.

The gun fired.

Shock and shooting pain spread through Pax as he fell in a crumpled heap on the floor. Justine screamed his name, anguish in her voice. *She cares?* The thought surprised him, even as warm darkness welcomed him.

Justine flung herself over Pax and cupped his face in her hands. They were softer than he expected. She groaned.

Clare called for help. *Too late.*

Cerulean crouched at his side, his grip firm and comforting. "Stay with us, Pax. We need you."

Quinn snorted, mocking as usual. His tone as dead as a rock in the desert. "Told you. Everyone has their limits. Time you learned yours."

Cerulean cleared his throat, his warm hand still gripping Pax's shoulder. "Beyond our limits, there is justice. Pax was never your enemy."

Clare heaved a sob.

A hot tear slipped down Pax's face. Even as night took him, the truth of Cerulean's words rose like dawn on a new day. *I never was anyone's enemy...*

Chapter Seventeen

-Newearth-

Once and For All

Taug leaned over his console screen, reading the newest message from *The Merrimack.* He rested his head on one tentacle, while his brows rode low over his narrowed eyes. With another tentacle, he scratched the side of his face and then wiggled it between his mouth and his breather mask. He tugged at the mask—his breathing rate quickened as he read the unbelievable news.

The lab door swished open, and Faye pranced through, a smile of irrepressible joy beaming through her eyes.

His eyes widening in horror at what he'd just read, Taug smacked his face with a third tentacle. He choked and fell backward, nearly toppling off his swivel chair.

Faye skittered forward and grabbed the chair, shoving it back into the proper position. "What's gotten into you, Taug?" She glanced at the screen. "You've been reading OldEarth thrillers again?"

Startled beyond belief, Taug shook his head in slow motion. "I can't comprehend it. Honestly, I'd always believed he was above suspicion."

Faye's smile melted into a confused frown. "Who? Did what?"

A chime turned them both toward the door.

Taug intoned, "Come in, Riko."

Riko, in his crisp white shirt and blue pants, strode into the lab.

Lang sashayed in right behind.

Faye's lips puckered.

Riko marched to Taug's desk and clasped his hands

together. "In case you haven't heard, the IAA has started formal evacuation procedures. Everyone is commanded to leave Newearth as soon as possible. The IAA authorities commandeered all ships to make sure that they're utilized to their full capacity."

Taug rubbed his head. "Well, that, at least, is not surprising."

Faye's scowl slid off Lang, bounced over Riko, and returned to Taug. She tapped his screen. "What's going on?"

Rising, Taug made room before the console and waved them forward. "Read for yourselves." He strolled over to the holopad and entered a series of coordinates.

Riko leaned over Lang, who leaned over Faye, who was bent over the console to scroll through the message. After a quick perusal, Riko turned away and waved at Taug. "Just give me the abridged version. I've got to get back. Wendell is acting as host for the day."

Faye righted herself and shoved past Lang, stomping toward Taug. "Surely, you don't believe it!"

Riko flapped his arms. "Believe what?"

Lang strode forward and squeezed Riko's shoulder. "According to Roux, your friend Cerulean is accused of treachery—seems he has plans to take over Newearth."

Riko froze. Only his eyes strayed back and forth as if reviewing a long series of memories. Suddenly, he boomed a thunderous laugh. *"Cerulean?"* He waved Taug's console into imaginary oblivion. "Don't be ridiculous. Cerulean has been on Newearth's side since the very beginning. The Crestas fought him, power-hungry humans fought him, even his own people betrayed him, but he never turned traitor."

Faye trembled. She crossed her arms high over her chest as she glared at Taug. "You, of all people, must realize how insane this is. Who is this Erik that Roux mentions? Who did he work for? Roux says something about a boss, but Erik's accomplice doesn't seem to know the details." She jabbed Taug in the chest. "You ought to know better than to doubt your own friend."

"Associate, really."

Looking rather relaxed, Lang leaned against the counter. "On the bright side, if what Roux says is true, and Cosmos is now hunting *them*, then they can lead her away from us—at least for a time. That may be enough to shake her interest in Newearth. She's only a space glob, after all. I doubt she has a long attention span."

"Technically"—Taug pointed to a hologram of a distant space sector now rotating before him—"she is an interstellar, large-celled organism."

Lang swung toward the holopad with a sneer. "Space glob is easier for the public to understand—more literary."

Riko strolled forward and considered the hologram, tapping a finger against his thigh. "Seems to me we have a mystery on our hands. Someone really ought to investigate. Who would want to destroy Cerulean? And why?" He swung his gaze on Faye. "I agree; we need to know who Erik worked for. I don't like the idea of saving Newearth from a *space glob*, only to have it destroyed by a monster working on the inside." His gaze zeroed in on the Ingot.

Lang lifted her hands. "I'd love to investigate. You know I would. But I'm too well known. Few would entrust their secrets to a Newearth News correspondent."

Faye sidled up to Taug and stared pointedly at him.

Taug pursed his lips and glared back. He huffed and pointed to his lab equipment. "I'm *occupied*."

Faye sighed. "If only Clare were here."

A chime rang, and without ceremony, Riko's Uncle Clem marched in waving an accusing finger. "Taug, I've got a ridge to scale with you!" He stopped and peered at the bewildered faces around him. "It's a Uanyi expression—but you *know* what I mean. The units you borrowed against Riko's café to build this—"

Taug froze. *How did he discover that?* He glanced at Lang.

Riko hustled forward, gripped his uncle around the shoulders in imitation of a friendly hug, and stopped him cold. "We've already been over that, Uncle Clem. Right now, we have more pressing matters to attend to."

Puffing up like an outraged rooster, Clem shifted away from Riko's grip and tilted his head. "What's more important?" Suddenly, he blinked and deflated. His hands fell to his side. "Is there news?" His voice dropped to a whisper. "Cosmos?"

With a snort, Lang sashayed forward and elbowed him confidentially. "Catch on quick, don't you? With your fiery temper and good intentions, I think we could do business together." Her eyebrows wiggled in gleeful undulations. "And you have such an honest, innocent face." She glanced at Riko. "Mind if I borrow him?"

Riko blanched.

"I believe he'll make a wonderful detective."

A new light entered Uncle Clem's eyes. "Detective?" He raised an eyebrow at Lang with a hint of interest.

A crash and a yelp sounded from the café.

Riko rushed forward and shoved his head through the open doorway.

Wendell called out, "All right! No worry!"

Taug slumped. *I'll never get my work done.*

Rubbing his neck, Riko turned and appraised the mismatched group. "All right. Lang, you take Uncle Clem and find out who's telling tales about Cerulean." He turned to Taug. "You keep working on the bioweapon for Cosmos. Whether she gets distracted or not, it's best to be prepared." He nodded at Faye. "And keep him out of trouble—please."

Lang saluted and steered a beaming Uncle Clem through the doorway, a bewitching grin lighting up her face.

Riko called after them. "And stay alive—you two!"

Relief filling him, Taug chuckled. "If only you were a scientist, Riko, we'd have saved the universe long ago."

~~~

Wendell desperately wanted to enjoy the night stroll, but he had to watch his step.

Dressed in a black leather jacket, blue leggings, and brown boots, Zara did not stop to consider the millions of stars twinkling in the winter sky as she tugged Wendell along by his coat sleeve down the sidewalk.

The wind howled through stark branches as swift clouds trailed across the crescent moon. An owl hooted in the distance.

Wendell hunched his shoulders and spoke to his boots. "Go home now?"

Zara shook her head. "No, you have to help me first." She peered at Wendell. "I'm doing this for your own good. Ingots always get the worst of it from the Crestas. You of all people should know that."

Wendell shrugged. They turned down the vacant alley that led to Taug's lab, and Wendell stopped before the locked door.

Zara nudged him. "You got the key—use it."

Wendell ducked his head. "Lies bite back."

Morphing into a huge, fanged animal, Zara glowered at Wendell through fiery red eyes.
~~~

Hands shaking, Wendell lifted a tiny datapad. He pressed it against a square insert.

The door slid aside.

Zara shrunk down to her former size and hurried inside.

Wendell glanced up and down the alley and then slipped in behind.

Threading her way through the dark laboratory, Zara lifted a small flashlight and shot the beam toward Taug's desk. "Ah!" She quickly settled in place and started tapping the console.

Wendell's gaze worked its way around the lab. He meandered to the dissecting tube and peeked under the lid. A noxious smell greeted him. With a groan, he replaced the lid and wobbled back to Zara.

"Yes!" Zara's face, lit by the screen's green glow, appeared more monstrous now than when she had morphed into a fanged creature.

Wendell stepped back.

Zara's hands flew across the console before she tapped the last key with a flourish. "That'll do it." Rising, she motioned for Wendell to follow.

Wendell traipsed along. "Go now?"

Zara pressed a finger to her lips. "They'll be back soon. But I sent the message." She giggled as she slid open the back door. "Justine will be furious! She'll kill Taug with her own hands."

Wendell froze. "Justine return?"

"She will as soon as she gets my message. I told her that Taug tried to kidnap me and plans to dissect me." After stepping outside, the door slid shut with a notable click. She pointed to Wendell's pocket. "Replace that before Riko notices." Then using a vice grip, Zara clutched Wendell's shoulder and growled. "Remember—trust no one." She shoved him toward the café's front door.

Wendell tripped and barely caught himself. He hunched his shoulders as he started down the deserted alleyway.

With a guttural hum rising in her throat, Zara traipsed alone across the dark street.

Wendell stopped and stared after her. "*No one*?"

~~~

Faye held one of Taug's tentacles and smothered her giggles as they bustled into the dark laboratory.

Taug grunted, "lights," and ceiling inserts illuminated the room in a bright glow.

After dropping onto a chair, Faye rubbed her tummy. "That had to be one of the best Greens Riko has ever—" Her grin faded. "What's wrong?"

Sweeping his gaze across the floor, Taug frowned. "Someone's been here—without my permission." He hit a wall panel, and a bright red light highlighted the floor, outlining a confused mix of prints. Taug pointed. "There!" He glanced up at Faye. "You see, don't you?"

Faye circled around, staring at the prints. "Wendell? And Zara?" Trotting over to the console, she watched Taug's dexterous tentacles bring up a recent action log.

Taug blew air between his lips. "She sent a message to Justine."

In large print, the log detailed imaginary events and Zara's fears.

Faye slapped her hot cheek. "Accusing you of all sorts of nefarious deeds, too."

Suddenly, Taug's tentacles swept across the console, and his bulbous eyes widened.

"What?"
~~~

"Here's a message from Mirage-Reborn." Taug's gaze zigzagged back and forth.

Faye read over his shoulder. Her chest tightened in anxiety. *Where is Cerulean? What's happened to you, my friend?* She cupped her forehead in her hands and staggered to the counter. Leaning upon the sturdy surface, she stared at the empty holopad. "Mirage-Reborn is under attack? And like some idiotic hero of old, Roux flies to the rescue." Plopping onto a stool, she tried to clear her head and settle her fears. "Lang would love this—award-winning universal drama."

Taug stepped away from the console and meandered toward the dissecting tube. "If only Cosmos hadn't broken away—"

Faye trotted to the holopad and slapped the console. An entire galaxy rotated before her. "She could be anywhere. It doesn't mean she's heading back here."

Taug turned toward Faye. "At least when she was following them, I knew where she was. Now—I know nothing. She could appear on the horizon at any time."

"She's not that fast. Besides, she's probably confused. Maybe, she'll wander out into deep space—"

Taug eyed Faye curiously. "And attack someone else?"

Horror flooded Faye's mind, memories of her home world swirling before her eyes. "Oh! I didn't mean that."

Taug sighed. "It's up to us to stop her—once and for all."

Propping her head on her hand, drained of all strength, her gaze wandered back to the holopad. "Everyone needs help! *The Merrimack*, Omega, everyone on Mirage-Reborn…" She closed her eyes. "Is there anyone left to save us?"

Taug lumbered over and wrapped a tentacle gently around Faye's shoulders. "No. This time, we have to save ourselves."

Chapter Eighteen

–The Merrimack–

Who Can Save Us Now?

Max peered through a round window into a distance no one could truly fathom. Unease filled him.

It was not much of a window to the universe, but the speckled systems glowed in majestic glory, nonetheless. A single, irregular speck twirled away in slow motion.

Max's eyes fixed on the spiraling jot. A groan escaped his lips as he leaned on the balcony railing directly above the engine room.

Bala wandered close, glanced at Max's fixed gaze, and then stared at the spectacle. He swallowed hard. "That him?"

Max nodded.

The ship's engines hummed at a slightly higher pitch as their speed increased.

Shifting from one foot to another, Bala exhaled a long breath. "I know I should hate the guy for trying to hijack us and accusing Cerulean of crimes against Newearth, but—"

Max pushed off the railing. He turned to Bala. "Hate takes too much energy."

Bala scratched his head. "I've never known anyone with your understated astuteness."

Ignoring the term "understated" and realizing that he'd just been praised to the highest degree, a pleasant sensation flooded Max. *Astute? I am astute?*

Bala glanced at the window and winced. "Perhaps we should've put him in a storage unit and brought his body back to Newearth for identification. That's what Clare would've wanted. Now all we have is our memory and Chas's word."

Max tapped his head significantly. "You forget my memory capacity. I made records of everything, and I'll pass the information to the authorities as soon as we get back." He started forward and stopped. "Or do you think I should send it now? Maybe they can discover something before we get back."

Bala bit his lip, one eye squinting. "Not a good idea. We don't know who's involved—it'll be better to wait until we can conduct the investigation ourselves. Too many mysteries." His gaze settled on the bridge doors. He gestured with lifted eyebrows. "What do you think Roux and Yelsa are doing in *there*?"

With an indignant sniff, Max straightened his shoulders. "Working—of course. Roux told her to abandon the trader's ship and directed me to dispose of—"

Bala ran his fingers through his hair, rumpling his black locks into a curly jumble. "I know that! I mean—do you think he's gotten over his little...infatuation-thing?"

Max attempted to stare Bala into the floor.

Bala stood his ground. "Stop it! You know as well as I that he's a red-blooded—oh, no, I mean—a passionate Luxonian-type. And she's a very desirable Bhuaci female." He flung his hands on his hips. "Passion's not a crime, you know."

Tightening his jaw nearly to the locking point, Max glared at the wall and chewed his words. "I wouldn't know. But as Roux is the captain, and Yelsa is our—"

The door slid open, and Yelsa sauntered over the threshold. Her face beamed with a tinge of pink, her eyes sparkling.

Max stepped back and let her pass, his hands clenched at his sides.

Bala bowed with a knowing grin, his face glowing.

Yelsa hesitated. "We're free of the trader ship and now set for the Mirage-Reborn." She started forward again.

Max cleared his throat, calling after her. "No trouble from the doctor then?"

Yelsa turned and seemed to be considering Max. "She tried to have me confined to quarters. But I convinced the captain of my worth on the bridge."

His gaze falling to the floor, Max forced out a response. "Oh. Good."

Rolling her tongue around her lips like a hungry tiger, Yelsa leaned forward. "Your good doctor probably needs a little cheering up." Her eyes glimmered. "A visit from you would do the trick."

Startled, Max glanced up. "You want me to keep her occupied?"

Yelsa marched down the corridor. "Just keep her out of my way."

Frustrated by an undefined need for answers, Max peered at her retreating back. "Or what?"

"She'll never make it to Mirage-Reborn."

With a heavy sigh, Bala patted Max on the back. "Sounds like you've got your work cut out for you."

Smothering his first curse word, Max knew, without a shadow of doubt, that it wasn't his work that worried him.

~~~

Roux slid a tray piled with square sandwiches and a
~~~

tall drink across the table toward Chas and watched the huge man's eyes light up. "Didn't your master ever feed you?"

Seated on a chair at the central table in the ship's lounge, Chas gripped the top ham sandwich and shoveled it into his mouth. He chewed a moment before talking around the last morsels. "He wasn't my master. I just worked for him—a good cause and good money. I always ate well. Just never enough." He shrugged and dug into the next sandwich. "I could've done worse and worked for his boss, Simms."

Roux's eyes followed Chas's culinary accomplishments as he pulled out a metal chair and took a seat. "You know Simms?"

Chas dabbed a napkin to his lips. "No. But Erik mentioned that his boss wasn't the nicest guy on the planet—Newearth, I mean." He took a long swig from the glass. "You'll have to tell him what happened."

Roux rubbed his temple. "That's not an option right now, but I'd like you to explain your *cause* before we get to Mirage-Reborn. I have to make a full report."

Chas munched another sandwich. "Really, it's about the future. Simms is building the biggest docking bay this side of the Divide, and he's afraid that your Cerulean is going to mess things up."

Roux folded his arms across his chest and leaned back. The lounge was empty, and only the hum of the air circulation unit sounded behind them. "Mess things up—how?"

"Cerulean is in league with a Luxonian Secret Council and some Crestonian extremists who want to clear the planet of all—and I quote—'inferior elements' and use Newearth as the focus for their interstellar business. In short, they'd become so strong that they'd secure Lux and Crestar interests for millenniums." He burped and shoved the empty tray away. "That's what I figured from his cryptic hints anyway." He lifted his hands in helpless innocence. "It sounded like another all-too-familiar plot to wipe out the human race—can't blame me for being worried."

The lounge door slid open, and Bala stepped in with a datapad tucked under his arm. His gaze shifted from Roux to Chas.

Roux stroked his chin meditatively. "I like the new docking bay idea. It would be great for Newearth—but why does he think Cerulean—of all people—would want to—"

"Uh, sir?" Bala inched closer. "There's a message from Mirage-Reborn."

Rising from his chair, Roux reached for the datapad.

With formal stiffness, Bala passed it over and peered down at Chas's crumb-strewn plate. He chewed his lip as his gaze traveled to the food dispensary.

Roux tapped the pad, frowning. His eyes flickered across the screen. Then he looked up. "You know what this says?"

Bala ripped his eyes from the counter. "Only that Cerulean's alive, but most of its garbled. Sounded like some kind of civil war's going on out there."

Roux stepped around the table, still peering at the datapad. "Which doesn't make any sense. How could Omega let things get so out of hand? Where is he?"

Bala shrugged. "We won't know till we get there."

"And how soon will that be?"

Scrunching his face, Bala tipped his hand. "The planet was hidden from our sight— we have only the directions from *The Summons'* crew to go on. Heck, we might fly right past it."

Chas rose, a lopsided grin spreading across his face. "Or fly right into it."

Irritated, Roux's gaze jerked back to Chas. "Enough." He flicked a glance at Bala. "We need to know what happened to Cosmos. Or Cerulean is going to give me that I-really-hoped-for-more-from-you look. You know the one."

Bala's eyes widened alarmingly, as if innocent of such shocking horrors.

Amused despite himself, Roux waved Bala off. "Well, I know it. And I don't want to see it again." He started for the door. "Let's see if we can send another message. Maybe Cerulean will answer this time."

The door slid open, and Jazzmarie sauntered in. She offered a formal nod to Roux. Her gaze skipped over Bala and pounced on Chas. With pursed lips and relaxed hips, she sauntered over to him.

Confused, and dearly wishing he wasn't seeing what he thought he was seeing, Roux tried to redirect her. "Doctor, I hope you are not still concerned about the matter we discussed earlier?"

Jazzmarie barely spared a second glance for her captain. "I will remain concerned as long as this ship and its crew are in danger of destruction." She lifted her hands in mock surrender. "But I trust you have things perfectly under control." As if seeing Bala for the first time, she stared him full in the face. "You there, when will we meet up with *The Summons*?"

Bala's eyes widened. "Oh, Lord! Paint me for a fool."

Roux stopped in the open doorway. "What?"

"*The Summons* has a homing signal. I can tap into it. We don't need to look for Mirage-Reborn at all. We just need to locate *The Summons*, and we'll be there in no time."

Genuine relief flooding through him, Roux grinned. "You get us to Mirage-Reborn, Bala, and I'll recommend you for a captaincy."

With a snort, Bala chuckled. “Then I’d outrank Clare. And she’d kill me.” He squeezed past the captain. “I’ll get us there, sir. No worries.”

Jazzmarie shook her head. “Have you forgotten Cosmos?”

Chas laughed with a dismissive wave. “The monster is probably heading for deep space.”

Jazzmarie’s sniffed comment, “I doubt that very much,” rang in Roux’s ears all the way to the bridge.

~~~

Jazzmarie exhaled a long well-placed sigh and peered at Chas who stood in the middle of the lounge like a perplexed mountain.

“Please, no formalities. Sit. Relax. I’m the ship’s doctor, the most skilled surgeon this side of—” Clucking her tongue, she wandered to the food dispensary. *I doubt he understands, much less cares.*

Chas lumbered to an arrangement of cushioned furniture and plunked down. Stretching out, he groaned in sensual delight. “Eek, gods, I haven’t had a decent rest in days.” He peered out of one open eye. “Maybe you could give me something to help me sleep.” His other eye opened a slit. “Maybe you have a few tricks up your sumptuous sleeves?”

Jazzmarie’s flowing blouse sashayed to the rhythm of her hand as she tapped the console. “Taco salad, pecan pie—oh, and a large banana shake.” She turned from the dispensary and cocked her head, scrutinizing the lounging hulk. “I’d sooner—”

The door slid open, and Max marched in. He glanced from Jazzmarie to Chas and back to Jazzmarie. Turning
~~~

on his heel, he seemed to think he could affect a full retreat without her noticing.

Her heart quickening, Jazzmarie moseyed forward, one hand beckoning. “Wait! Relax a bit, Maximan. That’s an order. You’ve been working hard, and I don’t want you to break down before we arrive at Mirage-Reborn.”

Chas sat up and leaned on one arm. “What is this Mirage place you keep talking about? I’ve never heard of it, and I’ve traveled—extensively.”

Jazzmarie swerved her gaze from Max to Chas. Two males focused on her. She purred with exotic energy. “Well, why don’t you come and sit with us and let me tell you about it?”

Tramping to a game shelf, Max plucked up a silver box. “I’d rather play chess.”

Stymied, Jazzmarie blinked. “*Chess?* When did you take up playing chess?”

“When I heard that it takes hours of serious concentration.”

Chas snorted. “That leaves me out.”

Stroking Chas’s arm with a light finger, Jazzmarie squeezed onto the couch. “Roll that table over here and bring my food, Maxi, and we’ll see if we can’t accommodate you both.” Winking at Chas, she nudged him back. “I’ll teach you a few tricks.”

Chas’s gaze rolled over Jazzmarie, a glint of appreciation in his eyes. “I bet you can.”

With a coy tap on Chas’s arm, she offered a sexy pout as Max pulled the table over and set the food before her. “Now don’t you be jealous, Maxi. It’s not becoming of a man of your quality.”

Max peered down at her scrunched intimately with Chas. “Perhaps I should leave you two—”

Suddenly chilled, Jazzmarie lifted her fork. She

pointed at his heart and grinned. “Not if you value your life.”

~~~

Yelsa leaned over the railing and stared at the ship’s engine as if by will power she could make it work harder.

Roux strolled up close and placed one hand on the railing behind her. “Still mad at me?”

Her emotions tying her stomach in knots, Yelsa gripped the railing. “You mean, am I still concerned that we’re rescuing your friends instead of protecting an entire planet’s population—hmmm—” Her jaw tightened.

Roux leaned on the railing, his gaze wandering to the window and the glowing universe. “I’m not abandoning our mission—in fact—this may be the most direct way of stopping Cosmos.”

Furious beyond clear thought, Yelsa jerked up. “Direct? Let me clarify—Cosmos is heading toward food, and that means some innocent planet is about to be devoured. Your friends are in another direction—they can wait!”

Roux turned and faced Yelsa. “My friends can stop Cosmos—if given the chance. Cerulean—”

“Luxonians have their own interests at heart. Trust me, I know. No matter how good their intentions, they can’t stop Cosmos.”

His eyes flashing, Roux pounded the railing. “But you can?”

Cornered, Yelsa turned away. “I told you—there is a solution.”

Roux clasped Yelsa’s arm and drew her close, staring
~~~

into her eyes. "We're not going to blow ourselves up in the hope of destroying her. It won't work, and I have no desire to die in a vain attempt at heroics."

"Love takes sacrifice."

"That's not love—that's pride! Pride and arrogance."

Yelsa tried to jerk her arm free, but Roux kept a firm hold.

"Listen, I never want to hear you talk about sacrificing yourself again. I don't think you understand what you're saying."

Though bitterness filled her, sarcasm tasted sweet. "But *you* do?"

Roux flung her arm away. "I do." Pounding to the window, he stared at the universe awash in vibrant colors. "I wasn't an only child. My parents had another son—older than me. He was sent out as a guardian."

Shocked at this personal revelation, Yelsa held her breath. She stared at Roux's back.

"The population he was assigned to observe lived—and died—in a constant state of war. He managed to get the necessary information back to the Supreme Council, but he never made it home." Roux bowed his head. "My parents were frantic when I wanted to become a guardian, but they died before I was stationed on Newearth." Sucking in a deep breath, Roux shook out his arms as if to rid himself of clinging memories.

Hesitant but drawn in against her will, Yelsa stepped forward. "I'm sorry." She dropped her voice softer. "Then you understand how I feel."

Roux turned and wrapped his arms around her waist, pulling her close. "Better than you know." He rested his head against hers. "Trust me. Cerulean has some kind of gift—things work out for him. We'll find him, and together, we'll destroy Cosmos."

"You really think he can help?"

"If there's one person in the universe who can save us—it's Cerulean."

Yelsa's heart sank. Such faith was doomed to fail.

~~~

Bala sat cross-legged on his unmade bed and stared at his datapad. Kendra smiled from a worry-wrinkled face. He chuckled. "Better late than never." He tapped the screen.

Kendra's soft voice echoed across the silent room. "Hi, sweetie! I just wanted to catch you up on all the goings-on around here. Seth is married now and has two kids; Bari joined the circus—like he was always threatening to do. And Rachel entered medical school." She grinned big time. "Ha! Got you that time—didn't I?"

Her smile faded as a humming noise grew in the background. "Listen, honey, there have been a few surprises. Zara—"

She glanced behind her and scooted closer to the camera, her voice dropping. "Zara's been having a few *issues.* She's not exactly what we thought. I'm afraid that Justine may be in for a bit of a surprise when she returns."

A squall erupted in the distance. Kendra turned and yelled, "Seth, take the little ones outside—please!"

She returned to the screen, her frown more pronounced, dark circles shadowing her eyes. She hunched forward. "If Cerulean were here, he might know what to do, but Faye and Taug are definitely getting worried. And frankly, so am I. But I don't want them to do anything—" She glanced back and dropped
~~~

her voice another decibel. "Unreasonable." Heaving a long sigh, she gripped the edge of the datapad. "I don't want you to worry, but if you ever bump into Cerulean or Justine—you might want to tell them to hurry home. Newearth needs them. Zara needs them."

Her eyes filled with tears, and she peered intently into the camera. "*I need you.*"

The humming grew louder. Kendra swallowed. "I've got to go."

The screen blinked to black.

Bala hunched forward, dropped his head into his hands, and rocked like a distraught child.

Chapter Nineteen

–Mirage-Reborn–

Hope Laid Waste

Justine combated rising horror. Quinn had shot Pax in cold blood, Cerulean crouched over the prone figure, trying desperately to keep him alive, and when she challenged Quinn, he shot her! Burning fibers and bio-ware filled the kitchen with an ugly stench. *Never underestimate evil!*

Quinn ripped his gaze from her smoking wound to Lucius' backyard. Rage took horror's place inside Justine.

Two figures hustled by the window.

Frowning, Quinn called through the open doorway, "Hey! I'm in here!"

I will kill him this time, no mistakes. Justine launched herself forward.

Quinn ducked out of the way.

A man called out, "Quinn? Lucius escaped. He's—"

"Hold on!" Leveling his gun at Cerulean, Quinn spat his words at Justine. "I'll shoot *him* next."

Justine lifted her hands and stood her ground.

Cerulean cradled Pax's upper body in his arms, rocking back and forth, his head down, like someone who had lost all hope and reason.

A broad-shouldered, middle-aged man with a peevish frown hustled forward. "Did you hear me? Grace told us—" He took in the scene.

Vera stirred with a groan.

Clare leaned over the counter to help her sit up. "Are you okay? That bloody maniac knocked you out with something."

Vera blinked in the afternoon light, a dazed expression in her eyes. "Just give me a minute to clear my head."

Gripping her damaged arm, Justine glared at Quinn.

The stranger's gaze swung back to Quinn. "You said Lucius tried to kill you—they're trying to kill you too?"

Quinn shoved the man backward. "Don't question me, Kilroy. I'm the one in charge." He stepped over the threshold. The other man followed.

Justine tromped after them. *If I can get him away from the others, I'll rip off his head and then...*

A smaller, thinner man bustled forward. "You're supposed to keep the peace, Sheriff!" He glared at Quinn's gun. "That doesn't appear too peaceful to me."

Swinging his gun in an arc, aiming at each person in turn, Quinn backed away. "You want to live like slaves—fine. There're other men in this town who'd prefer to be free."

The two men shuffled in place, their gazes bouncing between Justine and Quinn. The small man murmured, "I want to be free, but not a murderer."

Pity flooded Justine. *Fools with too much power.* She lifted her hands. "I've no slaveholding ambitions at present."

Quinn lowered his gun and stepped up to two men. "Abbas isn't coming back. We are on our own. You better decide who you'll follow real quick because mob rule never works." After flinging a last glare at Justine, Quinn pounded to the road. The two men hustled up alongside him.

Clare called from inside the house, "Justine, get in here! We need a doctor."

Justine hurried inside.

Cerulean stopped rocking and groaned, "No. We don't."

Freezing in mid-step, Justine stared as Cerulean laid

Pax gently on the ground, closed his sightless eyes, and pressed his forehead against Pax's, murmuring under his breath, "Peace, my friend."

With tears in her eyes, Clare helped a wobbly Vera off the table and led her to a chair.

Vera cradled her head in her hands, sobbing.

Justine sucked in a breath. *How do I fight Quinn without becoming just like him?*

—The Summons—

Justine scowled as she climbed the boarding platform onto *The Summons'* main deck. She tromped through the corridor to the bridge and joined Cerulean. Instead of relief or joy, confusing images swirled through her mind. She clenched her hands. Fury was her best friend these days.

Leaning over a console, Cerulean grunted. He straightened and turned to face a wall-sized view screen.

Clare stepped out from behind a holographic image of this sector of the universe and zeroed in on the main communications console.

Justine tapped through a series of commands on the engineering database. "I think someone's been trying to disable the engines, but luckily, they messed with an obsolete system. I had already switched everything over to the M-2700, so I think we're good to go." Her gaze raked over Cerulean. "*Whenever* that might be."

The Summons, unlike *The Merrimack*, was constructed during the first flurry of resettlement, when Newearth bustled with new arrivals—humans returning home from Lux and aliens looking for a fresh start on a new world. Originally, as class A-003, it boasted the first of its kind technology.

When new systems arrived from alien sources, they were patched into *The Summons* with all the skills available on the overwhelmed world. By the time Cerulean managed to command *The Summons*, she had been rebuilt twelve times. Nothing on the bridge matched. Console colors warred with swivel chairs of all varieties and created an eye-blazing menagerie of mismatched parts, which everyone pretended not to see.

Tapping her fingers, Clare focused on the message board. "Really, Cerulean. You're going to have to suggest the IAA scrap this model. Messages take forever, and I'm not even sure we're getting everything."

Cerulean paced in front of the main view screen, his gaze searching the stars.

"Ah!" Clare grinned triumphantly. "Here it is. Buried in space traffic, but I found it. *The Merrimack* sent us a message two days ago—they are heading in our direction."

Justine's mood darkened. "So, where's Cosmos?"

Cerulean heaved a deep sigh. "That's what I'd like to know." He faccd Clare. "Why are they coming here? Their main objective is to track—"

The door whooshed open, and Lucius ducked onto bridge, his hands lifted waist-high as if in surrender. "I just wanted to see if I could help. Grace thinks I should explain what we did."

Justine spun around. *"What you did?"*

Squaring his shoulders, Lucius nodded. "Yes. We sent a message to Newearth—I think. And one to the other ship on your message roster. We told them we were under attack and needed help."

Cerulean strode over. "Well, that explains why Roux is deserting his main mission. He thinks we're desperate." Folding his arms, Cerulean appraised the blacksmith. "Did it ever occur to you to check with us before you sent a message from *our* ship?"

Lucius' brows furrowed, his jaw tightening. "At the time, Grace thought you were all about to be killed. Asking for help didn't seem like a bad idea."

Justine harumphed.

Surprisingly, Clare stepped forward, putting herself inside Lucius' personal space. "It wasn't wrong. Nice try and all. But you see, *The Merrimack* is all we have between Cosmos and Newearth."

Lucius' gaze traveled from Cerulean to Justine and back to Clare. "I'm not worried about Newearth or Cosmos. Mirage-Reborn is about to fall into civil war—and that must stop at all costs."

Brushing off Lucius' stupidity as another example of human frailty, Justine strolled over to the communication's console. "Maybe I can get a message through, ordering them to return to their original mission" She sped through a series of commands.

Though stiff and frowning, Lucius didn't interfere. He faced the viewer screen, apparently studying the star-filled spectrum.

Cerulean pointed to a swirling section on the right. "Newearth is about there—more or less. Hard to say at this magnitude." His gaze slid to Lucius. "You are human—right?"

What could only be classified as a sarcastic chuckle escaped Lucius. "Human as they come."

Knew it. Justine glanced over.

Cerulean shook his head, wonderment in his eyes. "But you don't care about Newearth?"

With a grunt, Lucius faced Cerulean. "I cared—with all my heart. I was a faithful citizen and did good work. But that wasn't enough. Even after losing—" He shook his head and stepped away from the screen. “Never mind.”

Justine straightened. *There’s more going on here…*

Cerulean gestured to indicate a red glare on the screen. “Bothmal is about here.”

Swearing under his breath, Lucius stabbed the air to the left of the red mark. “Actually, it’s here. This is an old map; it’s mislabeled.” He turned and glared at Cerulean. “So, you know about my ignominious past?”

Cerulean leaned against the railing. “Yours and Quinn’s. I’d say, between the two of you, Quinn—”

An emergency signal flared over the message board in bright red letters. Justine reached up and scrolled over cryptic words. “What?”

Clare jogged forward and peered over her shoulder. “Something wrong?”

Though her heart couldn’t really race, Justine suddenly understood the expression. “Zara sent a message—from Taug’s lab. He’s holding her prisoner and plans to—dissect her!”

Cerulean rubbed his face. “Bloody hell.”

Forcing her way in front of the message board, Clare frowned. “I don’t think so.” Her gaze flickered back to Justine’s face. “Taug’s ambitious—and I wouldn’t put any sly scheme past him—but he’s not stupid. There’s no way he’d try this. He knows he’d never get away with it.” She turned and faced Cerulean. “Besides, if he was intent on such a thing—she’d never have gotten a message through.”

Justine’s clenched her hands. “You don’t know him like I do. He spared Derik only to get as much information as he could. That traitorous—”

Cerulean lifted a hand. “One crisis at a time!” He stepped to the console. “Did you get your message to *The Merrimack*?”

Heaving a deep breath, Justine squared her shoulders. "Yes. I sent it. How long it will take to get to them—anyone's guess."

Cerulean turned back to Lucius. "In the meantime, we have to keep this planet in one piece. Has Grace made the funeral arrangements?"

Lucius nodded, and his expression softened. "She's working on it. I said I'd help as soon as I checked on you."

Clare looked over. "How is Vera?"

"She's still weak but recovering. Grace took her in. A protector of sorts. Losing Dimi devastated her." His gaze hardened. "I need to go. I've got something to do."

Clare frowned. "What?"

"Since no one will save us, I'll have to exterminate Quinn myself."

Horrific memories clashed in Justine's mind, sending volcanic rage through her. "That's my job!"

Cerulean grabbed Lucius' arm. "No! We'll solve this another way. If he gets killed in the process, I won't shed a tear. But we've got to keep this planet from erupting into any more violence." He looked Lucius in the eye. "Is that what you want for Vera?"

Lucius jerked away and pounded out the door.

Flummoxed by contradictory desires, Justine dropped onto a chair.

Cerulean glanced her way.

With a wave, Justine ignored the concern in his eyes. She ran through her systems, searching for a malfunction. Once upon a time, killing had been part of her job description. For the first time in her life, and with a twinge of horror, she realized that, now, she looked forward to it.

~~~

Gary Nelson leaned back in the comfort of his living room, settling himself in an overstuffed chair, and grinned at Quinn. "So, you've come to pay your respects, have you? How kind. And to think, I imagined that you had no manners."

Quinn rubbed his nose and stared down at the old man, his face an unemotional mask. "I know you've probably been told all sorts of evil things about me. Your daughter sure doesn't hide her hate."

The old man shifted. "Grace is sensitive. Like her mother."

A flicker of understanding rippled over Quinn's features. "Yeah. That's what I've come to chat about. Rumor has it, that your second wife, a Bhuaci siren of some renown, died under mysterious circumstances. Certain Bhuaci authorities believed that she was murdered."

Lifting his chin, Gary stared at the door and raised his voice. "Grace, make me some tea."

Silence.

Frustration jabbed him. "Oh, damn, I forgot. She's out with that LuKan—making funeral arrangements, no doubt." A teasing thought made him smile. He refocused on Quinn. "There are plenty of rumors about murder around here, I assure you."

Quinn dropped onto a padded chair and rolled his hat in his hands. "Listen, I came here to make you an offer. I know about your past—the murder of your wife and how Omega snatched you away from the Bhuaci authorities. But"—he leaned on one elbow and dropped his voice—"I don't care about your past. I only care about your future. All our futures."
~~~

Nelson heaved himself out of his chair and grabbed his cane. “Guess I’ll have to make that tea myself.” He tottered to the kitchen, the cane pounding the floorboards with each step.

With an exasperated sigh, Quinn followed. “Mirage-Reborn deserves better than demi-gods.”

Entering the brightly lit kitchen decorated with lacy curtains and apple stenciling across the walls, Nelson chuckled, rumbles emanating through his chest. “Demi-gods indeed!”

Quinn pouted as he slapped his hat on the counter. “We’re intelligent beings! We don’t need to be watched over and coddled.” He straightened. “It’s time we demand self-rule.”

Nelson filled the kettle with water and talked over the rushing spray. “What about Abbas and Omega?”

“To Bothmal with them, for all I care. Not our concern. Besides, the Cresta finally got their revenge for an atrocity Abbas committed against them a long time back. Crestas never forget. Lost a third of their population—just for making discreet inquiries. At this moment, Omega might be dead, and Abbas will certainly never be the same.”

Placing the kettle onto the stovetop, Gary sniffed his disdain and lit the fire. “Hardly sounds like the mild-mannered Abbas I know. Killed a whole slew of Crestas? I doubt it.”

“What do you know about it? With such unchecked power, he and his son could go around destroying whole populations for their amusement, if they so desired, and no one would be the wiser.”

Nelson grabbed a cup, snatched a teabag from a canister, and dropped it in. His gaze roved the kitchen. “Where’s the bloody sugar?”

With a blank expression, Quinn looked around the

room. He frowned, snatched a bowl brimming with brown granules, and slid it across the counter. "In the coming days, I need to know who I can trust—you understand, old man?"

Nelson leaned against the counter and scooped sugar into his cup. "Sounds like you can't trust anybody."

Scowling, Quinn pursed his lips.

A child in a man's body.

The kettle whistled, and Nelson wrapped the handle in a plaid kitchen towel. He poured steaming water into his cup. Satisfied, he turned and faced Quinn. "Don't get all gloomy now. I happen to agree with you. I prefer freedom to tyranny—even soft tyranny. I never asked anyone for anything—except for Grace. She's pretty much given me her whole life." He sipped his tea and nodded. "That's enough burden for any old man."

~~~

Vera stood at the head of one grave, while Clare stood at the head of the other in the crowded graveyard.

The open side-by-side graves yawned like black holes. Nearby, tendrils of a weeping willow swayed in a gentle breeze.

Two lines of people snaked their way through the cemetery. One comprised of Mirage-Reborn citizens, including four hefty men, Lucius among them, carrying a coffin on their shoulders. The other comprised of only Cerulean, Justine, a Cresta, an Ingot, and a young boy. Justine carried the brunt of the coffin's weight upon her shoulders, though the Cresta and the Ingot took up the balance, and the boy wandered along forlornly behind. The two lines met at the graves and set down their
~~~

burdens. Lucius circled around and stood at Vera's side.

Cerulean strode to the center and stood before the two graves. "We are grieved to be assembled here today for such a cause, but these two, Dimi and Pax, deserve our highest respect. Both suffered injustices, yet neither bore grudges nor offered anything but their quiet devotion to—"

A voice called out from the back. "What do you know about it, Luxonian? You've just arrived—you're not really a citizen anyway, are you?"

A murmur of voices rose in agreement.

Vera's gaze fell on the speaker. *A friend of Quinn's?*

Cerulean lifted his hand in a conciliatory gesture. "Would anyone else like to speak?"

Vera stumbled forward, blinking in the strong light. Her hand, bandaged with a thick wrapping, shook as she slid it under her arm. "Cerulean is right. Dimi did suffer—but not from unfeeling fate. He suffered from the cruelty of others. Our planet was destroyed, and we were lost in a cold universe. Omega saved us from slavery, and for that, I'm grateful. But Dimi's death was not by chance." Her gaze searched faces in the assembly. "Our house was set alight by someone who wanted—"

Quinn's voice rumbled over the assembly. "This is hardly the place to make accusations, Vera. You should honor your brother—not defile his memory with speculations." His gaze rummaged through the crowd. "I know that some of you think I started the fire that night, but it's not true. I have Mirage-Reborn's best interests at heart. I don't go around killing people—unless there's no other way." His gaze flickered to Cerulean as he lifted his arm and his voice. "This world needs to grow up!"

Frustration fought grief as Vera scowled. She retreated into the crowd.

Cerulean cleared his throat. "Let's keep this as a

memorial to the two who lie here." He looked around. "Does anyone else have anything to say?"

The young boy by Pax's grave stepped forward. "I didn't know Mr. Pax very well, but I used to watch him and his friends." His gaze slid over to Justine and Clare. "He talked to me in the park once. Told me about some of the trips he used to take, trading cargo and such."

The boy's gaze shifted. "Pax looked kind of worried. So, I asked him if he was okay. He said that life was a mystery and rarely okay. But he laughed when he said it. I knew what he meant—my family was hunted too." He glanced at Vera. "But that's what makes this home—we've all been afraid." His gaze landed on the coffins. "I don't want to feel that way again." He turned and ran off into the woods.

A lump rose in Vera's throat.

Cerulean watched the boy's retreating figure, swallowed, and faced the crowd. "Any religious or ceremonial customs you'd like to observe?"

A Bhuaci woman stepped from the crowd. "Since we do not know exactly what Dimi would've wanted, and there are no LuKan Bishops to oversee their proper rituals, Vera asked that I bid a traditional Bhuaci farewell to our two friends."

Cerulean stepped aside.

The Bhuaci woman raised her arms and fastened her gaze upon the sky. Her voice rang out in a clear bell-tone.

Soaring like a mystery into a world unknown,
Lift your spirit to the joy of home.

We grieve—alone and bereft,
Lament our loss—a universal theft.

Loved, embraced, shared.
Pain and loss never spared.

Now cold in form but not forgot.
The Spirit fled but ever in thought.

An unspoken vow.
We'll forever share our spirits now.

Four men on each side stepped forward and, using straps, lowered the rectangular boxes into their proper graves.

Grief stabbing her soul, sobs welled up inside Vera.

Lucius wrapped his arm around her.

She wasn't the only one crying. Tears even coursed down Clare's cheeks.

But Justine stood on the edge of Pax's grave, stone still.

Quinn turned and marched toward Main Street.

As the crowd thinned, the throng wandering back to their homes and the business of the day, Grace stepped closer and pressed Vera's shoulder. "You ready to go?"

Lucius rumbled, "She'll stay with me until things settle down. No knowing what Quinn will try next—or another of his kind."

Cerulean sighed. "I was waiting until after the funerals to deal with Quinn."

Lucius stepped around Vera and confronted Cerulean. "What're you going to do? Hold a trial? As sheriff, he doesn't think he committed a crime, and he's got half the town convinced that he's their savior. The man is power-mad!"

Cerulean locked onto Vera's gaze. "You should stay with Grace a little longer. We're going to keep you safe."

Justine and Clare nodded.

With a heavy sigh, Vera patted Lucius' hand. "I don't want any more trouble; I'll stay with Grace."

He whispered in her ear. "You sure?"

Vera nodded. "It's safer for both of us this way."

Grace took Vera's arm and led her across the graveyard.

The gravediggers got to work. Men's grunts punctuated the air. Dirt smacked against wood as Dimi's and Pax's graves were filled with dirt.

In time, green grass would cover them. Amazed at the thought, Vera squeezed back tears.

At the street corner, Cerulean turned toward Quinn's office. Justine and Clare followed behind.

Vera glanced aside and met Lucius' gaze. He nodded, offered a quick smile, and then hurried after the others.

"An unspoken "vow" rang in Vera's ears.

~~~

Cerulean stopped at a fallen tree in the park and propped his foot on a log. He pulled out a datapad.

Justine took up a position on one side of Cerulean while Clare took the other. Lucius stood before him with his arms folded.

Cerulean scanned the datapad. "*The Merrimack* is getting close. We'd better make plans quickly, or there will be more graves to dig."

Lucius' eyes narrowed. "I know one grave I'm going to fill myself."

Waving off Justine's protest, Cerulean lifted his datapad. "Abbas sent me a message."

Justine grabbed the pad. "On a datapad? It must be a forgery!"
~~~

Clare leaned in to see, but Justine lifted it out of reach.

An ache throbbing through his head, Cerulean rubbed his temples. *Grown women on the outside, children on the inside*. "Stop!" Peering at Lucius, Cerulean ignored the two women squabbling over the datapad. "Abbas has negotiated with the Crestas for Omega's return."

Justine shook her head as she scrolled through the data. "The Crestas can't negotiate with Abbas! They aren't nearly powerful enough."

Exhausted beyond reason, Cerulean sat on the tree trunk. "Power isn't enough. Not when you're trying to save your son."

Justine glared at Cerulean. "Abbas could decimate their entire planet."

"But he wouldn't. Others of his kind, maybe. But not him. The Cresta don't need to exact revenge on the actual perpetrators. Only on someone from Abbas' race who won't retaliate. They can save face with just a bit of malice."

Justine huffed deep breaths. Her confusion fought with her fury.

Lucius cleared his throat. "Word in Bothmal was that the Crestas have been working on a new weapon called the mind twister. It scrambles the wits of any sentient being—to the point where they are less than worthless. Instead, they're dangerous and erratic for the rest of their lives. Even Bothmal doesn't want them after the Crestas are done."

Clare collapsed onto the log next to Cerulean, slapping her hands on her thighs and shaking her head.

Her normal composure gone, Justine spluttered, "This time, you can't stop me! Quinn is going to pay."

Cerulean stood up and looked from Justine to Lucius. "Don't be fools, you two. Quinn didn't do this. He found out somehow and merely used it to his advantage." He glanced over at Clare. “Besides, on some level, Quinn is right. If Omega’s mind is ruined and Abbas is growing old—Mirage-Reborn is going to have to grow up. Soon.”

Chapter Twenty

–Newearth–

Into the Melee

Lang wrinkled her nose as she tugged a slack-jawed Uncle Clem to the gatehouse of a huge manor. "Stop gawking! You look like a sightseer."

As structures go, the edifice on 1001 Universal Drive stood apart from the norm. Designed in the style of an OldEarth mausoleum, the Taj Mahal, Simms Palace stopped Newearth arrivals dead in their tracks. Over two thousand meters tall and nearly the same wide, the structure dominated an entire section of Lincoln Township, which, as the largest township near the Pacific shore, was an impressive feat.

The winter sun shining off its brilliant white exterior blinded the unwary, while the surrounding labyrinth gardens, now sleeping in seasonal hibernation, enchanted even the busiest passerby on a summer day. Each week, crowds lined the ornate iron fence encircling the retro-marvel, but few ever made it beyond the first gate.

In the distance, a space shuttle of modern design lodged comfortably on a radial multilevel docking bay with boarding tubes connected to Simms Palace.

Dressed in a long heavy coat, thick pants, and suede loafers,

Uncle Clem blinked like a man startled out of sleep. He hustled along at the Ingot's side, his gaze glued to the magnificent home. "How many people live there, you think?"

Though well protected in her bio-ware, Lang wore a bright pink cardigan, tight blue pants, and black combat boots. She shrugged. "Just Simms and a few of his favorites. He owns a harem, from what I hear."

She paused and considered the orange gatehouse door with the attached sign: *Trespassing—a serious offense—punished accordingly.* She chuckled and sniffed at the house. "I've heard that he has room for his Zinzinara team, a cooking staff, garden staff, medical staff, paid political pundits…" She waved dismissively. "You can imagine."

His imagination clearly running wild, Uncle Clem pointed with a shaky finger. "I'm not sure I should go in there." He nodded back the way they'd come. "Riko probably needs me at the café. Besides, a guy this important won't talk to an out-of-work Uanyi who's living with his nephew."

Lang gripped Uncle Clem's shoulder and, despite the heavy coat, squeezed hard enough to stiffen the Uanyi's spine. "That's why you're not out of work today—and why we practiced your brilliant new identity for three city blocks!" Her glare bore into him as her grip tightened. "Everyone is counting on you, remember?" She stopped before the main gate and pressed a buzzer, which resounded like a deep-toned bell.

A squeak escaped Uncle Clem. Gathering his composure, he sucked in a deep breath, clamped his jaws shut, clenched his hands, and took a wrestling stance. "Right. Serious investor. Mysterious friends. Connections to Bothmal."

Lang sneered. "Bothmal? I never said anything—"

A burly eight-foot Ingot opened the door and stepped outside, dwarfing Lang and throwing Uncle Clem into shadow. "Can I help you?"

Eyeing the tall, handsome Ingot, Lang sizzled in her element. A grin wandered across her lips. "I'm sure *you* can." Her gaze ran over his shoulders, down his chest—

and— She stopped herself. “But for now, please show us to Mr. Simms’ office. He’s expecting us.”

Uncle Clem swallowed convulsively.

The guard stretched out his hand. “Pass?”

Lang rolled her eyes. “By the Divide, do you honestly think I’d try to deceive one of my own kind?” She dug a datapad from a wrist strap and passed it over.

As the guard scanned the data stream, Uncle Clem gave Lang a what-are-you-doing? wide-eyed stare.

Without looking his way, she pinched his shoulder. *Stop acting like a squirming worm!* Lifting her chin, she pointed to the datapad. “Surely you recognize the Universal News logo and signature. I’ve been assigned to do an interview with the greatest developer Newearth has ever seen.” She tapped her foot. “You don’t want to keep Mr. Simms waiting.”

The guard appraised Uncle Clem. A snarl escaped. “What’s he for?”

Lang’s eyelids dropped to half-mast, as she struggled against the typical can’t-think-outside-a-box-mentality. *How disappointing.* “He’s Clem—a PR man—the finest celebrity representative since Hung Hong. Been touring the outer systems. We’re lucky we snatched him for a couple of days.” Plucking back her datapad, she huffed. “But if you’re going to waste our time—”

The guard stepped aside. Sweeping his hand forward, he chuckled. “I know your reputation, Lang, so I only believe about half of what you say. But since you are on today’s roster, you can follow me.”

Surprised and pleased beyond reason, Lang sauntered through the doorway.

Uncle Clem stood stiff as a possum playing dead.

Without a hint of respect, Lang reached back and yanked him along.

~~~

Simms liked contrasts. As he poured a drink, he looked himself over in the mirror behind the bar in his office. He loved how his olive complexion contrasted sharply against his pale-yellow shirt, white pants, and the bright silver chain he wore around his neck. And his masculine features—strong jawline, steel-gray eyes, and black hair—contrasted well with the ruby ring on his right hand and the lapis lazuli bracelet on his left. Diamonds of various sizes filled in any gaps on his fingers and ears.

Leaning back in a leather office chair, Simms, undeterred by the winter season, licked a chocolate chip ice cream cone.

The newest in a long line of admirers, two visitors bustled into the room. His secretary, Sue-Lee, a lithe Bhuaci female with sparking green eyes, announced them with her usual calm precision. "Lang from Universal News and her assistant, Clem."

Simms raised one finger in acknowledgment.

Sue-Lee bowed out of the room, a loyal servant before her master.

Lang folded her arms over her chest while her eyes danced, clearly amused.

Clem took in the luxurious room with his mouth hanging open, like a Neanderthal, clearly not accustomed to the finer things in life.

Simms wiped his lips with a white linen napkin and tossed the unfinished cone into a recycling bin embedded in the wall. He grinned. "We're not barbarians like they are on OldEarth. They've wasted so bloody much!"
~~~

With her attention fixed on Simms, Lang reached out and closed Uncle Clem's mouth. Her gaze never strayed from Simms. "You're a paragon of industry, sir. I'd love to hear about your grand plans for Newearth. Every glorious detail." Her gaze swerved to the couch.

Simms swiveled off his chair and grinned. *Oh, this is going to be fun.* He reached out, took her hand, and clasped it tightly. "I've wanted to meet you for a long time, Lang. We travel in the same circles, don't we? The rich and powerful, the makers and breakers of Newearth." He led her to the couch and flopped down with a contented sigh. "I've waited my whole life for this moment!"

Scooting to one side of the couch and crossing her legs primly, Lang glanced at Uncle Clem, who still stood frozen where the secretary had left him.

Simms followed her gaze and frowned. "And you are?"

With a languid wave, Lang made the introductions. "Come here, you clever man! Don't play Mr. Modest with us." She winked coyly at Simms. "Clem flew in just to assist me with your story." She arched an eyebrow. "He's the best PR Rep this side of the Divide. You're lucky I was able to convince him to take you on."

"Never heard of him." Simms shrugged. "But I've been too busy building the greatest docking bay in the universe to follow Newearth News."

Throwing eye-daggers at the little Uanyi, Lang pointed to a chair.

Resembling a frightened bird, Clem perched on the edge of the chair as if ready to take flight.

Simms snorted. *Must be one of those artsy types—great with illusions but can't handle reality.*

Lang's sultry tone snagged his attention. "Please, tell us about your work, Mr. Simms. Why does Newearth need another docking bay?"

Simms redirected his thoughts and met Lang's appraising stare. "It isn't just a docking bay—it's a way of life." He tapped a datapad embedded in his wrist and passed his hand through the air. Suddenly, a one-meter holographic image floated before them. "Just imagine—a welcoming home for everyone, offering whatever lifestyle you choose with complete freedom and fairness."

Lang frowned. "How do you know what people want? There are so many kinds that you'll spend all your resources making adjustments."

Simms grinned. "Not so. Remember who is paying? Companies petition us for membership and then send us the specifics necessary to make their receiving receptacle appropriate for their needs. Everyone is welcome and accommodated."

Clem muttered under his breath. "As long as they pay an exorbitant price, I'm sure."

Simms ignored the interruption. "Education systems are placed throughout the complex to assist new arrivals with communication adjustments. We have the necessary custom awareness and all the information anyone could possibly need for a safe, enjoyable stay on Newearth. Monitoring systems give me eyes everywhere, training personnel are located at strategic checkpoints, and assistants, human and otherwise, are available to anyone in need. Food, housing, medical care, entertainment, even gift shops, are on every level."

The hologram rotated in complex splendor before their eyes.

"A world within a world." Simms sat transfixed by his creation.

"If you can pay for it." Lang stroked her chin as her gaze followed the rotating image.

Clem lifted his hand like a hesitant child. "If you don't mind, Mr. Simms, could you give us a little tour sometime—maybe?"

Renewed energy thrilling through him, Simms bounded to his feet and clapped his hands. "Wonderful idea! I was going to wait until the official opening next month, but a little preview won't hurt." His gaze savored Lang as she rose from the couch. "You're all the representation I'll need."

Uncle Clem hurried ahead and stood by the door while Simms called through an intercom. "Sue-Lee, we're taking a tour of the facility. Get my jeep ready."

A disembodied voice answered. "Of course, sir."

Simms took Lang's arm and strolled over the threshold. "You'll love my vision."

Uncle Clem started to follow but hesitated at a glowing sign situated right above the door: *Want not—waste not.* He frowned.

Simms called, "Hurry up, Clem. Last is least in my way of thinking."

~~~

Clem sat in the back seat of the open jeep as it rolled on autopilot through the largest facility he had ever seen. His mouth kept dropping open.

Unceremoniously, Lang repeatedly forced him to close it with a twitch or a glare.

Clem took to scratching his head instead.

Circling high above Newearth, the docking bay lobby staggered his imagination. He couldn't see the end in any direction. Lifting his gaze, he peered at the railings spiraling up numerous levels into an indefinable
~~~

distance. The peak rounded into a skylight dome. The noses of various ships protruded into the lobby for disembarking crew and travelers, while hundreds of other bay doors above undoubtedly awaited incoming ships.

Simms grinned, pointed, and chattered to Lang in high glee.

Lang's gaze traveled the busy perimeter. "You're already in business?"

Simms chuckled. "Not officially. But we do have a few friends who enjoy a secure environment—free from the public glare."

Lang nodded, a glint growing in her eyes.

Clem leaned forward. He gripped the back of Lang's chair as he whispered in her ear, "What about the signs? Ask about them."

Lang turned around and frowned at him.

Pointing, Uncle Clem waved to a neon pink sign hanging from the ceiling: *Want not—waste not.*

As if in a surrealistic dream, Simms watched Clem's waving fingers. "Oh, that's a reminder and a warning." His expression darkened.

Lang tilted her head, her expression alive with questions.

With a mild hum, the auto-jeep continued its tour. Simms leaned back, clasping his hands over his firm middle, and took an instructive tone. "A friend who served in Bothmal prison showed me the wisdom of never wasting anything, not a particle of matter, not a single opportunity." Simms tapped the jeep console, and the vehicle stopped at the entrance. "To be successful, one must make choices. So, we recycle. Even the unwanted. We find a use for everything."

After stepping out of the jeep, Lang stretched to her full height. Her gaze lifted to the skylight exposing the starry universe. “And the Luxonian named Cerulean? How do you plan to recycle him?”

Horrified by the boldness of her question, Uncle Clem scrambled out of the jeep as fast as his legs could carry him.

With an abrupt laugh, Simms pounded the jeep’s frame. “By the Divide! I always said you were fascinating.” His amusement simmered to a light chuckle. “Cerulean is doing what Luxonians do best—making humans distrust aliens. He’ll destroy himself before too long. Then, I’ll figure out how to recycle him. Maybe he’ll become a proverb for the price of Luxonian overreach.” He eyed Clem. “Think of a slogan for that, and maybe I’ll pay you for the honor of using it in my docking bay.”

Propping her hands on her hips, Lang grinned. “From all reports, I would’ve thought the opposite of Cerulean.”

Simms climbed from the jeep and waved to an attendant. “You don’t have friends on the inside, do you? I mean, objective friends who can see clearly.”

Nausea rising, Uncle Clem glanced at Lang, who remained fixed on Simms.

An attendant halted in front of Simms.

With a formal wave, Simms gestured them forward. “Let’s go to dinner. I’ll arrange a party.” He sauntered forward with the attendant falling behind. “You’ll enjoy meeting my Cresta and Ingot compatriots, I’m sure.” He glanced back at Clem. “I don’t have any Uanyi friends—yet.” His grin returned. “But I’m sure I’ll find use for you soon enough.”

Clem heard a strange rushing sound in his ears. Like water roaring over a cliff. *There goes my peace of mind. And I wanted that…*

~~~

Riko leaned back on a plush chair, folded his hands behind his head, and tried to relax. *No one asked me to save the world, right?*

Faye bustled about his dim living room and snapped on lights. She stopped at the image of Riko's mother on a wide shelf perched on the edge of an ornate incense tree. She frowned at the empty ash bowl. "You haven't made any prayer offerings lately?"

Riko shrugged. "Mom wanted me to live in the present. Not the past." He sighed. "Though I wonder what she'd say about my life. Probably call me a Yurtlun."

Faye flipped on one more light, brightening the neat but sparsely decorated living room considerably. She pursed her lips. "I don't know the term."

Riko hefted himself into an upward position. "It's a fancy way of saying you're acting like an idiot." He rubbed a spot of grease on his sleeve. "Translated literally—a childish adult." Pulling a datapad from his pocket, he scrolled through spam adverts and old messages. "When do you think they'll get—?"

A chime rang.

Faye scurried to the door and opened it. "Finally!"

Lang shoved a limp Uncle Clem through the doorway, marched across the room, looked around, and then stared at Riko. "You have any strong drink around here?"

Riko and Faye exchanged glances. He pointed to a shelf on the back wall. "I have a couple of—"

The chime rang again, the door slid open, and Taug bustled in. In each tentacle, he clutched a different colored bottle. "I come bearing gifts." He glanced at
~~~

Riko. "Hope you don't mind, but I made a good exchange recently and—well—I like to share." His gaze rolled across the room, from Riko to Faye's frozen expression, to Uncle Clem leaning askew against the wall, then to Lang's burning frown. "Perhaps this is not the best time."

"You couldn't be more wrong." Swooping like a hawk on a rodent, Lang snatched the burgundy bottle and twisted off the cork. "In fact, we'll all need a strong drink in a moment."

Heaving himself out of his chair, Riko ambled across the room and pulled out a tray of sturdy wine glasses. He shrugged. "I never know when friends will drop by." After passing them around, he stepped back.

Lang did the honors, pouring a healthy dose of the dark brew into each.

Taug frowned. "You'll have us all out cold for a week."

Lang tossed back the majority of her drink and licked her lips. "I can only wish."

Helpless and growing ever more anxious, Riko flapped his arms. "Out with it. What happened? Uncle Clem looks like someone ran over him with a garden tiller."

Uncle Clem groaned.

Lang marched forward, reaching for another bottle, but Taug swung it behind his back. "Talk first. Then you can obliterate your brain cells."

Perching on the edge of Riko's end table, Lang folded her arms. "Simms owns a palace big enough to house the entire IAA. His docking bay is a world within a world, and at his little party, we met a few of his nearest and dearest." She threw back her head and gazed at the ceiling. "Ay, the man is so connected, orb weavers across the universe watch in amazement."

Taug slurped a long draught from his breather helm, then cleared his throat. "Connected how?"

Uncle Clem limped to a chair and slumped into its embrace. "He has the ear of the three members of the Luxonian Supreme Council, two members of the Ingoti Magisterium, four Ultra Commanders of Sectine, and even a member of the Bhuaci Kestrel were there."

Lang waved her empty glass. "And that's not the worst of it."

Riko wiped fresh sweat from his brow. *Powers above, have mercy!* "It gets worse?"

Lang snatched a bottle from Taug's limp tentacle. "The man has a glorious vision where everyone on Newearth will grow and prosper. He has no favorites. Every race should have everything they want. We'll all become first among equals!" She ripped the cork off the bottle and sloshed another healthy dose into her glass.

Confusion battling with panic, Riko bit his lip. "I don't see how that's so terribly bad."

Faye stared at Riko. "Now you're really acting like a Yurtlun."

Taug chuckled. "It's a mirage as grand as anything Omega ever thought up."

Riko shrugged. "But why? Can't a man have a grand vision and try to make it possible? What's so wrong?"

Listing to one side, Lang swung to Riko's computer console and tapped in a series of commands. The central holoscreen, banked by the back wall, brightened. "Here's why, my friend."

Lang's smiling face appeared larger than life as she toured Simms' Docking Bay. Lifting her arm in a wide arc, she embraced the same vision Simms had poured upon her and Uncle Clem that afternoon. Uncle Clem stood in the back crowd, blinking and smiling like a star-struck fan.

A frown dug its way across Riko's forehead. "You two became his PR reps?"

Uncle Clem leaned forward and buried his face in his hands. "He knows where you live, Riko. He knows about all of us!" Wiping his red-rimmed eyes, Uncle Clem lifted his head and found Taug's focused gaze. "He knows about your lab and your transmissions to the doctor aboard *The Merrimack*. He knows about the mortgage on the café, and"—he swallowed, his eyes swiveling to Faye—"he knows where each of you go every day."

Taug dropped his bottle, and it rolled across the room. His face blanched as his eyes narrowed. "He threatened you—us—I mean?"

Lang tossed back another large gulp and spluttered. "Not at all. He's too smart for that. He just made sure that we know that he knows *everything* about us."

Faye pulled the last bottles from Taug's tentacles and placed them on a side table. "Did he say anything about Cerulean?"

Uncle Clem stood and ambled across the room. He wiggled Lang's glass out of her hand. "Only mentioned that he never wastes an opportunity—and that Cerulean represents a great opportunity for Newearth."

Faye sighed. "He does, indeed."

Waving one hand, Lang leaned on Uncle Clem. "Oh, but the best part. You don't know Simms' motto: 'Want not—waste not.'"

The room fell silent. All eyes focused on Lang.

Lang swept her hand in an arch through the air as if displaying a vision. "Cerulean—a perfect scapegoat for treachery."

His whole body trembling, he glanced at the portrait of his mother. *You couldn't save us then… I can't save us now.* He faced his friends. *But I can stay true, even to the end.*

~~~

Kendra stood by the open front door dressed in a long thick robe and watched Zara plod up the porch steps in the black of night. Exhausted with worry, she tapped her fingers together as she peered down at the girl. "You know what time it is?"

Zara shoved her way across the threshold and pounded into the kitchen.

Kendra followed and slapped on a light. "We had dinner waiting for you hours ago." Leaning on the counter, with one hand propped on her hip, she sighed. "It's considered polite to let people know where you are and when you plan on returning."

Wrenching a bag of crackers from a cabinet, Zara growled low in her throat. "You're not my mother."

A headache threatening, Kendra swooped forward and snatched the cracker bag from Zara's hand. "No, I'm not. I'm your friend. And your mother's friend. You might try showing a little respect!"

Like an angry bee, Zara swung around and gripped Kendra's arms, using more strength than her little body suggested possible. After shaking Kendra hard, she opened her mouth and then bit down on Kendra's arm.

Burning pain shooting through her, Kendra smothered a scream and struggled against the miniature demon, jerking both of them across the room. In their struggle, they banged against the kitchen table, toppling breakfast glasses and sending bowls clattering to the floor.

Her eldest son, Seth, rushed in, his tousled hair standing at odd angles. With a cry, he launched himself
~~~

at Zara and grabbed her around the waist. Before long, Barnabus and Rachel arrived and scrambled into the mêlée. The younger children crowded in the doorway, their eyes wide and frightened.

Zara swung around, facing her opposition and spittle bubbled on her lips.

Kendra flung her arm wide and pointed to the door. "Get out!" Her fury built on fear offered no mercy. "Go and don't come back—ever!"

Diminishing, like a wilting flower, Zara stepped backward, her gaze fixed on Kendra. She flung open the door. As she stepped over the threshold, she transformed into a hideous vulture and screeched, "Traitor!" With a raucous cry, she flew into the night.

Heart wrenched and her body trembling, Kendra leaned against the table. Her children crowded close.

Seth swallowed, heaving deep breaths. "I didn't know she was so strong."

Rachel spat her words as tears spilled down her cheeks. "She's a demon!"

Reflexively, Kendra pulled her sleeve over the bite. "Demon or not, she'll never come back here." Kneeling, she wrapped her children in her good arm as they snuggled closer. "Taug was right—she's too dangerous.

Chapter Twenty-One

-The Merrimack-

Do What You Can

Roux sat on his captain's chair and ignored his gut, twisting in anticipation of finally asking Cerulean's clear-eyed advice. Surrounding him in silence, his shipmates watched. He spoke directly into the intercom. "So, can we come down?"

Cerulean's voice, sounding tinny and weak, filled the bridge. "At your own risk."

Roux glanced at Yelsa, who started to speak, but Roux lifted a finger. "I'll leave Yelsa and the doctor here and bring Bala—"

Cerulean's voice sharpened. "No, leave Bala on board but bring Max and the doctor. We have a patient she might find—interesting."

Jazzmarie, standing next to Max, lifted one eyebrow.

Like one of the good kids, Max waited patiently on the sideline, his hands at his sides.

Unsure how to broach the topic, Roux swung his gaze from the ceiling to Max. "Oh…I also have a prisoner—sort of."

Cerulean's soft chuckle wafted across the bridge. "Bring your prisoner—he'll feel right at home. And Max can work on repairing our ship."

Flummoxed, Roux frowned. "Your ship is broken, sir?"

Cerulean's disembodied voice grew weary. "In more ways than I can count. Sabotage—I think. I'll explain when you get here."

Perturbed, Roux straightened and waved Max over.

Disturbingly, Max barely controlled a grin.

Bala's forlorn body drooped over the communications console.

Yelsa gripped his shoulder. "It's better that we stay on board. We can search for Cosmos."

Bala glowered, his lips extending in a serious pout. "They'll have all the fun."

As Roux swung toward the door, Cerulean's voice rose again. "Bala, don't forget, I'm coming to your house for dinner when we get home."

A new light animating his eyes, Bala straightened. "Yes, sir! I haven't forgotten. Kendra already has the meal planned. And the kids promise not to take you captive this time."

With an eye roll, Roux clapped his hands authoritatively. "Come on; let's go." He gestured to Jazzmarie. "Could you rouse Chas? Despite the fact that he's been sleeping for the last three days, he's coming with us."

Jazzmarie clasped Max's hand as she entered the lift. "If I can't wake him, Max will carry him to the shuttle. Won't you, darling?"

Shaking his head, Roux entered the lift, waved goodbye to Yelsa and Bala, and intoned, "That'll do, doctor."

—Mirage-Reborn—

Roux stepped off the shuttle landing platform, strode forward, and gripped Cerulean's arm with no plans to ever let it go. "Good to see you, old friend." Leaning in, he ignored the crowd milling around the small grey ship and muttered in Cerulean's ear, "Leadership is killing my desire to live."

Pulling back, Cerulean gestured to the crowd, a weariness in his eyes. "Welcome to Mirage-Reborn." His gaze swept to the mountainous figure next to Roux. "Chas? The prisoner, I believe?" He sighed. "Well, I have no desire to put you in jail, so you might enjoy a tour about town instead." He nodded to a dark-haired woman hovering on the edge of the crowd. "Grace, would you show our guest around?"

Grace's eyes widened as she stepped closer, stopped, and bit her lip.

Chas grinned.

She smiled shyly. The two ambled away.

Clare drew near and nodded formally at Roux. "Thank you for coming. Though I still think you would have done better to locate Cosmos."

Attempting to hide his annoyance, Roux lifted his hands in a gesture of self-defense. "We can only prioritize according to the information we get. From the sound of it, this whole planet is in immediate danger." He shrugged. "Besides, we might do better working together."

Clare glanced at Cerulean, frowned, and then suddenly switched focus.

Roux's nerves twitched. *She's not happy with him…doesn't trust him?*

Approaching Jazzmarie, Clare's tone warmed. "Doctor? We need your medical expertise—if you'd be so kind."

Jazzmarie bowed, her flowered skirt rippling in a light breeze. "Always glad to be of assistance." She turned to Max. "Come on, Maximan. Let's not keep the good people waiting."

Feeling very much like unwanted baggage, Roux followed behind.

Clare led the way to a stately white house on a hill

with a wide porch wrapped around three sides. Jazzmarie and Max followed, and Cerulean took up the rear. Roux maneuvered to his side.

Ambling along Main Street toward a large house about a stone's throw away and set as the dominant feature on the landscape, Roux took in the small-town scenery. He cast his gaze at Cerulean. *Looks all right but he doesn't feel right.* Then it hit him. *He's not Luxonian anymore. Is he...human?* Horror shuddered through Roux.

Once inside the elaborate main hall, Jazzmarie swung her arms in an arc. She sucked in a deep breath and exhaled dramatically. "This is magnificent!"

A large fireplace anchored one end of the room, while oversized leather furniture, oak end tables, embroidered carpets, hanging tapestries, and myriad candles, flowers, paintings, and statues decorated every inch of available space.

Coming up from behind, Cerulean took the lead. "You haven't seen anything yet." He maneuvered her to a side room as tastefully, but not so densely, decorated. A single four-poster bed butted against the back wall, and two figures sat near—one, an old, hunched man, and the other, a beautiful, stately woman.

After coming through the doorway, Jazzmarie froze. "Justine?"

Entering the room last, Roux rubbed his chin, one eyebrow rising. *What's this? Love enkindled or endangered?*

Max halted on the threshold.

Justine rose to her feet and faced them.

Squaring his shoulders like a man collecting his nerve, Max strode right up to her.

Justine's eyes almost appeared to glimmer. Tears? *She can't—can she?*

Max wrapped his arms around her, hugging her tightly.

A whimper slipped from Justine as she responded, flinging her arms around him, a drowning victim grasping a lifeline.

Amazed, Roux grinned. "Love, if ever I saw it. And between androids! I'm mighty curious to meet their creator—Omega must be talented beyond measure."

Still standing in the middle of the room, Jazzmarie stared at the scene, transfixed.

Cerulean cleared his throat and gestured toward the bed. "Your patient, Doctor."

Pulling back from Max, Justine refocused on the prostrate figure.

Jazzmarie walked stiff-legged and stopped before the bed.

Cerulean nodded to the old man in the chair. "Abbas, this is Doctor Jazzmarie, one of Newearth's most renowned physicians."

Hunched in his chair, Abbas nodded shakily, his smile faltering. "It is good of you to come. But there's nothing to be done. The Cresta know their business too well."

Apparently recovering her senses, Jazzmarie passed her hand lightly across Omega's forehead, down the side of his face, and onto his chest. She turned and glared at Cerulean. "He's not human—so, why is he still in human form?"

Abbas wrung his hands together. "He probably thought it was amusing to be charged with mass murder and wanted to play the part of a human supplicant appealing to blind justice—while facing the Cresta Ingal."

Stepping up behind the doctor, Max frowned. "He's a mass murderer?"

Jazzmarie waved Max aside. "Not now." She leaned

toward Abbas and dropped her voice. "What did the Crestas do—exactly?"

Abbas' gaze wandered to his son. "They found him guilty—on behalf of all of our kind. They knew he wasn't personally responsible, but since thousands of Crestonians died, they wanted to send a clear message. Destroying his mind in a way we've never seen before accomplished that mightily. Crestas never forget, and they certainly never forgive."

Jazzmarie flicked a stray hair out of her face and turned to Max. "Return to the ship and bring my portable medical kit—sensors, scanners—everything." She returned to the patient. "What's his name?"

Cerulean stepped closer. "Omega. The founder of Mirage-Reborn."

Profound grief filled Roux. *Why do we do this to each other? For what end?*

As she moved past, Jazzmarie nudged Roux. "Once my things are brought down, you can return to *The Merrimack* and continue your merry chase."

Roux glared at Cerulean. "I heard that you were in the midst of a civil war!"

Cerulean took a step backward. "Abbas and Omega are home now. It's their war. Not mine."

His mind nearly numb with confusion, Roux tried to focus on Abbas. "But since Omega can't help, will you defeat Cosmos and save Newearth?"

Abbas sighed and refocused on his son. "Cosmos hardly matters now. If we do this to each other—we're already destroyed."

Roux looked to Cerulean and, to his horror, saw only agreement.

Bala leapt from his chair, his eyes wide as saucers.

Yelsa jerked around and faced him. “What? Has she devoured another planet?”

Crouching over the communications console, Bala shook his head. “Zara attacked my wife—bit her and—Oh, Lord!”

Yelsa tromped over to Bala’s side and glared at the screen. “*Who* is Zara?”

“Justine’s little girl—one of Omega’s creations.”

“Sounds like a monster.”

Bala tapped the console, cold sweat breaking over his brow.

Yelsa grabbed his hand. “What’re you doing?”

“I’ve got to tell Roux—we need to leave.” Dragging his fingers through his hair, he groaned, “Justine will want to come. Zara is her responsibility.”

Yelsa gripped Bala by the shoulders. “We’ve got bigger monsters to catch—Cosmos is out there—wandering free—getting hungry!”

Bala pulled free. “We can’t do anything until she comes in range of Newearth. We might as well head that direction.” He pleaded with his eyes. “I need to go home. I’ve got a wife, seven kids, and a little demon on the loose.”

After pounding back to her station, Yelsa tapped through a series of commands. “You might be right. Cosmos is back on her original course and heading for Newearth. If we hurry, we can intercept her.”

Desperate hope ignited into flame, tensing Bala’s muscles. “You won’t stop me if I contact Roux and suggest we leave immediately?”

Yelsa lifted her hands in acquiescence. “No argument here. Go ahead.”

The bridge door slid open, and Max marched in. “I’m retrieving the doctor’s—” His gaze shifted from Yelsa to Bala. “What’s wrong?”

The engines hummed at a higher pitch.

Max tilted his head, listening. “Are we going somewhere?”

“Something doesn’t sound right.” Yelsa shoved by Max and entered the lift. “I’m going to check the engines before we leave.”

Waving in dismissal, Bala returned to his communications console. “We’re heading back to Newearth.” He glanced at Max. “Everything okay down below? Cerulean keeping everyone out of trouble?”

Max stepped up to Bala, his gaze sweeping over the monitors. “Omega is in some kind of trance—retaliation for an unjust punishment inflicted on Crestar ages ago. Unrest appears to be building to a flash point, but Cerulean says it’s not his problem anymore.” Max slid onto a chair across from a bank of ship monitors, his expression blanker than usual. “I’m confused.”

Bala harrumphed. “We’ve all got problems.” He tapped the console and leaned toward the microphone. “Roux—can you hear me?”

Justine’s voice rose. “Just a minute, I’ll get him.”

His anxiety levels still rising, Bala tapped his fingers and blew air between his teeth.

Max stood, his shoulders slack. “I must get the doctor’s equipment.”

Hardly seeing him, Bala nodded, while his stomach did summersaults. “Fine.”

As the door slid shut behind Max, Roux’s voice rose into the air. “Bala? Something wrong?”

Bala hunched over the console. “Well, sir, it seems

that there's a significant problem on Newearth—Justine's daughter Zara has run amok, and, oh, lucky us, Cosmos is heading toward home again." He sucked in a deep breath. "Sir, Yelsa and I would like permission to leave orbit within the hour and head home to Newearth."

A crashing sound came over the intercom, as if someone had just kicked a chair across the room.

Bala bit his lip. "Sir?"

Roux's voice roared onto the bridge. "Is Max bringing the doctor's things down?"

"Yes, sir."

"Good. As soon as he gets her medical equipment set up, I'm coming up and—"

His nerves twitching, Bala eked out, "Yes, sir?"

"I plan on wringing your neck—right after I have a few words with Yelsa."

Like a man bracing himself for death, Bala nodded in wide-eyed composure. "And Justine—will she be joining us?"

Justine's voice rang clear and true. "You're bloody right, I will. Just wait till I get my hands on Taug!"

Bala sank onto his chair, his fingers hovering over the directional console.

—Mirage-Reborn—

Cerulean nudged Roux into the café booth and motioned for the waitress. "Two cups of black tea—extra strong—and some warm rolls."

Once seated in a booth, Roux hunched over the table and hissed his words at Cerulean. "I don't have time for this. Bala and Yelsa are so anxious to go, they wouldn't notice if they left me behind."

Surprisingly relaxed, Cerulean maintained his composure. *Am I dead inside?* He shook the thought away. "You'd be surprised what you have time for." He stared at his hands. "I'm really human now—you know that?" He chuckled. "Abbas saved my life by imprisoning me in a human body. I should be delighted. I've always felt more human than Luxonian. And now, I don't even need the Luxonian sun. Of course, I can't move at the speed of light, and I feel all the aches and pains of human flesh." He leaned in. "But perhaps, it's better this way."

Roux glared. "If you've got a moral to impart—just spit it out."

Cerulean shrugged and sat back. "I just did."

The waitress slid two steaming mugs in front of the men and laid a basket of warm rolls with a side dish of butter on the table. She smiled. "Anything else you folks need, just call."

Roux flashed a smile.

Cerulean nodded and gestured toward the food. "Vera and Lucius invited me over for dinner tonight. I'm saving my appetite."

Roux rubbed his forehead. "You've lost your mind as well as your Luxonian nature, haven't you?"

Cerulean clasped his hands contemplatively. "The rolls are delicious, not as good as Eve's homemade bread, but few can compare to her as a cook or a woman."

"Thanks for the stroll down memory lane. I was worried. Now I'm depressed." Grimacing, Roux ripped a roll in two, slathered butter on one end, and took a bite. He chewed and waved at Cerulean, as if encouraging him to say something.

Cerulean took a sip of tea and grinned. "Don't waste time worrying about me. I don't care anymore."

In mid-chew, Roux froze. He swallowed hard. "What?"

Cerulean nodded to indicate the murmuring café crowd and then motioned toward the window, indicating the bustling passersby.

"Ever since my father first brought me to Oldearth, I was smitten by humanity. I fell in love, not just with humanity but with the fragility of life itself. Everything mattered. Every fight for justice was my fight. Every call for help called to me."

Roux's shoulders slumped as he leaned back, his voice dropping low. "Has that changed?"

Taking one last slurp of his tasteless tea, Cerulean shoved the cup away. "I don't care anymore. Lux—Oldearth—Newearth—Mirage-Reborn, beings everywhere. It's all the same. Everyone fights for control, and innocent people suffer. No one ever grows beyond their own selfish vision." His eyes glimmered. "I guess I've lost faith."

"Faith in what?"

"In everyone."

Roux's hands clenched. He leaned forward. "Well, sorry, but you can't. I need you! I'm in love with a suicidal Bhuaci. I can't maintain control of my crew, and a monster is about to eat Newearth. I came here to save you—and now you tell me there's nothing to save." Jumping to his feet, Roux slapped his napkin on the table. "I'm heading back to my ship."

Cerulean rose and reached for Roux's shoulder.

Roux pulled away.

"Do what you can, while you can, Roux. But there's always another problem to solve, a new victim to help, another sad fact to face." He stepped away from the booth and waved to the crowd. "You'll die trying to help—but it never really makes any difference."

Roux flung back his shoulders and shook his head. "You didn't lose your *faith*, Cerulean. You've lost your humanity."

—The Merrimack—

Roux slumped onto the captain's chair and considered the bright mass of stars on the view screen. Cerulean's words rang in his ears. Depression settled in for a long stay.

Bala manned the communications console, his face tight and anxious.

Yelsa stood over the directional console. She looked at Roux. "The course is set—we're ready, right?"

Roused into some sort of action, Roux sat up. "Where's Chas?"

Bala mumbled, "The big guy is staying below—helping to reconfigure *The Summons*."

The door slid open, and Clare stepped onto the bridge. An uncertain smile wavered on her lips as her gaze zeroed in on Bala. "Aren't you going to welcome me aboard?"

Wide-eyed, Bala jumped to his feet and scrambled across the bridge. He stretched out his arms as if wanting to give her a hug and then abruptly smacked her in the arm. "Finally, we'll have some fun. I haven't beaten anyone in chess for ages."

Clare smirked. "Been getting thrashed by your betters, have you?"

Flapping his arms, Bala returned to his console. "No one dares to play with me. Too intimidated."

Clare grinned, her natural beauty, so often hidden under a frown, shining through.

The ache in his chest relaxing just a touch, Roux waved to an empty station. "You can track space chatter, Clare. See what's going on around us, like the good detective you are."

Bala slid into place and swiveled his chair in Clare's direction. "Just think! It'll be like old times. You'll tell me what to do—and I won't listen."

Strangely amused by what should have annoyed him, Roux controlled a chuckle and nodded to Yelsa. "Take us out of orbit, Yelsa."

Yelsa's hand hovered over the console. "What about Max?"

Roux clasped his fingers steeple style. "He's staying with Cerulean. May be just the medicine that man needs."

Yelsa lifted one eyebrow and finished her command sequence. "And Justine?"

"She is taking his quarters. Said to offer her apologies. She's not feeling well." Roux didn't bother trying to explain since everyone knew the truth. Even an android could have a bad day.

The ship's engines purred to life, and the ship sped into the stars.

Bala leaned toward Clare. "Why'd Cerulean have you come aboard?"

Darting a glance at Roux, Clare sunk her head on her hands and frowned. "I don't know. He seemed confused. When I left, he said, 'Goodbye, Anne.'"

His mood plunging over a cliff, Roux closed his eyes and desperately tried to remember what home looked like.

Chapter Twenty-Two

–Mirage-Reborn–

Save the Innocent

Max sat in the red café booth and peered from his hands to Cerulean, and then he glanced around. He didn't scream, "Help!"—though every centimeter of him wanted to. He had barely had a chance to talk with Justine before she boarded the ship. She had stepped away with only one backward glance. Their gazes had lingered as the world rushed around them. Now he faced Cerulean, a friend who felt very much like a stranger.

A petite woman in a blue uniform hurried forward with a pad and pen ready. Wisps of blond hair escaped a tight bun, and black eyeliner heightened the shadows under her eyes, adding dreariness to her weary face. But to Max's surprise, instead of intoning the menu, she chirped an introduction. "Hi! My name is Calinda, but everybody calls me Cal. What'll you boys have today? Blow my socks off!"

Max snuck a look at the waitress' feet.

Leather sandals encased rainbow socks, her toes wiggling merrily. They announced a happy-go-lucky spirit looking for excitement in a couple of fun customers.

Max hated to disappoint, but he rarely deviated from his usual order: hamburger, fries, and a cherry soda. Surprise tingled over his body when he asked for a Reuben sandwich, onion rings, and black coffee.

Cerulean stared at his hands resting on the blood-red tabletop. "Burger, fries, and water."

Beaming, the waitress spun around and zipped off with her marching orders. "Be right back, boys!"

Max shrugged. "Apparently, the pen and pad are just for decoration."

Cerulean flexed his fingers.

Tilting his head, Max tried to interpret the obscure action. *Preparing to massage tight muscles?*

"Have you ever killed anyone?"

Or strangle an unwary victim? Max glanced around for the waitress.

No one about the place. Most tables stood forlorn and empty at two in the afternoon.

Bracing himself, Max faced Cerulean. "Not with my hands, if that's what you mean."

Cerulean leaned back, throwing one arm along the back of the booth. Calm. Composed. After taking in the view, he dropped his gaze on Max. "But you have killed people. On purpose."

Horrified at his sudden lack of control, Max's vision blurred. *Tears or was his ability to focus compromised?* He nodded, though his mind swam with perfect-recall memories—conflicts where he had blasted the enemy from his employer's vicinity. A good job but not a *good* job.

Cerulean kept his gaze level, as they had their man-to-man chat about murder.

Max gripped the mug. "At the time, I wasn't aware that I was killing anyone. I followed orders. Back in those days, I was more machine than man. Survival instinct ruled since I needed the job. I eliminated dangerous people."

"It didn't bother you?"

Max ran his fingers through his hair as he'd seen done a thousand times by humans under stress, but the motion offered not a particle of comfort.

Cal sauntered up with a pot of steaming coffee and a glass of water with a slice of lemon floating on top.

“Here ya go.” She set the glass on top of a napkin in front of Cerulean and poured Max’s coffee. She nudged the creamer and sugar in his direction. “The burger and sandwich will be right up. Cook was napping.” She dropped her voice to a conspiratorial whisper. “We don’t say nothing. He’s a good sort. Up before dawn to get this place ready every morning.”

Max considered Cerulean. “Do you want to ask her if she’s ever killed—”

Cerulean choked. “If she did, it was unknowingly. Drowsy cook and all.”

Cal’s eyes widened. “Well, this conversation just got interesting! But you know, Quinn doesn’t have my vote, so I won’t tell.” She spun around and disappeared into the kitchen.

“Bet she’ll tell the cook that we’re up to no good.” Cerulean took a long draught and chewed a sliver of ice.

Max took a sip of coffee, licked his lips, and poured in half the creamer pot and three spoonfuls of sugar. He stirred, sipped again, and nodded. Culinary success took the gloom off any conversation. “Are you thinking of killing someone?”

“I’d like to kill Quinn. But I’ve never killed anyone. I don’t have it in me.”

Max considered this notion. “You’re human now. Humans kill other humans. So, technically, it is possible for you to kill Quinn.”

“Thanks.”

The ironic tone was not lost on Max. “I’m just saying that it is possible. Not that you want to. Or that you should. I’ve never met Quinn, but Justine told me his background.” Max took another enjoyable sip of coffee. “But she’s more concerned about you.”

“Me?”

“You called Clare Anne when she left.”

"Did I?" Cerulean shrugged and peered out the window. "I know how Anne felt. Trapped. Being a devoted human, she couldn't leave Earth. Her whole existence revolved around the people who lived there. In the end, was she doomed or reconciled?" He met Max's gaze. "I couldn't save her."

"You couldn't make her Luxonian the way Abbas made you human." A sudden thought jumped out at him. If Abbas made a Luxonian human, could Abbas make an android…? Max wondered if his chest was caving in.

Clasping his hands, Cerulean sighed heavily.

Using every particle of self-control he could muster, Max redirected his thoughts. "So, you think *you* failed? That killing Quinn might even the score and save a planet full of desperate people?"

A quick shake of the head, and Cerulean dropped the conversation.

The waitress trotted over with a tray carefully balanced on one arm and a coffee pot in her free hand. She set the pot on the table, slipped the plates into place, and grinned. "Cook wants to know what you two are plotting and if he can be in on the action." She refilled Max's cup.

Max poured the last drops of creamer into his steaming cup and blinked at the empty creamer pot. He knew just how it felt.

~~~

Grace stood before the spaceship's open bay door and stared at the hulking giant in front of her. She swallowed a scream rising in her throat.

Vera patted Grace's arm and stretched on her tiptoes,
~~~

leaning toward Grace's ear. "He's harmless. Really. Just rather large. Not bad."

Chas grinned. "Yeah. At first sight, everyone is afraid of me. But once they get to know me, they push me around like an idiot. 'Cause I kinda am. Sometimes anyway."

Hysterics warred with amusement inside Grace. Amusement won. She snorted.

Vera dropped flatfooted to the ground.

Grace glanced aside. "Sorry. I'm not usually so edgy. Just, with so much going on…" She grimaced. "I need to shut up. You just lost your brother. I have nothing to complain about."

Chas shrugged. "People always find something to complain about. But it's a waste of breath." He patted *The Summon's* doorframe. "Now this beauty just needs a bit of tender loving care, and she'll be as spry as a Bhuaci dancing girl."

Vera blinked, a scowl forming on her brow.

Grace laughed. "We'll leave you to it then, Mr. Chas. Captain Roux said that you have a knack for fixing machines." She shrugged. "We have mechanics and scientists here, but no one wants to leave. So, fixing a ship is low priority."

Chas stroked his chin. "I wondered about that." He dug a datapad out of his oversized pocket. "Nice place and all. But still, people get bored. I always like something new and exciting." His brows danced, his eyes inviting. "Don't you?"

With an arm yank, Vera redirected Grace's attention. "We've got to go. Lucius is waiting. And you have to talk with your dad—remember?"

Grace's spirits dropped from heady heights. Her gaze lingered on Chas before she turned away.

The large, muscle-bound, soft-spoken human focused

his attention on the datapad. With a polite wave, he stepped inside the ship, never looking back.

Harrumphing, Grace met Vera's impatient gaze. "All right. Let's go. I suppose I'd better find out what Dad has been up to."

The two hiked back to town.

The blacksmith shop's large double doors stood wide open, allowing a breeze to break the stultifying heat of the central forge. A huge anvil stood to the side while a variety of hammers, tongs, vices, chisels, and wire brushes were laid out in neat rows or hung from hooks along the wall.

Lucius stepped outside his shop, sweaty and flushed. He grinned as they approached.

Slowing her pace, Grace offered a polite wave.

Vera trotted right up to Lucius, her eyes sparkling.

Well, she's not shy. Not anymore, anyway.

Lucius awarded her with a welcoming grin.

Annoyed, Grace left the two love birds and trotted to her house. *Hers?* The pronoun lied. Nothing was *hers.* Not even her life. *A fake reality for people who can't—* She shook herself from her negative thoughts, climbed the porch steps, and stepped inside the foyer.

Silence.

"Dad?"

"That you, honey?"

Habitual anxiety twisting her stomach, Grace hurried into the living room. *What kind of mood is he in today?*

Old Man Nelson sat ensconced in a large recliner with his feet up, looking like a child's toy tucked safely out of the way, a book in hand, his gaze fixed on her.

Grace plastered on a smile. "You're doing okay? I went to see if the new guy needed anything to fix *The Summons*. Quite a ship! Never seen anything like it before. Wouldn't be something to fly off—"

Old Man Nelson reared his head. "What's wrong with you, Grace? You've never babbled before."

Stung, Grace stiffened. "Oh, sorry. Had too much coffee at the café. That's where I met Vera. She had to go check on this guy, Chas, a human guy, like us, just a lot bigger. She dragged me along for safety or something. Never seen such a man. He's huge. I mean—"

"Grace!" Her father leaned forward as if planning to spring out of the chair.

Grace pressed her lips together and clamped her hands till the tips went white. "Sorry. I'll heat dinner. I have a casserole ready."

Her dad's comment, "You do that," followed her to the door. A memory tripped her steps. She stopped and spoke to the open doorway. "Vera said that Quinn came by."

"So?"

Grace turned around, her knees knocking and her heart clenching. "Just wondering what he wanted. He's not well-liked. People say that he set the fire that killed Vera's brother, and then he shot that innocent guy—"

Her father's glare could still intimidate her. "Innocent? He was an imposter, an Ingot pretending to be human. You know what Abbas always says: We have to be honest about who we are—orphans, failures, addicts." He shrugged, his gaze dropping. "Even *murderers*. Doesn't matter. The guy was trouble." He clasped his hands and smiled sweetly, meeting Grace's gaze. "Like you, he has a duty to protect me."

Her throat closing, Grace fought panic. She couldn't breathe. She stared out the window.

Down the block, the jailhouse door opened, and Quinn stood in the doorway. His gaze darted from side to side, angry and alert.

A dead calm settled inside Grace. *I know who I am.* She looked at her father. "I'll get supper on the table."

"That's my girl. Once all these foreigners leave, we'll go back to our regular lives. Omega will get better, and Quinn will settle down. You'll see."

Across the street, Vera and Lucius stepped out of the blacksmith shop hand in hand. The slim LuKan grinned like a schoolgirl as Lucius swung her arm playfully. Happiness incarnate.

Not far away, Quinn's eyes, burning with grievous hate, followed them.

Grace recognized it, and sadness filled her.

~~~

Jazzmarie held Omega's hand as he lay on his plush bed, his eyes squeezed shut in a perpetual grimace. She felt nothing. *I'm a doctor, after all. Professional detachment is a good thing.*

She reviewed what she knew, shoving aside guilt about what she did not feel. Roux had told her about Cerulean's illness and how Abbas had healed him by transforming him into a human state for his stay on Mirage-Reborn.

Like most of Newearth citizens, she already knew about Omega's part to play in Justine's trial. Thankfully, *Newearth News Reports* had obligingly filled in Taug's history as the one to awaken Justine in order to manage his father's half-breed creation. And Taug's little friend Faye was actually the defacto Bhuaci leader on Newearth. *Surprise, surprise. They are devious, as I always suspected.*

Recently, she reviewed the historical records detailing
~~~

the Mystery Race's attack on Crestar. *Such horror!*

She patted Omega's limp hand and sighed. *The Crestonians' revenge will merely make one more juicy tidbit for reporters and historians alike.*

Being apprised of the basic facts didn't offer any current assistance in saving Omega's life. If Abbas could not save his son, she had little reason to think that she, a mere human doctor, could.

Abbas paced before the huge fireplace. Though appearing elderly with white hair fanning over his shoulders, a grey beard sprouting from his chin, and watery sky-blue eyes, his firm steps suggested hidden strength.

Flames licked enormous logs in the hearth, but the temperature remained mild.

Her datapad buzzed. She glanced at it.

Taug?

She should've guessed. With a professional nod to a young Bhuac assistant standing at a respectful distance, she laid Omega's hand on his chest and stepped to the farthest corner of the room. She tapped the speaker. "What do you want? I'm in the middle of something."

Taug's face beamed from the screen. A happy pod ready to impart good news. "She's heading here, and I have the perfect solution already."

Amazed that she'd completely forgotten about Cosmos, Jazzmarie blinked. "Of course, you do."

Taug's usually bulbous eyes narrowed considerably. "What are *you* doing?"

Unashamed, Jazzmarie chuckled at her professional advantage. "You'd kill to be in my shoes right now."

"Your shoes would probably destroy my will to live."

Swiveling, Jazzmarie turned the datapad's camera toward Omega's inert form lying on the bed and Abbas pacing at the other end. "I'm trying to save two members of the Mystery Race. Really, I am hoping to save Omega's life and his father's heart." She turned the datapad around, grinning delightedly at Taug's wide, bewildered eyes.

Taug's pasty face drained of every trace of pink highlighting. All bubbles ceased. A low hum rose.

A stunning thought raced through Jazzmarie's mind. "Oh, but wait! You could save him. Crestonian that you are, you could find out what they did and how best to heal the injury."

Taug's gaze strayed from her face to something over her shoulder.

Cold flowing over her, Jazzmarie glanced aside.

Abbas stared at Taug's image on the miniature screen, his jaw firm and a hint of menace in his eyes. "Can you save my son?"

Taug glared at Jazzmarie. "Newearth is about to be attacked, and you're assisting an enemy that murdered a third of my people?"

Jazzmarie rubbed her face, weariness enveloping her. This was getting complicated. "Transports are clearing Newearth before Cosmos gets there. It's not like *you'll* die unless you stay and get eaten. You said that you have the solution—so use it! As for me,"—she glanced at Abbas—"I'm a doctor. I must do my duty and save the innocent." She shrugged. "Hardly the case with Crestonians."

Taug harrumphed.

The screen blackened.

Jazzmarie faced Abbas. "Don't worry. I'll find a way to save your son."

Glaring red fire, Abbas poked Jazzmarie. "Get him back."

Jolted by his daring to touch her in such an unfriendly manner, irritation sizzled through her. "No one orders me around!"

Max speed-walked across the room.

How long has he been watching? Jazzmarie's mood shifted. She winked at Max.

Clearly in no mood for romance, Max stopped next to Abbas and faced her. "Do what he asks, Doctor."

Furious at being flouted, Jazzmarie recalled Justine's and Max's devoted gazes. "On one condition, Maximan." *You can't offer me a future, well then, I'll just have to make one for myself.*

Chapter Twenty-Three

-Newearth-

Maybe Mom Was Wrong

Riko, in his blue uniform pants and white shirt, flushed hot with embarrassment and stared at his uncle, wondering for the umpteenth time what family DNA really did for a person.

The immaculate kitchen stood silent as his loyal but neglected cook sat lounging with his chair tilted against the back wall, his eyes closed, and his feet resting on an overturned scrub bucket.

Dressed for comfort in matching blue sweatshirt and sweatpants, Uncle Clem ambled up to the sleeping man clad in a chef's uniform and nudged him on the shoulder. "Go home, Mickle, and pack your stuff. Everyone is leaving Newearth."

The culinary master opened his weary eyes, rubbed his face, and sat up. His feet hit the floor with a thud. "Way I see it, we've got as good a chance here as out therc."

Tapping his foot, Riko wanted nothing more than to clear the room and consider his options in peace. He glanced from his cook to his uncle and didn't attempt to cover the sneer in his voice. "Show him the way to Simms' new docking bay. I hear he's taking desperate cases."

Uncle Clem rolled his eyes and snorted. "He'll certainly take everything a desperate person could offer to get a room in one of his luxury liners." He nudged the cook again. "Be reasonable, man. You've got a wife and kids. Don't take chances. Get on one of the Inter-Alien standard ships. You'll be safe once you get out of orbit."

With a bedraggled sigh, Mickle stood and stretched. "I don't see why I have to go while you two get to stay."

Clasping his chef's shoulder, Riko led him to the door. "I own the place. Plus, we're expendable. To your family, you're not."

Mickle met Riko's gaze, shrugged, and extended his hand. "Soon as the planet-eating beast is gone, I'll be back. Count on it."

Riko winked. "Just don't share any of your culinary secrets with the competition while you're away."

Muttering, "They'd hafta kill me first." Mickle shuffled into the bright light of a cold winter day.

With a shudder, Riko shut the door and faced his uncle. "Now that's done, let's get this place secure."

"From a planet-eating beast?" Uncle Clem waved the thought away. "No, we have more important matters to discuss. Like whether you and Lang should get married in the spring or the fall."

Stopped in his tracks, Riko stared at his uncle. "You don't seriously think that Lang cares about me, do you?" Blood roared in his ears as his whole body warmed at the thought. "In *that* way."

Uncle Clem trotted into the café dining room, sidled over to Taug's lab door, and cocked his head. "He in there?"

Riko shrugged. "Don't think so. Faye said that they were going to see Kendra. More trouble with Justine's kid. I wish they'd just let her be. She doesn't mean any harm."

Dropping onto a stool, Uncle Clem tapped his fingers on the counter, plunking out a tune. "The way I see it, Lang likes you, but she knows it's impossible—you being Uanyi and her being an Ingot. She likes me, too, as a friend, an uncle, you know." He lowered his brows. "But she's lonely. A man like Simms, now, he could entice a lonely heart."

A laugh burst from Riko before he could contain it. "Simms? That recycled human? He's got more replacement parts than the decrepit ship Cerulean took to Mirage-Reborn."

Uncle Clem hefted himself to his feet and stopped in front of Riko, glaring meaningfully. "Lang is an Ingot. She knows all about replacement parts. Been doing it all her life. She's also ambitious, spirited, and real lonely."

Waving his arms in the air, unconcerned that his voice was rising several decibels, Riko roared, "What do you want me to do? Romance Lang so she doesn't get cozy with some vainglorious human?" He chuckled as a new thought knocked Clem's theory to shambles. "Besides, she hates the guy."

The front door opened, and the bells jangled.

Hardly dressed for the weather, Taug shuffled inside with cautionary glances in every direction.

Riko glanced at the closed lab door. "Did you forget how to use the other door? Or do you want meal service?"

His head jutting forward, Taug scuttled across the room—an awkward spy on an important mission. "My door is being watched. Faye sent me over."

Riko folded his arms over his chest. *For this, I can hardly wait.*

Uncle Clem leaned in.

Taug eyed the kitchen. "Though, considering the circumstances, a refreshment might help. Might you have a little Green on hand? I'm parched."

Exasperated, Riko motioned toward the kitchen. "This had better be important."

Uncle Clem hurried to Taug's side. "Any news about Cosmos?"

Taug shrugged. "She's still heading this way, but I've

got a perfect solution. If only I could get a certain doctor to use her influence with the Cresta Ingal, traitor though she is. The High Tribunal will agree to anything the Ingal suggests. And the Ingal will do anything to get an upper hand in the Inter-Alien Alliance. Besides, it would do much to atone her guilt in aiding the enemy."

Uncle Clem slapped himself on the cheek and then held the door wide to allow for Taug's girth. "I have no idea what you're talking about, but it always comes down to politics, doesn't it?"

In the kitchen, Riko slammed the freezer door shut with his foot, lugged a gallon bucket to the counter, and then snatched a tall glass off a shelf. "That's the way in the real world." He waved a large spoon at Taug. "What do you want from the Ingal that you can't get yourself?"

"The good doctor and I came up with a paralyzing formula that should stop Cosmos in her tracks. Problem is, how to administer it. She's got a thick hide, that one."

Uncle Clem slumped down in the chair vacated by the cook. "Back to square one."

"Not really. The Bhuac aboard *The Merrimack* came up with a solution, but no one else wanted to try it."

Riko poured a foamy mixture into a glass and squeezed lemon juice on top of it. "Why not?"

"They would've had to drive straight into Cosmos' mouth to administer the paralyzing agent."

Riko handed the drink to Taug. "Can't think why no one wanted to try that."

Uncle Clem shrugged. "You could just send up a bot with the agent."

One tentacle held high to stall the conversation, Taug poured the drink into his breathing helm. He slurped and sighed, a smile spreading across his face. Then he shrugged. "No bot we have is powerful enough. You know the Inter-Alliance regulations on that."

“So, send up a whole bunch.” Clem’s eyes lit up, dreamily. “It’d be amazing—a million innocent bots surrendering their existence to save Newearth.”

After frowning at his uncle, Riko leaned on the counter. “If only Omega or Abbas would come to the rescue. Surely the Mystery Race could destroy her outright.”

Taug poured the rest of the liquid into his breather helm and slurped with gusto. He sighed and held up a tentacle, a proclamation ready. “The Crestas have learned a lot from the Mystery Race. We don’t need them anymore.”

Uncle Clem’s jaw dropped.

Riko jogged over to Taug and stared him in the eye. “What are you saying? We’re saved?”

~~~

Faye hated to get angry, but irritation bubbled from deep inside like lava from a volcano. *Where is Taug?* She glanced out her apartment window and chewed her lip.

The sun had set, leaving an orange glow on the stark horizon. Black birds soared from naked trees in Eden’s Garden, an ill-named park situated across the street. Few autoskimmers hovered along the streets, while a couple of pedestrians hustled along the sidewalk, their survival instincts demanding that they get somewhere warm as soon as possible.

She had left Kendra eating a quiet supper with the kids, though her bandaged arm stood out like an Interventionist at a children’s party. Finding no sign of
~~~

Zara, she had sent Taug to the Breakfastnook to discover Wendell's whereabouts. Her only hope to quell the budding monster lay in the hands of a simple-minded Ingot.

She tapped her datapad again.

No response.

A chill raced over Faye. *What if Zara tries to kill Taug?*

Without another coherent thought, she shoved open her window, climbed on the ledge, morphed into an eagle, and flew into the bronze sky.

~~~

Faye reached the Breakfastnook in good time, aided by a strong north wind. She alighted on the bench situated against the brick wall, tapped her beak against the picture window, and peered inside.

Taug lounged with not one—but two!—empty glasses before him, his limp tentacles testifying to his current state of inebriation.

Riko and Uncle Clem appeared to be sharing an amusing story.

Controlling the urge to morph into an oversized gorilla, tear the café door off its hinges, and stomp inside, Faye tapped the glass with her beak.

With a startled expression, Riko looked over.

If intense golden eyes and a sharp beak had anything to say, they said it now.

Riko jumped from his seat, scurried to the door, and jerked it open.

Morphing back to her usual form, now dressed for the weather in a black sweater dress, a thick coat, and tall
~~~

boots, Faye stood before him in all her Bhuaci beauty. "Evening, Riko. May I join the party?"

Riko swallowed, cleared his throat, and peered over his shoulder.

Faye swept past him.

"It's not a party, really. Taug came over, saying something about—"

Taug struggled to his feet, a wide grin hovering on his lips. "My sweet dear! I was just about to ask them about her."

Uncle Clem straightened. "About *her?* Who are we talking about?"

Faye marched up to Taug and clamped her hands on her hips. Every millimeter of her small form bristled. "You do realize that a dangerous misfit is on the loose? It's a miracle that Kendra escaped with a minor injury, and poor, innocent Wendell might be fighting for his life!"

His attention caught, Riko strode forward and clasped Faye's arm. "Wait up. What about Wendell?"

"The little monster attacked Kendra and ran, or flew, out the house. Wendell is the only person she trusts. She may order him around, but she really thinks—"

Uncle Clem waved his datapad in the air. "Stop!" He blushed when all heads turned his way. "I just want to mention that *The Merrimack* is heading home with Justine. She can take care of the Zara brat."

Riko scowled. "She's not a brat. Just troubled. Thinks that she can save people from evil characters"—he pursed his lips—"like overbearing Crestonians."

Taug harrumphed.

Riko poked Taug's shoulder. "Zara thinks that you're willing to do anything to gain scientific advantage."

Faye slid her gaze to Taug.

Taug hiccupped. "Not *anything*, exactly."

Faye stretched on her tiptoes, attempting to glare into Taug's eyes. "You never planned to dissect her?"

"I don't dissect living people!"

Faye looked around the room, trying to comprehend her own anger and the situation at hand. *There's more here than he's saying...* "Something put the idea into her head. Who are you going to dissect?"

Caught like a fish on a line, Taug flung his tentacles in all directions. "The doctor and I planned to hold off on Cosmos' execution long enough to learn a little about her. A little dissection on a dangerous beast. That's all! There is no crime in advancing scientific knowledge." He glared at Riko. "You might want to try it sometime."

Fay shook her head, sadly disappointed. "You'd risk Newearth just to gain friends with the Ingal?"

Taug's tentacles hung limp as he shuffled to the door. "The Ingal are very powerful. With their assistance, I could help everyone—Omega, Zara, even Wendell."

No one else moved.

He swung open the front door.

Nearly knocking Taug backward with surprise, Lang stood in the doorway. Brushing past her, he stepped outside. With his head down, he stumped away, shuffling aside new-fallen snow with each step.

Riko sighed. "Like Zara, he was just trying to help, to be a friend."

Shaking her head, Faye exhaled. "If we don't watch out, our friends will kill us."

~~~

Wendell stopped at the park entrance. Ill dressed for the weather in slip-on shoes and a thin gray jacket over
~~~

his short-sleeved uniform shirt, he wracked his brain for a solution. Unlike the children he'd played with at the orphanage, Zara had combustible moods and could not be calmed with a running game. He couldn't ask Riko or Uncle Clem to help since she might hurt them. She already hated Taug and distrusted both Faye and Kendra.

A powerful man who got things done— rang in his ears, part of a conversation he overheard at the café between Lang and Uncle Clem. *Simms? A man of means…*

He glanced up and scanned the park. Zara messaged that she'd be on the swings. He frowned at the snow but shuffled to the swing set.

The rhythmic clink-clank, as the swing's metal connectors rubbed against the top pole, broke the silence of the frozen park.

Zara's thin legs kicked up as she leaned back, propelling her slim body high into the air. Back she came with a swoosh, screaming a high-pitched "Ayeee." She mounted the sky again, her eyes and mouth wide with the gravitational thrill.

"Cold?" Wendell could not understand her joy in light of her bare legs and arms in the frozen air.

Zara leapt from the swing in a fluid motion and landed before Wendell, gasping with laughter. "I love swings! I love winter!" She raised her eyebrows and grinned mischievously. "And I love you!"

"I love you, too." No truer words could be said. Wendell's mom had explained countless times that his highest duty was to love everyone. She would stroke his cheek when she said it and then laugh at her next words. "You're a natural-born saint."

He never understood the reference since, as an Ingot, he was not naturally born. Not like humans. He knew better than to correct her. She was right. He didn't understand. Life was like that.

Zara linked arms with him and tugged him toward the street.

Fresh snow fell in fat flakes.

"Where to?"

Zara laughed. "You're cold, and I know just the place."

Wendell let himself be steered back the way he had come. After marching in silence with their heads bowed against the swirling snow, they didn't turn right at the corner toward home as he expected. Instead, they turned left and headed toward the café. Though he'd never had the headgear of most Ingots, he did have receptor implants that allowed him to pick up the slightest sound. He heard footsteps ahead, padding loud and quick. Then a large figure appeared, plowing through the snow toward them.

Dressed in a long red coat and wearing tall black boots, Lang didn't resemble an Ingot any more than Wendell did. Yet her armor and slender headgear under her stylish clothes availed her of every ounce of techno advantage. He shivered when she intercepted them.

"Wendell, Zara, glad I found you."

Zara stopped and looked up, fists clenched and ready for a fight. She blinked at the tall figure before her.

Lang grinned. "We've been worried about you. Taug was supposed to bring word that you and Kendra had a difference of opinion, but naturally, being a Cresta, a Green completely unmoored his mind."

A grin quivered on Zara's face.

Wendell studied the Ingot woman. She had always been kind to him, but some café patrons whispered together in their booths about her secret schemes. Uncle Clem once said that she had feelings for Riko. Riko refused to smile when she stopped by the café, but a smile glowed in his eyes anyway.

Wendell glanced at Zara.

Zara hunched her shoulders. "I'm busy now, but we can go to the café later. Tell Riko to make us something good and hot." She gripped Wendell's arm as if taking possession. "He hasn't eaten all day, and he's freezing in this pitiful uniform."

Lang's shoulders relaxed, an amused cat willing to play. "Busy, eh? I wish I had something interesting to do. Now that everyone—well, not *everyone*—but most people have left the planet, I'm stuck with no story to report and no audience to care."

Zara stared at Lang, head tilted as if contemplating something. "Do you trust Taug?"

Lang held her gaze, immobile, impossible to read. "Not a bit."

Zara leaned forward, excited, her breath released in white puffs. "You want to help me save Newearth?"

Lang shrugged. Apparently, she had nothing better to do at the moment. "Sure."

"Good. Come on. I'm going to make sure that once Justine gets home— after she kills that stupid planet-eater—she tears that ugly Taug limb from limb."

Wendell's heart pounded. He rubbed his head, hoping to stay upright. More than once, he had short circuited and fallen to the ground. His mom always worried. Riko yelled. He didn't know what Zara might do.

A frown worked over Lang's face. "You do look a little peaked—for an Ingot, I mean." She clasped Zara's hand—friends on a mission. "We'll get this fellow something to eat and a warm drink, then talk to Riko about your plan, and—"

"No! Riko won't help. He's friends with Taug. He gave him a lot of money."

Lang halted, her expression growing tight. "How do

you know that?"

Zara smiled. "I go places and see things." Her grin turned sour. "I know you like Riko. But you hate Taug more, right?"

Wendell couldn't see how it would help, but the words tumbled from his mouth. "We go see Simms. He gets things done."

Zara cocked her head and concentrated on Wendell, a robin eyeing a worm. "Simms?"

"He built a big space dock. He say, 'Want not, waste not.' He make good use of Taug."

A slow smile spread over Zara's enlightened face.

Lang's eyes bulged, and her fingers tapped her thigh as snow mounted around them.

Doubt filled Wendell with a fresh wave of dizziness.

Zara dropped Wendell's arm and stared at Lang. "I'll leave Wendell with you and see Simms myself. He might be worth knowing." She blinked away.

Her mouth gaping, Lang stared at the spot where Zara had stood a moment before.

Nausea twisted Wendell's stomach. "This not good. Riko not happy. Me in trouble."

Lang gripped his arm and started marching toward the café. "You're a fool with a good heart, and he's my friend, so I won't let him kill you."

Wendell sighed as he trudged beside one of the few beings that actually understood him. Besides Mom.

Chapter Twenty-Four

-The Merrimack-

After All Is Said and Done

Roux lay on his bed, his eyes closed, his body relaxed. Wearing loose-fitting dark blue pajamas, he exhaled a long, slow breath. *Bala practices breathing exercises...seems to help.* Roux sucked in yet another breath and exhaled.

Sensual images of Yelsa as she appeared when he'd first met her on the beach swayed before his eyes. She had been wearing shorts and a tight shirt, highlighting the youthful, feminine figure she adopted when appearing humanoid. Her almond-shaped eyes, pouty lips, high cheekbones, tanned legs, muscled arms, and eager, independent spirit had aroused every sense in his body.

He groaned.

Heaving himself off his bed, Roux padded to his console and tapped the databank awake. He rubbed his chin where he experimented with a short beard. *The rugged look—confident and appealing, right?* He murmured at the intercom, "Intimate relationships between Luxonians and Bhuaci."

A stream of links popped up.

Surprised at the assortment, he squinted and started to scroll through. "I'm not alone, eh?" His eyes stopped on a particularly intriguing title: *Diary of a Bhuac Married to a Luxonian—Universal Love*. His edges blurred as heat ran through him. "Good glory, she doesn't have many inhibitions!"

He read and swallowed a lump forming in his throat, his mind whirling with every sizzling sentence.

A loud buzz splintered his concentration. He jerked his gaze off the screen.

The buzz burst again.

Roux pounded to the door and slapped the unlock button. "You better have a good—"

Yelsa, wearing her crisp, standard uniform, stood before him.

Despite opening his mouth, Roux couldn't get his words out. He choked.

Yelsa reached forward, her eyes concerned. "You all right, sir?"

Roux sucked in a steadying breath and stepped back. He waved her inside. "Fine. Caught me…napping. Please, come in."

Sauntering forward, Yelsa's shoulders and hips swayed naturally.

A Bhuaci thing? Roux tried to redirect his mind—as well as his eyes. "What can I do for you?"

Yelsa stopped in the middle of the room, her gaze flickering over the sparse furnishings and the barely rumpled bed. "I just wanted your permission to follow up on transmissions the doctor made with the Cresta Taug on Newearth. Rumor has it that the Crestonians finally got revenge on the Mystery Race. If they've become that powerful, they may be able to destroy Cosmos outright. After all, they have as much a stake in Newearth as any of us."

Roux shrugged, uncertainty undermining his fragile confidence. "The Cresta aren't known for their generosity."

Yelsa frowned. "It would be for their own good."

Heat flushed Roux's face. Furious at himself, his body started to glow. "You're right. But—" A longing to touch her soft skin dissolved all coherent thought. *What is wrong with me?* "I'm just lonely."

Yelsa's eyes widened, a cat caught in a net.

He plopped down on his bed and rubbed his stubbly chin. "I didn't mean to say that. Sorry. Totally unprofessional."

Flummoxed out of her usual impassive expression, Yelsa stammered, "Don't be—sorry, I mean. It's been a trying time for all of us." She stepped closer. "Are you ill?"

Misery sent a throbbing ache through him. "Yeah, maybe." He stared at Yelsa. "How well do you know Cerulean?"

"Only a bit, mostly by reputation."

"Well, he's not acting like himself, and that worries me. I need his clear thinking, and Lux needs his direction. Add to that, the Cresta have managed to beat the Mystery Race at their own game. I may not have trusted Omega, but I never thought he was a bad guy. Just reckless. But give a Cresta hope for scientific advancement, and they won't hold back. They'd dissect their neighbor if it'd add data to a pet theory."

Yelsa sidled closer, then perched on a chair by the bed. "So, you're missing your friend? That's why you feel lonely?"

His confusion melting in a swirl of desire, Roux clasped his hands to keep his fingers from getting him into trouble. "You ever get lonely?"

Yelsa swallowed. "Yes. But I don't think about it. The best way to get home is to do my job."

"Not long ago, you were going to kill yourself to do the job."

Yelsa shrugged. "Perhaps the doctor was right about some things, but really, I want to make it home again."

Roux reached over and pressed her hands.

Yelsa stiffened.

Roux waited, not moving a muscle.

Springing to her feet, Yelsa stepped out of reach. "I can't. Not now."

Roux climbed to his feet, his gaze holding hers. "I wasn't asking for anything. Not yet anyway."

A bing echoed from the console.

Yelsa glanced aside, her panicked expression dissolving into relief. "That's probably Taug. I sent out a practice message to see if I could communicate with him—on the expectation that you'd be okay with my plan." She started toward the console. "May I check?"

Roux started to nod but then remembered that he hadn't closed his last file. "Wait! I just have to—" He nearly knocked Yelsa down in his rush to get to the computer.

As he peered at the screen, bewilderment froze his hand. The screen stood blank. He tapped it. Still blank. The file was closed and the computer asleep. He tapped it awake again.

Yelsa backed to the doorway. "I should go to my desk and take it there anyway. It might look odd coming from here."

A fresh burst of the door buzzer broke through Roux's confusion.

Yelsa slapped the open button.

Unsmiling and in standard uniform, Bala stood stiffly in the doorway.

His heart sinking, Roux watched Yelsa slip away and hardly noticed when Bala strode up to him.

~~~

Bala stood right in front of Roux and didn't know how to begin, though he had practiced his speech eight times
~~~

as he made his way to his captain's quarters. "Sir? We need to talk…Look, man, I know how it is…Roux, you've got to get a hold of yourself!"

Roux reared back from Bala's too-close proximity. With a sigh, he strode to his liquor cabinet and pulled out two glasses and a red bottle. He placed them on the table and yanked the cork out with a significant glare at Bala. "Sterling taught me the value of intoxicating beverages during times of high stress."

Well, this isn't going according to plan. "Sounds good, sir. Just one thing—"

Roux poured healthy doses into each glass. "What?"

"I haven't told you the reason I came."

Handing over one full glass, Roux chuckled. "It can't be any worse than what just happened here."

Bala clutched the glass stiffly. "Your last search was on the public setting. It came across Clare's notice, so she pointed it out to me. I closed the file as discreetly as possible, but I just thought I'd mention—"

Roux tossed his drink to the back of his throat and gulped it down. Then he poured another.

Rolling his eyes, Bala marched over and snatched the bottle from his captain's hand. "Sir, you can't do this. We have important matters to settle. Like saving the lives of every living being on Newearth, which includes my wife and kids."

Spitting in fury, Roux flailed his arms. "You think I don't know that? I am perfectly aware of the fact that millions of lives depend on me and that I am not up for the task. By the Divide! I don't have a clue what to do. Sterling was always my mentor, and Cerulean was my friend. But now, Sterling has been ordered to retire, forced from his position on the Supreme Council. And Cerulean is having some kind of mental breakdown and decided that he doesn't care a hoot what happens anymore. I'm stuck on a ship chasing a monster with a gorgeous, alluring Bhuaci who just wants to get the job done and go home."

Normally, dramatic details inflamed Bala's already overzealous imagination, but this time he kept his expression deadpan. "Thanks for spelling out the messy details. But none of that changes the fact that you are the captain, and your feelings can't interfere with your *job.*"

"Really?" Roux glared at Bala. "Feelings for Kendra and your kids have never interfered with your professional abilities?"

Discombobulated by Roux's logic, Bala stole a moment to think. He sloshed the red liquid down his throat, only dribbling a bit, then wiped his chin with the back of his hand. "Touché, Captain. Your point is well made. But, frankly, so is mine. Yelsa isn't the woman for you right now because you can't obsess about anything other than tracking Cosmos and getting us home safely."

"*And* figure out how to destroy a planet-eating monster."

"Got me again, sir."

Chuckling, Roux patted Bala's shoulder. "It helps to admit the mess I'm in."

Bala forced a smile. "You're not alone."

Like a man about to face hand-to-hand combat, Roux shook his arms loose, then strode to his console. "I've got work to do. Yelsa is communicating with Taug, thinking she can get the Cresta Ingal interested in doing our job for us. It's worth a try." He sighed. "I wish I could get Cerulean to talk to them. He could convince the Ingal to grow wings if he wanted to."

Bala shrugged. "Somehow, I don't think that would help. But Taug might have a solution we haven't thought of yet." He started for the door. When it swished open, he stopped on the threshold and looked over his shoulder, meeting Roux's perplexed stare. "Don't worry about Cerulean, sir. He's just depressed. It happens to humans all the time. But if he's the man I think he is, he'll come through it."

As he strode down the foyer, Roux leaned out the doorway and called after him, "When might that be?"

Bala called back, "When he gets to the other side."

~~~

Clare ambled across the ship's main deck, her long green tunic swishing around the comfortable tan leggings she wore. She stopped near Yelsa, who stood at the communications console, and nudged her shoulder. "You want to talk about it?"

As if the proposal involved illicit dealings, Yelsa's disgusted expression spoke volumes. "I have nothing to talk about."

Clare shrugged. *Sheesh. Just trying to be friendly.* Tact not being her strong point, Clare had never bothered to cultivate it. "If my superior wanted to get romantic with me, I'd want to talk to someone. But no matter. Be cold and indifferent. Though, really, Roux isn't a bad guy, alien though he be." The fact that she was talking to a Bhuac squirmed through the edge of her consciousness. She shoved it away.

Yelsa slapped the sleep button on her COM panel and faced Clare. "Who in Bothmal do you think you are? Roux is my captain. I have a mission aboard his ship. That's all there is to the situation."

Yeah. And I'm just as gorgeous as Justine, and Cerulean doesn't mean a thing to me. "Okay. Don't get
~~~

huffy. I'm only asking since I saw what he was looking up when—"

Yelsa tilted her head, her gaze fixed on Clare.

Lasers have nothing on this woman.

Clare lifted her hands, a quick surrender. "Forget it. Not my place to say another word." She tapped the console. "So, what's Taug up to? Got any useful info?"

"I was just going to read his reply when you interrupted."

Her interest piqued, Clare waved Yelsa aside and opened the file. "Well, now that is important. Let's see what Mr. Taug has to say!"

Grumbling, Yelsa leaned over Clare's shoulder.

Taug's insignia and smiling face appeared beside the written transmission.

Hello, Merrimack,

Thank you for your interest in my work!

The good doctor didn't offer me much hope for a final solution, though we did manage to perfect a paralyzing solution that will hold Cosmos in status for an undetermined period of time. We now only need an effective means of administering it.

~Yours Truly,

Taug, Crestonian scientist 1st class stationed on Newearth

Clare typed a response.

Hi, Taug,

How about the Cresta Ingal? Will they rescue Newearth, preserving their investment in the planet and impressing the Inter-Alien Alliance with their glorious abilities?

~Clare, Human Services Investigator on good terms with bootmakers

Clare turned away from the console, leaned against the railing, and crossed her arms. "It'll take a few minutes, but he'll reply quickly. Boots are very important to him."

Rolling her eyes, Yelsa plopped down on her chair. "Who cares about a Cresta's boots?"

Clare chuckled. "Taug has terrible foot problems, but I found the greatest bootmaker this side of the Divide. The guy makes the best-fitting terrestrial boots for Cresta feet, and I gave a pair to Taug before we left."

Yelsa's tone dripped with sarcasm. "You're *friends* then?" She shook her head in disbelief.

"Not exactly. I just know that he'll remember me with fondness. And when I need a question answered, he'll likely respond quickly."

"Mercenary manipulation then?"

Their cordial relationship sinking fast, Clare adjusted her tone. "Well, not completely. I do sort of care—"

Bing!

Yelsa and Clare bumped shoulders as they hovered over the screen.

Taug's beaming face appeared only slightly wavy. "Hello, Clare! The messaging system simply isn't adequate when I have a friend to converse with. Plus, you're in range now. How wonderful! Let's chat."

Yelsa looked as if she might regurgitate her lunch.

Rather amazed at the surge of joy racing through her,

Clare didn't have to force her grin. "Hey, Taug. It's good to see you, too. How is everyone? Riko…Faye…Kendra…"

Tentacles flying, Taug's eyes rolled in the abundance of all he wanted to say. "There's so much to tell! I can hardly wait to cozy up at the café and share intoxicating beverages with you."

With what sounded like a strangled scream, Yelsa shoved forward. "Listen, Cresta, there's little chance of anyone cozying up anywhere if we don't stop Cosmos from destroying Newearth, so would you mind focusing for a bit?"

Taug's happy expression crumpled. He glanced from Yelsa to Clare. "Short fuse, eh? Must make for an interesting journey."

Clare sighed. "Much as I hate to admit it, she's right. We need to talk about the Ingal. Will they help us?"

Glancing away, looking a lot like a little boy casting about for a suitable fib, Taug flapped a tentacle at the screen. "They're thinking about it."

"Thinking about it!" The melding of their voices actually sounded symphonic as she and Yelsa reacted as one.

Clare jerked her mind back to matters at hand and took the lead. "What's that supposed to mean? Either they'll help us or they won't."

Offering a nonpartisan shrug, Taug dropped all attempts at an informal chat. "They want to know what Newearth will offer in return."

"Bloody Bothmal!" Yelsa stomped across the deck, her fists clenched and her jaw a hard line, underscoring the burning rage in her eyes.

Clare leaned in and lowered her voice. "Listen, Taug, we know what the Cresta did to Omega, and I don't think that the Mystery Race is going to take Cresta's revenge in an all's-fair-in-love-and-war spirit. The Ingal may think that they have made their point, but this is hardly the time to burn their bridges. The Cresta might want to have at least one friend left when the Mystery Race decides to even the score."

His large golden orbs glimmering, Taug nodded. "No truer words were ever said, Clare. To be quite honest, I'm terrified of the Cresta legacy—remembered only as a part of a selfish, obsessive race."

Clare wanted to nod in wholehearted agreement, but she was too flummoxed. *An introspective Cresta?* The thought positively boggled the mind.

Yelsa's hard tone broke through. "At least when your race dies, you'll deserve your fate."

Taug gasped.

A direct hit.

The screen blinked to black.

Clare straightened and stared at the main viewer, showcasing the glory of the myriad universes. *We can't end like this.*

Chapter Twenty-Five

Mirage-Reborn

Seeds of Tomorrow's Day

Saving grace of lives well lived,
Do faithful offerings make.

Far away from familiar love,
A libation for my sake.

Weakened desire
Burns fresh anew
At the temple of my need.

Kindness forges strength,
In the spirit of good deed.

Exile in life
Partner in strife
Wandering
Free.

Family ties replaced
Reformed
Chosen dear
Paths made clear.

Death has no hold when life beyond limit grows.
Blessed are the merciful, for mercy they shall know.

We sow in fresh-turned clay,
The seeds of tomorrow's day.

~Bhuaci Servant Song

Cerulean read the poem twice. He looked up from his datapad and stared across the park full of lingering leaves dangling from exhausted trees and wondered how autumn had managed to rush upon him so suddenly.

Lucius Pollex marched in his direction, a serious look in his eyes, his mouth a tight, determined line.

Oh, Lord.

Lucius stopped short and bowed a formal salutation.

In proper form, Cerulean nodded back. He patted the empty place on the bench next to him. “Sit and help me understand autumn.”

A surprised grin quirked over Lucius’ face as he took the offered seat. “As far as I can figure, the seasons come and go according to Omega’s mood. If he’s happy, then spring bursts forth, and when he’s upset, a winter freeze stops us cold. Most often, it’s perpetual summer.”

A spark of hope igniting, Cerulean straightened. “Then perhaps Omega is rousing from his stupor?”

Lucius stared at scarlet leaves falling in a fresh breeze. “But not feeling like springtime, apparently.” He threw one arm over the back of the bench and crossed his legs in repose. “I need answers.”

Cerulean chuckled, the understatement lifting his mood considerably. “You and me both.”

“As you’ve probably become aware, Vera and I have deepened our friendship to something more.” His intense gaze made his meaning clear.

Cerulean tapped his datapad, old anxiety rising.

“We want to marry and have a family.”

Cerulean shrugged. “I’m no expert, but LuKan and Human physiology might be compatible. You could ask the doctor, Jazzmarie.”

“It’s more than physical with us. Even if we can’t marry and have children, we’d be soul mates, faithful and loving for the rest of our lives."

Pain clutched Cerulean's heart. A memory of Anne rose before his eyes.

"I want to know what Luxonians and the other races are going to do about Mirage-Reborn if Omega doesn't revive. I know that you don't have the authority to decide these matters, but surely you have some inside information."

Cerulean rubbed his eyes and slid his datapad inside his pocket. "You have excellent timing, I must say."

Lucius raised an eyebrow.

"Sterling just informed me that he is retiring, and I am to take his place on the Supreme Council." He tapped the datapad. "He even sent me a poem to make the situation more palatable."

Lucius' eyes widened, and his mouth fell open. "So, you *do* have the power to decide what will happen here."

Cerulean shook his head. "Not at all. This isn't my world. It's Abbas you must ask. I'll return to Lux soon."

Lucius frowned. "But what about us? Quinn wants independence at any cost, but Omega is weak, and Abbas is old. And besides, what about Newearth? Weren't you going to save it from Cosmos?"

"As I said, my responsibility is on Lux." He stood and patted Lucius' shoulder. "Perhaps I can do some good there, and—just maybe—I'll find a reason to keep on living."

~~~

Abbas clutched his son's hand. "Omega, can you hear me?"

A spasm rippled over Omega's body.
~~~

Jazzmarie stood alert and observant at the bedside. She gasped, "He's coming out of it."

Abbas nodded. "He's closer to the surface. I can feel his presence again." A shadow slid just beyond his conscious mind. "He knows we are here, certainly, but he's still too far under to awaken fully."

Checking the monitors she had attached to Omega's body, Jazzmarie pursed her lips. "If he were human, I'd say he was recovering from a coma."

"If he were human, he'd be dead now." Abbas patted Omega's hand, then placed his son's hand on his chest in picturesque repose. He paced across the room to the door.

Watching him, Jazzmarie frowned. "Where are you going?"

"I need to speak with Taug."

Crossing her arms over her chest, Jazzmarie's frown deepened. "Why? He can't tell you anything. Besides, Omega's coming out of it. We don't need the Cresta anymore."

Abbas glanced over his shoulder and stared at Jazzmarie. *Such a waste of intelligence.* "I don't need them; they need me. They just don't know it yet."

~~~

Max had never seen himself as a matchmaker, but then, life often surprised him. He stood in Grace's living room and tried to look as trustworthy as possible.

Chas' endless commentary concerning Grace made the situation as plain as rainbow socks. He had approached Grace in the store that morning with the suggestion that she take the mechanic something good
~~~

to eat. Grace had practically spun herself silly, hurrying to her house, dashing into the kitchen, and packing a huge picnic lunch.

She lugged the basket from the kitchen into the living room and stopped before him, her hair freshly brushed, her clothes changed—*three times, but who's counting?* She gripped the basket looking as nervous as a deep-sea diver ready to take the plunge. "There's a tray for Dad in the kitchen. You'll keep an eye on him?" A frown replaced her smile. "He's been acting strange." She glanced out the window. "I don't want Quinn bothering him." She reached into the basket and plucked out a plump sandwich. Hesitatingly, she held it out.

Max's digestive synapsis fired in anticipation. He accepted the offering. "Thanks. I'll ask your father about his adventures. Humans always like talking about themselves."

Grace blinked. "Good thinking." She eyed the sandwich. "I wasn't sure if you could eat."

Surprised at a pleasant feeling bubbling inside, Max wondered if he was developing a sense of humor. He offered a confident smile. "I have the ability to digest food, though my sense of taste is not terribly discriminatory. Now, go feed our mechanic so he won't perish before repairing the ship."

Grace practically skipped out the door.

Certain now that he and humor were no longer strangers, Max entered the kitchen. He poured himself a glass of cider and added fishpaste on rye to his culinary experiences. Next, Max started wiping down the counter with a clean dishcloth.

A shout demanded his attention. "Grace! I'm hungry. Get me something before I die, would you?"

Prepared for this eventuality, Max swung into action. A plate filled with a neat sandwich, chips, a dill pickle, and apple slices waited on the tray at the end of the counter. Imitating Riko's café etiquette, Max hefted the tray in one hand and carried a large drink with the other. He grinned. Might as well see how far his newfound sense of humor extended. He marched into the living room.

Old Man Nelson rubbed the last of his nap from his eyes and stared hard at Max. "Who are you? Where's Grace?"

"My name is Max, and I'm another of Omega's creations, here to assist you while Grace is away. The mechanic fixing our ship needs food. She's providing necessary sustenance."

The old man grunted. "Long as that's *all* she's providing."

Max searched his databanks. Aghast, his eyes narrowed. "Chas is an honest man, and Grace appears to be a levelheaded woman. Good judgment must rule the situation."

With a shake of his head, Old Man Nelson pointed to the tray. "Did you carry that in here for decorative effect?"

A burning sensation replaced the bubbly feeling. *Annoyance?* He shoved a paperback novel—a bodice-ripping romance if the cover meant anything—a glass of water, and a deck of playing cards aside and set the tray on the table by the wheelchair.

The old man grunted again. His fingers shook as he snatched up the sandwich. "Mechanical men don't need to eat, I suppose."

Surprised again, Max clasped his hands in an attempt to maintain a professional demeanor. "I'm not a mechanical man. I'm a man with a mechanical armature."

Spluttering as he put the drink to his lips, the old man

dribbled juice down his chin.

Max yanked the napkin off the tray and held it out.

Old Man Nelson ignored it. He chewed and gulped his meal and swigged his drink with obvious relish. When finished, he wiggled his fingers dismissively—a restaurant patron instructing the waiter to clear away the mess.

Max ignored him.

A large black piano stood against the far wall. Intrigued, Max remembered a song that Yelsa had once hummed. He sat on the stool and plunked out the melody.

The old man leaned back, apparently content to listen to the day's musical entertainment.

Max swiveled around. "I asked Abbas about you."

Old Man Nelson grinned. His tongue flickered between his teeth as he licked his lips.

"He told me about Grace poisoning your second wife to save you from the clutches of a manipulative siren. It would have been a very risky move and does not fit her personality."

Something malicious stirred in the old man's eyes.

Lunch boiled in Max's stomach, his fish paste and cider churning into something unpleasant. *There's always a downside.* He got up, strode across the room, and lifted the curtain to peer outside.

His decrepit voice wavering, the old man chuckled. "Grace loves me. What can I say?"

Max did not bother to turn around. "You did it, though, didn't you? You simply allowed your daughter to assume the guilt, maintaining a tight grip, so she'd never leave you." Max could practically feel Nelson's gaze burning into his back. Luckily, he did have a mechanical armature. He turned around.

"You can't prove anything." Saliva dripped from the

corner of the old man's mouth.

"I don't need proof. Abbas certainly knows."

A shrug of dismissal. "He won't tell. He'll maintain the lies that Omega used to bring us here. Omega needed citizens for Mirage-Reborn, and I needed a new home. It worked out fair and square."

Max crossed his arms. "Except for Grace."

Like a dog staking his territory, Nelson barked his words. "She's used to it!"

Max felt his humor rise again, but this time it felt twisted and cut deep inside. "She shouldn't be." He picked up the dishes and carried them to the kitchen.

Chapter Twenty-Six

–Newearth–

I'm Alive

Riko stood at the back of his café and couldn't imagine why he didn't spontaneously combust on the spot. He wanted to slug and hug two very different people at the same moment. After ordering Wendell to "Go get something to eat and then clean up around here," he refocused on Lang. His heart pounded, and sweat trickled down his back, but he must stick to the main crisis at hand. "She just blinked away?"

Lang nodded. "I'm not sure what Wendell was thinking when he suggested asking Simms for help, but it might not be such a bad thing."

Riko slumped down in the nearest booth and slapped his hands on his cheeks. "That wild child, together with Simms, the guy who wants to recreate Newearth in his own image?" He shrugged in exaggerated cheer. "What could possibly go wrong?" He glanced up and met Lang's inscrutable gaze.

"I have an idea."

Riko's heart rattled in his ribs. It wanted out of his body as much as he did. "Yeah? Can I help?" *Good glory! What am I saying?*

A smile tugged on Lang's lips. "Let's find her and check on Simms. See what's really going on."

Though his heart froze in stark terror and his brain swirled in a cloud of confusion, Riko heard himself say, "Okay," with relative calm. He stood and started for the door. Coherent thought made a sudden reappearance. "Hey, Wendell—"

The kitchen door swung open, and Wendell leaned

out. “Sir?”

Riko grabbed his coat off a hook by the door and tugged it on. “Lang and I are going out. We’ll be back in a bit. If Taug or Faye return, tell them we’re checking on Simms and Zara.”

Wendell edged the rest of the way into the diner, his eyes wide and anxious. “She be powerful. He be dangerous.”

Lang laughed as she grabbed Riko’s arm and pulled the door open. “We be brilliant!”

Riko glanced at Wendell’s frightened face one last time before Lang swept him outside.

Halting on the curb, Lang tapped her datapad. “I called for taxi a few minutes ago.”

Riko stared at her, uncomprehending.

“I figured that if you didn’t want to come, I’d go anyway.” She shivered. “It’s too blasted cold to walk anywhere.”

Vandi Transport stopped on the curbside, and the back door slid open.

I don’t have a bit of control over my life... Riko pulled his dignity together and stepped in. “That’ll work. Especially considering the fact that I have no idea where we’re going.”

~~~

Riko stood on the street side and stared at the gigantic structure looming before him. “This is a house?”

Lang shrugged as she pressed the buzzer on the guardhouse. “A combination home, place of business, and the shell of an enormous ego.”

A tall, muscled man with cyborg accoutrements,
~~~

including specialized headgear, stepped from a side door. "It's late, and there are no visitors on the schedule, folks. You'll need to make arrangements for the tour another time."

As the hulk bore down on them, all but dwarfing his Uanyi frame, Riko suddenly repented of the puffed-chest intimidation tactics he often used on stray cats. Being the little guy could be darn scary.

Lang, on the other hand, rose to the challenge. She laughed, flashed her perfect teeth, fluttered her anything-but-innocent eyelashes, and leaned in. "Simms told us to come anytime. He's been waiting for me to bring him a wonderful surprise." She eyed the embroidered nametag on the man's lapel and caressed it with a tender touch. "My dear, McDowell, would you please let the boss know that his good friend Lang has brought him the most divine cook this side of the Divide to enhance his culinary experiences and bring even greater renown to his soon-to-be-universally-famous establishment?"

Chuckling, McDowell shook his head. "Nothing doing, sweetie. I'm not losing my job due to your charms."

Desperate times called for desperate measures. The truth would have to suffice. Riko squared his shoulders. "Then would you please inform Mr. Simms that an out-of-control Luxonian-human named Zara is rampaging about Newearth, ready to kill anyone she deems a threat, and she wants to make use of *his* abilities to settle an imaginary score?"

McDowell considered the two carefully. He stepped back into his guard booth, keeping his gaze fixed on them until he disappeared inside.

Slapping her hands on her hips with a huff, Lang glared at Riko. "What're you doing? You should never tell the truth to the enemy! Never!"

Riko swallowed a lump in his throat. "Ma used to say that the truth sets us free."

With surprising vehemence, Lang's eyes nearly popped out of her head.

McDowell reappeared. He pressed a datapad on his wrist, and the gate swung open. "Follow the guide drone. Simms is waiting for you." He crossed his arms and sighed. "I hope you know what you're doing."

A stern mask fell over Lang's face as she grabbed Riko's arm.

Riko gulped and tried to keep up.

~~~

Riko's first thought upon entering the inner sanctum and seeing Simms was—*not a happy guy.*

Simms, dressed in a lush blue robe over silky white pants, grinned wickedly as he stood in the center of the room. His pearly white teeth gleamed. "You've brought me another treat, eh, darling?"

Like butter on hot toast, Lang's stern expression melted.

Irritation squeezed Riko's innards in a decidedly unfriendly manner.

Bowing low, Lang swept her hand toward Riko. "I've brought you my favorite Uanyi, the most renowned cook on Newearth. He's been hidden away in a quiet corner of the world, until he could be offered a just recompense for his services. Knowing what you have planned for the greatest docking bay this side of the Divide, I believe you'll discover a match made in heaven."

As if needing time to think the matter over, Simms toured his exquisitely appointed den. Bookshelves lined
~~~

two walls, expert sports equipment lined a third, a grand holoscreen held center stage near the far end, and an OldEarth-styled mahogany desk stood gloriously in its appointed place by a bay window. Comfortable furniture arranged in a U shape before a fireplace created a quaint scene by itself.

As if he had all the time in the world, Simms rambled back around and halted in front of Riko. Next, his eyes surveyed the Uanyi from head to toe.

Feeling strangely violated, Riko stared across the room, a dumb animal being appraised for its worth.

Simms shrugged. "You can serve lunch for my next business conference, and I'll see what Lang is making such a fuss about. But I must tell you, I've already got the best hostess Newearth has to offer. I picked her up right after I got here. A Bhuaci beauty that can add spice to more than stews, if you get what I mean." His eyebrows danced over a memory. "I even snagged an expert on inter-alien cuisine heading off planet. He kept babbling about his family, but I made him a deal he couldn't refuse. His family will survive best if he pleases me first."

Hot fury seared through Riko. He lunged forward. "I'll serve you, all right, on a platter with an apple in your mouth!"

With extraordinary reflexes, Lang snatched Riko's arm and held him in place. One quick shake, and she brought him into compliance. She flashed a smile and redirected her attention to Simms. "Actually, there's a more serious matter we've come to discuss—"

Simms replaced his perpetual grin with a serious pout. "The idiot child? I had to restrain her." He plunked down on the soft couch nestled near two plush chairs framing a cozy corner. "I tossed the suicidal, half-breed into a padded cell. She'll remain comatose till I find a good use for her. Though I'm tempted to hand her over to one of my Cresta friends." He shrugged. "They pay well for lab rats."

Riko closed his eyes, not daring to meet Lang's gaze. *Just wait till Justine gets back.*

~~~

Riko slid off his coat, hung it on the rack, and faced Lang as she followed him into the Breakfastnook. "That certainly went well."

Lang leaned against the counter and nodded. "Better than I expected, actually."

Wendell trotted forward with two steaming mugs. He set them on the counter and hurried off again.

Riko watched him duck into the kitchen, and then he slid his gaze to Lang.

Perched on a stool, she sipped from a cup with a slice of apple floating on top. Her eyes widened in delight. "Hot cider?"

Riko nodded. "While you made your goodbyes to Simms, I messaged that we'd need something hot and spicy when we got back."

Lang grinned. "Simms has done what we couldn't. For now, Zara can't hurt herself or anyone else. Despite being an immoral charlatan with visions of grandeur, he deserves credit for that much."

Balancing a tray with hot apple pie slices, Wendell slid one plate in front of Riko and the other before Lang. He waited until Riko nodded his acceptance and then ambled back toward the kitchen, humming. Suddenly, he halted and turned on his heel, an unformed question on his lips.
~~~

Lang looked up and met his gaze. "Zara is fine, Wendell. Simms promised that he'll just keep her sedated, and he won't do anything else with her until Justine gets back. The idea of tangling with an irate human-android-mom doesn't appeal to his successful-businessman nature."

Appeased, Wendell retreated into the kitchen.

Riko savored a bite of his pie, sipped the cider, and then jumped into the deep end. "So, Lang, you ever think of getting married and having kids?"

~~~

Taug hated it when Faye was mad at him. His whole system slid into a miasma swirling between depression and hyperventilation. He watched her stir a bubbling pot on her OldEarth range set against a red brick wall.

Her well-appointed kitchen gleamed in country-style charm, while she mixed with all the vigor of a Bhuaci religious leader, making a stimulating brew for her next inter-alien guild meeting.

Taug wrung his tentacles together beseechingly as he sat slumped at the small round table. "You must understand, I tried to get them to listen, but the Ingal are rather set on their priorities. They said they'd get to Newearth as soon as they can. What more do you want?"

Laying a large wooden spoon aside, Faye huffed and grabbed a spice bottle from a full rack. She tapped the aromatic sprinkles into the pot. "I understand that they will help when it's in their best interest to do so. I just think that you could have made it clear that if Newearth succumbs to a plant-eating beast, we won't be available to help them if they ever need a friend." She turned to a
~~~

large bake oven and pulled the door wide open.

The scent of hot bread wafted into the room.

Chastened, Taug traced swirls in the table's woodgrain. "What else I can do?"

Tugging on oversized oven mitts, Faye faced two loaves of hot bread and drew them out, her face flushing with the effort. "Yelsa is a very resourceful person, and she has the most up-to-date information concerning Cosmos' and Omega's conditions. If she spoke with the Ingal, I think they might listen to her."

With effort, Taug rose from his seat and sidled next to Faye, his nose twitching from the heady scent of hot yeast. "Would you like to speak with her first, Bhuac to Bhuac? I could arrange that." A flicker of hope dispelled his gloomy mood.

Faye flipped the two loaves onto a wooden board and watched the steam rise. She tugged off the mitts and faced Taug, her expression softening. "Yes, I would. Thank you, my friend."

He sighed in relief. When she nudged one of the loaves in his direction, he knew all was forgiven. How he would ever get the bread into his breather helm was another matter altogether.

~~~

Wendell stood in the center of Kendra's living room and watched her four youngest children run in circles around him. Relief and happiness seeped through his weary limbs.

Kendra, her pregnant stomach extended, strolled forward with a stained laundry hamper tucked under one arm. "Don't let them run you ragged, sweetie."
~~~

Wendell zigzagged between the children, reaching for the basket.

A collective groan rose from the broken circle.

Kendra chuckled. "Go play in the fresh air, kids." She handed Wendell the basket and continued to the kitchen.

After a struggle in the back foyer with coats, hats, and assorted mismatched gloves, the kids rampaged into the great outdoors, leaving the kitchen door half open.

Wendell closed it with the toe of his boot. He took the hamper to the cleared kitchen table and dumped the contents in a wide arc. Then he proceeded to fold the clothes.

Kendra stood back, amazement plain on her face. "Can I hire you? Or adopt, maybe?"

Wendell frowned. "I work for Riko. He need me."

"I mean when he doesn't need you." She picked up a pair of stained pants and pressed her hand along the seams, straightening them as she went. "Any time would be good for me."

"Mom need me, too."

Kendra sighed. "You're a good kid. You know how I know?" She grinned at him. "Because everyone needs you."

Trying to hold back the confusion that hounded his every step, Wendell shook his head. "Mom think me a saint. Zara think me a child. Riko think me an idiot. Lang think me a fool."

Kendra laughed. "So many people thinking about you! Must be a pretty special guy." She laid her bandaged hand on Wendell's arm. "You're always trying, and that's what counts. No one is perfect, honey. Seems to me that you've got more heart and good sense than most humans or aliens I've met."

Wendell looked at Kendra, peace and love soothing all doubts. "Zara not hurt you again."

"We get hurt when we care, Wendell." She shrugged. "But it's worth it. Caring is what keeps us alive."

Wendell nodded through a sigh. "I alive."

Chapter Twenty-Seven

–The Merrimack–

Redefine Hero

Justine paced before the closed bay door, her arms wrapped around her waist and her gaze down. Conflicting sensations slammed her sensibilities like gladiators at an OldEarth blood sport. *I'll kill him! No, I'll interrogate him first. Find out how he did it. Then I'll—*

Yelsa tapped her shoulder. "You ready?"

Suppressing the urge to break the innocent Bhuac's arm for intruding on her vivid method of chosen torture, Justine seared the woman with her glare. "Can I head down now?"

Unperturbed, Yelsa stepped aside. "The transport is ready, but Bala is still making arrangements with Simms' docking bay. You ever heard of the guy? Apparently, he's managed to direct all Newearth traffic to his personal empire." She smirked, amused by human foolishness. "Chaos has been great for the man's business."

Justine's body clenched. Ignoring Yelsa, she ran Simms' personal file before her eyes once again.

A human in his sixties, Simms appeared to be an ordinary man, though the facts hummed a different tune. He paraded his well-toned body in a yellow shirt and brick-red pants that most men would have sense enough to shy away from. With enough high-quality replacement parts to make an Ingot proud, he didn't really need all the jewelry he sported, screaming devotion to youth, wealth, and power. His cultish obsessions were obvious.

If he hadn't put Zara into a coma, she'd shrug off his existence as she would a gadfly flittering about Newearth with no particular advantages except for his business acumen. His antipathy against Cerulean made him stupid, not dangerous. But his actions against Zara made him a target of her wrath.

The bay door slid open, revealing the entranceway to a small shuttle.

Yelsa stepped in front and lifted her hand. "Let me check things on this end before you fly off. Besides, Bala would kill us both if you left without him. He's as worried about his wife and kids as you are about Zara."

Justine clipped her words. "I know how to fly a shuttle. I've been working longer than you've been alive."

Yelsa shook her head. "Parenting must blind people." She scowled as she tromped ahead. "I'm not worried about you making it to the Newearth. I just want to make sure that you don't set Cosmos in road rage, racing after you. Your flight plan better give it wide berth. While you and Bala scurry home, I'm keeping an eye on her progress." She strode to the main console. "Remember, it's not just your kid on that planet. Every person on Newearth is someone's kid."

The only thing that held Justine's arm in check was the fact that Yelsa happened to be right.

~~~

Yelsa jogged down the sterile white corridor toward *The Merrimack's* main deck, her heart pounding. In Bhuaci circles, Faye had grown into legend. Though her past swirled in mystery, her personal sacrifices on behalf
~~~

of her people instilled the highest regard in every devoted soul. Even the Bhuaci spiritual leader Song spoke of her with due respect. An opportunity to consult with her was an unexpected honor.

The main door slid open, and Yelsa halted in her tracks.

Clare stood before the holopad, chatting with a beautiful Bhuaci woman whose eyes spoke of vast experience and ancient wisdom. Her attention snagged, Clare turned and grinned. “Here she is. I knew she wouldn’t miss the chance to talk with you.”

The holographic image shimmered as Faye’s head turned, and she fixed her eyes fixed on the newcomer.

The desire to transform into a bird and fly away nearly overwhelmed Yelsa. Stiffening her spine, she stepped forward and bowed. “Yelsa at your service.”

The holographic Faye smiled, a benefactress bestowing her generous spirit on those in need of comfort. “Faye at *your* service.” She glanced from Yelsa back to Clare. “There is a lot to be done, and we are running out of time. Cosmos is closing in.”

Her professional persona kicking in, Yelsa locked onto the important facts at hand. “Through Taug, I was able to make a formal proposition to the Ingal, and they have accepted my offer.”

Rearing back, Clare stared at Yelsa. “What proposition? I didn’t get anything from Inter-Alien Alliance Committee stating that they’ve reached an agreement.”

Yelsa cleared her throat. “I told them that they can have anything they want—even Newearth itself—if they save the planet.”

Spluttering, Clare blew strands of hair from her face and slapped her hands together as if in an effort to keep from strangling Yelsa. “Are you mad? The Cresta will most certainly take you up on that offer! What's the point of saving the planet from one beast only to hand it over to another?"

Yelsa scowled, flittering her gaze from Clare to Faye. "The Cresta are too intelligent to want anything but the best for Newearth. The planet's extensive natural and cross-cultural resources allow them to prosper through their unique system. Not like Cosmos, who just wants material to digest."

Faye tilted her head and peered at Yelsa. "Though I agree with Clare, the Cresta are not capable of prioritizing the best interest of Newearth, especially since they always put their own interests first. Still, I approve your action."

Clare did an about-face and glared at the image. "Approve? Why?"

Faye laughed. "Because one thing I have learned from Taug is that, though Cresta value scientific research above anyone's personal interest, they must save face in the process."

Her belligerence fraying at the edges, Clare kept her gaze focused on Faye. "And that helps us how?"

A brilliant idea clarifying itself in her mind, Yelsa leapt forward, nearly colliding with the holograph. "When they come to save the planet, we can publicly announce an award they will receive for their generosity and goodness. They'll become universally renowned patrons of Newearth, allowing the planet to serve all races equally as it did before Cosmos threatened it!"

Faye's laughter cascaded like spring rain over Yelsa's dry spirits. "And I know just the people to splash that message all over the universe." She glanced up as if considering a new thought. "Even Simms might like to help. After all, it's his business too."

Biting her lip and pacing away, Clare tapped her

fingers together. "That's not bad. Not bad at all."

Faye's image shimmered. "I have to check in on Taug and discuss matters, but rest assured, if the Ingal has agreed to your proposition, then they will do their utmost to save Newearth." She frowned. "I just hope that they're as smart as they think they are." She offered a farewell sign. "Until we meet again." The holographic image faded away.

Clare sighed and turned to Yelsa. "That went pretty well. We have a shot at saving Newearth with us acting as the support team. And you just met your hero."

With new thoughts challenging her preconceived notions, Yelsa returned to her monitor. "We just might have to redefine hero."

~~~

Roux stood before his private communications console in his quarters and stared at the face he knew so well. Sterling was his friend, mentor, and superior in every way. At the moment, he hated the smug face with a passion. "I can't come home now!"

Sterling flicked that concern away with a two-fingered wave. "Don't be ridiculous. You can come home any time you want. And since Cerulean is returning home, finally and forever, I can think of no better place for you to serve."

Every molecule in his being revolting at the thought of Cerulean stuck on Lux for the rest of his natural existence, Roux had to hold himself together. "You can't expect Cerulean to give up his place on Newearth. Humans have been his life's work. His passion."

So bloody sure of himself, Sterling offered a half-
~~~

smile. "He's already agreed to take my place. I'm retiring from the Supreme Council. It's time for a fresh perspective, a younger influence to guide us into the new era."

Baffled, Roux cupped his hands over his ears as he'd seen Bala do when stymied by input overload. For the first time in forever, he felt truly connected to a human. *Oh, Lord, I'm channeling a married guy with seven kids. Get a grip, Roux!*

His expression switching from amused to annoyed, Sterling snapped his fingers at the view screen. "Is this thing working? You seem frozen in place, Roux."

"I'm all right, but I disagree with your decision. Cerulean is already depressed. Being cut off from Newearth will kill him. And what *new era*? Just because the clock is ticking at regular intervals does not mean that ancient wisdom has changed or old truth doesn't still apply. You can retire if you want, but don't drag Cerulean from the life he loves into a position you can't wait to get away from."

Clearly stung, Sterling pursed his lips. "Watch yourself, Roux, or I may devise a perfect revenge."

The fire within dying, Roux felt his body go cold. Tears threatened. "I'm not trying to be disrespectful, sir. But I don't think you realize what you are risking."

His words clipped, Sterling lifted his chin, ready to take whatever arrows Roux had to fling. "What am I risking?"

"The soul of the only person this side of the Divide who can hold our universe together." Without another word, Roux hit the end button, and the screen blinked to black.

~~~
~~~

Bala leaned in and grinned stupidly at the viewscreen in the cramped shuttle. "Hello, sunshine. I am *so* glad to see you."

Looking anything but bright and sunny, Kendra, with dark circles under her eyes and a glowering expression, stared back at Bala. "It's been cloudy, snowy, and bitter cold around here. Don't know where you're seeing sunshine. But I must say that you're a sight for sore eyes."

Bala waved that thought into interstellar space. "Ah, Justine over here would probably be happy to toss me overboard. But just so you know, we're speeding home as fast as our little engines can take us."

Light flickered in Kendra's eyes. "You're coming home! That means you took care of Cosmos, and everything is okay now?"

Holding down his jittery nerves, Bala tipped his hand back and forth before the viewscreen. "Well, we don't have all the details worked out exactly. But it looks like the Cresta are coming to the rescue. They managed to learn a trick or two from the Mystery Race, used it on Omega, and now they can rattle big brains with ease."

Kendra's gray pallor seemed to go grayer. "I haven't a clue what you just said." She squinted, then lifted a finger and wagged it at Bala. "If you didn't kill Cosmos, then where is she?"

Bala swallowed the chunk of ice rising in his throat. He tried not to squeak when he spoke. "Well, she's following right behind us. Apparently, she likes shuttles. Probably thinks we're a tantalizing snack. But don't worry, Justine is manning the shuttle…or should I say womaning it?" He shook himself off the distraction and scratched his head. *How to explain this so it doesn't sound nearly as bad as it really is?*

Kendra stared, waiting.

"Don't look so worried, honey. Justine is the perfect person to give chase to a planet-eating monster. And she sure is eager to get home to Zara. So, all we have to do is keep ahead of the monster and dock at Simms' Docking Bay." He rolled his shoulders, leaned in, and dropped his voice low. "Then I've just got to keep Justine from killing Simms and steal back Zara, who hopefully won't do anything too terribly drastic. Next, I'll just run down Taug, of course, keep Justine from killing *him*, convince the Cresta multi-time traitor to get the Ingal to destroy Cosmos *before* she changes menu plans and targets Newearth for her dinner special." Drained, Bala ran out of breath.

Kendra stared blankly into the screen. "Well, if that's all, darling, then our worries are over. If there's anyone I'd entrust to such a mission, it's you, man o' mine." A sparkle entered her eyes. "You've always been my hero."

Then his wife smiled at him. With tears in her eyes, granted, but a real smile that beamed all the way through black space and struck deep into Bala's heart. With love like that, there was no mission impossible.

Chapter Twenty-Eight

–Mirage-Reborn–

One Ray of Hope

Omega's mind swirled with grisly images he could not control. Pain seared his body like fire burning through a forest. *Please, someone, help me!* Hunched over and powerless, splattered with blood and gore, his own or others he could not tell, he grunted like an animal while tears of anguish, humiliation, and fury poured down his face. He tried once more to rise, but the clasping tentacles that held him squeezed even harder, sending throbbing pain through his whole system.

Oh, God! Have mercy!

The swirling mass slowed. The pressure lightened. Then Omega lifted his gaze and perceived what floated before him—mangled bodies. Cresta bodies. Millions of bits of flesh and, to the left, an odd image, vaguely familiar—a woman made of clay falling…then shattering…in slow motion. His mind screamed, *It's not my fault!*

More images slithered around him. Crestas of all kinds, male and female, young, old, proud scientists, and humble workers collecting the remains…the scattered flesh. Eyes vacant. Motions jerked. A final gathering and return to the water. Polluted ocean. The life-giving liquid choked with rotting dead.

Horror filled Omega. Sincere and absolute sorrow filled every particle of his being. And for once, he grieved not for himself.

~~~
~~~

Abbas stepped away from his son's bedside and beckoned Cerulean forward.

Cerulean paced up, his gaze darting to the figure covered by a light blue blanket. "Is he any better?"

With a nod, Abbas offered the same hope that he comforted himself with. "He is not dead. He's holding on—to something. I'm not sure what."

Rubbing his hand over his mouth, Cerulean appeared to smother a snort. "He has my sympathy." He sucked in a breath. "So, what are your plans? Have you asked the Cresta how to heal the damage?"

Abbas gestured toward the door. "Let's take a breath of fresh air. I could use a bit of sunshine. So dim and murky in here."

Accepting this proposition, Cerulean followed Abbas down a long passage, turned two corners, and finally stepped outside into a large, well-kept sunken garden with a fishpond at the center. "Very nice."

Abbas rubbed his hands together and lifted his face to the rays of the sun. Warmth spread through him like a benediction. "I know why they did it. I understand now."

Cerulean shook his head. "Excuse me? Why who did what?"

"Why the Cresta attacked Omega."

Cerulean frowned. "Revenge for what happened on Crestar—I thought."

Amazed, Abbas found himself smiling. Not a happy smile but a reflex that spoke of understanding, relief, and completion. "Yes and no." He clasped Cerulean's arm and led him to a finely wrought iron bench. He sat down and waited for Cerulean to join him.

Cerulean sat, a frown etched across his brow.

Abbas leaned forward. "They showed Omega the results of the destruction and all the pain the Crestar population suffered." Tears filled his eyes. "I felt my son's pain, and in turn, I felt their pain too. It was grievous to the extreme. The pain from losing my wife could not even compare. In consequence of that decimation, the Cresta very nearly despaired. They lost faith in all they held dear, and that has changed them forever. Whatever modicum of innocence they once held died then."

As if he could not take another blow to his own fragile mind, Cerulean leaned back on the bench and closed his eyes. "So why did you cause such destruction to the Cresta in the first place? Over a breach of etiquette? Because some Crestonians dared to ask too many questions, you killed a third of their population?"

Choking on the memory of the terrible pain, Abbas eked out his words. "I didn't. I had no part to play in the whole affair. And in truth, my race was only marginally responsible. The Cresta wanted to know how we created new lifeforms, how we made barren planets habitable. Our intelligence had come at a cost. We don't share easily because such knowledge is a dangerous thing."

"But to kill the innocent along with the guilty—I hardly see how you can minimalize the tragedy with words like *marginally responsible*."

"You do not understand what I am saying: my people gave the Cresta what they wanted. We gave them powerful information, and Crestonians suffered the same lesson we did."

Cerulean opened his eyes and sat up. He stared at Abbas.

"As we experimented, we set terrible forces into play that rebounded on us. As a by-product of self-healing experiments, we created adaptable diseases, which decimated our population. When we created mixed races with the intention of combining the best of each, we created powerful beings with no allegiance to anyone, who then terrorized innocent populations on distant planets. At home, turmoil burned through our worlds, setting our people against each other. As a result, there are few of us left." Abbas clasped his hands before his face. "In truth, the Cresta killed themselves. We didn't send a disease to gain revenge; *they* created it, let it loose unknowingly, and then blamed us."

Cerulean bowed his head.

Abbas patted his friend's shoulder. "There is one ray of hope in all of this. I believe that if Omega survives, he will finally understand—we make terrible gods."

~~~

Vera stood before her brother's grave mound, while tears slipped down her face. "I will never forget you, Dimi. No matter what happens, you will always be my best friend and truest love. Your pure heart will guide and guard me even still, I know."

Three Uanyi youths jostled playfully back and forth as they ambled through the graveyard.

Vera wiped her face and sniffed back the last of her tears. A hand dropped on her shoulder and pressed it in gentle sympathy.

Grace stepped out from behind and stopped at Vera's side. "I didn't want to startle you. But I came to have a quiet moment with Dimi, too. Guess we all need someone to talk to, eh?"

Vera nodded and looked over at the gray-haired, stoop-shouldered human. "I saw you with Chas at the ship. Looks like he's got it working perfectly if his test flight is anything to go by."
~~~

A grin quirked over Grace's face. "He's amazing. I've never met anyone like him." The light in her eyes faded. "But he'll probably head back to Newearth now and find work at the new docking bay they've got started there. Once he learned that Cerulean is actually a good guy, he was ready to move on. Though, he grew up on another planet and hardly knows Newearth…still, since he's human, it is his home world."

"I thought Newearth was threatened by a planet-eating monster."

Grace shrugged. "Word is that the Cresta have offered to save the planet with a new weapon they've created. It'll immobilize the creature, and they'll tow it off to Crestar, where they plan to study it to their hearts' content and then kill it at their leisure."

Boiling nausea rose in Vera's middle. "Something might go wrong. I can't imagine taking such a thing home and hoping to contain it, even if it is a scientific prize."

Grace laughed. "You don't know the Cresta if you think they'd give up a chance to study something this big just for safety reasons."

Vera shook her head, unconvinced. "Still seems like a bad idea." She glanced over her shoulder, her gaze searching the immediate environment. "Any news on Omega? Is he any better?"

Following Vera's example, Grace did a quick look around. "Chas thinks that Omega will survive, but he may never be the same." She bit her lip. "How about you and Lucius? How are things going there?"

Suddenly shy, Vera didn't know what to say. "I think he wants us to be together, but he's also obsessed with Quinn. How those two ever managed to keep the peace on this planet as long as they have is a mystery."

Grace shrugged. "While Omega was in charge, things

were contained. With him out of commission, there's been a power hole, and nature abhors a vacuum." She pressed Vera's shoulder again. "Lucius loves you. It's as obvious as the sun in the sky. And if you feel the same, which I think you do, then don't let Quinn get in the way. Love is too precious to be run over by a rampaging ego."

Joy fluttering through her, Vera shivered in momentary delight. "I like how you think, Grace." She crouched and patted the earthen mound over her brother's grave. "I'll be back and visit again soon, Dimi." She rose and took Grace's arm. They headed toward Main Street.

Grace laughed. "Hey, isn't your house the other way?"

"My house is. But I'd like to meet the mechanic I've heard so much about. Perhaps there is room in that ship for one more?"

Blinking, Grace wrinkled her brow. "*You* want to go to Newearth?"

Vera laughed. "Not me, silly. I just think that a wonderful woman I know would make Chas a great wife, and you both need a home."

~~~

Lucius washed his hands clean, dried them on a towel, changed his shirt, combed his hair, and then checked his appearance in the mirror. Satisfied, he stepped outside of his blacksmith shop into the brisk evening air. With a bracing breath, he strode down Main Street and stopped before the jailhouse, lit by a dim overhanging bulb.

Jeremy Quinn sat at a table, scrolling through a datapad.

Lucius stepped inside and stopped short. "You know that datapads are contraband."
~~~

With a sharp flick of his hand, Quinn waved Lucius away. "What's Omega going to do about it? Or Abbas, for that matter?"

Lucius marched forward and stood over the dark, bowed head. Disturbed by Quinn's utter coolness, he hesitated.

Slowly, Quinn slid his datapad aside and looked up. He leaned back in his chair, calm and composed. "You come for a reason?"

"Justice."

With a snort, Quinn rose languidly to his feet. "*I am* justice, Convict." He faced Lucius. "You, on the other hand, are as good as dead if you get in my way."

His initial intentions blown to smithereens; Lucius forced himself to stay calm. "I wanted to give you one fair chance just so I can remind myself that I tried. Even after every horrible thing you've done, I really tried to treat you with decency."

Two large men ambled out of a back room, their hands clasping guns at their sides.

Lucius shook his head. "I was going to offer you the chance to run in an election against me, but I see that I was just fooling myself. You aren't capable of an honest run at anything. It's all about brute force with you, isn't it?"

Quinn grinned as he rubbed his chin. "I use charm when I have to."

Lucius stepped closer and got right into Quinn's face. "You set the fire that killed Dimi, and you shot and killed an innocent man."

With a quick turn, Quinn retreated to the counter. "Fires happen. Especially in old houses. And I merely took out an undesirable element. Neither Crestas nor Ingots like being reminded of their mistakes. One thing they'll actually agree on—mistakes should go away."

Fighting a rising tide of fury, Lucius clenched his fists. "I guess we'll all agree on that. Question is, which one of us is a mistake."

"That'd be you, Convict."

His mind suddenly clear, Lucius relaxed. "I may have worn a prisoner uniform, but I was never as imprisoned as you." He turned on his heel and headed for the doorway. Without looking back, he flung his words like a challenge. "Mirage-Reborn is growing up for good. And we can't afford *any* mistakes this time around."

Lucius left the jail behind and headed for the one man who could help him, Old Man Nelson.

~~~

Max wandered through the peaceful park at the break of dawn, watching a pair of nesting birds feeding their young. *Must be nice. Fluttering about with no concern other than finding your next meal.*

A large black bird dove in, cawing raucously, toward the nest.

Two smaller bluebirds raced forward and intercepted the attacker, screeching as they darted about, their beaks stabbing.

The park came alive with chattering squirrels running commentary as they raced along the treetops. A frightened rabbit leaped into a hole in the embankment. Three other bluebirds and two yellow-throats threw themselves into the fray, twittering and cawing between dives.

Max watched, amazed and chastened. "I rescind my hasty assumptions, my feathered friends. I had no idea how violent your world could be."

A voice called from across the park. "You talking to
~~~

yourself, Maximan?"

Max glanced over, and a sigh heaved itself up from deep in his middle, ready to jump overboard. *Jazzmarie—doctor and charlatan.* He looked at the bluebirds chasing off their predator and closed his mouth.

Jazzmarie ambled forward, her long flowing skirt rippling with every move. "I can barely drag my exhausted body another step. You wouldn't mind getting me something to sustain my overwrought nerves, would you, darling?"

Confused, Max located the café in his sights and pointed. "Didn't Abbas feed you while you were attending to his son?"

Her eyes wide with shock, Jazzmarie shook her finger at him. "You're such an innocent, Maxi. I forget. You're like a newly hatched bird. Don't know a thing about devious powermongers who want to take over the universe. I wouldn't eat his food for the life of me!"

Suddenly feeling sluggish, Max fought sticky webs trying to wrap themselves around his mind. *I need coffee.* Startled by this thought, Max faced main street. "The café serves quality food." Without further ado, he started in the proper direction with quick steps.

Jazzmarie wailed as she hurried up behind him. "Wait! I haven't slept for two days, my nerves are shot, and that stupid Abbas ignored me when I offered him my secret information."

Hating himself for his weakness, Max had to ask, "Secret information?"

"Taug has a solution for Cosmos."

Max frowned as he slowed his pace. "You might be behind the times. Cerulean was with Abbas yesterday, and he already knew that everything was well in hand. He told me to rest easy and went to bed as soon as the sun set."

Jazzmarie squinted and appeared to study Max, as if a hidden truth were written on his face. "I don't know about you sometimes. Either you are smarter than you act, or you're a handsome fool." She shrugged. "In either case, I adore you, but I must have some nourishing food."

In weary assent, Max hurried toward her salvation.

Once settled at a window-side booth inside the café, Max caught an attendant's attention and ordered a serving of bacon and eggs, a full plate of French toast, a fruit salad, black coffee, and a large milkshake.

Jazzmarie stared at him for a moment and then cleared her throat. Wiggling happily, she announced her wishes to the waitress. "A cup of tea with *fresh* squeezed lemon. No bottled stuff, please. A vegetable quiche with plenty of white cheese, crispy hash browns, a large orange juice, and four sausage links on the side."

To her credit, the young waitress kept her face expressionless and strode to the kitchen, merely tapping the order pad against her thigh as she went.

Chattering and a few friendly shouts filled the early morning air as waitresses, busboys, and a couple of cooks tried to keep up with the breakfast crowd. A couple of Uanyi farmers scarfed down their food, chomping and chewing, with only a few clipped words exchanged. A Bhuaci mother with twins struggled to feed them alternate spoonfuls while their dad sipped coffee and chatted with the guy in a booth across from him. An older Cresta perched on a stool at the counter and poured a tall glass of Green into her breather helm.

Rather early in the morning for that, I'd think.

"Max! Are you even listening to me?" Jazzmarie slapped his hand in what was clearly meant to be a playful move between friends.

Max didn't like it, but he couldn't reason out why.

"I am telling you that we have to do something. I don't think Omega will be fit to rule this planet, and Abbas doesn't seem able to make the hard decisions necessary. It's like being back on *The Merrimack* with Roux in charge."

His interest piqued, Max kept his gaze focused on the doctor even as the waitress poured coffee in his cup and then set a steaming mug of hot tea before Jazzmarie. "What do you think we should do?"

Gripping her pots, the waitress strode off to find other empty cups to fill.

Jazzmarie leaned in. "*We* can manage things, of course. I'll convince Abbas to go home and get the rest he so desperately needs, and you'll immobilize that failed Bothmal guard, break his legs beyond repair or something. Then we'll announce to everyone that you and I are now Mirage-Reborn managers. We can even say that we have Inter-Alien Alliance approval, so they'll feel like part of the larger universe—connected—you know. It makes people feel special to be part of a bigger system."

While stunned by the sheer audacity and raw evil of the suggestion, Max was surprised that he also felt curious enough to ask a follow-up question. "And Cerulean?"

Jazzmarie smirked. "He's human now. Easy-peasy. Just tell him that he can either accept our decision or go back to Lux. You probably wouldn't even have to break his legs or anything."

When the waitress returned with their meals, confusion swirled through Max. His hunger synapses weren't firing. Even his sense of smell seemed to have deserted him.

Struggling with the various plates, the waitress

scrunched her brows in concentration as she placed each dish in just the right place. Finally, she straightened and smiled. "Have an enjoyable meal." She trotted off happier than Max had seen her all morning.

Jazzmarie sipped her tea, then dug into her quiche like a cat going for a mouse nest.

His mind whirling, Max leaned back and tried to collect his wits. *Old Man Nelson and Jazzmarie could be evil twins.* He stared at his luscious-looking food. Uncomprehendingly, despite his sickening company, the bacon and eggs whispered facts about high nutritional values and calming overwrought synapses. He picked up his fork, scooped up a healthy serving, then held it in tantalizing anticipation as a vivid thought struck him. "There's someone I want you to meet. He'd be just the right assistant for you."

Jazzmarie talked around chews as she continued to scarf up her food. "Yeah? Not you, huh. Who's that?"

"A certain gentleman who thinks much like you. He'll probably have some very good ideas."

She laid down her fork and peered narrowly at Max. "You sure you don't want to be my right hand, Maximan, and manage this world with me?"

"Once you understand who you are dealing with, you'll want the Inter-Alien Alliance's assistance."

Jazzmarie sipped her tea, dabbed her mouth with a napkin, ran her gaze over Max, then shook her head. "I'll meet this guy, sure. But honestly, if you aren't with me, then I'll work alone." She shrugged. "If it makes you happy, he can think he's helping, but that's never really the case. As for the Inter-Alien Alliance, no thanks. I've never been very partisan. Really, I'm all about me."

With stunning accuracy, Max finally categorized Jazzmarie in her proper place. A piece of his innocence traded places with shrewd understanding. He took his first bite and decided that this, too, was part of being human.

Chapter Twenty-Nine

–Newearth–

Doesn't Bear Thinking About

Kendra knew the warning signs well enough to pack her overnight bag, shuffle to the door of her bedroom, and call her fourteen-year-old son for help. "Seth! Come in here, boy, and give your fragile mama a hand." *Thank you, Lord, for weekends and good strong boys.*

With long hair barely swept out of his eyes, wearing baggy pants and an oversized sweater, Seth hurried down the hall, his gaze fixed on her. "You all right, Ma?"

There were so many answers to that question, Kendra's mind swam with possibilities—*Define all right… I will be once I get this little one outta my ribcage… Focus, woman!*

The baby kicked, and her stomach muscles cramped, making her knees impersonate noodles. Her legs buckled.

Seth grabbed her arm, his eyes wide with fright. "Mom!"

Kendra held onto her son, breathing through the contraction. Once it subsided, survival instincts rushed up from the deep. "Get my bag, honey, and carry it to the curb. I already called an autoskimmer to take me to the maternity center, so I'll be fine. But you, my love"—she cupped his face in her hands—"are going to have to survive as chief, cook, and cleaner until I get back. Can you do that for me? Normally your father would handle things in his frazzled, maniac-dad sort of way." She shrugged. "But you know."

Seth swallowed and wrapped his arm in hers, carefully leading her down the hall. He called into the boys' bedroom as they passed, "Hey, Barni, Mom needs her bag. Go get it, would you?"

Barni sat on the floor, building a city with intricate blocks, assisted by his two younger sisters—a slim eight-year-old Rachel and a very self-assured six-year-old Veronica. His four-year-old brother David crouched before them. At eleven and well beyond his cherubic stage, Barni glanced up. "You going somewhere, Mom?"

At the sight of her brood playing so pleasantly, Kendra's heart swelled in gratitude. *You've done well, woman. One more won't break you.* She looked around and spied little Martha, the two-year-old clothes-queen, who was valiantly tugging one of Rachel's sweaters over her head. *Oh well, at least she's in her element and not in the kitchen.*

Kendra's stomach muscles started to contract again, squeezing painfully. She talked through the discomfort. "I'm about to welcome your baby sister into the world. I need a maternity room to collapse in, but Seth knows what to do, and you'll help him, won't you, Barni?"

Barnabas jumped to his feet and skedaddled down the hall, shouting as he went, "We're fine, Mom. I'll get your bag. Just get going before anything weird happens!"

Chuckling despite the last twinges of the contraction, Kendra let her oldest son open the door for her and then clutch her arm as she waddled down the porch steps and to the curb. He stood guard at her side as they waited for the autoskimmer. She sighed. *Still young'uns, but they're sure coming along nicely. Amazing what a lot of love will do.*

~~~
~~~

Faye's heart pounded in exhilaration, fear and joy bombarding her soul with so many unexpected quandaries. She bustled about her kitchen, adding the last spices to a steaming pot of homemade soup, and then checked the oven for a batch of her strengthening muffins. *If there's anything that will do Kendra good, it'll be my muffins. She never eats enough, that woman.*

The doorbells tinkled.

Faye glanced out the window.

Darkness hid the winter woodland view.

Scrunching her brows together, she hurried to the door, checked the entryway camera, and flung open the door in surprise.

"Riko! And Lang! What are you two doing here at this time of night?"

Lang, as imposing as ever, grinned like a cat that had just swallowed the last of the cheese. "We had to wait until closing to come by. It was Riko's idea."

Staring straight ahead like a man in a lineup waiting to be hauled off to Bothmal Prison, Riko shook his head. "Not me. Uncle Clem came up with this one. But Wendell agreed, so I figured, well, we do need help."

Bewildered beyond words, Faye waved to the warm kitchen. "Hurry up and come in. The winter winds won't stop at the door. Besides, I've got a pot of soup brewing, and I want to arrange my basket of goodies for the morning."

Lang ambled after Faye, her sultry tone now curiously casual. "Goodies? You've got something special for Taug? Trying to get on his good side, maybe?"

Faye hurried to a pot on the range, turned off the heat, and stirred the mixture, annoyance flying amid her other concerns. "No, of course not. I'm *already* on Taug's good side. It is he who must stay on my good side. This, my friends, is going to be an elixir for our dear Kendra, mother of her glorious seven."

Riko pulled out a stool and slumped down. He sniffed the aromatic scents wafting from the pot. "That smells good. But Bala and Kendra only have six." He frowned. "I think. Though it's hard to count straight, the way they're always moving around."

Lang leaned on the counter and placed a hand on Riko's shoulder. "You forget the one she's carrying. It may be tucked inside, but it counts just like all the rest. Especially when it comes to taxes."

Surprised and a little gleeful at the opportunity to break the news, Faye twirled her spoon in the air. "So, you haven't heard? Kendra had her baby girl this morning. Little Alexa!" She frowned. "Very little since the baby was premature, and Kendra is quite weak. Hence the need for my nutritious goodies!"

His eyes rounding with concern, Riko straightened. "Oh, say, then we probably shouldn't be bothering you now. You've got more important things to do."

Faye shook her head and placed a cover on the kettle. "Don't be silly. I have enough muffins to share with you two. And a calming cup of hot tea would do us all good. Besides, you said you needed help?"

Lang stood aside as Riko filled the tea kettle at the sink, almost as if he were in his own kitchen. He placed it on the stovetop and tapped the console for three minutes. "Well, it's rather hard to explain…"

Lang took a seat at the counter and clasped her hands. "No, it's not. We want to know if a Uanyi and Ingot can get married."

Clutching three mugs, Faye froze. She stared at Riko and then at Lang. "You. Two. Marriage?"

Lang kept her gaze steady.

Riko appeared to be memorizing the floor tiles.

Rousing herself from shock, Faye placed the mugs on the table and retrieved the tea caddie. She set it front and center and considered her options—pretend ignorance or be honest. She chose a third path. "First, I need you to explain what you mean. Are we talking sex and see where things go or a life-long commitment to each other's welfare?"

Riko lifted his head, his eyes wide and clear. "I'll go for the life-long commitment thing."

Lang grinned. "Sounds good to me."

The topping on a good-news day—joy bubbled up inside Faye. "In that case, I'll expect to see you both here tomorrow morning bright and early."

His face blanching, Riko choked out his words. "What for?"

Lang tilted her head, her brows doing an inquisitive dance.

Faye shrugged. "If you really want to understand commitment, there's nothing like taking care of a family to test your resolve." She clapped her hands like a schoolmarm calling the class to order. "Help me settle in as I take care of Kendra's family while she recovers in the maternity ward. I plan on staying a week. You two just need to survive a few hours."

Slapping her face, Lang shook her head. "Six children? We'll be outnumbered."

With a snort, Riko reached over and rubbed her shoulders. "Relax. Kendra does it all the time. And if we need serious help, I can always call in Wendell. I hear he's got a special way with kids."

Faye poured steaming water into each cup and smiled. *Wait till I tell Taug. Growing families and new love interests. The Ingal will be agog with Newearth possibilities.*

Her gaze swept over Riko as he held Lang's hand, and

her happy mood fell to Earth. *Life-long commitment—not for the faint of heart.*

~~~

Taug shuffled down the sidewalk against the bitter wind, a bottle of the best liquor available this side of the Divide wrapped in each tentacle. They had been a good find and only available to Crestas with special connections. He huffed rhythmically through his breather helm, bubbles hissing like gas escaping from a pressurized tank. Images of his lagoon back home on Crestar warmed his chilled flesh. *Darn bio-suit hardly keeps out the blasted wind.* He remembered his celebratory drinks and grinned, despite the frozen blasts hitting his face.

"You sure would make a great snowman with your white suit covered in frost!"

Startled, Taug halted and glanced around the dark street.

Uncle Clem stepped out of the shadows and came closer. "It's only me. I was out scouting for news since Riko and Lang went to see Faye. Figured I'd see who's left in town and what the local gossip says about Cosmos."

Taug found himself strangely suspicious of the annoying little Uanyi, who he suspected was actually much more intelligent than he let on. After all, no one could be so blithely ignorant. *Must be an act.* "Learn anything useful?"

"Nothing you don't already know. But Filbert, the courthouse guard, said that nearly all the higher-ups have reformed the government aboard the *Newearth*
~~~

Alliance in orbit. And Shusha from city security said that Simms has brought in extra help to keep lowlifes from getting any ideas while homes and businesses are left vacant. A good thought, though I'm just not sure what he gets out of it. He must get something. That man does nothing from the generosity of his soul." Uncle Clem shivered and pointed in the direction of the café. "I need to check on Wendell before I call it a night. Mind if we finish our chat inside?"

Relieved, Taug nodded and started forward again, his toes numb in his worn boots.

The two huffed along in silence. Only the occasional clank of the bottles in Taug's tentacles broke the silence. Crossing the icy street became a treacherous undertaking as the day's slush had frozen to a sheet of ice. Alarm spread through Taug as images of breaking his precious cargo sped through his mind. A huffed snort, almost resembling a whimper, rose into the clear black sky.

An owl hooted in the distance. A goose honked a plaintive cry.

Uncle Clem stopped in the middle of the empty street with his hands tucked deep into his pockets. "Something wrong? You're all hunched over."

Time to fess up? Oh well, nothing for it but to stick to the facts. "I have acquired a number of treasures which I had planned to share with our friends, but I'm afraid that I am losing my grip, and the ice may be too much for my worn boots."

His eyes widening at an alarming rate, Uncle Clem gushed in response. "Oh, say, I had no idea! Sorry about that. Didn't realize that you were carrying a load. And here I go, chattering on while your breathing helm is icing over. Here, let me carry a few of those. No, I can take three, and you take the others. Then we'll be even and can help each other across."

Relieved beyond measure and amazed by the sincerity in Clem's voice, a chummy feeling spread over Taug. Once relieved of half his burden, he hustled along at a brisker rate, and they plowed right into the café kitchen like teammates after a winning game.

Wendell hustled forward, his voice squeaking. "Cosmos here?"

Uncle Clem set his three bottles—red, green and blue—on the counter and laughed. "Naw, just trying to beat the freezing wind before it turned us into Newearth popsicles."

Grateful beyond words for the steamy warmth, Taug carefully set his three remaining bottles next to their mates. He turned and appraised Uncle Clem. The Uanyi was tugging off his scarf and coat, smiling at Wendell, who grinned in return. The honest camaraderie between the two delighted him. "I think we should celebrate!"

Uncle Clem hung his coat and scarf on a peg and then turned, his face windblown red but still smiling. "Yeah? Why is that?"

Wendell didn't wait for a reason but hurried and gathered three goblets.

Taug swiped the Green off the counter and lifted it high. "The Cresta will save Newearth! The news is spreading as we speak, and everyone can come home as soon as the Cresta ships are within range of Cosmos."

Stunned, both Wendell and Uncle Clem stared at Taug with open mouths.

Taug cracked open the top of the green bottle and poured a dollop into each glass. "It's true. We learned a great deal from the Mystery Race, and now we rise to heroic feats."

Wendell frowned. "How learn?"

Taug passed the glasses. He poured a healthy dose into his thawing breather helm, slurped, and sighed in relief. Then he dragged over a large stool and got comfortable. “Well, apparently, the interview process with Omega started out well enough, but when he shared memories with them, it became uncomfortably clear that the Mystery Race had not actually set out to destroy a third of our people. Rather, in our eagerness to study them, we did not take proper precautions. We inadvertently unloosed an alien disease which killed Crestas immediately upon contact.” He took another long draught, slurped, and sighed. “Ironically, it is that very toxin that we can now use against Cosmos. Even so large, she is not immune. I tried it on her little cousins, and it works to devastating effect.” He pointed to the doorway. “Would you care to see? I can show you.”

His eyes wider than ever, Uncle Clem nodded and followed as soon as Taug got to his feet.

Once in the room, Wendell stayed in the doorway, hesitating.

The liquor having softened his mood into an expansive generosity, Taug waved the young Uanyi into the room. “Come in. It’s not often that one gets a sneak peek at the world’s salvation.”

Wendell inched into the room and stopped at Uncle Clem’s side.

They stood before a large vat that Taug presided over like a proud merchant showing off his wares. He lifted a lid and wagged a tentacle. “See, they were a happy little family of Cosmos cousins swimming about in the vacuum of my mini-space station. But now, they lie limp and powerless.” Heaving a long sigh, Taug wiped his face with a tentacle. “It’s been a long day, and I must check in on Faye tomorrow to see if she needs help.” He dropped the lid on the vat and turned away.

Uncle Clem took the hint and tugged Wendell’s sleeve. “We should go. He might undress, and I can’t have that image haunting me forevermore."

Wendell frowned and pointed back to the vat as they walked to the door. "But one move. I saw."

Taug harrumphed. "Nothing of the sort. A shadow. Nothing more." He waved goodbye to Uncle Clem with a fresh burst of warmth filling him. "We'll have a sign made with your brilliant slogan, 'Crestas are the Best-as.' And this time—it'll be true."

~~~

Kendra placed her hands over the incubator and stared at her tiny baby. Her heart throbbed with the desire to reach inside and clasp her little one to her breast. But Alexa was sleeping in a secure unit and needed all the rest she could get.

"I want her." Rachel propped her hands on her hips like a young matron with needs that should not be ignored.

Kendra smiled at her crew. Some bundled around, while others stared with their faces pressed against in the nursery window. "Soon enough we'll have her home, and you can help me take care of her."

Veronica made a silly face at the baby, and Seth yawned as he jiggled Martha in his arms. David stared upward, looking peaked and hungry. Barnabus frowned. "Will they let us take her when we leave Newearth?"

Startled, Kendra pulled back and considered her son. "Leave Newearth? Where're we going?"

Rachel patted her brother's arm. "Aww, we don't have to go. Daddy is coming, and he'll take care of Cosmos. He'll beat it up if he has to."

Smothering laughter, Kendra waved her kids down the hall. "Alexa needs her beauty sleep. Let's go to my
~~~

room. We'll order a big dinner since you all look like you're about to faint from malnutrition."

The clan padded after her as she accepted Martha from Seth's arms. Kendra leaned in close to her son. "When you get home this afternoon, tell Faye that Justine is coming, and she might want to be prepared. An angry android is nobody to mess with. I'll call Simms myself—after all, he might have done the right thing. But no parent likes it when their kid is sedated and locked in a cell."

Rotating his stiff shoulder, Seth grinned at his mom. "Only a fool would get between you and your kids. I can only imagine what Justine might do."

"Doesn't bear thinking about. Good thing Daddy will be home soon." Relief filled Kendra as she entered her fully furnished maternity room. Plunking down on the bed with her kids climbing on beside her, she grabbed her datapad and messaged room service. "Let's see, how many pizzas can we eat?"

Chapter Thirty

-Shuttle-

The Next Step

Bala crouched over his console, unable to stand upright as the ship accelerated, and prayed that the last thing he saw in life was not a blinking red alarm notice.

Justine muttered under her breath, "Bloated macro-organism! Get off my tail!"

The engines whined in loud complaint as they reached maximum speed.

Bala dearly sympathized. He lifted his head and glanced aside at Justine's scowling face. "Think that going faster only makes her want to chase us more?"

"Why would speed have that effect? Doesn't make sense."

In imitation of one of his kids, Bala dearly wanted to throw a fit. "You've never spent much time in the wild, have you?"

Sparing a brief glimpse, Justine continued to work the directional console, her fingers flying. "I've seen plenty of wild in my time, don't you worry. Besides, this maggot should get tired soon."

Using every muscle in his aching arms, Bala heaved himself to an upright position. "Just swerve aside and slow down. See what happens."

Her expression deadpanned, Justine snorted. "Have it your way!"

The ship tilted at a sharp angle, the engine roar dropped, and their speed slowed considerably.

Gripping the edge of the railing and tapping through the locator, Bala followed Cosmos as it sailed by. Its trajectory still ran toward Newearth, but its speed soon dropped to a more sedate pace.

Justine swiveled around in her chair and eyed Bala. "I have no idea how you knew to do that, but thank you for your insight. It would have run us over in a few more minutes. Not a pretty image, no matter how you play it."

Pride never got much of a platform in Bala's life, and his natural humility demanded that he make a joke of the situation. He cracked a smile and tried frantically to think of a good one-liner that Justine would comprehend.

Oblivious, Justine swiveled back and tapped a code on the console, and the main viewing screen focused on a central image—Newearth. "Home sweet home. Though Cosmos is ahead of us, I'll sneak around, and we'll get there a day ahead of her. Then we can watch the Cresta's solve our problem from a chair on the front lawn."

Bala closed his eyes in relief, his chest heaving as if he had just run a marathon. *Thank God!* Kendra's weary eyes, his kids' faces, and the shadowy image of the baby he had yet to meet filled his mind.

Justine leaned back. "At this speed, we'll dock at Simms' port in eleven hours. And, oh boy, am I looking forward to that meet and greet."

Bala opened his eyes, swiveled his glance at Justine, and was surprised to see her staring right at him. *Waiting for my reaction? Or permission?* He laughed. "What if we go maximum speed?"

Justine actually smiled. "We'll be home before you can plan dinner."

—Newearth—

Kendra marched down the long corridor of Simms' central office building, feeling like she'd left her heart at home, but she was determined to see this matter through. It was a point of honor, and Bala was big on honor. She wasn't going to let him down. Or Justine, for that matter. Despite her android physique, Justine was a mother now, and mothers had to stick together in this crazy world.

The corridor of doorways and branching hallways created a dizzying complex. *Was it third turn on the right and the second door or second hall on the left and third door?* Stymied, Kendra halted in her tracks.

A young Bhuaci woman trotted forward from a left-hand branch, smiling in a smug sort of way.

Kendra controlled an eyeroll. *A beautiful, young know-it-all. Just what I need.*

The petite woman stopped before Kendra, a datapad in her hand. "You must be Kendra? I'm Sue-Lee. I've been looking for you everywhere. Mr. Simms was expecting you in his audience chamber this morning, but he said he'd squeeze you in for a minute now if you hurry and follow me."

Flummoxed, Kendra stayed put. "Audience chamber? What, is he the pope or something?"

A fluttery laugh and Sue-Lee started forward, one hand towing Kendra along like necessary baggage. "Oh, there's an idea. But don't tell Mr. Simms that or he might take you seriously! Just what Newearth needs, another pope!" She giggled again.

Uncertain whether to be incensed by this blasphemy or grateful for the warning, Kendra plodded along, scrambling to get her thoughts in order.

The audience chamber dwarfed anything Kendra had ever seen in a public setting. The vaulted ceiling and arched doorways reminded her of St. Peter's Basilica in the OldRoman section of Newearth. Though no saint statues or holy artworks adorned the niches and walls, the huge round windows allowed a steady stream of morning light into the wide-open space. Awestruck, she stopped just inside the audience chamber doorway and stared.

A luxury jeep motored forward, and a thickset man leaped out. His bright yellow shirt and dark green pants practically bounced off his jet-black hair and well-oiled skin.

Shocked by the two amazing sights, the glorious structure and the dubious man, Kendra found herself at a loss for words. Not a typical experience.

Simms took her hand, pumped it in welcome, and pulled her closer, a grin spreading wide over his face.

For some unaccountable reason, Sue-Lee backed away and snapped pictures of them together, shaking hands.

Kendra immediately drew her hand back. Reflexively, she wiped it on her pant leg.

Cupping his hands together like a delighted child, his fixed gaze never wavering, Simms voice boomed, "So, we finally meet! I've read up on you, woman. I know all about your illustrious lineage, and I must say that your husband's various exploits have made entertaining reading as well."

Her mouth as dry as any desert she could name, Kendra forced herself to croak out a few words. "I came about Zara…to see if she's all right."

A brief chin scratch and a glance away spoke of Simms' disappointment that she had clearly missed the value of their iconic meeting. He shrugged. "The little hellion is fine. *Now.*" He grinned again and pointed to huge docking bay doors. "Bet you're glad that the Cresta ships have stationed themselves outside my docking bay. Just in time to greet the mega-monster, arriving sometime tomorrow, I hear."

Kendra nodded, though her mind replayed his words,

troubled by them. “What do you mean, *now*? Was she not all right before?”

The beaming smile vanished. “Look, you know as well as anyone that she is trouble. A Luxonian-human child with anger issues is nothing to mess with. Good thing that I have some very savvy Crestonian friends who were only too glad to help out. Just like they’re helping with the Cosmos threat. They deserve a bigger place in Newearth’s future. Overseers, I’m thinking. The perfect culture to lead us out of the malaise of Luxonian inefficiency.”

Kendra shook her head. Was she hearing right? “Malaise of inefficiency? The Luxonians rescued us and took the human remnant in, while Crestonians tried to blast their way into a power position.”

“Ah, you listen to too much Newearth News. We have to look forward, not back. Even the Inter-Alien Alliance Committee can’t solve all our problems.” He looked over his shoulder as if giving a nod to his docking bay. “Contrary to the old order, I’m going to give Crestonians prime position on my docking bay. They deserve it.”

Shivers ran down Kendra’s spine. “The whole point of the Inter-Alien Alliance is to ensure that no one gets into a prime power position and to enforce laws which state that every race must respect humanity’s inherent dignity.”

Simms rolled his eyes. “Look, if you want me to hand over the little menace, then we need to have an understanding. When I have a problem, the Cresta always assist. So, when they wanted a sneak peek at the hybrid, I was happy to oblige. Lucky for everyone, they saw the problem and fixed her. When the mechanical mom shows up, she’ll get a dream daughter.” He waved his hand in dismissal. “You can thank me later. Sue-Lee will lead you out. I’m going up to watch the show. Got a front-row seat on one of my luxury shuttles for when they take down the monster."

Kendra hardly noticed when Sue-Lee took her arm, chattering as she went, and led her down the corridor. The words "fixed her" rang loud in Kendra's ears.

—The Merrimack—

Roux stood behind Yelsa at the directional console and realized that he no longer felt the magnetic attraction of her presence. An empty feeling rose into the void. *What's wrong with you, man? You never seriously wanted her kind of trouble.* He shook himself.

Yelsa glanced over, her eyes narrowed.

Cerulean's voice played in Roux's head: *Everyone fights for control, and innocent people suffer. No one grows beyond their own selfish vision.* A new image rose in his mind. Himself dressed in Supreme Council robes, listening, traveling, advocating for the noble virtues too often sacrificed in life's daily combat. "*I* could serve well."

"Sir?" Yelsa had turned to face him, her eyebrows arched like question marks.

"Just a thought…an idea that might make a world of difference."

Yelsa pursed her lips but left her next question unspoken.

Blessedly beyond the chains of lust, Roux almost laughed. "Don't worry; it won't involve you. Though"—he grinned—"Song may have something to say about it."

Shaking her head, Yelsa returned to her console. "Fine, so long as you don't make any deals with the Cresta behind our backs." A scowl worked over her face.

"I'm still not convinced that the Cresta can really manage Cosmos. Their superiority complex has gotten them into trouble on more than one occasion."

Roux rubbed his bristly chin and returned to the captain's chair. *Now is as good a time as any to see what I'm made of.* "Call Mirage-Reborn and see if you can connect with Abbas. Let's hear what he thinks about the Cresta's chances of defeating Cosmos."

With a decided nod of approval, Yelsa worked her way through several connections until Abbas' voice finally rose from the communications console.

"Yes, Roux?"

Roux rose to his feet and squared his shoulders. Though he wished he could see Abbas personally, he was just as glad that Abbas could not see him in his unassuming human façade. "Hello, sir, I am the captain of *The Merrimack*, heading back to Newearth, ready to intercept Cosmos if need be. We have been assured that the Crestas have the situation well in hand and will soon attack—paralyzing and then towing her back to Crestar for further study and eventual destruction."

No response.

Both Yelsa and Abbas maintained a discrete silence.

Summoning his strength, Roux plunged on. "Would you tell me your assessment of their abilities? Can they succeed in this bold venture?"

A prolonged stretch of quiet perplexed Roux. His mind whirled. Had he just infuriated one of the most powerful beings in the universe?

Finally, Abbas' voice broke through dead air. "The Cresta are quick studies, and they are capable of a great deal of harm. My son is reviving, but he will never be the same. When they attempted to make him harmless, they ended up making him mindless. He simply cannot think in a linear direction anymore. His thoughts are scattered, and he will never act on his own again."

Yelsa stiffened, her breath stopping.

Roux tried to hold back the rush of grief resonating through vast space. "I am very sorry for your loss, Abbas. But it is good news for the Cresta's chance of success, at least."

Silence.

An abrupt intake of breath and Yelsa tapped the console. The screen before them brightened with the image of Newearth on the right and Cosmos slowly approaching from the left.

Though relieved at the thought of Newearth's salvation, Roux knew the burden of Crestonian's heightened power would now haunt him for the rest of his life. "Thank you, sir, for clarifying the matter. We will soon arrive at Newearth and allow the Crestonian's room to achieve this noble end, though it will never make amends for your loss, I know."

Silence.

Roux waited.

Yelsa's hand moved over the console as if in expectation of breaking communications.

Abbas' voice vibrated through the air. "They won't destroy her. You realize that, don't you?"

Roux swallowed back the taste of bile. "Excuse me?"

Abbas' voice, infinitely sad, rose like a vaporous cloud, dimming the entire universe. "No, that's never how it works. Once power at this level is reached, killing is much too easy a conquest. Slavery is the next step. They will own Cosmos. And in consequence, they will attempt to rule."

Not merely chilled but frozen in horror, Roux saw the Supreme Council break apart like icicles blasted by a Dustbuster.

Yelsa's voice rose, wavering, yet determined to know

the worst. “And after slavery? Is there another step?”

“The final one, yes. Absorption. In your rage and retaliation—you become just like them.”

Dead silence.

Communication broken, Yelsa looked up, tears in her eyes, pleading for answers.

Two opposing thoughts whirled in Roux’s mind. And strangely enough, Roux knew they were both true. *My life is over. My life has just begun.*

He placed his hand gently on Yelsa’s shoulder, not a lustful spark left in his being, and he reassured her with his command. “Pick up speed, Yelsa. We have a universe to save.”

Chapter Thirty-One

-Mirage-Reborn-

To Stop Evil

Lucius eyed the crowd of beings from six different worlds, damaged humans, exiled Luxonians, Cresta defectors, disillusioned Bhuaci, malfunctioning Ingots, and one orphaned LuKan, as he stood on the bandstand in the center of the park. Well over half the town had gathered before him. Sucking in a deep breath, he prayed that Vera would stay in the far back. *This whole thing could blow up in my face.*

Next to him, Old Man Nelson sat ramrod straight in his wheelchair, his gaze fixed ahead. What power of persuasion the old geezer could possibly hold over the milling throng was lost on Lucius.

I still can't believe he's helping me. Uneasiness tightened Lucius' gut. *Why I should trust him is beyond reason. But still, I need—*

Quinn shouldered his way to the front of the crowd. He lifted his head and called over-loud, as if Lucius were deaf. Or stupid. "Hey, Convict, riots lead to jail time. You know that, right?"

His anxiety rising, Lucius searched the crowd again until he found Vera on the right. Like a drowning man gripping a buoy in rough seas, he locked onto her steady gaze. Her grave expression showed no fear; she'd vent her feelings later. Too tough to break, she'd stand there holding his gaze even if a tornado blew through.

Encouraged, Lucius raised his arms, a respectful request for silence.

The crowd settled and focused in. On him.

"You all know me, Lucius, the blacksmith. And those

who know me well realize that my life has never been easy. As Quinn likes to remind everyone, I was a convict sentenced to time at Bothmal."

A few people gasped, and a couple of older Crestas looked scandalized.

Quinn smirked, his gaze sliding to his men on either side of him. A shared look of triumph between them.

Lucius pushed on. "I was convicted of a crime I never committed. Or rather, it was not a crime in my eyes. During a disaster, I had a choice— save my superior or save her baby. I did what *she* wanted. But I was held negligent of my duty and found guilty. Quinn" —he pointed right at the man— "was my guard at Bothmal."

Quinn's voice piped up. "And I loved every minute of it!"

A few snickers and jeers from the crowd.

Startled by the ugliness before him, Lucius hesitated.

Old Man Nelson snorted and banged his cane on the arm of his chair. "Listen up, you menagerie of half-wits and malcontents! Don't stand there in smug judgment when you all know perfectly well that if Omega hadn't hauled each one of you out of whatever mess you were in, you'd all be dead. Or worse—stuck in Bothmal with the likes of Quinn abusing you at his pleasure! So shut your mouths and listen to one of the few innocent men here. And pay attention! You have a choice to make. Omega can't save you now."

Shocked but more than a little pleased, Lucius scrambled to regain his train of thought.

Quinn cursed in vile language and spat to the side.

Like a man ready to take the plunge into the deep end, Lucius stepped to the edge of the platform and surveyed the crowd. His body tensed, ready for anything. "Nelson is right. Word is that Omega will never recover, not completely. Abbas is with him and will see to his care.

Mirage-Reborn must take care of itself from now on. We will hold free elections and decide who should lead us into a new future."

Quinn bellowed. "Who's this *we* you're talking about? You and your Luxonian friends? Or are you going to model us on Newearth and form an Inter-Alien Alliance? You'd replace Abbas and Omega for a whole universe of managers!"

Flummoxed, Lucius froze. Inter-Alien Alliance support would be a relief, allowing them time to grow into their own mode of government. But it was a risk, too. Once power is given away, it's rarely given back.

Petite as she was, Vera elbowed her way forward. "There is nothing wrong with asking for help. We're hardly in a position to form a self-contained government at this time. We have no shared history, coming from different planets, cultures, and belief systems. We need help to do this right."

A man shouted from the back. "Maybe you need help, LuKan, but humans have been self-governing for time out of mind. People just need to decide what's important: self-rule or slavery!"

A Cresta waved a tentacle. "We allow no onc to rule us. Omega was merely our host. We have always lived freely here, and that should not change now."

In the background, murmuring grew to heated conversations and a few shouts.

An Ingot thrashed forward and faced the agitated crowd. "Don't act like naive children. If Omega doesn't rule this world, then someone will certainly come from another world and take over. Power always plays the master, even when it wears a kindly face."

Lucius' stomach clenched. *Not good. Things are getting completely out of control.*

Coming from behind, a smiling Jazzmarie swished her

way forward. She leaped onto the platform and stood between Lucius and Old Man Nelson. She turned to face the crowd and lifted her hands to speak. Her voice rose, cultured and authoritative. "Hello, Citizens of Mirage-Reborn! I am Doctor Jazzmarie from Newearth, and I have the perfect solution to your problem—"

The unsettled throng didn't much care to listen. Bustling conversations erupted from every corner, and a fight broke out between a Cresta and a human. An Ingot threw himself into the fray and was joined by a feisty pair of Bhuacs.

Quinn fired his gun into the air, startling the crowd. "See, this is what I mean. Given a chance at self-rule, and all hell breaks loose. As far as I am concerned, you all owe time in Bothmal, and since I'm still the warden, you'll either do as I say, or I can take you down."

Lucius wanted to beat the man.

Shaking in fury, his face nearly purple with rage, Old Man Nelson rose from his chair and threw his cane at Quinn, shouting, "Take that, you damn tyrant!" He tottered.

Shocked that someone else had the same urge, Lucius jumped in close to keep the old man from overbalancing.

The gunshot astonished him.

The bullet plowed right into Old Man Nelson but didn't stop there. Pain seared through Lucius' shoulder as he slipped to the ground. Vera's scream echoed faintly in the distance.

~~~

Grace ambled among the prairie flowers and looked up, surprised by a sharp pop sound in the distance.

Chas, strolling at her side, stopped suddenly. He glanced at her, then yelped, "That was a gunshot!"
~~~

Her heart jumping to her throat, Grace grabbed Chas's hand and started running. "My father!"

Leaping alongside, Chas huffed his words. "Your father shoots guns?"

Unable to explain her jumbled thoughts, Grace raced faster through the quiet prairie, heading for Main Street.

Once at the crossroads, the angry, jostling crowd in the park was easy to spot.

Barely catching her breath, Grace took off again.

Chas hurried after her. "Wait! What's going on?"

Fear filling her, Grace choked out the only words that made any sense. "My world is ending."

~~~

Cerulean stood across the street from the fractious mob and devoutly missed his Luxonian abilities.

Two Luxonians morphed into six-foot dragons and mindlessly attacked the crowd. Three Bhuaci flew off in eagle forms and began screaming as they circled overhead, looking for a good position to attack. Other shapeshifters had taken new forms, while Crestas and Ingots used their natural strength to strong-arm those around them. No one made any headway. Even Quinn had stopped shooting, waiting for his men to come back with more guns. Apparently, no one had properly planned for civil war.

Coming up beside Cerulean, Max planted his hands on his hips and shook his head. "You want me to go in there and stop them?"

Cerulean snorted. "You'd get ripped to shreds for your effort. Good intentions won't help us now."

Max tilted his head as he spoke, his voice low and a warning in his tone. "People are getting killed."

Old Man Nelson lay sprawled lifeless on the
~~~

bandstand as Vera tried to staunch the bleeding in Lucius' shoulder.

An eagle dove in, attacking an Ingot who had a chokehold on a human. A tide of men with shotguns, small sidearms, and pistols jogged toward Quinn.

Intercepting them, Quinn grabbed the largest gun available and started shooting into the crowd. An Ingot and a Cresta fell, followed by an Eagle.

Max started forward.

Frantic in his helplessness, Cerulean attempted to hold him back. "They're going to kill each other, if not today, then tomorrow, and nothing we do will stop that. You can't win."

Max peered at Cerulean with what looked very much like disappointment. "Whenever I confront evil, I win."

Cerulean watched his friend enter the fray, his heart breaking. Not so much for Max but for himself and the truth he had lost. *What would Anne think of me now?* He looked up as darkness fell amid the bloody scene, and sadness filled him. *She already knows.*

Thirty-Two

-Newearth-

Burden of Regret

Riko dropped onto his couch, his tense muscles relaxing for the first time in days. *Don't know when I've been so tired.* Images of Bala's kids racing in circles, while Lang rocked the baby and Kendra made supper brought a smile to his face. *They're not bad people—Bala's family. A quality sort, really.* Lang's deep-throated hum as she cradled the infant played in his ears. *She'd make a good mama.* His stomach clenched. *If given the chance.*

With a weary sigh, he pushed himself off the comfortable cushions and ambled to his pantry. After an exhausting day, he hardly felt like making a meal, so he grabbed a bag of munchies and surveyed his drink options.

Familiar shuffling footsteps approached the door, and a voice called out, "Ri-ko? Any-one-home?" *Taug can sing-song with the best when he puts his mind to it.*

Riko squeezed his eyes shut a moment, gathering his composure. *Pity he never puts his mind to leaving a person in peace.* Knowing that assessment was blatantly unfair, Riko popped his eyes open and paced back into his living room.

Taug stood grinning just inside the doorway, with an ornate bottle clutched tight. "Thought we should celebrate! I come bearing stupendous news!"

Attempting to fight off his bad mood, Riko waved Taug inside. "Great news would be welcome about now. What is it?"

Ever the protocol aficionado, Taug flapped a tentacle. "Glasses! I must pour first, then announce."

Too weary to argue, Riko grabbed a couple of mugs off a shelf and handed them over. "Go on. Tell all."

A frown flashed at the uncouth drinking ware. Taug quickly bypassed his momentary displeasure and twisted the cork off the lavender bottle. He graciously filled the cups and handed one to Riko with a flourish. "Cosmos has arrived, and the Cresta ships started their bombardment. She should be immobilized by sometime tomorrow."

Relief cascaded over Riko's body. "Then everything will be okay? You'll get promoted for your good deed, we can get rid of the mortgage on the café, and life can go on like it was before?" He nearly collapsed onto the floor.

Using quicker reflexes than Riko expected, Taug led him across the room with surprising tenderness and let him drop onto the couch.

A few drinks later, Riko wasn't feeling a particle of pain, and his tight muscles had thoroughly uncoiled. He lolled back in the cushions, while Taug relaxed on a padded chair with his booted feet propped on the ottoman.

Taug eyed him with a grin playing on his lips. "So, you enjoyed your foray into domestic life? Bala will be grateful, and he's a man everyone wants as a friend."

Riko reached up to a switch and brightened the lighting, which had grown murky as the evening closed into night. "I didn't help out to gain points from Bala. It was Faye's idea, really, to see if Lang and I really enjoy being around kids."

Taug straightened, his eyes narrowing, a look of concentration etched on his face. "Why would she care if you like kids?"

Flustered by his blunder, Riko stammered, no coherent thought salvaging his slipup. "Uh, er, well, just…because…”

Taug leaned forward, his expression earnest now. “I’ve seen you two together, and I assumed that you both have sense enough to know that, biologically speaking, you’re not suited. Even with all the physiological alterations the greatest Cresta minds could endeavor, there comes a point in which the *you who cares for her* would not be *you* anymore. Or she would not be *her*. If you understand what I mean.”

Irritation flashed like fire through Riko. “What about you and Faye? You two seem to make things work, and you’re not exactly *suited,* biologically speaking. It’s hardly fair that you engage in your own relationship pleasantries with another race but insist that it’s impossible for the rest of us.”

Taug leaned back. “You are mistaken. I understand your frustration, so I will excuse your tone and the oblique accusation. But Faye and I have a purely spiritual and emotional bond. We have not tried to make it what it can never be—carnal.”

Icy clarity washed over Riko. “Are you, a Cresta scientist of the highest renown, trying to tell me that there are limits to what we can do?”

His tone sad, and perhaps edged with a hint of bitterness, dropped low. “It’s not something I gladly accept. Our mortal existence demands wholeness, which no mere scientific approach can replace. If reason and science ruled all, then I would not regret so much. But instead, I carry the burden of regret—about my father, Derik…and others.” He recorked his bottle, dropped his feet to the floor, and maneuvered to the edge of his seat. “If you really care about Lang and she does want offspring of her own, then be honest and let her find a mate who can allow her biological nature to flower. Don’t pretend that you can offer her what you can’t.” He forced himself to his feet with a groan.

With depressing clarity, Riko recognized the painful truth as it swarmed over him. He climbed to his feet, reached out, and pressed Taug's shoulder. "I appreciate your honesty. I know many Crestas who would've happily played me for a fool in order to experiment on us, only to discover that they'd done more harm than good."

With an agreeable nod, Taug brightened. "Platonic friendship has its rewards too, you know. But I'll keep an eye out for a nice Uanyi female for you." The cilia on his head wiggled waggishly. "I can be quite the matchmaker when I set my mind to it."

Riko suppressed a rising groan as he led his friend to the door.

~~~

Uncle Clem tried to pretend that Wendell was mistaken. But the horrific possibility that the Cresta's had—once again—overestimated their scientific abilities portended disaster for Newearth.

Last night, Wendell had cleaned up and gone home to bed, oblivious of the fact that his doubts concerning the demise of the Cosmos cousins had kept Uncle Clem tossing and turning in his bed half the night.

By morning, Uncle Clem knew that he could not leave the matter to chance. There wasn't a soul he could trust with his fears. Riko was riding a doomed relationship into unknown territory, Taug would never admit he was wrong, Faye would trust Taug, and Kendra had more than enough to manage without being told that, despite their best efforts, her home world might be eaten in the next day or so.

The words "Want not—Waste not" rang in his head.
~~~

Without conscious deliberation, Uncle Clem jumped onto one of the last autoskimmers still available and directed it to Simms' palace. With unfeigned panic, he announced himself to the guard— "I have urgent news! Simms' docking bay, as well as the whole planet, is at risk. You must let me speak with him!"

Amazingly, the guard passed the message along, and Uncle Clem soon found himself back in Simms' gloriously ornate office.

Swiveling in his chair before his oversized desk, Simms didn't look particularly pleased to see him. "You got urgent news? Spill it fast. I'm late for the Cresta versus Cosmos show, and I don't want to miss the finale. They say that Cosmos is nearly completely comatose already."

In horror, Uncle Clem realized that he had nothing to back up his fears but the anxious mutterings of an Ingot reject. Defying his inner qualms, he squared his shoulders, crossed his arms, and took a bold stand. "The Cresta won't actually kill Cosmos. They'll only—"

Simms shook his head and shot to his feet. "That's it? You're upset because they're planning to haul her off and experiment on her?" Simms shot from his scat and started for the door. "I've got better things to do than to worry about your pathetic moral code. So, what if she isn't dead when they experiment? How do you think we learn anything—by keeping our hands clean?" Laughing at the absurdity, Simms tapped the datapad on his wristband and headed for the door. "Tell 'em I'm ready. Be there in a couple of seconds."

Uncle Clem watched the gaudily dressed human disappear through the doorway without so much as a backward glance. The refrain "Want not—Waste not" was playing in his mind.

~~~

Bala nearly screamed as Justine weaved their shuttle through the crowd of ships arrayed in perfect symmetry halfway around the beast while the Cresta bombarded Cosmos with persistent regularity. Justine was perfectly capable of avoiding the main action. But the surrounding shuttles—foolish onlookers—were creating havoc in space. The throng jostled each other, darting every which way, apparently trying to get the best view.

Too anxious to sit still another moment, Bala unstrapped himself from his seat and leaned on the railing before the view screen. "What are those idiots doing? This isn't a circus show for their amusement!"

Justine smirked. "You know humans. Everything is entertainment. Even tragedy."

Bala's stomach jolted as she directed the shuttle in for a quick landing.

"Don't think Simms will mind if I slip into one of his new docking bays, do you?"

Bala forced his breakfast to stay in place. "You wouldn't change your trajectory even if he did."

Justine's fierce gaze only emphasized his point as she landed the ship in a perfect position.

Bala readied himself as fast as his arms and legs could move. *Lord, have mercy. I can't wait to get out of here!*

After exiting the shuttle, Justine checked the docking bay's mapping system and started for the large doors on the right.

Bala huffed along beside her, trying to keep pace. "I know you want to see Simms, but can we make it quick so I can get home before my youngest heads off to college?"

Her eyes glinting like polished steel, Justine stopped and faced Bala. "There is no reason for you to come with
~~~

me. I just want to find Zara. You head home, by all means."

His insides quaking, Bala could hardly decide whether to explode or implode. "I'm not leaving you to face Simms alone. Partly for your sake and partly for his. I don't want you to start a planetary war so soon after Newearth has been saved from destruction. Too much drama for my taste."

Justine hustled along, following a path that Bala could hardly comprehend. The docking bay was much larger than he ever imagined, and as they ascended to the top floor, where Simms' office was located, Bala tried to call his wife.

Kendra picked up after the first ring. "Hello, darlin', would you mind picking up some bread on the way home?"

His funny bone tickled, Bala struggled to deadpan his reply, "Absolutely, sweetheart. Anything else?"

Kendra's warm and inviting voice dropped to a sultry level. "Oh, I have a few things you can do for me when you get home, man o' mine."

His face in a steaming flush, Bala faced the elevator wall.

The door slid open, and Justine darted out.

"Got to go, sweetheart. I'm trying to keep Justine from interrogating Simms with undue force. Hopefully, he'll just hand Zara over, and we can head to Vandi—"

Kendra's tone cut across the miles with sharp anxiety. "Simms is in space watching the show. Didn't he leave directions…about Zara?"

Bala stopped in his tracks, smashing the phone against his ear. Kendra had used her warning tone, the one that told him that he'd better step carefully. "Directions?"

Justine stopped and retraced her steps to Bala. "I thought you were coming. That implies movement."

Her tone dropping to whisper level, Kendra offered no comfort. “Be careful, my love. Zara isn’t what Justine is expecting.” A pause. “Ask Sue-Lee about Zara. I’m sure she’ll know.”

Justine’s hearing, as perfect as ever, didn’t miss a word. Her words took on a menacing tone. “Sue-Lee? Who’s that? And what should I be expecting, Kendra?”

Bala ended the communication before things became any more unsettling. He tapped Sue-Lee into Simms’ Docking Bay Identity Key and soon had a meeting scheduled with the secretary at Simms’ office.

He and Justine tramped down the corridor to the luxurious doorway. *Oh, Lord, You were kind enough to keep us alive so we could come home. Now, if You’ll just get us out of Simms’ docking bay without murder or mayhem, I’d mighty appreciate it.*

Thirty-Three

–*The Merrimack*–Orbiting Newearth–

Misplaced Mercy

Roux stood on the viewing deck of his shuttle and stared with fascinated horror at a close-up of the beast they had been chasing for what seemed like eons.

Cresta ships surrounded her on three sides, shooting harpoons into her skin. Lines grew taut as the Cresta ships first anchored their spears, then positioned themselves in a line, and finally drew away, pulling the lines tight.

She's repulsive. Really sickening. But still, this is merciless, brutal even. Roux shook himself. *What am I thinking? That thing ate people!*

Clare padded next to him, her hands clasped behind her back, her gaze absorbed by the scene.

Fighting his repulsion, Roux glanced from Yelsa at the directional console to Clare at his side and tried to take the long view. "Think she's dead yet?"

Clare shrugged. "That wasn't the Crestas' intention. They plan to experiment on her. Figure out how she even exists."

"That doesn't bother you?"

Clare shook her head. "Not a bit." She glanced aside. "Should it?"

Roux rubbed his chin. "I have some reservations. I mean, who gets to decide if she is worthy of basic respect? Yes, we eat lifeforms…lower ones, albeit, but still, shouldn't there be a formal process to decide if she is worthy or not?"

Yelsa lifted her gaze from the console and narrowed

her eyes, focusing on Roux. "She's not cognizant, has no self-reflection or ambition other than to eat and reproduce. Higher lifeforms, by nature, determine if lower lifeforms can aid us or add something to our existence. She adds nothing. Only threatens."

"So, we can do what we want with her?"

Clare huffed. "I'd kill her outright if I had my way. She is little better than a virus feeding off the universe."

Roux shook his head. "But what if we discover that she's a part of something more? Maybe she can communicate, but we just don't understand. Maybe she does have feelings, but we just don't care?"

Yelsa snorted. "You're making the Cresta's case for them. They want to learn all about her."

Clare shook her head and returned to the communications center. "Until I know better, she is merely a dangerous beast that ought to be destroyed before she kills again."

Yelsa returned her attention to the console.

Roux flapped his arms in helpless frustration. "What about the Cresta? What if they enslave her so they can grow more powerful—use her as a threat against us?"

A bitter laugh rose from Yelsa, though she kept her eyes on her screen. "Then *they'll* be the beast that ought to die."

Irritated by the cold logic, Roux took one more look at the viewscreen before returning to his captain's chair. He stopped dead in his tracks.

An enormous luxury liner maneuvered into the open space behind Cosmos.

"What insanity is this? Who is that? Only a fool would try to turn this into a photo-op."

Frowning, Clare tapped through myriad checks to identify the shuttle. "It belongs to Mr. Simms—the mastermind behind our huge new Newearth Docking

Bay."

Yelsa stared at Roux, her perplexed expression reminiscent of a woman trying to pull up a lost memory. "Didn't that raider, Erik, work for Simms? Wasn't he trying to get Cerulean out of the way in order to pave the way for Simms' rise to docking bay dominance?"

Scowling, Roux leaned in closer to the view screen. "Why would Simms want to get close to Cosmos?"

Clare shrugged. "Maybe he's helping. Word is that the Cresta have invested heavily in the new docking bay."

Anxiety mixed with fury, compelling Roux to do something. "Stupid idiot shouldn't be out there! Once he gets close, others will think they can do the same. It'll cause havoc." Roux hurried to his captain's chair and tapped in a code.

Yelsa crossed her arms, clearly perturbed. "What're you doing?"

"Calling for backup. I'm not facing down a mega-ego like Simms by myself."

Laughing, Yelsa turned away. "We're circling a planet in the middle of a monster transfer. Who on Newearth will come now?"

Smug, Roux crossed his arms and waited.

A moment later, Sterling blinked onto the deck, annoyance written all over his face.

Roux grinned.

Clare rolled her eyes.

Astonished, Yelsa plunked down on her chair.

Sterling rounded on Roux. "What do you want? I was in the middle of a very enjoyable meal and watching a rather boring drama. Really, I don't know what all the excitement is about. She may be big, but she hardly seems threatening. I'd just as soon watch a worm being dissected."

"We need to stop Simms from interfering."

"Who?"

Roux jabbed the air in the direction of Simms' shuttle. "Simms is the mastermind behind the new docking bay. He also wanted Cerulean taken out so as to eliminate any unpleasant questions, *and* he's a big investor in Cresta studies—including their work on Cosmos."

Sterling rubbed his face. "Should I be worried? Insulted, perhaps…but worried?"

Roux stepped closer, invading Sterling's personal space. "Can we really trust the Cresta to keep Newearth's best interest in mind? How about if they replicate Cosmos…use her offspring to threaten others to do their bidding? Some dangers are too powerful to contain. They get out of hand eventually."

With his gaze locked on Roux, a slow smile spread across Sterling's face. "You are not the Luxonian I knew." His eyes glinted in amusement. "That's a compliment, by the way."

With a shriek, Yelsa slammed her hand against the console. Alarms started blaring, and orange warning lights flared from every ship in space.

Roux glared at the screen.

Clare gasped.

Like a child breaking free of webs, a wide-awake Cosmos turned and opened her mouth. Three Cresta ships and an Ingoti trader disappeared into the gaping maw.

Roux clenched the railing for support. *Yelsa was right. My mercy was misplaced.*

Thirty-Four

–Mirage-Reborn–

No Words

Abbas clutched his hands together to keep them from trembling as Omega took his first steps across the room toward the door. Once in the hall, the muted lighting created a gloomy feel, but Abbas was sure that moving around and seeing people would stir his son's mind back into some semblance of clarity. It often took action to reorientate the mind and adjust the synapsis so that they made the necessary connections.

His face slack and gaze wandering, Omega appeared more like a lost child than a mature being in the prime of his life. He stumbled on the rug, his arms flailing.

Abbas reached out and steadied him. "Take it slow, my boy. No rush. Just one step at a time. You want to see the townsfolk. They've been waiting for you. There's even a gathering in the park you can enjoy."

Slowly, awkwardly, Omega shuffled forward. His expression did not change. He was either concentrating or oblivious to everything but his next step. Abbas felt immense relief when they crossed over the threshold of the front door and stepped into sunshine.

A strange murmuring roared from the center of town. Abbas frowned. *Now what? I left Cerulean in charge, but he hardly seems up for the task. No one cares to manage things properly. All wastrels and fools!* Depression pressed on his shoulders as his son followed the noise.

Omega's blank expression offered no clue to his

thoughts. If he had any.

As the noise level grew, so did Abbas' anger. At the park, a jostling, fighting, screaming crowd had gathered. Crestas were slapping everyone within reach of their tentacles, Ingots wildly punched victims at random, humans were wrestling other humans, and Bhuaci in various forms: dragons, eagles, wild cats, and wolves attacked with claws extended. Seething fury took Abbas. He transformed from a stoop-shouldered elderly man into an iron-fisted warrior waving a staff of lightning. *Enough of this! No more!*

Leaving his son's side, Abbas rushed into the crowd and leaped onto the bandstand.

Old Man Nelson lay on his back with blood spreading across his chest. Grace pressed her hands against the wound and sobbed, while a strange man stood at her side, tears in his eyes.

The blacksmith, Lucius, sat propped against the LuKan, Vera, while the android, Max, attempted some form of first aid.

Cerulean stood across the road. *Helpless.*

Such pitiful sights would normally have tempered his wrath, but pushed beyond all merciful boundaries, Abbas lifted his hands, the staff flashing with unspent charges, and called out in a booming voice, "You are not worthy of life! My son gave you a second chance, and this is how you repay him?"

A figure shuffling toward Abbas caught his attention. Omega drew near, fear and confusion in his eyes.

In his mind, Abbas saw their doom, the judgment they deserved—complete desolation of the planet and all life upon it. There was nothing and no one worth saving.

From behind came a noise that rose like the whine of an insect.

"Hey—hey! I'm coming. No worries!" Jazzmarie

hustled forward and sidled in close, a coy smile playing over her face. "I know it looks bad, Father-Being, but *you must* forgive them. They're just unruly children and can't handle freedom. Most people can't. They need someone to be strong for them. Let me take them off your hands. You've been burdened long enough." She glanced at Omega, who had reached the edge of the bandstand and stared up at her, uncertain fear giving way to a new emotion. *Anger?*

Stunned by the woman's audacity, Abbas almost laughed. "You think *you* could do better?"

A knowing gleam sparkled in Jazzmarie's eyes. "I'd never compete with you, of course, but I can do better than this." She gestured to indicate the crowd. "And I won't have to shoot anyone. Not like Quinn. As a doctor, I have more humane ways to control a population. After all, everyone wants to stay healthy, right? I have just the medicine they need." She grinned.

The possibility of handing the mess over to someone else danced tantalizingly before Abbas. Doubt flickered, and he hesitated.

Omega did not. Sweeping his hand through the air in a grand arc that soon encircled Jazzmarie, a sucking sound rose, and she was transformed.

Jazzmarie's body turned from flesh to clay, utter amazement and shock on her face. In an instant, she had become a frozen statue, resembling her former self in every detail—except life.

Horrified, the crowd halted. Arms stopped in mid-swing, punches held back, birds forgot to flap, claws retracted, and jaws did not bite.

No! Abbas reached for his son.

Impishly, Omega tipped Jazzmarie off the stage.

The clay figure toppled and fell headlong, breaking into pieces with a shattering crash.

Abbas collapsed into his son's arms. *And I was going to kill them all...*

~~~

Max tied the makeshift bandage tight around Lucius' arm, then patted Vera's shoulder as he offered what advice he could. "Keep him still until we can tend to his wound better."

Vera nodded, her attention fixed on Lucius.

Max headed toward Old Man Nelson, though he knew that he could offer little help there. The man's ashen face and sprawled body spoke volumes.

Quinn stepped in front of Max, blocking him, and faced the crowd. "Time for you all to go home now." He waved his gun. "Don't make me use this again. I know you're upset, but I have the situation under control. Always have. Omega and Abbas never really ran this place. I did, and you all know it. I'm the Justice of the Peace and, as long as you all obey my justice, we will have peace. Simple as that. We don't need them."

He waved a gesture of dismissal to Abbas and Omega. "You saw what Omega just did—he's a crazy man. A dangerous crazy man! And Abbas can't manage us anymore. He's been trying to get out of here for years. We owe him this kindness, at least. Let him go home and enjoy the last years of his life."

With myriad expressions of bafflement, resignation, fear, and annoyance, the throng broke apart and began to disperse, spreading in different directions across the park. A few grumbles and murmurs echoed along their lines, but the fury of moments before appeared spent, like the aftermath of a tornado.

Max turned his gaze to Cerulean, who still stood silent
~~~

and alone across the road watching, but not taking a single step.

A gasp caught Max's attention. He turned.

Jeremy Quinn crouched at Grace's side, grasping her bloody hand. "Don't be sad, Grace. He was a demented old man. It's a relief, really—and you know it—to be free of him. Now, perhaps, you can make a better life. With someone who can really appreciate you." He drew her resisting body close and wrapped his arm around her.

Old Man Nelson's eyes opened, his mouth set in a grim line. He slithered forward, snatched Quinn's gun from its holster, and fired at close range. Then he collapsed again.

With a grunt, Quinn fell over, clutching his chest.

Grace's scream reverberated throughout the park, sending black birds cawing into the air.

In a swift movement, Chas stooped low and lifted her from the scene. He spared a glance for Max as he clumped down the steps. "I'll appreciate her. God knows, no one else around here understands what the word means."

Max crouched at Old Man Nelson's side and placed his arm under his head. He had no idea what to say, but words came anyway. "Is there anything I can do—for you?"

Spluttered words bubbled on the old man's lips. "Don't forget…us." After a short spasm, his body relaxed, and his soul fled.

Max laid the old man's head down and closed the sightless eyes. Then he leapt off the bandstand and gathered the pieces of Jazzmarie. He placed them at Old Man Nelson's side.

Sobs rose in crashing waves, stabbing and splintering his very being. Unable to form words, he screamed his fury at the sky.

A firm hand pressed his shoulder.
Cerulean offered no words. Only compassion.
Max finally understood.

Thirty-Five

-Newearth-

Simple-Schmimple

Justine stood at a large plate glass window inside Simms' luxurious office and watched Sue-Lee lead Zara along the long, bright corridor.

Zara's gaze stayed fixed ahead, unswerving, uninterested. Completely passive. Her brown shorts and pale-yellow tunic-top set off her youthful figure without a hint of the fierce passion she had shown earlier.

Bala stood off to the side, unobtrusive and quiet. *Thankfully.*

Chattering away, apparently unaware that her audience could not have cared less, Sue-Lee stepped aside at the doorway and, with a gentle hand, steered Zara in her mother's direction. "Say hi to your mother, child."

Unaccountably hesitant, Justine moved to the middle of the room and waited.

Zara paced the necessary twenty-one steps and stopped in front of Justine. "Hello, Mother."

I should be feeling something... Yet there was nothing. Perhaps a tinge of dissatisfaction mixed with melancholy. No relief and certainly no joy. "Hello, Zara. You look well."

"I am well." Zara finally lifted her eyes and met Justine's gaze. "Are you well?"

Impossible question!

In his intuitive, magical-like way, Bala seemed to know just what to do. He sidled over and crouched at Zara's side. "Hey, kiddo, glad to see you again. Kendra has been worried silly about you. Want to come over and see the family sometime?"

Her eyes rolled up as if searching her memory. Click! A smile brightened her face. "Yes. I'll come with Mother."

Suddenly, Justine knew what relief felt like. A cascade like cooling rain on a hot day rolled over her. She had to repress an unaccountable urge to hug Bala.

Bala straightened and grinned, his hand resting gently on Zara's shoulder. "We'll make it a date then. I'll talk to Kendra and the kids about a good time."

A wistful expression rippled over Zara's face. "Tomorrow?"

Justine glanced at Bala and begged with her eyes.

Swallowing hard, Bala sighed. "Sure. Tomorrow. If I get to see my family today, we'll call it a deal." He glared meaningfully at Justine.

Justine nodded decisively, a plan forming in her mind. Yes. Bala could get reacquainted with his family today, and then she would take Zara to visit Kendra, the wisest human she knew, tomorrow. Perhaps Abbas could join them. For tea, or something. Between the two, they could help Zara. She stared down at the quiet girl. The child wasn't right, though she wasn't all wrong either. Just not herself. If only Omega…

Sue-Lee broke into her thoughts. "Mr. Simms was sorry that he couldn't be here to participate in your happy reunion, but he was called away on urgent business."

One of Bala's eyebrows rose—if disbelief were rude, then his expression practically slapped Sue-Lee in the face.

Justine sighed. *A good man but so little tact.* "Urgent business?"

"He's supervising the Cosmos collection."

Bala snorted. "What? Is he taking pictures for an art

center?"

Justine jabbed him in the side gently, though Bala's expression suggested otherwise. "You mean he is assisting the Cresta as they take possession of Cosmos?"

Clearly bewildered, Sue-Lee nodded. "As I said."

Satisfied, Justine took Zara's hand. "Fine. I will speak with him when he returns. I expect a full explanation of everything that happened to my daughter while I was away. I especially want to know about the Cresta's part to play."

"She's been well-cared for." Sue Lee beamed at Zara. "A perfect child. You can trust Mr. Simms and his Cresta associates implicitly. Everything was done for the best."

Bala started for the door. "If only I could believe that, I'd die a happy man."

Once out the main doors on the street level, Bala saluted Justine and Zara. "I'm off to meet my newest progeny and all my other assorted progeny, with the grand hope that my wife has already done the breakfast dishes. Wish me luck." He jumped onto an autoskimmer and zipped away.

Justine started down the busy street, clasping Zara's compliant hand. She ignored the array of Cresta ships in the sky encircling the latent monster. If Zara didn't notice, all the better.

A swath of green in the distance with an old-fashioned fence encircling it announced the city park. "How about we stop at the swings before going home?"

Zara grinned through an emphatic nod.

A flicker of happiness warmed Justine, and she added this feeling to her ever-widening definition of motherhood.

~~~

Bala raced up the porch steps and bounded into his house, yelling at the top of his lungs, "Dad's home!"

Stunned silence, and then wild pandemonium broke loose. Shouts and screams mingled with the pounding of footsteps as children exploded from every room in the house. A baby's wail only added melody to the cacophony. *Glorious sounds!*

Kendra emerged from the kitchen, carrying a whimpering infant. A substantial quantity of flour dusted her face, arms, and her favorite apron. "I suppose you'll want bread to go with your dinner, huh?"

With all the attention, Bala could hardly huff out an answer. Arms encircled his legs. Arms squeezed his waist tight. Arms clutched at his chest. Arms even wrapped around his neck—as his eldest son hugged him.

But when their eyes met, no words were necessary.

This is the woman I married, the love of my life, the mother of my children, and my best friend, all rolled up into one gorgeous human being. Bala was not entirely certain that he could keep his heart contained in his chest.

Her eyes glimmering, Kendra gestured toward the kitchen. "If you survive the welcome home committee, you can come in here and help out. The breakfast dishes have been waiting patiently."

Laughing till he was nearly crying, Bala carried, dragged, and manhandled his kids across the room. A flicker of movement in the sky caught his eye. Against his will, he looked out the window.

Red lights flared from every Cresta ship. A siren's scream rose in the air.

The kids fell from Bala like autumn leaves and rushed
~~~

to the living room window.

Bala pulled the lacy curtain aside, dread filling him.

Cosmos was on the loose and, apparently, very hungry.

~~~

Riko didn't want his relationship with Lang to end this way, but he couldn't take the heavy load of guilt another day.

The diner was filled to capacity, everyone in a festive mood. Shiploads were returning to Newearth every hour, and Newearth citizens wanted to enjoy the Cosmos roundup spectacle with favorite drinks and snacks.

Lang stretched her legs in the aisle as she shared a booth with Faye and Taug. Wendell loaded their empty glasses on a tray and took an order for another round.

After finalizing the last order for a large table in the back, Riko hurried over, flipping a clean dish towel over his shoulder and wiping his hands. He hesitated when Lang offered him a long stare.

Clearly in an expansive mood and well lubricated by two full glasses of Green, Taug waved a languid tentacle at Riko. "I told you that everything would work out. All we had to do was study the situation carefully, run extensive tests, and then come up with a plan. Simple-schmimple."

Faye nudged Taug's rotund side. "You've had your worries, and don't try to deny it." She looked around, her eyes searching. "Where did Uncle Clem get to? He should be celebrating with us. He'll get a plum job as PR man for Simms' Docking Bay when this is over."

Lang rolled her eyes. "I don't think he likes Simms too much. Besides, he's needed here at the café. Riko has plans to expand."
~~~

Belying his stupor, Taug sat up sharply. "What? This is news to me."

Lang licked her lips. "Well, he wasn't going to tell anyone just yet but—"

"I wasn't! Not really." Riko blushed and stared at Lang. "I can't expand. Not in the way you think. It's impossible." He glared at Taug and waved. "He told me as much!"

Faye dropped her head onto her hands as Lang sat upright and glared at Taug. "What did you tell him, Cresta?"

Blinking with a look of innocence, Taug spoke, "I didn't tell him anything that you two shouldn't already know. An Ingot and a Uanyi can't have offspring. You aren't suited biologically speaking, and there is nothing science can do to fix that, short of destroying you, which would rather defy reason, don't you think?"

Lang shot to her feet, towering over the assembly. "This shouldn't even bother me. I've got much more important things to deal with." She charged down the aisle.

A yelp from the doorway claimed the room's attention.

Uncle Clem stood with the door wide open and called, "Riko, get out here! Cosmos has broken free, and she's eating the Cresta ships!"

Lang rushed out the door.

As nearly the entire café emptied, patrons hurrying outside, Riko stood stupefied in the middle of his diner.

Taug hadn't budged. He looked up and met Riko's uncomprehending stare. "But I did all the experiments. I had all the necessary data to back up my conclusion."

Wendell shuffled to the table and started clearing away the last of the dishes. He hummed as he worked.

Riko shook his head. *The boy may be slow, but he is the only one with any sense.*

Thirty-Six

-The Merrimack-

Do Your Part

Roux could not believe his eyes. Shock seemed to slow everything down and magnify the details. He swore he could see tiny Crestas screaming for help, though his logical mind told him that it wasn't possible.

Leaping across the deck, Yelsa maneuvered between Roux and Sterling and got right into Roux's line of vision. "We have to stop her once and for all!"

Sterling sucked in a deep breath and stared at Yelsa. "And what would you suggest?"

His tone was as ragged as his breathing. He stared at Yelsa. "And what would you suggest?" His tone was as ragged as his breathing.

Clare stomped forward. "I heard about that—a suicide mission it was called."

Clapping his hands together like an impatient schoolteacher rounding up a rowdy class, Sterling snapped his words at Yelsa. "You are a hysterical Bhuaci child, and I won't hear another word about self-destruction. We have other options."

"It's called self-sacrifice, not self-destruction." Morphing into a much larger, more muscular version of herself, Yelsa towered over Sterling. "Some of us believe in a worthy death."

Clare scowled. "Some of us want to hear about the other options."

Roux pressed Sterling's shoulder. "We need to board Simms' ship and move his luxurious hulk out of the way—then the remaining Cresta shuttles can maneuver better and reestablish their attack."

Sterling nodded, and the two blinked away.

—Simms' Bridge—

Roux flashed aboard Simms' ship with Sterling at his side.

Without the slightest sign of surprise, Simms laughed. "What's this? Two Luxonian guests boarding my ship at such an auspicious moment?"

In no mood for games, Roux ignored the stylishly dressed crowd standing around, holding drinks and eyeing him in excited clutches. "Don't you realize that people are dying out there?"

Simms shrugged. "The Cresta knew the risks. This was their big chance to prove themselves." He sighed dramatically. "Now it looks like I will have to save the day…and Newearth. Oh, my, such a heavy burden of responsibility. I hope *someone* will reward me for my brave and benevolent nature."

His edges glowing with barely suppressed fury, Roux stomped closer. "What do you think you're going to do, sing the beast to sleep?"

Laughter all around. A few gigglers spilled their drinks, sending others into hysterics.

Ignoring the side drama, Simms kept his attention focused on Roux. "Not at all. I just happen to believe in backup plans. I packed enough tranquilizers to knock this monster out of her skin. All I have to do is send in my well-armed shuttle and let it do the dirty work." His grin widened. "I might even man the thing myself. There's nothing quite like being a superhero, is there? Saving the planet should earn me a paragraph or two in the history books, don't you think?"

To Roux's amazement, Sterling actually smiled, relief relaxing his shoulders. "I'm impressed. And here I thought you were just one of the idle rich."

"Oh, I'm never idle. That would go against my motto. Once I save our dearly beloved planet, I do expect fair recompense. A majority vote on the Inter-alien Alliance Committee should do nicely."

Roux swore under his breath.

The crowd waited, their eyes shifting in the direction of the conversation.

Appearing suddenly irate, Sterling stomped off and disappeared down a corridor.

Simms frowned at Roux. "I thought Luxonians were used to being helpless. Oh, well, let's give him a few minutes to collect himself. In the meantime, do *you* agree?"

Roux stared at the ceiling, trying to focus through the mayhem of fears, agitations, and confusing lies. *What is Sterling doing? He's not one for fits of fury...*

After a few whispered words to a sober attendant, Simms grabbed a drink off a sideboard and gulped it down. He offered one to Roux.

Roux snorted and started down the corridor after Sterling.

Before Roux could get halfway across the deck, Sterling strolled back in looking as if he'd just returned from a week's holiday at the sea. "Excuse my taking a moment, but I needed time to consider all sides." He gestured expansively. "I must bow to the reality of the situation—we have no other options. Time is running out. Go ahead, Simms, and do what you must. I'll make the necessary arrangements with the Inter-Alien Alliance when the time comes."

Simms smirked. "No tricks now. I have recorded our

conversation."

Miffed, Roux glowered. "You do your part. We'll do ours."

Roux and Sterling blinked away.

—*The Merrimack*—

Roux went to the directional console and immediately reconfigured their position. "I'm pulling us back—out of the way."

Their mouths agape, Clare and Yelsa stared at Sterling and Roux.

Recovering first, Clare flushed with fury. "Where in Bothmal did you two just go?"

With his usual aplomb, Sterling dropped onto the captain's chair, leaned back, and closed his eyes as if to blot out the rest of the universe.

After giving in to an eyeroll, Roux sighed and glanced from Clare to Yelsa. "Simms says that he"—air quotes—"packed enough tranquilizers to knock this monster out of her skin." Roux shrugged. "He's even manning the shuttle to hit her as close as possible."

With a strangled scream, Yelsa shook her head and waved her arms. "A shuttle won't have enough power! He's just wasting time, annoying her. More people will die!"

Her eyes narrowed in concentration, Clare stepped closer to the main viewing screen.

A large battle-ready shuttle emerged from the lower section of Simms' luxury liner. It moved with remarkable speed, leaving a vaporous trail.

"Why is he taking this risk? Business tycoons never put themselves at personal risk."

Roux stepped beside Clare. “They do if the reward is big enough. Simms wants majority control over the Inter-Alien Alliance.”

With a scoff, Clare waved that idea away. “Hope you told him where to put that notion.”

Yelsa paced over to Roux, crossed her arms, and stared right at him, waiting.

Roux glanced at Sterling and realized how ridiculous pointing his finger at the patriarchal figure would appear. *Oh, Lord, there is no good way out of this one.* He refocused on the screen.

Since every Cresta shuttle had cut their lines, Cosmos appeared to have scraggly hairs trailing from all over her body, making her more grotesque than ever. Two Cresta shuttles were still at risk, built for strength rather than speed.

As Simms’ shuttle approached, instead of merrily gulping down the last appetizers before her main meal, Cosmos maneuvered for a turn.

Simms ship couldn’t reverse fast enough.

Before Roux could process what was happening, Simms’ ship was in her gaping mouth. *Oh, God, no!*

Breaking the silent drama, a sudden flash blinded them, followed by an explosion—brilliant colors flaring in all directions.

Bits of Cosmos goo spiraled through space, while her main body writhed, glowing innards leaking from an enormous wound.

Unnoticed, Sterling had joined them before the viewing screen. He clasped his hands behind his back and watched the unfolding scene as the remaining Cresta ships drew a safe distance away, and Cosmos floated like ocean debris into space. He sniffed. “You’ll have to follow her and make sure that she doesn’t magically rejuvenate.”

Her eyes shining with unspent tears, Yelsa shook her head. "Simms did what had to be done. He could've stayed safely onboard his luxury liner. But he didn't. He saved everyone else."

Clare huffed. "I don't get it. He was supposed to kill her—not sacrifice himself. She had two perfectly delicious Cresta ships right in front of her; why did she turn?"

The vaporous trail... Roux stared at Sterling. "The shuttle was more appealing."

Sterling heaved a long sigh. "He was going to his death anyway. I just made sure that his sacrifice was not in vain. Want not—waste not."

Clearing her throat, Clare continued to stare at the mesmerizing screen. "I studied up on Simms. He hired Erik to kill Derik. The man was an unrepentant murderer. But even still…"

Sterling turned away. "We all die, but he'll be remembered for his sacrifice—last minute though it was. Far better than he deserves." He stopped in the center of the bridge and saluted Roux. "I have much to discuss with the Supreme Council. Change is part of growth, and we need fresh leaders. After all, not everyone has to be a hero. He just has to keep his head when everyone else is losing theirs." He stared meaningfully at Roux.

Roux swallowed a lump in his throat. "After we've made sure that Cosmos is truly dead, we'll dock on Newearth. Then everyone can finally move on with their lives." He nodded to Sterling. "I'll see you at home."

Home.

For the first time in his life, Roux looked forward to his return.

Thirty-Seven

–Mirage-Reborn–

The Best of Our Natures

Abbas kept a firm grip on Omega's arm as they stood in the grand hall one week after the disastrous park assembly, and he watched the entire Mirage-Reborn citizenry gather before them—one last time.

Well aware that Omega's expression of vacant-eyed disinterest unnerved people, he tried to cover for him by nodding at each person as they entered.

As a well-rested Lucius and a smiling Vera stepped over the threshold, he tightened his grip and leaned toward his son. He lowered his voice. "Lucius and Vera were just married, and they'll be the managers of Mirage-Reborn with the assistance of Grace and her fiancé, Chas."

Grace, in a simple summer dress, entered with Chas towering on her right.

To keep his own spirits up, Abbas continued his recitation of recent events. "The human giant has a remarkable history. You'd probably have rescued him if given the chance, but this time, he seems to have saved himself."

Hunched and squinting, Omega leaned in as if following every word of his father's monologue.

It took an exasperating amount of time for the whole town to arrive and assemble themselves on hardwood benches before the dais.

Lucius and Vera stood on Abbas' right, while Grace and Chas stood on Omega's left.

This time, Abbas kept his silence. He had no orders to give and no advice to impart. The murder of Dr.

Jazzmarie had been ruled an accident by all those who cared to voice an opinion, though Omega had never shown the slightest sign of remorse.

"Clearly, he had no idea what he was doing," Max had stated in the inquiry the day after. And no one had disagreed. The incident was deplorable but soon dropped.

Abbas was also well aware of the fact that he had been within milliseconds of destroying the entire planet had it not been for his son's madness. Omega's rash act had saved every single person sitting with hopeful expressions before him. Abbas had nothing to say in the face of that terrible truth.

Once everyone had quieted, Lucius stepped forward. "Though everyone has mixed feelings about recent events and our future lives here on Mirage-Reborn, most of us realize that we owe a debt of gratitude to both Abbas and Omega. They did not have to take us in during crucial moments in our lives—but they did. No matter how trapped some of us have felt, we've still been given a home, honest work, and the opportunity to reform our lives.

"For the first time, we are now able to take full responsibility for Mirage-Reborn. The transition will not be easy, as recent days have shown. No one expects such a diverse assembly to follow an old model. We must craft a new government tailored to our unique identity, but we need help to do so. The Inter-Alien Alliance has offered to send six assistants, representing each of the races on this planet, to help us move forward." Gravely, he surveyed the listening crowd. "I will not take this momentous step without your approval." Lucius stepped back and dropped his gaze.

Grace stepped forward. "All who will accept the Inter-Alien Alliance's assistance, please stand. Those who wish to refrain, know that you still have a voice and can speak to any of us privately about your concerns."

Nearly the entire assembly rose to their feet.

Then Vera stepped forward and stood next to Grace. "The motion has been carried. The Inter-Alien Alliance will be formally invited to join us next month. With this decision made, we'll now walk over to the cemetery and bury our dead.

Gripping his son's arm, Abbas took the first step. It was time to move on. Sending three lost souls onto a better world was a good place to start.

~~~

Cerulean stood aside and stared at the three graves that he and Max had just finished digging. Two large black coffins and one small golden container waited beside their perfectly proportional holes. Old Man Nelson's casket stood first in line. Then the casket for an elderly Ingot named Gemstay, whose patched bio-ware connections did not withstand his vigorous attacks on a Cresta twice his size, and finally the box containing the shards of Jazzmarie.

Everyone else wounded in the fray had been successfully tended to.

Sweat poured down Cerulean's back, and his muscles ached. But he also felt strangely refreshed, as if hard work, sweat, and muscular strain were somehow good for the soul.

The crowd filtered into the cemetery following Abbas, who led the way, tugging a reluctant Omega by the arm.

Cerulean found it hard to catch his breath. Bodies reacted in such troubling ways to emotional distress, he could hardly believe any human managed to stay upright
~~~

throughout the day. He forced himself to hold his position beside Max as Omega and Abbas drew near.

Suddenly slack-jawed, Omega halted and stared directly at Cerulean. His eyes lit up, and a crooked smile broke over his face. He shook free of his father's restraint and galloped forward, rushing toward Cerulean.

Shocked but not dismayed, Cerulean accepted the joy gushing from Omega and wrapped his arm around him.

As Abbas and the rest of the citizens encircled the graves, perplexed looks and a few whispered comments broke the solemn silence.

Cerulean didn't care. Part of him was relieved that Omega didn't see fit to turn him into a clay figure and break him into pieces, but mostly he felt the rightness of their moment together. Omega had loved as best he could. Though his intelligence was greatly dimmed, he could still recognize a kindred spirit. Peace washed over Cerulean.

The funeral ceremony reflected the spirits not only of the dead but of the living left to carry on. Grace placed a red rose on her father's coffin. Three of Quinn's men fired rounds into the air in a final salute. A Cresta sloshed a bucket of seawater onto the grave, mumbling a promise to meet him in the great beyond. Finally, Vera timidly stepped forward and lifted her voice.

Every sunrise gives way to day.
We're out the door and on our way.

Momentous adventures yet to see.
Hope springs, anything might be.

Noon peaks
Glory seeks.

Accomplishment! Fulfillment! Time flies!
Then weary…wandering…shadows rise.

Too soon, sunset gives way to night.
Every mortal's honest plight.

In the end, we can do no more.
Merely, hope and pray—our souls will soar.

After the last cadence fell, the somber assembly broke up, trailing in small groups to homes and meeting places. Someone called out, asking if the café would be open.

A chorus of, "Please, do!" brought a smile to the proprietor. Two of Quinn's men even offered to help, which drew a humorous response from one of the waitresses. "You'll look pretty as a picture in my apron, Cal." Cal laughed as loud as everyone else.

With Omega still standing at his side, though no longer hugging him, Cerulean reveled in the happy atmosphere. "I never thought I'd see the day."

Abbas stepped forward and nodded. "In truth, I have only now come to see what my son has accomplished here. Omega offered each person a new life. But for the first time, everyone has agreed to live it."

Cerulean dropped his gaze. "I've had a chance at a human life, something I'd thought I always wanted—to truly understand the fullness of humanity." He sucked in a deep breath. "But I realize that they have their experience—and I have mine. The grace to live fully can only be given to one living in accordance with their own nature, not someone else's.

Abbas placed his hand on Cerulean's shoulder. "You have been healed in more ways than one."

Warmth spread through Cerulean; his whole being vibrated with Luxonian energy. Wholeness filled him once again.

Max strolled over with Lucius, Vera, Chas, and Grace following close at his heels.

In turn, Vera and then Grace hugged Cerulean goodbye. Lucius shook his hand. Chas kept his place and smiled.

"You'll come and visit us, won't you?" Grace motioned toward her house in town. "I'll always keep a room ready for you."

Lucius wrapped his arm around Vera and grinned at Cerulean. "And if you know anyone who needs a new home, Mirage-Reborn always welcomes the homeless and forlorn."

A heavy burden lifted, Cerulean smiled, and for the first time in ages, joy filled his soul. "I'll return—and when I do, I'll bring friends."

Taking a step closer, Max cleared his throat. "The ship is ready for lift-off. Are *we* set to go?"

Cerulean clapped Max on the shoulder. "Yes, Max, let's take to the stars and see where we are led."

Thirty-Eight

-Newearth-

Three Months Later

Heroes Within

Riko loved the sound of clattering dishes, chattering crowds, and sizzling vegetables on the grill. He stood in the back of his Breakfastnook Café and eyed Wendell leading a wobbly line of bickering school kids to a table. Sympathy for the bedraggled teacher rose inside Riko. *Fieldtrips? Huh, might as well be honest and call them torture trips.*

Suddenly, Wendell started to hop on one foot. All the kids started to hop exactly like him. The weary pedagogue at the back of the line laughed. In no time, they were all seated, their drinks ordered, and happiness restored.

Riko chuckled. "That kid knows how to manage things, all right."

A chuckling voice sounded in his ear. "You know it, Boss. He's a class act, that one."

Heat rushed over Riko's face as he considered Jayla, the petite Uanyi waitress that Uncle Clem had "found." Unable to think of a clever response, Riko dropped his smile and started for the kitchen.

Jayla wasn't done with him. "Hey, Boss, your Cresta friend just ordered another large Green. Think he can handle it? I don't want to get anybody in trouble, but Uncle Clem makes them pretty strong. Poor guy might end up under the table."

Riko glanced at the new drink bar that Taug had designed. It could sit seven with extra-wide cushioned chairs, especially accommodating for unique Cresta needs.

Happy as a puppy with a chew toy, Uncle Clem had insisted that he could run it himself since he knew how to make every fashionable drink this side of the Divide. And if he needed help, Taug would gladly assist.

Riko sighed and nodded at Jayla. "Yeah, Taug can handle it. He handles a lot of things—even failure—with remarkable ease."

Sitting in a booth across from Faye, Taug's rotund body jiggled like jelly. Then Faye's high-pitched giggle broke through the dense chatter, but no one noticed. They were always telling each other stories and laughing.

Jayla nudged Riko. "You've got a lot of great friends, Boss. I love working here. Just so you know."

Surprised out of the power of speech once again, Riko stared after Jayla as she flounced back to the kitchen. He hated to admit it, but… *She is rather adorable…*

Just then, the door chime rang. He looked over, and his stomach dropped to his toes. *Oh no, Lang…*

After Newearth was finally free of the Cosmos threat and patrons returned to the café in droves, Riko got busy, and life took over. Jayla's presence only helped to shove Lang's existence to the back of his mind—not out of it.

Now she was back—and staring right at him.

"Hey, Riko! Just the Uanyi I want to see."

Riko practically shook in his boots. *Is it too late to hide?* He surveyed the room.

Taug glanced over, Faye's eyes following his, and they both watched as if utterly fascinated.

Forcing himself to bravely stand his ground, Riko clasped the back of a chair. "Um, yeah, hi, Lang. Nice to see you. Been a while."

Oh, Lord, stop me from babbling.

A soft smile broke over Lang's face. "Yeah…a while. But I've been busy. Had to cover the opening of the Newearth Docking Bay and Simms' Memorial. I must say, I'm impressed with the android team, Max and Justine, managing everything. Course, they're getting a bit of help from that patriarch Abbas. Having advice from the Mystery Race, who isn't so mysterious, does have its advantages."

Surprised by this extraordinary gossip, Riko gestured Lang over to Taug's booth. "We'd love to hear the details if you'd care to share."

Leaning forward, Taug nodded, and Faye slid over and patted the seat next to her.

Riko held up his hand. "Let me get you something to drink."

Jayla popped up at his elbow. "I'll get it, Boss. No worries." She eyed Lang in open-mouthed admiration. "I know you—Lang from Newearth News! Wow, I admire your stuff more than anything. What'll you have? If we don't have it, I'll find someone who does."

With all tension broken, Lang grinned and slid into the booth next to Faye. "Anything with chocolate. The more, the better."

"I like the way you think, sister!"

Taug lifted his empty glass. "And Greens for everyone!"

Jayla grinned. "Sure thing. Be right back." She skipped away.

Forcing himself not to watch Jayla's frisky departure, Riko leaned on the table and focused on Lang. "So, what is this about Abbas? He's helping Max and Justine run the Newearth Docking Bay?"

Taug slapped his cheeks with two tentacles. "You don't say!"

Faye shushed him. "But what about the son—Omega?

What happened to him?"

A new look came into Lang's eyes, a thoughtful, almost mystical expression. "Abbas was kind enough to let me interview them, so I got to spend some time with Omega. He's remarkable. Though he'll never be able to think in a linear fashion, and he acts on impulse like a child, still, he manages to exude an honest innocence. A quality of soul that one rarely finds in our menagerie of intellects."

Taug sniffed. "I'm not sure I understand what you mean by that."

Faye's eyes brightened. "I do."

Riko glanced over to Wendell, who was making faces at the school kids as he cleaned the table next to them.

Lang reached up and pressed Riko's hand as it rested on the back of the booth. "In the aftermath of Cosmos' destruction, a lot of orphans have been brought to the docking bay. Justine asked me to help her found the 'Newearth Is Home' Foundation." Lang's eyes misted. "It's quite an honor. Zara is going to be our poster child, and Abbas and Omega will help us find patrons among their own kind." She jutted her jaw toward the drink bar. "I plan on asking Uncle Clem to be our PR man."

Riko clasped Lang's hand in both of his. "I am really glad, Lang. You're the perfect person for such a job. A noble soul for a noble cause."

Glancing around, Faye cleared her throat. "Well, if you are sharing your good news, we might as well share ours too."

Uncle Clem hurried over. "Hey, are you all talking about me? My ears were burning—and that's as sure a sign as any."

Lang smiled. "I'll give you a full report in a minute. But first, we want to hear—"

Riko frowned at Taug. "Yeah—what?"

Taug's naturally pale pallor pinkened. "Well, after my little mishap with the little Cosmos cousins, Faye and I brought a proposal to the Inter-Alien Alliance Counsel. We plan to organize a Science Discovery Oversight Committee." He shrugged. "Even the best science can be made better if understood from more than one viewpoint."

Charmed, Riko shook his head. "An act of *humility* from a Cresta? Well, Newearth is off to a fresh start! Nothing like learning from our mistakes, I always say."

Uncle Clem clapped his hands. "Hey, I've got it! The perfect slogan! 'Want a new life? Head to Newearth.'"

Bounding from the kitchen, Jayla ambled forward with a tray loaded with fresh drinks and a towering chocolate creation.

Noise and laughter in the air, Riko considered his bustling café and smiling friends. *I couldn't agree more.*

~~~

Max strolled at Justine's side down the long Newearth Docking Bay corridor as Zara ran in zigzags ahead.

Justine called after her, "Don't get too far, now. We're heading to the central dome."

Zara slowed and called over her shoulder. "I know. You told me already. But I want to see Grandpa."

Justine snorted. "She sounds so human!"

Max sighed. "Like a child who wants to grow up fast. We all strain forward."

Justine stopped at the clear-paneled elevator and beckoned her daughter. "Zara, Grandpa and Omega are waiting for us at the central dome. If you wander off, you won't get to see them."
~~~

Running as fast as her feet would carry her, Zara raced back. Then she scooted into the lift as soon as the doors opened and hopped up and down until they arrived at the top.

Justine rolled her eyes at Max. "Do you think we should've left her as she was? I mean, the Cresta didn't actually damage anything, just suppressed her impulses a bit."

"She needs to manage her impulses. There's no better time than childhood to learn how to behave."

The elevator doors opened to a well-lit large circular room with a clear-domed ceiling. The glory of constellations too numerous to count showered down on them.

Zara bounded out and rushed into Abbas' waiting arms. Omega grinned but held his place at Abbas' side.

Various people, from young Bhuaci families to elderly Cresta dignitaries, strolled along the outer promenade, while attendants supervised assigned flight decks. Ships of all sizes, including luxury liners, trading merchant vessels, and a sizable number of shuttles, flew in and out of the ports encircling the central bay.

Zara tugged on Omega's hand. "Come and see your old home! Mama showed me. It's just over there. Looks like a speck even with the magnifier, but there's a zoom link. Max said we'll go and visit some time."

Omega let himself be led by the child, a bemused look in his eyes.

Max strolled up to Abbas with Justine at his side. "What do you think of the place? Do you think we can make something of it?"

In response, Abbas lifted his arms wide as if to take in the room, the docking bay, and perhaps the entire known universe well. "We don't make something of a place. We make something of ourselves. Though I am old, Omega is damaged, Zara has a future unimaginable, and you two are unique by all the annals of creation, we are making something of ourselves—discovering our meaning in the process."

Pleased with life unfolding before his eyes, Max reached for Justine's hand. She intertwined her fingers in his.

~~~

Bala snuggled close to Kendra, her warm body every bit as enticing as it was the first night they were married. "Thanks be to God. I am so glad to be home."

Kendra laughed. "You say that every night."

"It's true every night."

In the moonlight filtering through the window, Kendra's eyes sparkled. "You know, you need your rest. You'll have your first full day of work tomorrow, and Clare will be expecting you *on time*."

Bala yawned. "Are you kidding? After three months of debriefings, trainings, and instituting new protocol procedures for the Newearth Docking Bay, not to mention manhandling my abundant progeny around here while you sneak in multitudinous naps, human services will be a breeze! And for your information, Clare doesn't intimidate me one tiny, itsy bit."

Snorting, Kendra covered her mouth with her hand. "Uh-huh. I believe in you, honey."

Unabashed laughter always brought out the best in Bala. He wrapped his arms around his wife and planned on showing her what true faith looked like.

Kendra practically purred in his arms.

A baby's wail pierced the air.
~~~

Even as he slipped his feet into his cold slippers and rose from his warm bed, Bala knew that his proclamation was as true as ever.

Thanks be to God.

~~~

Cerulean sat on the top step of his cabin porch and reveled in the glory of the night sky.

Sterling and Roux stood on the path, sharing the view.

"There was a time when you didn't care for humans." Cerulean kept his face fixed on the stars.

Sterling looked over at Cerulean and shrugged. "Your extraordinary passion bewildered me. As did your father's love for all things on Earth."

Roux sighed. "A bit before my time, but the truth is, it's not easy being a guardian. Belonging to two worlds but forever exiled in the choice of one or the other."

Sterling met Cerulean's gaze. "You are at peace with your decision?"

Cerulean nodded. "I never asked to be a Supreme Council member. I almost lost myself as a guardian. But strangely enough, after failing so badly, I feel a closer kinship to both my Luxonian biology and my humanity."

Silence held a moment.

Then a wolf howled, and two owls hooted in quick succession.

Cerulean considered Roux in the starlight. "Are you sure you're not just making it easier for me? You might want to travel and make a life with…someone."

Roux looked up, facing a distant galaxy. "Yelsa is back on Helm, where she belongs, serving alongside Song. I'll learn my new role and—just so you know"—his voice rose a notch— "I might end up being the best
~~~

Supreme Council member Lux has ever known."

A smile warmed Cerulean's mood.

Sterling clapped Roux on the shoulder. "And we'll all expect regular updates on Mirage-Reborn. They are a new star rising in our universal family. Changes keep us young at heart, even if our bodies tell a different tale."

Cerulean snorted as he rose to his feet and climbed down the steps. "You will never grow old, Sterling. You'd have to grow up first, and that shall never happen."

Roux offered a deferential bow. "Next time you see me, Cerulean, I'll be expecting reports from you." He nodded farewell and then blinked away.

Before Cerulean could brace himself, Sterling clasped him by the shoulders. "I once said I never wanted a son, but I lied." He stepped back. "Though I never had a child, I have been blessed with an honest friend. In the end, I am well compensated."

Choked up, Cerulean tried to respond, but no words would come.

Sterling patted his arm. "I'll train Roux as you trained me—with lots of understated humor and abundant patience. I'll also pray to God that he won't come to his first Supreme Council meeting with his shoes on the wrong feet."

Tears filled Cerulean's eyes as Sterling blinked away. Relaxed down to the molecules of his being, he climbed back onto his porch and sat down on his favorite rocking chair.

A whistling tune caught his ear. *What the—?*

"Hey, Cerulean, you still up?"

Shaking his head, Cerulean could hardly believe his ears. "What would you do if I wasn't, Clare? Jostle me out of bed?"

Clare climbed the last of the incline and then huffed

up the porch steps. "Something like that." She dropped onto the bench. "Gosh, but I forgot what a hike it is to your place."

Cerulean rose and gestured toward the door. "Want to come in for a cup of tea? I picked up a new spicy mix in Vandi the other day."

Clare hopped to her feet. "Sounds good. So long as I can get to sleep tonight. I've got a big day tomorrow. Bala is meeting me at the Breakfastnook, and we have to go over a new case."

Cerulean held the door open, and golden light spilled across the floor leading to the kitchen.

Clare stepped in and made her way to the kitchen. "It's a murder investigation. I guess near-planetary-extinction doesn't stop some people from dastardly deeds."

Cerulean stepped to the stove and put the kettle on. He listened as Clare described the case—an elderly man who had refused to leave during the Cosmos crisis. "Though none of his expensive art objects were taken, it was clear that someone was looking for something important. The place was ransacked from top to bottom. And he lay dead with a stab wound to the heart. Almost like a message." She shrugged. "I could use your help on this one. After all, you're Newearth's hero."

Stunned, Cerulean turned with a mug in each hand and felt very much like dropping them. "Don't joke, Clare. I couldn't save OldEarth, Newearth, or even act like a decent human being when given the chance. On Mirage-Reborn, I fell into despair—a crime against humanity, if anything."

Clare took the mugs from him and set them on the table. "Where's that tea you were bragging about?"

Feeling snappish, Cerulean yanked a box off the high shelf and slapped it onto her open hand.

Daintily, Clare dropped a tea bag in each mug, then

poured steaming water into each. She savored the wafting scent, smiled, and handed one mug to Cerulean. Then she leaned against the counter and eyed him. "You know why I am a pretty darn good detective; why Roux is rising to the Supreme Council; why Max and Justine are able to take over the Newearth Docking Bay; why Abbas and Omega are making their home here; why Taug and Faye, Lang and Riko, Bala and Kendra and their abundant offspring are doing so well? It's because you aren't *always* a hero. Because you have shown us what makes a hero, and then you let us rise in our own way. If it is a crime, it's a hero's crime, Cerulean."

Flummoxed, Cerulean took a sip of tea. Spicy warmth spread through him. He offered a grateful smile.

As if the tea had given her super speed, Clare drank her entire mugful, then exhaled a long breath. "Well, good. I just wanted to touch base with you before I meet with Bala tomorrow. If you hear anything that might help, you know where I am."

With that, she placed her cup in the sink and headed for the door.

Cerulean followed, still cradling his cup. "Say hello to Bala from me. I'm supposed to go over for dinner next week."

Clare huffed as she started down the steps. "I'll remind him. That man is so forgetful, it's amazing that he can keep all his kids straight. Just hope he's not late on his first day back!" With a backward wave, Clare bounded down the incline.

Cerulean stood in the brilliant moonlight and stared at the glory of the stars above. A hulking trader ship blinked across the sky as it headed for the docking bay. Steam from his cup wafted upward in spirals like silent prayer offerings.

He thought about his father, Teal, who had for long

years watched over the clans of Aram, Ishtar, and Neb, then followed their descendants into the first century with Georgios and, centuries later, found an honest man in Melchior. As the last of her kind, Anne taught Cerulean the true meaning of love. And when Justine awoke, though he offered kindness, she showed courage to face whatever end.

Cerulean's heart swelled with unaccountable joy.

You were right, Father. The best in humanity always humbles those who only see the worst. We're reaching for heaven and discovering heroes within.

About the Author

Mother, Educator, Writer, Manager,
and Captain of my ship

As a teacher with a degree in Elementary Education who has taught in big cities and small towns, Ann Frailey homeschooled all of her children. She manages her rural homestead with her kids and their numerous critters. She writes books and a Friday blog alternating between short stories and her My Road Goes Ever On series.

Her nonfiction work focuses on the intersection of motherhood, widowhood, practicing gratitude, and rediscovering joy.

Her fiction novels expand from the OldEarth world to the Newearth universe—where deception rules but truth prevails.

She earned a Masters of Fine Arts Degree in Creative Writing for Entertainment from Full Sail University.

In her spare time, she serves as an election judge and as secretary/treasurer of her small town's cemetery.

She is currently finishing a new science fiction novel in the Newearth world and a historical fiction & science fiction blend in her OldEarth series. To check out her stories, novels, inspirational books, and her film and tv scripts, visit https://akfrailey.com/

www.ingramcontent.com/pod-product-compliance
Lightning Source LLC
Chambersburg PA
CBHW070612310726
48982CB00001B/57
9798986180335